Praise For Wind

"The Dandelion Trilogy comes to
non-stop action and a cavalc
transforming society." - Burt Kempner, author and filmmaker

"*Winds of Change* awakens you to the individual and collective power of participatory democracy. It's brilliant, elegant, and utterly simple. We just need to show up." - Natasha Léger, Executive Director, Citizens for a Healthy Community

"*Winds of Change* really pulls the series together as an instructive allegory of what continued activism for nonviolent change can look like. It makes it look not-so-hard to live a life dedicated to meaningful community action and change!" - Seán P. Duffy, Executive Director, Albert Schweitzer Institute, Quinnipiac University

"Eloquent, visionary and accessible, this book energizes and expands upon the epic stories told throughout the Dandelion Trilogy. It encourages us to realize that revolution is not the end of conflict, but the beginning of a messy, communal voyage towards justice." - Susie Beiersdorfer, National Community Rights Network

"These practical and inspiring examples of direct democracy are exactly what we need to move forward as society." - Marissa Mommaerts, Gabriel's Garden

"While set in a 'time that looms around the corner of today', this book is filled with detailed descriptions of tools and strategies my students can use here and now." – Dr. Mark Stemen, California State University, Chico

"This novel lets us imagine what is possible in our work for peace with justice." - Patrick Hiller, War Prevention Initiative

Winds of Change
- a revolution of dandelions and democracy -

Winds of Change:

a revolution of dandelions and democracy

Copyright © 2021 by Rivera Sun

Rising Sun Press Works
P.O. Box 1751, El Prado, NM 87529
www.riverasun.com

Library of Congress Control Number:
2020920997

ISBN (paperback) 978-1-948016-12-4
(hardback) 978-1-948016-13-1
(ebook) 978-1-948016-14-8
Sun, Rivera 1982-
Winds of Change

*For Tom Hastings, who rooted for the dandelions
from the moment we met,
and spread their seeds far and wide in the world.*

Other Novels, Books, and Poetry
by Rivera Sun

The Way Between
The Lost Heir
Desert Song
The Adventures of Alaren
The Dandelion Insurrection
The Roots of Resistance
The Dandelion Insurrection Study Guide
Rise & Resist
Billionaire Buddha
Steam Drills, Treadmills, and Shooting Stars
Rebel Song
Skylandia: Farm Poetry From Maine
Freedom Stories: volume one
The Imagine-a-nation of Lala Child

RISING SUN PRESS WORKS

A Community Published Book Supported By:

DeLores Hollister Cook
Mary Pendergast, RSM
CV Harquail
Jayanne Sindt
Jaimie Ritchie
Maja Bengtson
David J. Spofford
Rev. Elsie McGrath
Rick and Carol Brown
Caroline Corum
Lindsay and Collin Palkovitz
"Dr. Mark" Stemen
Burt Kempner, author and filmmaker
Susie Beiersdorfer, National Community Rights Network
Elizabeth Russell, Dreamfruit Almanac for Earthlings
pk mutch, publisher: LiisBeth.com; Greg English and Augusta
Michael Mirigian
Scott Springer, Waldorf Teacher, The Bay School, Maine
Glenn & Darien Cratty
Robin Wildman
Brian Cummings
Marirose NightSong and Daniel Podgurski,
Len Beyea
Rocki Ranellone & family
Chet Gardiner, Author
Rev Michael Omar Harrington, OccupyFaith
Nancy Audette, RSM
Lorraine Dickin
Cody and Leo
Mary Shea Kealey Kustas
Leslie A. Donovan
Tom Hastings
Beth Remmes
Sharon Reiner
Johnny Mazzola

Cassandra R & Jenjoah B
Sasha and Mika Tornberg Agetorp
Adam & Dolly Vogal & Family
Patrick Hiller
Daniel A O'Brien
Caitlin Waddick, Úrsula Zia, Anika Zia, Rustum Zia, Asim
Zia, and Calcifer; Raffay, Raheel, Rauf-ud-din, and Arya
Elizabeth C. and Petey Cat In Vermont
Eva Marie Bonanno
Hilda J Richey
Andy Katsetos
Bruce A. Shay
Jeralita Costa
Joni LeViness
Gerry Henkel
Natasha Léger
Marissa Mommaerts, Gabriel's Garden
Barbara Gerten
Seán Patrick Duffy
Eva Marie Bonanno, Joe Bonanno, Tejah and Ebel Echenique
Rev. Silvia A. Brandon-Pérez,
People Without Borders Justice Temple

... and many more. Thank you.

Winds of Change
- a revolution of dandelions and democracy -

by
Rivera Sun

Table of Contents

Table of Contents, cont.

AUTHOR'S NOTE

. . . . .

From Rivera Sun

It's been a wild eight-year journey from the moment my pencil first touched the paper to scribble out the words: *in a time that looms around the corner of today.* The Dandelion Trilogy began in the wake of the Occupy Protests and finished as Donald Trump attempted his coup of lies during the 2020 election. In between, we've seen the eruption of the Movement for Black Lives, Idle No More, the Standing Rock resistance to the Dakota Access Pipeline, #NoKidsInCages and campaigns against migrant family separation, March for Our Lives, #MeToo, Fridays For the Future, Extinction Rebellion, and so many more campaigns for justice. It's been tumultuous, invigorating, awe-inspiring, terrifying, and certainly the stuff of legends.

Winds of Change brought the Dandelion Trilogy to a close as we endured a global pandemic, weathered the storms of the intensifying climate crisis, and witnessed the United States' largest protests in history (20 million people outraged by police brutality, racial injustice, and the murder of George Floyd). We already know that the next ten years will be marked with such profound change that the past eight years of tumult will pale in comparison. Change is an imperative. We must rapidly transition away from not only fossil fuels, but the entire industrial growth society that relies on systemic oppression, racism, and the destruction of ecosystems.

Facing such complicated, entwined crises, what can a work of fiction offer our world in these times?

Hope. Vision. A sense of possibility. This novel offers a recognition that a solutionary future is not purely speculative, but pragmatically possible. *Winds of Change* is built from the bare bones of the best ideas of our society, bringing to life the brilliant work of participatory democracy projects, intergenerational movements, climate transition plans, Rights of Nature, Solutionary Rail, reviving the commons, and much more. Our saving grace in these perilous times is that the answers to our most pressing problems are at hand. We do not lack solutions. We merely lack the political will to implement them.

Winds of Change explores what happens when ordinary people come together to make decisions about the things that affect our lives. The scenes may seem surprising if you haven't seen participatory democracy at work. I have. I've worked in co-operatives, lived in co-housing situations, shopped at member-owned grocery stores, fixed my bicycle at tool co-ops, taught in collective skill-sharing networks, banked at member-run credit unions, organized participatory groups projects, and much more. I've seen people sort out tough conflicts over and over. It can be messy. It is always powerful. (People-powerful!)

I choose to write about these ideas because I think they matter. We don't have time for the gloom-and-doom horror stories of dystopian fiction. We don't have the luxury of reading 80,000 words about how bad things could get. It's an indulgence we can't afford. Fiction must rise to the times and offer us ideas that help us not just survive our predicament, but tap into the courage required to radically re-wire our society.

Times of great change require stories of great change. They demand that our fictional heroes and sheroes are bold and visionary. We need to emulate the characters who are willing to disrupt business-as-usual in pursuit of a way of life that stands a chance of continuing on this beautiful planet. If we are going to navigate this looming transition and ensure the survival of our species, the next ten years will, by necessity, be times of upheaval and transformation. They will challenge us all to live with uncertainty. They will call upon our willingness to radically adapt. We need stories about people who live life-less-usual and dive into the adventure of a lifetime. We're going to be living those stories all too soon.

My writings, and especially this novel, are aimed at giving us stories for these times. I write about characters who journey through massive change so we won't feel so alone as we ditch the expectations of a culture built on greed. I write chapters packed to the brim with possibilities so that we'll lift these ideas off the page and put them to work in our communities. I draw from the most inspiring examples in real life so that we'll know such things are not only possible, they're happening all around us.

I hope the adventures of the dandelions have brought joy to you as you read these novels. I hope you see yourself in these pages and that the scenes inspire you into action. These are wild times. With any luck, we'll learn to fly like those silver dandelion seeds, soaring on the winds of change.

With love,
Rivera Sun

Winds of Change

It was a time of giddiness and babble, when the world seemed hopeful and lost all at once. Possibility lurked on the edge of each moment. Disaster loomed across every horizon. With humanity at a crossroads, the clock ticking in the earth's heartbeat, the Dandelion Insurrection took a deep breath . . . and went flying on the winds of change.

CHAPTER ONE

· · · · ·

After the Fireworks

The night hung dark in all directions. Across the pooling black of the lake, distant drunken whoops shot out. A pitched shriek echoed over the water. A crackle erupted in the sky. Starbursts lit up the night. Cheers lifted on the shore. An off-key anthem praised rockets' red glare. The smell of charcoal briquettes swept past and vanished.

Back when that song was written, it would have been the stench of burning flesh, Charlie thought cynically.

He lay on his back in the bottom of a metal rowboat in the middle of a lake on the Fourth of July. Red and blue hues of fireworks electrified his features in brief flashes. Angular and aching, his face bore the lines of a youth who has seen too much and knows secrets that wake him up at night. His sandy hair gleamed green for an instant as a firework bloomed above him. The crackling pink trails of the explosion turned his blue eyes violet.

The light fizzled. Darkness dropped like a shroud. Charlie Rider disappeared from sight once again. Only the strip of glow tape and the solar lights attached to the stern and bow remained, bobbing like drunken stars stumbling in the black sky. The sound of splashing arose, rhythmic and confident. A murky figure swam up to the boat. The metal pinged with the slap of a palm. Zadie Byrd Gray's laughing eyes lifted over the gunwale. The vessel lurched in the water.

"You should come in," her breathless voice enticed.

3

"It's too cold," he answered, not budging from the comfort of the blankets layered in the hull. He grimaced. She'd soak him when she clambered back in, dripping and naked, teeth chattering and skin bluish under the cover of darkness.

"Makes you feel alive," Zadie urged, releasing the edge of the boat and diving back into the inky waters.

The triple flowers of the next fireworks illuminated her face when she resurfaced. Her black curls were plastered tight against her skull by water-weight. Her pale skin gleamed for a second, limbs strange and froglike under the surface of the lake. *Typical Zadie Byrd Gray,* he thought with a small chuckle, *skinny-dipping under the Independence Day fireworks.*

It had been his idea to row out and escape the mayhem of the shore. His massive extended family had all gathered at the gravely beach for corn-on-the-cob, hotdogs and burgers, and apple pie. His cousins had contributed a devastating vat of homebrew. Zadie's father, Bill, launched into a tirade on the shortcomings of the Founding Fathers - a lecture they'd both heard a thousand times. When Charlie whispered in Zadie's ear, she leapt at the chance to slip off. They shoved the boat into the water and rowed out to watch the fireworks. Charlie texted his mother so she wouldn't suddenly glance up with panic thundering in her chest when she didn't see him. She'd lost too many nights of sleep over her revolutionary son. He'd been shocked to see grey streaks in her hair when he had returned home to Northern Maine.

The boat tipped as Zadie heaved her torso out of the water. Charlie sat up and countered the weight. He handed her a towel as she rolled in, sopping.

"Brrr," she gasped, "I swear there's still ice at one end of the lake."

"Wouldn't surprise me in the least," Charlie answered.

4

Though the spring melt had long passed, the water in Northern Maine wouldn't lose its frigid edge until August - and even then, only in the top few feet of sunlight-pierced waves.

A good metaphor for revolutions in this country, Charlie thought darkly. *They never went deep enough to keep out the chill of centuries of injustice.*

Another collection of fireworks boomed overhead.

They'd fought and struggled for so long, shining bold as dandelions, piercing the darkness of the hidden corporate dictatorship, making so much progress, and yet . . . the sheer weight of injustice still thundered like an oncoming train wreck through the lives of the people. The backlog of misery accumulated by centuries of rich people's rule had a momentum of its own. A nation could only be neglected for so long before the moth-eaten holes of the social fabric crumbled into dust. It would take a hundred years to dig out of the mess of the hidden corporate dictatorship.

And they didn't have a hundred years.

They'd ousted the corrupt politicians, replaced them with decent enough officials, thwarted a counter-revolutionary take-over, and halted the corporatists' continued efforts to steal anything that wasn't nailed down. It still wasn't enough. He and Zadie had worked non-stop to get bills passed through Congress, held an emergency election for a single-term transitional president, and ensured that hundreds of corrupt officials were prosecuted by the legal system. It had been a herculean effort, worthy of a thousand medals of honor, but the reports kept rolling in, bad and getting worse. Drought in the farmlands. Corporate businesses declaring bankruptcy and vanishing to avoid penalties on a decade of unregulated abuse. Global banking sanctions. Threats from other superpowers. A military on the verge of mutiny. Crumbling infrastructure. Debt balloons collapsing with a pffftzzing whine. Turmoil and chaos.

And now, the rising rumble of fear was triggering a backlash. The law-and-order crowd was calling for stability, traditions, and the good old days. Behind them, the good old boys lurked in the shadows, trying to regain power. There were no easy answers to the problems anymore. It had been so simple to oppose the tyranny of the old regime - everyone despised the hidden dictatorship - but it was so much harder to get people to agree on the solutions and next steps.

Charlie flexed his aching fingers. He'd been writing all afternoon. Dusk had fallen, unnoticed, by the time Zadie unexpectedly slapped his laptop shut. He glanced up, bleary-eyed from staring at the glaring screen.

"Time's up," she declared. "It's a holiday, remember?"

"Humph," he snorted.

"Don't start that," she warned, shaking her black curls. "Suspend your cynicism. Enjoy the fireworks, for once."

Charlie groaned, but rose to his feet. They had a deal: he could scribble away the afternoon, reflecting on revolutionary themes for his next essay, but then he had to watch the fireworks over the lake with her. Charlie had agreed to come only after she threatened to throw his laptop in the water and run off with one of his cousins who knew how to have a good time.

"We're national heroes, Charlie, m'boy," she teased him. "Come grin-and-bear the Fourth of July. At least we didn't have to go to any parades in DC."

After his series of blistering rebukes to politicians about the lack of progress on social reforms, their public appearance schedule had cleared out considerably.

"Keep criticizing Congress and we can finally retire," Zadie joked.

But it was no laughing matter. Revolutionary truth-tellers rose and fell on waves of change, propelled or repelled by the opportunists of the hour. The same people who applauded them for tackling the hidden corporate dictatorship detested them when Charlie turned his mighty pen toward their shortcomings. Charlie never forgot that Thomas Paine, for all his *Common Sense*, died obscure and alienated from his peers, disillusioned by counterrevolutions in France and the constitutional conservatism in the United States.

As it was, both he and Zadie had been politely disinvited from the Fourth of July ceremonies in Washington, DC. It was an honor they neither sought nor mourned. Instead, they came north to spend time with family - or at least, Zadie had. Charlie cloistered himself in the back bedroom of his grandfather's camp by the lake and tried to ignore the patriotic fervor of the weekend. It nauseated him. Though he loved his country fiercely, he couldn't stomach its shows of patriotism.

A starburst of a crackler erupted as they settled down on the bottom of the boat. Zadie curled tight to his side, the chill of the metal muffled by the towels, scratchy wool picnic blanket, and his churning furnace of body heat.

"Did you ever wonder," she asked, "if we wrote the Constitution today, would we do it the same way? I mean, that was two hundred and fifty years ago. People rode *horses* to send messages. Most people couldn't read - heck, most people weren't even considered people - enslaved Africans were counted as three-fifths human. Indigenous Peoples were considered 'savages' that needed to be conquered or controlled by white people. White women were considered the property of their husbands and fathers. The poor, including indentured servants, couldn't vote or run for office."

"Most of our political history is the story of how we rewrote our Constitution to include more of us," Charlie answered.

"Yeah, but if *all* of us could have participated in the crafting . . . if we designed a new system, right now, what would we, the People, create?" Zadie rolled onto her side and leaned on her elbow, cheek propped in hand, eyes aglow with thought. "Would we stick with a representative republic? Would we include more direct democracy? Would we add anything to the systems of checks and balances? What about consequences - like docked pay or getting fired - for officials who refuse to enact the demonstrated will of the people?"

Charlie could almost see the ideas exploding in her mind as she spoke, fireworks of possibility lighting up the darkness for brief, vanishing flashes. He'd spent plenty of sleepless nights mulling on these same concepts. They always fizzled out by morning. Crumpled paper littered his writing area like fireworks casings on the Fifth of July shores.

"People don't even know what democracy is," he reminded Zadie. "They've been taught that the unparalleled brilliance of the Founding Fathers gave us the best system in the world, and there's no need to change it."

"American Exceptionalism is such a deadly brainwashing technique," Zadie grumbled, flopping back down on the blanket and setting the boat rocking. "It makes us unwilling to improve."

"If we rowed back to the beach and asked anybody - except your dad, he doesn't count - if we should rewrite the Constitution, they'd throw a hotdog at you and dunk you in the lake."

That was the irony of the Fourth of July: there was nothing revolutionary about it. The nation celebrated patriotic loyalty to an unjust system rather than the revolutionary willingness to upend the world in search of greater equality and justice. On the day that honored the courage of those who defied global superpowers, their descendants followed rote patterns of tradition without deviation, year after year.

Charlie might not have minded if it happened on September 17th, Constitution Day. Then, at least, the obvious self-worshipping rhetoric wouldn't be hypocritical. But a day commemorating revolution ought to be, well . . . more rebellious. People should spend the day asking the very questions Zadie had just raised, thinking critically about the political system, and working to correct outstanding injustices so that the "truths held to be self-evident" could be reflected in the politics and practices of the nation. They should spend the day advancing the quest for life and liberty. They make sure the pursuit of happiness could be actualized by every citizen, not just by some.

And then, he admitted with a chuckle, *after a long day of making meaningful strides toward liberty and justice for all, then we might set off a few fireworks and slice up the apple pie.*

"This holiday is the same as all our others - militarized, commercialized, corporatized beyond recognition or meaning," he grumbled. His bitter comment hung on the summer air, hollowed by the metal boat and softened by the lapping waves. "If we want a deeper kind of democracy, it'll take another revolution to get it."

He could feel the curl of Zadie's smile even in the dark.

"Good thing," she replied, "we know a revolutionary or two."

A trio of fireworks lit up the sky, red, white, and blue, one right after the other. Charlie watched the colors illuminate Zadie's face in shades of warning, hope, and possibility. The red faded last, an uncanny glow of rockets' glare, a reminder that tradition did not die easily and that patriotism sometimes fought against change.

CHAPTER TWO

. . . . .

Constitution 2.0

"They're gonna tar and feather you."

Tansy Beaulisle's skepticism huffed in each syllable. Her pencil-thin black eyebrows rose to the hairline of her bleach-blonde orb of curls. The Black lawyer massaged her temples with a groan. Her fire engine red fingernails circled. Charlie and Zadie exchanged a nervous look. Maybe this conversation should have waited until Tansy's Fourth of July hangover wore off. It was nearly noon, but their impulsive video call had found her in her bathrobe, hunched over her first cup of coffee.

"If you ever use those words in public," she grumbled, "I'll personally find the rail to ride you out on."

"Constitution 2.0?" Zadie teased, a gleam of wicked mischief in her eye. "What's wrong with saying we need to upgrade our operating system?"

Tansy leveled her a look that could have stopped a runaway freight train. She had seen Charlie Rider and Zadie Byrd Gray through hell and high water. She'd defended them in a circus act of a court trial. She'd let them stay at her house in DC despite death threats and assassination attempts. She loved those two kids like a pair of pets that chewed the carpet. She had never abandoned them, no matter how hard it got. But this?

Tansy considered giving them up for adoption.

"There are nine kinds of trouble waiting for you if you start calling for a Constitution 2.0. Y'all been charged with treason

11

before and I got you off, but if you go actually playing with treason-fire, you're gonna get burned."

"Tansy, we weren't - "

"Uh-huh."

She wasn't buying it.

"Look," Tansy told them, "Americans love the Constitution almost as much as they hate politicians. Makes no sense, but there you have it. They may be convoluted, bad rules, but they're *our* rules. Y'all call for a whole new kit-and-kaboodle set of rules, you're gonna get booed off the field."

"The Founding Fathers revised the Constitution constantly," Charlie argued.

"They didn't have two hundred plus years of history stacked up on top of 'em. You do."

Tansy's tone of voice tried to flatten them into a withering pool of contrition - a trick she'd picked up from her mother. It had worked wonders in the courtroom. They appeared immune. Zadie tried to explain that they just wanted to spark a nationwide discussion on democracy.

"That's all fine and dandy, but don't say the phrase *Constitution 2.0*. Y'all gonna get charged with treason so fast, lightning'll seem slow. You wanna change the law, bit by bit, you do that - baseball's changed since the first sandlot game - but if you're gonna make new rules . . . well, that's like turning a football team into a synchronized swimming squad. Ain't gonna happen. People fought and *died* for this Constitution - "

"Oh, for heaven's sake - " Zadie began.

"Not just in wars," Tansy reminded her, "but in movements, too . . . including ours."

Zadie scowled. She didn't need reminding. Not a day went by without her thinking of the drone strike that had killed her mother and many other Dandelion Insurrectionists.

"We weren't fighting for the Constitution, though - "

"Weren't we?" Tansy retorted. "*Restore* democracy, that's what we always said. Not invent it from scratch."

"But we've never had democracy," Zadie groaned. "Not really."

The Dandelion Insurrection had "reset" the country. But to what? They had a representative republic. They voted on the people who voted on the laws. Bills tiptoed or stampeded through Congress. Citizens petitioned for some, fought against others. And most people thought that was fine. The system seemed to be working closer to its ideals than it had for most of its sordid history.

And yet . . . like a housewife with a string of pearls, a wasp-waist dress, two perfect children, a new model car, a dog, a husband, and a white picket fence; Zadie wondered why she wasn't happy. Why wasn't this political process enough? Why did she feel like something was missing from the long-held dream of seeing their country back to normal?

Perhaps, she thought, *because it's not* our *dream.*

For hundreds of years, this had been the dream of rich white men who kept congratulating themselves on what a great system it was. It may have worked out dazzlingly well for them, but, for the rest of the people, it was a disaster. The citizens had been patching and amending the process for centuries, trying to make sure that we, the People, weren't robbed, enslaved, exploited, abused, or utterly ignored. Zadie tapped her finger against the desk in agitation. On the computer screen, Tansy winced at the sound.

"I didn't design this system," Zadie pointed out. "You didn't design it. No one we know did. And if we sat down today, the Constitution we would craft might look startlingly different from the one made in the 1700s and patched up ever since."

Charlie ran his hand through his hair, elbows on the tabletop. He'd let Zadie take the lead in debating with Tansy, but - even though he'd once written a fiery essay on the *need* for a Constitution 2.0 - he agreed with their lawyer. People would fly off the handle at the idea. He sighed. Outside, the sky ached blue. The summer sun glared. The spruce trees hunched dark and foreboding on the edges of the wind-tossed fields.

"We've got to shake things up," Zadie went on, nudging Charlie with her shoulder. "We can't keep starting our mornings like we did today."

"What happened this morning?" Tansy asked with a frown.

The shrill ring of Charlie's phone had blasted them awake just after dawn.

"Don't answer that," Charlie had mumbled, tossing the phone aside after a quick glance at the number. He hid his head under the pillow. "It's Brad Andersen. He wants my support on that weak bill scaling back fossil fuel subsidies and I already told him it was a pathetic attempt to undermine the efforts for meaningful change."

Zadie groaned. The Capitol Hill fixer - campaign manager, bill greaser, deal broker - had been pestering Charlie for weeks, wanting his support for one bill and his denouncement of another, his pledge to candidates, or better yet, a hint that he might consider a run for office. Brad Andersen never called Zadie, which both annoyed and delighted her. As the Dandelion Insurrection settled into the rosy glow of yesterday's news, Zadie's part of the story was already being downplayed by the authorities. Her heroics were being eclipsed by narratives that centered on Charlie's writings. Worse, it wasn't just Zadie getting shoved to the sidelines. It was all the Dandelions. The leaderful nature of the movement was being reframed into a convenient narrative of a charismatic leader: Charlie. She found

14

it aggravating most of the time . . . but not when Brad Andersen was waking Charlie up at dawn instead of her.

The phone silenced. Then it rang again.

Charlie reached for it. His shoulders ached. Last night, they'd drifted down the lake as the shine of million-year-old stars replaced short-lived firework explosions. They dozed off to the comforting cradle-rocking waves, waking with groggy disconcertion when they bumped up against the shore at one in the morning. With a groan, they rowed back to the camp. They'd staggered into bed just a few hours before Charlie's phone startled them awake.

"I thought we had a revolution to get rid of guys like Andersen," Zadie grumbled. "The sun's not even up yet."

Charlie sighed and sat up. Zadie rolled over and hauled him backwards.

"Lemme go," he protested, flailing against her hold. "He left a text. I should make sure nothing disastrous is happening."

The cool air rushed into his space as he slid away. Her skin prickled. She shivered. Was this how it was going to be for the rest of their lives? Every time DC needed a problem solved, they called Charlie and got him to mobilize the Dandelions' support or opposition. Zadie hated it. All the creative turmoil, the street-based rebelliousness, the energetic disruption of people power - all of that was getting funneled into a call-your-reps-and-senators-song-and-dance. It wasn't *wrong* . . . but was it really the best they could do?

They'd won. They ought to be happy. Zadie scrunched her nose. Once they had ousted the corporate oligarchs, she and Charlie had assumed that they could step back. They'd expected that the government would function at least adequately well, that it would plug along doing what was best for everyone, helping out the average citizen. But it didn't. Even with fairly elected officials, they had to threaten mass action to get even the smallest, most sensible bill through Congress. They had to sound the alarm every other week as some horrid piece of legislation tried to sneak into law. It was exhausting, frankly. Without constant vigilance, the rich people and corporations would unravel all their hard won gains.

"It's just . . . clunky," Zadie said, though what she meant was *moribund.*

The current political system was designed to deliver injustice while claiming that it did the opposite. It was slowly grinding her soul into sawdust. It was wearing Charlie down to the bone. Haggard lines hung under his stubble. That morning, she had watched the shadows beneath his eyes turned bluish as he fired up the coffee maker. His shoulders slumped as if he couldn't quite muster the strength to straighten his spine. He opened his laptop and flinched at the light.

"Close it."

Zadie rolled to standing and shut it with a firm click.

"Come back to bed. Sleep for a few hours. You're not at Andersen's beck-and-call. You're not DC's lackey. You're Charlie Rider, the Man From the North. You won a revolution and you deserve to rest."

He rubbed the back of his neck and nodded. She tugged the crook of his arm.

"Come on. There are three hundred and twenty million people in this country. Let some of them speak up. Or maybe the elected officials could actually do their jobs. All this begging and pleading with officials isn't democracy."

"*They* think it is," Charlie pointed out as he rolled back into bed. He wanted to argue that the very things Zadie objected to were what most people thought democracy was all about. But, he didn't. He was too tired. He collapsed against the pillow with a groan. Zadie wrapped her long arms around his chest, nestling against his back, holding him - and keeping him from leaping up ten seconds later when a burst of panic kicked him.

"You know me too well," he muttered.

Zadie felt his galloping heart slow beneath her palms. She did know him. She knew he woke up in cold sweats reliving the drone attack that killed her mother. She knew he had nightmares of the assassination attempts they'd survived. She knew he had panic attacks about how everything they'd done wouldn't be enough, that he could write his fingers down to the bone and the corporate oligarchs would still come back to power, that he could organize the people into mass action as inexorably as the tide, and yet the tsunami of the climate crisis could still sweep human life off the face of the Earth.

But Zadie had one strength he didn't: she loved him more than all the rest of the world combined. *He* might work himself into an early grave for the sake of humanity, but *she* wouldn't let him.

Zadie had no desire to run back to DC to solve the nation's problems. She refused to accept this slog of begging politicians to do the right thing. Zadie could sense a field of looming possibilities hovering over the country. She had inspired hundreds of candidates to run for local office with a Dandelion Politics platform based on compassion, respect, and taking care of people. It was a good start, but there was so much more to be done. She'd heard stories of democracy done differently. Her friend Inez Hernandez had been using neighborhood democracy for years. The community councils connected residents with movement organizers to solve local problems and build resilience. Some cities used participatory budgeting with citizen involvement in allocating funds. She had run across organizations that determined the direction of their mission through member polling and visioning circles. She'd heard of places that used community dialogues to unpack local problems.

Zadie lay awake as the morning light traced its fingers across the curtains, holding Charlie in her arms, her heart racing against his warm back, her mind leaping out beyond the horizon line of today's reality into the wide open space of tomorrow's potential. At last, excitement tingling in her veins, she slipped out of bed and threw on her bathrobe. She piled her tangled curls up on her head and turned on the coffee maker. When Charlie stirred at the delicious scent, she was ready with a cup and a question.

"What if," she asked, alert as an excited puppy as he rubbed the sleep out of his eyes, "we launched a campaign for real, participatory democracy at every level of government?"

He blinked. She rattled off a stream of ideas from town councils that engaged citizens in policy design to federal agencies that used robust public polling to decide on new policies.

"Is that even legal?" Charlie asked suddenly, frowning. "I mean, they're not the processes outlined in the Constitution."

"Maybe it's time for another Constitutional Convention," Zadie dared to suggest. "And a Constitution 2.0!"

So, they had called Tansy Beaulisle, a lawyer and Constitutional scholar, for her advice, fully expecting her enthusiasm . . . and running smack into her refusal to get involved with overhauling the founding laws of the nation.

"Y'all do this, I ain't gonna be your lawyer anymore."

"Tansy!"

"I can't. How can I represent you in court when you're throwing out the law?"

"That's not - "

"It is."

"What about the Right to Revolution?" Charlie countered. "We have a legal right to launch a revolution in times of tyranny and inadequacy of government. It's a theory of law based in part on the Declaration of Independence."

"Heavy emphasis on theory," Tansy grumbled. "And, is the new government inadequate or tyrannical?"

"Yes," Zadie stated emphatically. "If they have to call us at dawn to get anything done, I think so."

"Look, I don't wanna split this wood with y'all right now," Tansy groaned. "Lemme think it over when I don't feel like I have a hatchet in my head. But if you're really set on this folly, I'll give you a tip."

"What's that?" they asked warily.

Tansy fought the urge to tell them: *don't do it.* Instead, she sighed and suggested they go down to Massachusetts and talk to a young woman named Elisha Adams.

"Who is she?"

"A revolutionary," Tansy replied grumpily. "Y'all gonna get along like fire and powder kegs."

CHAPTER THREE

· · · · ·

Turning Up the Heat

Heat flattened the city. Asphalt gleamed, shiny and malevolent. Concrete endured in washed-out weariness. Anything green wilted and crisped at the edges in the inferno of the record-breaking summer temperatures. Heat waves curled off the concrete, steel, tar, glass, and brick. As he navigated traffic, Charlie battled the sense of doom pressing down on his perspiring brow. These scorchers plastered the country earlier and longer each year. It was the inevitable effect of corporatists lying about climate change, refusing to act, stalling all attempts to transition away from fossil fuels and factory farms and the carbon emitters that turned up the planet's heat like a gas oven.

Boston evoked images of rowers on the Charles River, minutemen mobilizing against redcoats, Harvard crimson and masses of college students, a harbor port and a tangled sea of serpentine roads and highways. When Tansy told them they'd find Elisha Adams at City Hall on Tuesday afternoon, their minds leapt to the small, historic steeple-and-column brick building that was now a museum. Instead, they pulled up in the parking structure of a hulking concrete monster that seemed to be auditioning for the Star Wars franchise.

"Wasn't expecting that," Charlie confessed.

Instead of evoking a sense of revolutionary times, the beige top-heavy building carried itself with an air of Big Brother and the weight of bureaucracy. It was a place where revolutions died under mounds of paperwork. With a sense of foreboding, they checked-in with the clerk, passed through the metal detectors, and strode through the dimly lit, low-ceilinged corridors until they reached the city council chambers. The semi-circle of councilors' chairs was flanked on either side by citizen seating. It was oddly reminiscent of bleachers at a high school basketball court. The meeting was well underway so they slid in quietly.

In the center, bearing up under the scowls of the officials, a young Black teen in a fuchsia T-shirt and blue jeans testified to the city council members. She held her chin high, arguing with precision and passion. Beside her, a girl with jet-black hair and chicory-toned skin clutched a stack of documents. Charlie squinted, but couldn't read the titles on the folders. Next to her, a pale Goth of a teen with a shocking blue-dyed, half-shaved haircut whispered to the others. The trio huddled shoulder-to-shoulder as they addressed the impassive faces of the council.

"Running that gas pipeline - an explosion waiting to happen - through our neighborhood is environmental racism," the Black teen argued. "Our area already has the worst rates of asthma and lung disease from the city incinerator, the industrial park, and the smog patterns. Now, you want to put in a leaky pipeline to a natural gas export terminal that will do nothing but kill us *and* the planet? Uh-uh. I don't think so."

"Ms. Adams, your time is up."

"Fine. Meera, you're up next."

She handed the mic off to the petite East Indian girl as the mayor tried to interrupt. Elisha ignored him, brown eyes fierce. She had petitioned for months to put this issue on the city agenda. She'd called them directly. She and her friends had organized sit-ins at the councilors' offices only to be told the same line over and over: it was a done deal and they should have spoken up sooner.

Elisha didn't buy it. Wrong was wrong. Slavery wasn't

acceptable just because the enslaved hadn't filed a petition on time. It wasn't right to steal the Indigenous Peoples' lands because they didn't send in enough public comments in opposition. Just because a group of money-grubbing corporatists had shoved this deal through didn't mean her community was going to roll over and die.

"Last weekend," Meera told the irate mayor in a quiet but clear voice, "a bunch of us blockaded the pipeline's construction route in two places. One was uptown in an affluent neighborhood. The other was on our block. Both groups were arrested, but if you look at these photos . . . "

She nudged the third youth to hold up poster-sized prints and swivel to make sure everyone saw the images. In one, a pair of white-haired, white-skinned grandmothers were being politely escorted into a police van. In the other, Elisha was pouring milk into the eyes of her tear-gassed twelve-year-old cousin. In the next photo, Meera's Puerto Rican neighbor was face down on the asphalt, bleeding as police hogtied him. In the third, a crowd of protesters threw their hands over their ears in agony as the police used eardrum-splitting sound cannons to force them to disperse.

"We're here today not just because this gas export project is deadly to all of humanity, not just because it is extracted from under the feet of outraged communities in Western Massachusetts, not just because this pipeline was rejected in a wealthier area and dumped on the poor; not just because the increased toxins in the air are yet another act of environmental racism, not just because the city police violently cracked down on lower income and people of color residents for doing the exact same thing as white and affluent residents uptown, and not just because the whole approval of this plan was sneaky and underhanded," Meera paused for breath. "I'm here because the entire system of so-called democracy has completely failed ninety-nine percent of your constituents in the short term, and all of us in the long term."

If they built this terminal, it would *be terminal* for people and planet.

"You are out of line, Ms. Sundaran, and your time is up. Please sit down, the three of you," the mayor ordered.

"No," Elisha refused.

None of them moved. Meera passed the mic to the third youth.

"For the record, I'm Frankie Mirelli. My family runs Mirelli's Bakery in the North End," the teen said, scratching the back of their skinny jeans with their sneaker. They'd been born Frances Mirelli, but they hadn't gone by that name since kindergarten. In middle school, they'd declared themselves non-binary - a fact that Frankie's Italian-American father still refused to acknowledge, even though their grandmother had explained gender neutral pronouns in two languages to him.

What do I care if Frankie's a boy or a girl or something special? Nonna had declared. *What's so hard about they/them pronouns? They're my grandkid, no matter what.*

Frankie adored Nonna. But they'd been crashing at Elisha's after the last shouting match with their dad - which was how they knew how bad the air was in that part of town.

"It stinks," Frankie told the officials. "And you won't do nothing about it. You won't talk about the pipeline or the export terminal. You won't hold hearings. You won't listen to us when we call. You won't put it on the agenda."

"We don't have time for everything," the mayor cut in.

"You have time!" Elisha shot back.

On the docket of today's council meeting were budget items that paid for scooters for Ivy League college students, city funds for yet another public-private development partnership for constructing high-end condos, and a stimulus program for large rock concerts in the privately-owned sports stadium. Today, millions of dollars would be approved for the already rich and privileged.

Elisha and her friends had had enough.

"We're not giving up the floor until you give up on this pipeline," Elisha shouted.

"Yeah," Frankie added, speaking into the mic. "We're shutting you down until you shut it down!"

The mayor cleared his throat impatiently. The teens had long surpassed their three-minute public comment allocation.

"You are violating others' right to be heard," the mayor tried to say.

"Bullshit."

The room flinched at Elisha cussing. The teen scowled back. She and her friends had asked this city council a hundred times to hold metropolis-wide discussions on climate adaptation plans. *That* would be honoring people's right to be heard. Elisha knew that the officials tracked how many times she, Meera, and Frankie had sent texts and emails about this. The city clerk could pull up their dossier in thirty seconds flat. The police officer assigned to the city council meetings was fidgeting, just waiting for the signal to throw them out . . . again. Last time, they'd been warned that they'd be arrested if they continued to disrupt the proceedings.

"We are in a global emergency," Meera spoke up again, earnest and impassioned. "Instead of building an export terminal, you should be listening to the people. They have solutions. They have plans and ideas. They should be empowered to be part of the process - no, scratch that, they should be at the *heart* of this process."

25

"I'm sorry, your time is up - "

"Maybe *your time* is up, Mr. Mayor," she rebutted. "You've had years to deal with these issues and all you've done is make the crisis worse. We don't have another decade to do nothing. We need change now."

Zadie's grin split her face at the teens' boldness. Tansy had grumblingly described Elisha Adams as a rabble-rousing, young troublemaker, but Zadie took that wording as a form of praise. She knew their lawyer had a soft spot for instigators. When pressed, Tansy had pursed her lips and said Elisha got into more trouble than anyone she knew - barring Charlie and Zadie, of course - and had gained local notoriety for both activism and pranks of a historical nature.

"Like a Boston Commons pop-up store and impromptu makers market, for example," Tansy told them, "or a memorial service for Crispus Attucks, the Black man who was the first - and often forgotten - casualty of the Revolutionary War. She even held a Thanksgiving Day small pox die-in at Plymouth. I've been her lawyer since she was twelve and decided to steal a horse to crash the Fourth of July Paul Revere Race dressed up as Sybil Luddington, the teenage girl who really rallied the minutemen."

But Elisha's stunts didn't stop at historical antics. She had been organizing for social justice since middle school, and today's challenge to City Hall was just one of a long series.

"Your time is up, councilors," she said. "It's time to cancel the pipeline project. It's time to stop that export terminal. It's time for people-power to replace your foot-dragging and inaction."

She spun to the bleacher seats, appealing to the scattered citizens.

"Who will stand with us?" Elisha Adams demanded, swiveling to look around for supporters.

Someone coughed. Another squirmed. A few people hastily looked away as the girl's gaze sought their solidarity. The long moment stretched painfully as citizens wrestled with their consciences. They still held out hope that the political process would work, that the councilors would rally to the crisis, that they didn't need to take drastic action.

Zadie pursed her lips, scowling. This, right here, was the very phenomenon she and Charlie had led an insurrection to prevent: citizens' concerns ignored, corporate officials dragging their feet on important issues, people cut out of the political process. She rose before Charlie could reach out and stop her. She strode down the bleacher steps to the center aisle. Astonished gasps and murmurs leapt up as people recognized her. She heard her name whispered from one person to the next.

Zadie drew close to Elisha Adams, Frankie Mirelli, and Meera Sundaran. She stilled.

Who will stand with us? the teens had asked.

"I will," Zadie Byrd Gray answered.

She tossed a grin at the astonished teens. The mayor signaled to the police officer. He charged forward and the room erupted into chaos.

CHAPTER FOUR

. . . . .

DARx

"That was brave of you," Zadie said.

She and the three teens sat in a chilly side room after getting strong-armed out of the council chambers. Zadie pulled the zipper of her sweatshirt tighter up around her neck and drew her hood over her hair. She rubbed the goose bumps down on her legs as the air conditioning pumped out an icy blast from the vent above them. Outside, the heat blistered the beige paint off the walls. Somewhere, Charlie was arguing with cops and calling Tansy for legal advice.

Before Zadie Byrd Gray's unexpected endorsement could spark a popular revolt, the mayor had signaled to the cops to remove them for "disrupting a tradition of democracy that went back to the Founding Fathers". Frankie had hollered that the Founding Fathers' town hall meetings looked more like a bar brawl than Robert's Rules of Order - a remark that did not endear them to the authorities. The police officer had hauled the teens and Zadie out of the room for "inciting a riot" and "threatening violence".

"It won't hold up in court," Meera exclaimed, protesting as they were put in a side room while the police considered whether or not to arrest them. "We're nonviolent! I said it in the public record earlier."

"Besides," Frankie muttered, "disruptive and rowdy are the hallmarks of the Bostonian political tradition."

The stilted, ritualistic town meetings had steadily grown more draconian over the years. The recent Fourth of July holiday only highlighted how far from its origins the civic process had deviated.

"They're an oligarch empire," Elisha reminded Frankie in a huff of righteous indignation. "We're insurrectionists for popular democracy. Of course they shut us down."

Zadie agreed. Power holders wouldn't give up their power without a struggle.

"Of course, you know the real reason they kicked us out, right?" Elisha asked. The young woman tossed Zadie a worldly look, lifting her eyebrow and pursing her lips. "They shut us down because we're women, non-binary, queer, Black and Brown, and teens. Basically, everything but white men. If we had stood up in fancy suits, flashing Ivy League degrees, and demanding a lot of money for our hot new civic innovation, they'd have smiled and nodded and set up a private meeting. If *Charlie* had stood up? They would have fallen over themselves trying to shake his hand. They want to put up a statue of him."

"Yeah," Frankie chimed in. "It's totally unfair. Charlie's, like, the new Founding Father. And you, Zadie? To them, you're just the wife."

"No, more like the girlfriend," Meera added. "The love interest."

"The after thought?"

"The sidekick?"

"Hah," Elisha snorted. "That's on a good day. Mostly, she's like the wh-"

The teen clapped her hands over her mouth. Her friends shushed her. All three threw guilty looks at Zadie.

Zadie felt the pit of her stomach drop like an iron weight. She knew the next word: *whore*. Truth and shock waged a wrestling match over Zadie's face, but there was no denying it. In the court of public opinion, Charlie Rider was tried and found heroic. He was lauded for his courage and for his revolutionary ideas. Even his critics focused on his writings. No one attacked him for being a man. But Zadie? When the hate mail came, it called her a slut, whore, bitch. When the empire struck back, it weaponized her gender into an epithet. When her enemies tried to knock her down, they attacked her for being a woman.

"How do you stand it?" Elisha asked her, shaking her head slowly from side to side. "I mean, they put you through hell."

Elisha remembered hearing it on the news. She'd been a freshman in high school when the corporate government labeled Zadie a terrorist, a sophomore when the tabloids concocted an affair between her and Will Sharp and tried to destroy her relationship with Charlie. The old regime had called her a slut and a whore, thrown her past in her face, and tried to wreck her reputation in the witch hunt of the century. Zadie's juvenile records had been cracked open illegally and her history of working in strip clubs had been slapped in her face in court. There was no denying the gendered nature of the attacks and the fact that, while Charlie was applauded for his role in "restoring democracy", Zadie's role was tainted by the scandals.

The way the city councilors lauded Charlie, none of them had any doubt that if Charlie had stood up and told the councilors to give real democracy a try, they'd have been rolling out a pilot program next week.

Instead, Zadie, Elisha, Meera, and Frankie had been tossed out of the room.

"This is what they do," Elisha commented, folding her arms over her chest and staring at the white-plastered wall. "Lock us up. Shut us down. Silence our voices. Shove our ideas out of sight. That's how they keep power, by pushing all challengers out of the room. The more your body threatens the power structure, the less willing they are to listen to you."

"Wait . . . what are you doing here, anyway?" Meera asked Zadie, curiosity breaking through the teens' escalating indignation. The other two fell silent, suddenly all ears and wide eyes as they waited for Zadie's answer.

"Charlie and I wanted to find out more about people-powered democracy," Zadie answered. "Tansy Beaulisle told us to come by and meet Elisha."

The whoop Elisha let out bounced off the hard walls and made the guard peer in at them.

"I think she meant it as an object lesson in the perils of calling for real democracy," Zadie warned as the girl tossed her locks and smirked at her friends.

"Nah," Elisha assured her. "She's giving you her wink-and-nod approval for whatever you're working on. This is her way of saying, *I can't help you because I'm a fancy-pants lawyer, but I'll tell you who can.*"

"You?" Zadie asked, trying to clamp down on her skeptical tone.

"Uh-huh." Elisha nodded, winking. "Tansy knows we're stirring up trouble for real democracy. She warned me to quit it or she wouldn't bail me out anymore."

"We did get a similar warning, something about getting tarred and feathered."

"We're interested in the same kind of trouble," Elisha pointed out.

"Revolution?" Zadie guessed.

"Real democracy," Elisha said at the same time.

"I suspect it's one and the same," Zadie replied. "And, for the record, *I* thought it was brilliant, shutting down City Hall."

Elisha rolled her eyes.

"It was something," she answered with a rueful chuckle. "Foolish, reckless, stupid, pointless - I can hear my mom already. Aunt Tansy'll read me the literal Riot Act - "

"Wait - Tansy Beaulisle is your aunt?!" Zadie gasped.

"Not by blood," Elisha clarified. "She's my godmother, my mom's best friend from growing up together. I've wanted to meet you for sooooooooo long, but Mom forbid it. First the laws, then the drone strike, then the assassination attempts - Mom thought Aunt T had lost her mind, letting you all stay with her."

Zadie had to agree. Their lives had been dangerous for the people around them.

"What you did back there was great," Zadie told them.

Meera sighed.

"It was doomed. I told you it wouldn't work," she groaned to the two others. "You can't challenge the old system until you grow the strength of the new system."

Elisha shrugged.

"Gandhi said - " Meera started.

"Don't *Gandhi said* me," Elisha burst out, laughing, "or I'll *Dr. King* you!"

Meera lifted her hands in surrender.

"Can you guess how we met?" Meera asked Zadie, pointing at Elisha as her friend covered her face with her hands and groaned. "A fistfight in middle school."

It was hard to imagine Meera tackling Elisha in the cafeteria, but it was true.

"I kept saying that Gandhi was a racist," Elisha admitted, "and Meera kept telling me I didn't know anything about anything, until finally, one of us - "

"You."

"- threw school lunch pudding at the other and received a punch in return."

"When we got suspended for the fight," Meera put in, "my parents made me write a report on Gandhi's nonviolence."

"Yeah, and the minute my dad heard about it, he made me write two reports: one on the claims of Gandhi's racism and another essay on Dr. King's nonviolence. We both had to present the two kinds of nonviolence to the whole school on the International Day of Nonviolence."

"It was pretty mortifying," Meera agreed, remembering the school assembly where she blushed so furiously she thought smoke would come out of her ears. Elisha had to explain to rows of bored and skeptical middle schoolers that Gandhi was a case study in overcoming racism. Educated in Great Britain, he both experienced and absorbed colonial racism. As a young person of color, he was discriminated against by the British, and in turn picked up discriminatory views toward Black South Africans. But during his time in South Africa, his racism was challenged and ultimately shifted. The Mohandas K. Gandhi who arrived there as a twenty-three year old was not the same Gandhi who left there as a forty-five year old.

"The interesting thing about Gandhi," Elisha had informed her peers, "wasn't that he was racist as a young person, and sexist and classist, but that he tried to unlearn those beliefs throughout his whole life."

In a world rife with discrimination, they were all taught to discriminate. Middle school was full of spoken and unspoken hierarchies: the pretty clique, the coolest, best dressed, geeks and nerds, jocks and brains. Ask anyone in the cafeteria and they could describe - in detail and down to the last person - the silent caste system to which they relegated each other, organized the lunch tables, and determined the pecking order of the bully chain. The color of one's skin, the price tag on sneakers, the latest model of phone, one's accent or attitude . . . Meera and Elisha caught on quick that they - and everyone they knew - had a backpack full of subtle biases that influenced their daily choices. These biases decided who they hung out with and whether or not they liked the students in their group assignments. They determined whether someone egged on a bully's teasing or stood up to defend their classmates. Young Mohandas Gandhi's experience in South Africa was one of intense change, a trial by fire of unlearning the racism he had been taught to hold toward himself and others.

"People tend to forget that Gandhi was a person of color, a person who held both privilege and oppression," Meera had read from her notecards during the assembly. Her voice barely squeaked above a whisper.

Elisha had shoved the microphone closer to her face and whispered the famous Gandhi quote in her ear: "Speak your truth, even if your voice shakes, right?"

Their eyes met. In that moment, as Elisha Adams held the mic up to amplify Meera's painfully shy words, their friendship began. In the coming years, they proved inseparable, becoming mutual instigators of student-led actions, and learning about the many ways that the Civil Rights Movement was deeply influenced by Gandhian nonviolence. There had been a long-standing and articulate discussion of the nonviolent approach in Black journals and circles for years by the time of the Montgomery Bus Boycott. Dr. King had even traveled to India after Gandhi's assassination to study with the Indian organizers.

"Remember what my Dad told me?" Elisha chuckled, nudging Meera in the ribs as they sat side-by-side on a pair of plastic chairs in the beige-walled room in Boston City Hall.

Laughing, the pair launched into an imitation of Elisha's

father, squaring their shoulders and shaking their fingers.

"Nonviolence is a technology. Nobody stops using their computers and cars because racists use them. If Dr. King didn't let Gandhi's stupid ideas when he was a youth get in his way of using nonviolent action to shake his country to the core, why should you?"

Elisha's eyes turned misty.

"I miss him, too," Meera said gently, giving her a squeeze.

Elisha nodded. Two years ago, her dad had a heart attack on the way home from teaching conflict resolution in the South End of Boston. Half the city came out to mourn; the ongoing program was endowed in his memory. He didn't just *believe* in nonviolence; he *used* it every day, forming groups to de-escalate conflicts, training people to intervene in bullying, helping youth gain peer-to-peer mediation skills, launching restorative justice programs. His lifework and example lived on in countless people, including his daughter.

"And how about you, Frankie?" Zadie asked, turning to the third teen. "How'd you get dragged in with these two revolutionaries?"

"Me'n Elisha were in the Descendants of the American Revolution together," Frankie confessed. "My mom's a member."

Zadie lifted an eyebrow.

"Mmm-hmm," Elisha answered. "People don't realize it, but African American history is basically as long as white history in the United States. In fact, white people were the minority of the people on this continent at the time of the American Revolution. Between enslaved Africans and Indigenous Peoples, most of us weren't white."

"A bunch of the fighters at the Battle of Bunker Hill were Black," Frankie added. "The only guy to be recommended for

valor there was a Black man. The first casualty of the Ame
Revolution was Crispus Attucks, a man of African and Natick
descent. A quarter of the American soldiers at the Battle of
Yorktown were Black."

Elisha grimaced. When history curriculums left out the
color, the past became a pale reinforcement of preconceived
notions of whiteness. Colonial history had bored her senseless
with its litany of white-centric narratives. Boston education
glossed over one hundred and fifty years of its slave-owning
history, applauded themselves on banning slavery in 1776, and
thought being an abolitionist stronghold got them off the hook
for the structural racism that continued to this day.

"The Descendants of the American Revolution come in all
races, genders, and political persuasions," Elisha stated. "I was a
member until they banned me."

"What?!" Zadie exclaimed. "What did they ban you for?"

"Wearing their T-shirt while reciting Abigail Adams'
Remember the Ladies speech at a student sit-in on the football
field. We were protesting the sexism of unequal sports team
funding. It was Frankie's fault."

"All the best ideas are mine," Frankie boasted.

Elisha grinned. It was true. Out of a slew of half-ignored
middle school history classes on dead white guys, Elisha had a
crystalline memory of the segment on Abigail Adams. Drama-
obsessed Frankie had picked the feisty first lady in the
"Historical Speeches" re-enactment assignment. Taking the
homework an extra step, Frankie had turned an entire series of
letters between John and Abigail into a one-person
performance. The lines fired back and forth on women's
suffrage were burned indelibly into Elisha's memory.

"Ole Abby was badass. Pro-women's rights at a time when
women were property, anti-slavery when it was legal and

normal everywhere in the colonies," Elisha reported. "Tell her, Frankie."

Zadie leaned forward, already smiling in anticipation.

"Okay, so everyone knows the *Remember the Ladies* letter - you know, where Abigail begs John to remember the ladies as he's writing the Constitution and treat them more kindly than the jerks who came before," Frankie explained. "But what people don't know is that Abby wasn't politely *asking* John - she was threatening to revolt against the patriarchy."

"Do it! Do it!" Meera urged, eyes lighting up. "Do the scene you did in class!"

Frankie leapt up and recited from memory, every inch the impassioned First Lady:

"*If particular care and attention is not paid to the ladies, we are determined to foment a rebellion and will not hold ourselves bound in any laws in which we have no voice or representation.*"

Zadie grinned. Frankie held up their hand in warning.

"But John Adams zinged back that she was being saucy," Frankie reported, shifting posture and mimicking a huffy John Adams. "He wrote: *We have only the name of Masters, and rather than give up this, which would completely subject us to the Despotism of the Petticoat, I hope General Washington, and all our brave heroes will fight.*"

"Despotism of the Petticoat!" Elisha repeated as she and Meera burst into giggles. "I can't even . . . "

"Wait - John Adams was threatening to violently suppress his wife's campaign for women's rights?" Zadie exclaimed, staggered.

Frankie nodded. That same letter series also revealed that his views on the "insubordination" of Blacks, Indigenous Peoples, and others were equally insulting to the dignity of humanity. All they'd wanted was the same things the rich, white men were demanding: life, liberty, pursuit of happiness.

"Ole Abby didn't let it get her down, though," Frankie reported, quoting the reply from Abigail, *"Not withstanding all your wise Laws and Maxims, we* (the women) *have it in our power not only to free ourselves but to subdue our Masters* (i.e. the men) *and without violence throw both your natural and legal authority at our feet."*

"She would have made a good Dandelion Insurrectionist," Zadie joked, applauding as Frankie bowed. "She had quite a grasp of nonviolent struggle."

"Well, she should," Meera remarked. "The colonies had just finished a decade of widespread resistance. One hundred and fifty years before Gandhi, they were spinning their own homespun and boycotting British imported cloth. They also used mass civil disobedience, organized widespread tax resistance, and built alternative institutions. The colonies were basically independent before the Revolutionary War - all Thomas Jefferson did was send a keenly-worded text to the monarch. The Declaration of Independence wasn't a wishful, idealistic, or unexpected declaration. It was a statement of fact, reflective of the strength of the revolutionary struggle. "

"This is the kind of stuff we thrived on with DARx," Frankie said with a chuckle.

"What does the 'x' stand for?" Zadie asked.

"Excommunicated," Frankie reported. "After they banned Elisha, a bunch of us started a spin-off."

"So, I have to ask," Zadie said, turning to the Black teen, "are you *that* Adams?"

"No," Elisha snorted. "I'm closer kin to the Addams family on TV than the president. There's a family rumor that we're Tituba's daughters - the Black woman framed by those nasty

39

Salem girls during the witch hunts - but mom says that's just hearsay. We do know that we come from a long and notorious line of rabble-rousers stretching back centuries."

"No wonder Tansy thought we should meet," Zadie remarked. "You probably aren't at all alarmed by the notion of a Constitution 2.0."

Elisha snorted. It was more like Constitution 9.0. The laws of the United States were, by nature, a work-in-progress. As a young Black woman, she could neither forget nor forgive the racism and sexism inherent in the rich, white Founding Fathers. She couldn't enshrine a constitution that empowered people who looked like them while subjugating ninety-four percent of the population. They chickened out of abolishing slavery, caving to the Southerners' demands. They established a new ruling class of landowners rather than empowering people of all classes equally. Women actually *lost* the right to vote in several states, including New Jersey. For a lot of people alive back then, the 1787 Constitutional Convention was a real setback.

"We did a DARx stunt about it," Elisha reminisced. "It was on a class field trip to Philadelphia's Liberty Hall. Frankie and I got suspended for that one."

"I still think we should have gotten extra credit for being able to impersonate those tour guides," Frankie grumbled.

Throwing on the blue vests of the museum officials, Frankie and Elisha had given an impromptu tour to their fellow classmates - and a handful of tourists - explaining how the tall windows had been covered with blackout curtains, guards had been standing at the doors, and James Madison's records of the convention had been sealed until after the deaths of all the participants.

"If that sounds like the setting for a coup, it's because it was," Frankie chimed in. "It was the death of the revolutionary

40

ideals of the independence movement - a political maneuver so underhanded that thirteen delegates stormed out in protest. Two came up with a protest document listing the civil liberties of ordinary people: the Bill of Rights."

It took thirteen years to ratify the Constitution, in large part because of the death of participatory democracy in the form of town halls and popular votes. New Englanders, in particular, objected to their loss of rights and power, and resisted being replaced with elected officials. The words *pursuit of happiness* in the Declaration of Independence literally became *protection of property* in the Constitution. Instead of *all men being created equal*, the Constitution laid out how quantifiably *unequal* people were. The newly-minted country laid its foundation in commerce, land acquisition, and the establishment of a strong federal military with which to put down slave revolts and Indigenous sovereignty struggles.

"The rest is history," Elisha said with a shrug.

But the future was still up in the air.

"I think knowing history helps us decide what to change in the present," Zadie declared. "I think we can do better than to cling to the tattered, tainted remnants of the past. We can take the ideals and see if we can meet them more fully with new ideas."

Meera asked if that meant the Dandelion Insurrection was working on real democracy.

"Yeah, because we want to help," Elisha burst out.

"Seriously!" Frankie agreed. "Everyone's, like, *vote 'em out,* and we're, like, *dude, we can't.* By the time we can vote, it'll be too late for the planet."

"I can't answer for the Dandelion Insurrection," Zadie reminded them. In a leaderful movement, everyone made up their own minds. "But, Charlie and I are - "

"Oh! Hang on. Don't tell us here," Frankie said with a groan. They pointed at the security camera in the corner of the room. If they were really going to talk about revolutionary ideas, they couldn't do it where the surveillance state had its eye on them. The other two teens clammed up instantly, eyes wide and mouths shut.

"When we get out, we could go to our office," Meera suggested in a murmur.

"You have an office?" Zadie replied. These "kids" were ten times as organized as she and Charlie had ever been. Better informed. More articulate. More prepared. They even had an office, apparently, that could thwart the all-invasive surveillance state. She was trying hard not to feel jealous.

The three burst out laughing. They nodded, but Zadie caught a mischievous gleam in their eyes.

"Just where is this office?" she asked.

The three couldn't stop giggling. Finally, Elisha pulled a straight face.

"We're teenagers. It's summer. Where do you think we hang out?"

Zadie grinned. She knew exactly where: the beach.

CHAPTER FIVE

· · · · ·

Self-Rule

The sand scorched their soles as they hurtled over the dry boardwalk. Leaping the bracken of the tideline, they sighed at the touch of the ocean's damp edge. Elisha and Frankie raced each other into the surf. Meera waded in more slowly, pausing at each swelling wave.

"They can't bug the sand," the teenagers had told Charlie and Zadie, and the ocean waves were likewise safe from surveillance.

"You know who they remind me of?" Zadie remarked to Charlie as they waded into the sea foam and saltwater.

"Yeah," he sighed, "us."

She flicked water at him.

"Stop grouching," she told him, diving into the cool waves.

Charlie bent with a stiff smile and splashed some water on his face to break the press of heat. Hidden annoyance at Zadie's unexpected arrest gnawed at him. She could have talked it over with him. She *should* have at least warned him. But when he had complained, she'd thrown him an incensed, narrow-eyed glare and hissed back.

"I don't need your permission."

Hidden beneath that hot scorch of her words was the frustration ignited by her conversation with the teens. Who was *he* to think he controlled everything? Charlie caught only the baffling lash of her temper, though, and missed the sub-context, leaving him wondering what he had done to combust her anger.

43

Was it so wrong to think they should have discussed risking arrest before she had impulsively leapt into action?

He stared out at the waves and tried to let the prickle of tension dissolve in the salty sea breeze. The charges had been dropped for all of them; Tansy had convinced the city attorney to frame the teens' outburst as mere disruption. It was better than making mountains out of molehills with a court case in which the notorious Zadie Byrd Gray defended her right to revolution. Tansy had chewed them out on speakerphone even as she got them released with a wrist slap and a warning.

"Y'all pull that stunt in Boston City Hall again, they're gonna toss you head first out of their marbled halls."

"Linoleum, actually," Elisha grumbled.

"Don't sass me," Tansy snapped. "Y'all lucky they didn't call it *undemocratic treason*."

"How can calling for democracy be undemocratic?" Zadie exclaimed.

"Because they think they've got a constitutionally-outlined democratic process and y'all weren't following it."

Charlie agreed with Tansy. Maybe. He felt conflicted. Much as he conceded that the old system was flawed, he wasn't convinced that Elisha's strategy was warranted. She'd shut down the civic process. She'd been willing to supplant democratically-elected officials. He was the last person to judge another person for staging an insurrection, but was this really the right time or place?

Fortunately, Tansy had deflated the fiasco into a moot point. For now.

In the deeper water, the teens leapt and splashed, bursting to the surface with shrieks and smiles. For one great, glorious moment, they were just three teenagers at the beach. The afternoon light hung like held breath and for that suspension of time, the planet's heat and perilous uncertainty receded from view. Charlie wanted to call out, to warn them - or no, to simply freeze them in this moment: happy, not yet targeted by government repression or dodging hate mail in their inboxes or tied to the relentless yoke of political pressures.

A wave rushed in and hit his shins. In that instant, the illusion shattered: they were Black and Brown and queer and female and non-binary. They were born into a world of discrimination. They all were, even him. If Charlie were brutally honest with himself, he was forced to concede that even white maleness was a flimsy protection without the reinforcement of wealth. His stance against the rich and powerful had etched a target on his back. The moment he had switched allegiance from the oppressors to the oppressed, the powerful had turned on him with the special hatred reserved for traitors. For that's what Charlie was in their eyes: a class traitor, a traitor to the supremacy of people who looked like him, a traitor to the ideologies they espoused and profited from.

Charlie rubbed down the goose bumps that stippled his pale skin. The blast of summer sun made sweat run down his back. His long shadow wavered over the water. Zadie spoke to the teens and they burst into laughter, tossing glances back at him that he didn't know how to interpret. An acidic taste clung to the back of his mouth, unexpected, but familiar. Fear. He'd charged into the Dandelion Insurrection half-blind with youthful idealism. Now, he knew the taste of terror, the hollow agony of loss, the jittery queasiness of worry. Charlie's muscles knew the toll of rising to challenges again and again and again. He'd scaled mountains of dangers, but he looked at the landscape before him - the one Zadie charged breathlessly into - and flinched. He sighed. There was no way out but through.

Charlie waded deeper into the surf. The water smacked his

ribs. He gasped and hesitated.

Courage is taking the next step even when you are afraid.

Charlie took a deep breath and dove in.

The ocean swelled and rolled. Beneath the surface, the din of the world muted. The cries of gulls muffled. The burning heat of the day eased. When he came up for air, the world felt kinder, gentler, refreshed, and ready for new ideas. Zadie swam over, all smiles and sparkling eyes. He kissed her and even murmured an apology against her lips.

"Whoot! Whoot!" the teenagers cheered.

They broke apart. Zadie splashed water at Elisha's teasing. Charlie caught Frankie's wide eyes jumping between them and recognized the starry-glazed look of a burgeoning crush. He wondered which one of them it was for. He hid a smile. If it was a crush on Zadie, he knew the feeling.

They waded into the shallows and circled back to earlier conversations. With the damp sand sagging underfoot and the sandpipers scattering ahead of them, they strolled down the beach toward the distant jetty. Charlie thought of all the long meetings he'd endured in dreary conference rooms and wondered if holding discussions outdoors would change them.

Of course, he conceded, admitting to himself that the salty air and cooling swim had done his temper a world of good. The teenagers hopped the incoming waves. Charlie and Zadie laced their fingers together and walked on the mainland side of the shore, weaving in and out of the glistening bracken line. Their footsteps danced around seaweed and periwinkles, mermaid's purses, pale driftwood, and blue-black mussel shells. Their silence allowed the tides to speak, to whisper their thoughts in the crash of surf and hiss of water over sand.

At last, Meera broke the quiet, her words emerging from the depths of memory and reflection.

"Do you know why Gandhi called India's Independence Movement, the Self-Rule Movement?" she asked.

Zadie shook her head, feeling the sunlight warming her shoulder blades.

"He thought that in order for Indians to govern themselves as a nation again after hundreds of years of the British ordering them around, they'd have to rebuild the capacity to self-rule, to determine one's own actions with wisdom, and to work with others to wisely govern together as a nation."

"We need to learn self-rule," Charlie admitted. "Rich people have been ruling over us for hundreds of years. We, the People, are a little rusty at making decisions together."

In many ways, the United States was in a parallel predicament to the Indians in the early 1900s. For years, they'd been ruled by a regime. Now, everyday people had to step up and govern themselves. But would they make wise decisions? Or would they replicate the destructive behaviors of their predecessors?

Meera stepped sideways as a high wave washed in. Elisha yelped as it soaked her shins. Frankie dodged the splash.

"Democracy is not a spectator sport," Meera said, quoting Marian Wright Edelman, "but it's also a lot more than petitions and phone calls."

Elisha snorted. That was an understatement. Calling senators, signing petitions, going to town meetings, making short public comments, voting every few years - these were just a smidgeon of the immensity of possibilities in the field of democracy. What about national conversations on crafting policy? What about wisdom councils on intergenerational civic planning? Or citizens' assemblies on how to resolve the inequities that plagued their society? They didn't have time for slow baby steps; the planet was burning up. Even here at the

, the scorch of the sun heated the sands to a blistering temperature. Further down the shore, a relic of a coastal beach house crumbled into the water, decaying after last year's surging tides and rising sea levels had eroded its foundation. The owners had abdicated their responsibility to pay demolition fees. The ruined building was now the subject of a court battle to determine if taxpayers were obligated to cover these costs. Elisha frankly thought that people who were wealthy enough to own beachfront property should pay the fees, not the taxpayers in her neighborhood who were struggling to meet rent and keep the electricity on.

"I think we need to get in their faces and disrupt the old system with new ideas," Elisha stated, "like we did today."

"I don't know about that," Meera disagreed. "Sometimes, you need to start outside the halls of power and work your way in."

"Yeah," Frankie put in, "the American colonists didn't ditch the monarchy by staging an insurrection in London. They did it by building up a whole different governing structure in the thirteen colonies. By the time Jefferson trumpeted out the Declaration of Independence, the towns and cities in America really were independent."

"So, if we built alternative systems - " Charlie mused aloud.

"In schools, churches, workplaces, small towns, large organizations, and so forth," Meera explained, picking up steam, "then someday, people will see how outdated our current system is and replace it."

There were ten thousand places where participatory democracy was perfectly legal and not at all treasonous. If they built up a viable new system until its implementation was self-evident, change would be inevitable.

48

"Fine," Elisha grumbled. "Just remember: we don't have all the time in the world. The clock's ticking, folks."

Meera grimaced and kicked the foam of the incoming wave.

"You're right, but are people ready for this kind of change?" she asked. "If the Dandelion Insurrection called for direct action to overthrow city councils with citizens' assemblies, I think it would backfire."

"Like it did today," Charlie murmured.

"There will always be people who hate new ideas," Elisha huffed.

"It's more a case of *not knowing* about the new ideas," Frankie pointed out. "Most people have no idea what you're talking about when you say the words: *participatory democracy*."

Charlie and Zadie exchanged looks. It was true. Most people drew a blank. They thought it meant more voting or polling, more calling officials and signing petitions.

"People don't know what real democracy is because nobody talks about it," Meera sighed. "Nobody reports on it. Nobody teaches it. Nobody hears about how there's thousands of little democracy projects popping up all over the place."

"Well, they need to know . . . and fast," Elisha muttered.

Charlie's grin gleamed in the golden light of the afternoon.

"Well," he said softly, modestly, "perhaps that's where we can help."

CHAPTER SIX

. . . . .

Dandelion Democracy

Before the dandelions leapt out of hiding, before their bold actions erupted across the landscape of the country, before anyone even knew resistance to the hidden corporate dictatorship existed, Zadie Byrd Gray, wanderer and adventure seeker, had traveled across the nation, collecting the scattered tales of tiny rebellions and local uprisings. She told them to Charlie who put pen to paper and word to wind, and sent the stories into the hearts and minds of thousands.

"We can do the same with democracy stories," Zadie told Meera, Elisha, and Frankie. "We can spread the seeds of these ideas far and wide. We can help propagate a movement for real democracy by collecting and sharing these tales."

They could make visible the invisible. They could show that real democracy was happening already, right under their own noses. There was nothing unconstitutional about that. So long as they didn't directly challenge the political structure laid out in the Constitution, they could plant real democracy in every inch and aspect of American life. They could embed its values in how nonprofits came up with their annual plans, or how grocery stores decided what products to put on their shelves, or how spiritual communities studied their faith, or how schools determined their curriculum.

"We rarely ask people to help decide these things," Zadie pointed out.

The "greatest democracy in the world" was decidedly undemocratic in every layer and level of its society. Its culture was still deeply hierarchical, with top-down orders, bosses in charge, elites handing out marching orders to minions, marketing departments figuring out how to shove products down consumers' throats instead of asking what they truly wanted, and politicians repackaging unpopular policies in deceptive new names. Few groups gathered and asked what the people wanted. Polls determined how much crooks could get away with, not what people dreamed about and yearned for.

These weren't the stories reported on the corporate news. The rich and powerful had no interest in telling ordinary people about democracy.

"Elisha joked about the Harvard suits earlier," Zadie said, "but projects in real democracy, community self-determination, neighborhood sovereignty, citizen control of schools, police review boards, and participatory budgeting aren't coming from the elites - they're happy with the status quo - the changes are launched in places where the people are being abused by concentrated power and corrupt officials."

So, it was up to them to track down the stories and send them flying across the country like the silver seeds of the dandelion.

"You should go to the Food-Op in Atlanta," Meera said to Charlie and Zadie. "It's a low-income nonprofit co-op where the members work out how to redistribute food surpluses from farms, groceries, and restaurants."

"Oh, they could check out Rise Up Together in Mississippi," Elisha exclaimed. "It's a Black resistance and resilience movement. They're doing everything: co-op businesses, neighborhood democracy, boycotts of corporations, revolutionary political alternatives, restorative justice, and more, all as part of a racial justice movement opposing white-dominated traditional politics."

"While they're in the South, they could go to Shared Altar in Alabama," Frankie added. "It's an interfaith collective where the whole group meets to decide the content for worship and services. I heard about it from my cousin."

"Oooh!" Elisha exclaimed, eyes widening with a thought. "Mobile Mobile! In Alabama, there's also this differently-abled collective. We learned about them when one of their members visited our class and talked about ableism."

"Yeah," Meera chimed in, "the Disability Rights Movement gave us one of the best democracy slogans ever."

The three chanted it out together: *No decisions about us, without us!*

They had dozens of other suggestions on democracy projects. Armed with Internet access, they followed the rabbit hole of search engine inquiries down into a brimming underworld of participatory democracy projects happening off-the-radar of the mainstream. Charlie and Zadie exchanged looks. They couldn't go to all these places and collect all those stories, not in a thousand years. There were too many.

"We can start somewhere and call for others to post their stories, too," Charlie suggested. "We can popularize the idea and then let the people speak for themselves."

They agreed to let the teens set up a blog and crowd source suggestions for where they should visit. The teenagers named the blog, *Dandelion Democracy.*

There are ideas that come to you only when you can't sleep, Charlie and Zadie wrote in their first post, *when the state of the world keeps you awake all night, tossing and turning. Yesterday, we spoke to three young people, Elisha, Meera, and Frankie, and heard their burning questions for our world. Today, we're embarking on a quest like heroes of old, a search for real democracy. For we hold this truth to be self-evident: we, the People, have more sense in common than the elites who have been running the world thus far. We know the heartbreaks and the challenges of our lives. We know the pain and suffering of the policies that have failed us. And, we know the solutions, too. Hidden in our towns and cities are the answers to our questions, the solutions to our problems. We are going to seek them out. Tell us where to find them.*

The answers flooded in. Inez Hernandez in New York City invited them to interview her neighborhood's autonomous governance board, set up as a resistance node years ago. The Suburban Renaissance asked them to write about the ways they networked and exchanged tools and resources laterally, rather than from the top down. The tech wizards who built the secure Alternet had Tucker Jones do a video chat interview explaining the consensus-based design model. Idah Robbins and her elementary school students coauthored a story on democracy in education, telling about their struggles to stop the privatization of their public school. The Dandelion Insurrection abounded with examples of participatory democracy. As a leaderful movement, the practices of making decisions *with* everyone rather than *for* everyone attracted people who already organized in a similar manner.

New stories came in through the submission form every day, often from the network of writers Charlie had invoked during the Dandelion Insurrection's collective vote to choose whether to disband or disperse. The Woman From The Southwest introduced community dialogues over controversial proposals. The Schoolteacher By The Lake told them about the high school student council that held school-wide listening circles on bullying after a sophomore committed suicide. The Soccer Mom In The Suburbs shared about facilitating citizens' assemblies for rezoning plans. The Granny In The Mountains helped people organize wisdom circles for reversing youth flight from rural areas. The Kid On The Coast helped neighborhoods figure out how to care for aging populations.

Charlie and Zadie heard about participatory budgeting projects that redirected police budgets into conflict and crisis prevention teams. People sent in photos of the fishbowl discussions conducted in their city to address disproportionate police contact with minority youth. An elder wrote to them about a collective planning experiment at a senior living center to determine a shared activities schedule. Charlie and Zadie reposted the articles people sent, called organizations to interview them about their practices, and wrote co-authored essays about the meaning of democracy.

Democracy isn't just about voting on officials ... or even just voting in referendums, they explained. *It's about who decides what the problems are, how we hear from those impacted, and the way we figure out how to move forward together.*

They traveled through cities and towns, stopping to visit as many projects as they could squeeze in. They patched together travel funds from a crowd funding request on the *Dandelion Democracy* blog and the occasional speaking engagement at local universities. Everywhere they spoke, they invited local democracy project organizers to take the stage with them and share their stories. Elisha, Meera, and Frankie called them frequently, urging them to take photos and make short posts. #DandelionDemocracy started to trend:

#DandelionDemocracy can be done anywhere, by everyone.

#DandelionDemocracy is how we decide, together.

#DandelionDemocracy gives us tools for self-governance.

They visited Athens, Pennsylvania, a town that had the distinction of being the nation's first Sortition Town. Drawing on the history of their namesake city, they filled public positions by random lottery - sortition - instead of by election. It leveled the playing field for people who didn't have time or money to campaign. It cut down on corruption. It ended nepotism. From school board to town council, the two-year terms rotated with regularity among the citizens.

Sortition is like how we choose people for jury duty, Charlie explained in their blog about the visit. *A Sortition Town chooses their officials by lottery. Ancient Athenians preferred sortition over elections and campaigning. They didn't consider elections democratic – it was too easy to steal them, or to make campaigning unaffordable or inaccessible to regular people.*

They crossed the state line into Western New York, where they dropped in on a series of countywide listening circles designed to turn animosity over a development into creative solution-building for urban-rural planning. From there, they traveled to Youngstown, Ohio. The library system was curating its collection and budgeting its resources based on the response to a regional participatory polling campaign. Using yes/no text messages, the librarians determined what books to add, how many computers to make available, what equipment to put in their growing tool library, which branches could use sewing machines versus 3D printers, and so forth. Posters at bus stops and community bulletin boards expanded on the "question of the week" texts. A quarter of the city regularly responded to the texts. Another quarter filled out the sixty-question survey. Charlie and Zadie listened as the librarians explained how they had assessed the responses for gaps. Who hadn't responded? Why not? How could the library serve the needs of the community better?

Resource sharing instead of mass consumerism is critical to saving our one-and-only planet, Charlie wrote in their blog post about the visit. *Democratic systems like this one tap into the phenomenal knowledge an entire city holds collectively. If two heads are better than one, all of us are smarter than some of us.*

They traveled onward in the rattling old station wagon that had once belonged to Charlie's cousin Matt. A French Acadian medallion of St. Christopher, patron saint of wanderers, swung from the rearview mirror. A jar of Easter water gathered at dawn from his grand-père's spring rolled around in the glove compartment. Zadie stuck her lucky wheat penny in the space between the cup holders, touching it whenever the engine wheezed too loudly.

As they headed west, the summer heat wilted the cornfields. Entire stands of trees sagged under infestations of tent caterpillars, signs of an ecosystem thrown off-kilter. In the distance, the blinking lights atop fracking towers marked the places where citizens' resistance to fracking had lost a battle. Over and over, the Constitution's representative republic had served corporations and rich people. Was it any wonder that people were searching for ways to make citizens' voices not only heard, but responded to? Was it any wonder that ordinary people wanted to be in control of the decisions that affected their lives?

Participatory democracy was spreading because the people had better solutions than the power holders. The timeline for change was shockingly short. They needed all hands on deck. Their world desperately needed the collective intelligence of billions of people to solve its most dire and pressing problems.

When you tap into the brainpower of your community, Charlie and Zadie wrote, *you not only get* more *responses, you often find* better *ideas and* wiser *solutions.*

Their next stop was in Cincinnati. A group of Somali and Indian workers had launched a creative mapping project to redesign the bus routes to serve the lower income neighborhoods better. Unfortunately, they'd run into a stumbling block: wealthier neighborhoods were pushing for the transportation funds for their areas as they sought to lower their carbon footprint by shifting from cars to public transit. The organizers were facilitating story-sharing circles to try to transform anger and bitterness into creative solutions. After several hours of sharing, a Honduran nanny wondered why the wealthier residents didn't start a carpool network. That's how she got uptown to work on the days she had to leave before the buses started running. Why couldn't they figure out what her community had? With that option on the table, the group decided they could augment peak bus times with ride shares. By listening across class barriers, they found the solutions that unlocked transit justice for everyone.

"We really are smarter together," Zadie said to Charlie as they drove onward.

"I don't know," Charlie replied with a sigh, "we can also be astonishingly stupid together."

"Yeah, but ideally," Zadie argued, "good democracy practices help communities transform collective stupidity into collective intelligence. And from there, hopefully, turn it into collective wisdom."

"Do you ever feel like it's an uphill slog?" Charlie groaned as they crawled through traffic under the industrial zone's glaring electronic billboards. "I mean, the corporate media churns out a billion stupidifying messages each day. It cranks out misinformation and polarizing half-truths by the second."

"Yeah, it's a real headache . . . which brings us to our next stop," Zadie announced with a laugh. "The Indy Media Center in Indianapolis, Indiana."

The Indy Media Center trained citizen journalists in

solutionary journalism for the express purpose of empowering citizens to solve their conflicts and problems. In the time of the hidden corporate dictatorship, media conglomerates had pumped out biased news and outright lies with a totalitarian control the Third Reich would have admired. Under claims of impartiality, they pitted one network's slant against the other in dueling sets of lies. Each pretended to be more factual than their rival channels, but everyone lied, deceived, misrepresented, concealed facts, veiled truths ... and profited off it. The networks were propaganda outlets for feuding clans of rich people. One group invested in fossil fuels would pump out climate denying pseudo-science. Another group investing in weather engineering would claim that only tech could save the planet. Meanwhile, no one spoke up for the dire reality that the planet couldn't sustain the current rates of human greed and overconsumption. If they wanted wise democracy, the media needed to be devoted to that goal ... not to the goal of generating wealth for the rich and powerful.

The Dandelion Insurrection had kicked the most corrupt corporatists out of the government, but Charlie saw how much more had to be done. Without change in the media, wealth redistribution, shifts in cultural beliefs, and more, the changes they had wrought would be rolled back before the decade was out. At the Indy Media Center, the collective was actively organizing to reclaim the media from the corporate take-over.

"Media shouldn't be propaganda for the elites," said one reporter, a Latinx man named Jorge Cervantes.

"We should be building understanding, not hatred," added a tech specialist, Allison Yuan.

"A network's programming should be determined by surveying the whole community," the new media coordinator, Finn McEvans, put in.

Charlie and Zadie joined the collective for a roundtable lunch discussion at the Center. A potluck meal of burritos, vegetarian sushi, curry and noodles - even peanut butter and jelly on homemade sourdough bread - was spread across the table. A baker's dozen of staff members had joined the conversation. They worked in all forms of media: television, streaming, social media, arts, journals, blogs, newspapers, zines, murals, graffiti, posters, movies, books, poems, and speeches . . . the list went on. Media came in a hundred formats, shared by millions of people. The Indy Media Center's crew included grandmothers and children, veterans and radical activists. The faces around the table came in shades of mahogany, cream, peach, caramel, sienna, and every shade of humanity. Each person had a piece of the truth to share. Charlie took notes, scribbling down quotes as fast as he could.

"We, the People, are ten thousand times more interesting, creative, and inventive than the corporate media's portrayal of us," Ali Suong said.

"Our mission here at the Indy Media Center is to empower communities to listen to people instead of corporations," Layla Mansoor added.

"We want our fellow citizens to tune into their neighbors instead of talking heads," Dev Gupta explained.

"We want to share people-powered solutions instead of advertisements for yet another stupid product," Amanda Nguyen contributed.

Imagine, they urged Charlie and Zadie, that every media outlet - every television station, news magazine, social media page, blog post, radio and podcast program, and so on - shared the purpose of disseminating accurate information in order to empower collective wisdom. Imagine if every time a problem came up in the news, the reporters covered what happened, who was harmed, the solutions and alternatives tried by others, and how people could take steps to meaningfully address what had caused the problem to begin with.

"It's restorative justice taken to the next level," Lakeisha Kuare told them. She ran the *Community Justice Through Media* program.

Media was powerful. For decades, it had been a tool of the rich. It had been used to divide and conquer the populace. The result? A nation at war with itself, a populace seething with self-loathing, a people on the verge of constant hysteria, afraid of one another and blind to the potential of change.

At the Indy Media Center, the team was campaigning to take back the television and radio broadcasting licenses from corporations and put them under democratic stakeholder - not shareholder - control. Thanks to the hidden corporate dictatorship, four companies had gained control over eighty percent of the media. But now, the bullhorns of the hidden corporate dictatorship's propaganda machine were being seized as politicians and CEOs were finally being convicted of bribery, corruption, insider trading, and a slew of other white collar crimes.

"We've been pushing to have these licenses and stations returned to the public as a form of reparations for the damage done by the regime's lies," Lakeisha and her colleagues explained.

Charlie wanted to cheer ... or cry with relief. The corporate-controlled media had caused so much pain, damage, and confusion with its lies about the nation's wars, the climate crisis, economic peril, and more. Reparations in the form of returning media resources to the people was a powerfully transformative idea.

"How can I help?" he asked.

With a series of articles, the Man From the North's endorsement of the Indy Media Center's efforts knocked the first domino over in a cascading set of changes. In rapid succession over the next few months, three court rulings shifted thirty percent of the media channels into public control. A bill slogged its way through Congress that restored older, fact-based reporting laws. On its heels, a second bill passed that evicted private companies from publicly-licensed airwaves. The private bandwidths were still concentrated in a few tightly-gripped fists, but it was a start. It would be a big help when it came to dealing with controversial issues.

Democracy had to be a way of life, not merely a political system. When push came to shove and conflicts turned heated, it helped if an entire society was familiar with the processes that proposed solutions, met needs, and even healed the pain and harms that had been done. Abortion, gun control, racism, colonialism, illegal wars: there was a long laundry list of hot button topics on the national agenda.

Could participatory democracy handle them? Charlie wondered. He recalled the countless shouting matches he'd witnessed when he covered local town council meetings throughout his valley in Northern Maine for the local paper. If civic process broke down over where to put in a boat landing on the river, how could it deal with polarized and divided issues riddled with pain and controversy?

He'd heard the stories of it being done. In 1971, for example, the decision to integrate the school departments in Durham, North Carolina, was made through a community-wide *charrette*. This was a process that gathered people over several days in a range of one-on-one, small group, and larger assemblies to discuss desegregation. Two of the main organizers were bitterly opposed local leaders, a Black woman and a Ku

62

Klux Klan member. Pitting their factions against each other, they wound up getting over a thousand people involved. Despite hatred and intense fear, the charrette led to a surprising outcome. The deciding vote in favor of desegregation was made by the KKK member, whose views had been changed by the experience of speaking directly with Black community members.

In Tennessee, Charlie had a chance to witness firsthand the way real democracy could be a transformative process for a community. They had been invited to sit in during a contemporary charrette process on defunding the police and reinvesting in alternative conflict teams. It was a condition set by a restorative justice circle for the mother of a Black teen who had been shot by the police. A local Black-led community justice coalition had organized it. Tensions were running painfully high. The police chief had ordered all off-duty officers to participate. Racial justice and white ally groups had mobilized thousands to attend. The Supporters of the Police League had sent their club members. The organizers put in sixteen-hour days, debriefing the team and putting out fires. But, the process held officials' feet to the fire and made them look into the eyes of the citizens impacted by their policies. Police and community members heard from one another directly. People who initially supported the police listened to firsthand reports of over-policing and racist policies. Black residents asked pointed and hard questions of police and officials. The inside-workings of the police department were laid bare, sometimes deepening the community's understanding of their challenges, other times revealing the blatant biases officers held.

It was intense, heart-wrenching, and eye-opening. At the end of the week, the city council agreed to overhaul the police department, defund several units, invest in community-led crisis response teams, revise the use of force standards and code of conduct policies, and implement a community review board with subpoena power.

It was not a perfect solution. It was not a panacea. Everyone could see there was more work to be done. Not all of the police officers left as racial justice champions. The Black community members still held pain, trauma, and skepticism. But something had shifted . . . and that shift opened the door for more change. As Charlie and Zadie said their farewells, they spotted one of the organizers speaking with the mayor about other ways charrettes and democracy practices could be used to address pressing issues in the city.

Remember, Charlie and Zadie cautioned their readers, *democracy is not a free-for-all. It's not some free market version of group process where the loudest shouter wins. There are structures and practices that can help collective wisdom arise in a group - even one deeply divided by hatred, pain, and fear.*

If done well, democracy could help dispel the ignorance that polarized issues. It could assist communities in finding their way to common ground. It could be healing and transformative, eye-opening and empowering.

People are wiser than we think, they wrote, *but the system is rigged against wisdom. Media and politics are both designed to pit us against one another. It is important to circumvent those and figure out ways to come together and come up with the solutions we need.*

And with Dandelion Democracy, that's what Charlie and Zadie were trying to encourage, one community at a time.

CHAPTER SEVEN

. . . . .

Mr. Megachurch

The television blared beyond the hiss of the motel's spotty shower. Zadie fiddled with the nozzle, hoping to turn the lame drizzle into a spray that could pierce her thick curls. They were in the vast, blank slate of the American Heartland. The endless flatness hid its size in repetitions of corn and soy fields. The monocrops had been prairie once upon a time. Long ago, they would have swayed in the wind's rhythm and sung in clusters of buffalo grass, ricegrass, nimblewill, and lovegrass. Three centuries ago, flocks of birds and herds of antelope and the Kansa people would have echoed the circles of the plants' generational journeys. Instead of lines and grids, this land's flatness would have carried waves and swells, edges and eddies, slow dances of advancing grasses interspersed with wildflower waltzes. Above herds of bison and burrowing badgers, the clouds told stories across the sky. Sharp, dramatic storms would have growled warnings to jackrabbits and silver coyotes. Gentle shushing lullabies of rain would have drummed on the rooftops of prairie dog colonies.

Instead, an eerie monotony of flat, green, flapping cornstalks surrounded them, endless and relentless. The plants clung to washed out soil, pale and listless, propped up by chemicals. It was a continent-sized holocaust masquerading as progress.

They'd booked a motel that night and ordered take-out Chinese from the place down the street. As Zadie showered,

Charlie began to type up his notes from their visit with their friend Tucker Jones in Kansas. As usual, the modest computer programmer was up to revolutionary mischief, along with his friend Alex Kelly, who was looking for a career shift. Alex had engineered a masterstroke of resistance, Operation Shut Down, which had locked down the major branches of the government in opposition to John C. Friend's bid for control. From congressional staffers to state department workers to IRS file clerks, thousands of federal employees had walked off the job and refused to serve the power-grabbing Interim President. Tucker had never been so proud of government bureaucracy in his life.

Alex's higher-ups, however, didn't appreciate it. The formal investigation had been inconclusive, officially, but fingers pointed, people talked, rumors hinted, and Alex's name went on the short list of suspected organizers. The FBI and NSA told Alex in no uncertain terms that she was no longer welcome in federal service. Since she had a secret history of covert leaks and whistleblowing, she accepted her severance package, emptied her desk, and bolted out of DC. Alex kicked around her mother's house for a few miserable weeks before leaping at Tucker's invitation to visit him in Kansas.

"If you want a job reprogramming robot tractors," Tucker told her, "there's a future for you here."

They laughed, but when Tucker's neighbor came begging for his help with his computerized tractor, she didn't hesitate.

"We've become tractor pirates," Alex told Charlie and Zadie with a laugh. "We hijack the corporate monopolies' systems, disable their tracking devices, unlock their coding, and liberate farm equipment for the benefit of humankind."

Back when tractors became fully automated, the agricultural corporations locked the hoods and started charging for all maintenance. Gone were the days when a farmer could tinker with the engine and do his own repairs. Now, repairs had to be done at licensed shops and farmers had to pay the corporations thousands of dollars when something broke. The expense was more than most farmers could bear. One by one, the mega-corporations squeezed the profit margin out of farming, sent the farmers into debt, and bought up their operations.

So, like pirates of old who sailed the seven seas evading the trade monopolies of the original imperialistic mega-corporations, Tucker and Alex were pirating the tractors, using code instead of cannonballs and hacking techniques instead of swordfights.

"If I could make those companies walk the proverbial plank, I would," Tucker sighed, shaking his head.

"Huh. I'd go for the non-proverbial plank," Charlie snorted. "Those agricultural corporations are responsible for hundreds of thousands of farmer suicides in both the US and India, famine-driven wars in Africa, the collapse of ocean ecosystems from nitrate run off. I could go on."

He didn't though. If he began listing the agricultural corporations' crimes, he wouldn't stop until dawn. Compared to that litany, pirating a couple of tractors was a drop in the ocean. Charlie planned to write an exposé on the strangling of democracy in machinery; everything down to the bolts was now proprietary knowledge. Tinkering was illegal on most machines, if not impossible by design.

While he wrote, Zadie futilely struggled with the faltering showerhead. Finally, she gave up and simply let the hot water run down her spine, easing the aching spot between her shoulder blades. She shut off the faucet with a squeal of old, shuddering pipes. In the quiet, she heard the muffled sound of the television rising and falling in the cadence of hellfire preaching. She frowned. What on earth was Charlie watching?

"God intended this to be a Christian nation. It is part of His divine plan. He intends to spread His reign to the furthest corners of the globe, to rout out heathenism and sin, and to bring salvation to the sinful and suffering, alike."

Zadie stood dripping on the postage stamp bathmat, listening. Where had she heard that voice before?

"God gave us our marching orders in the Bible. Only three things stand in our way: Democrats, the Devil, and the Dandelions."

"Did you hear that?" Charlie exploded, shouting over the sound of the man's voice.

Zadie came out, sitting down on the sagging bed, drying her wet hair with a towel. Charlie spluttered at the television as the preacher called upon his worshippers to remember that the Lord wanted them to be humble gardeners toiling in his fields - not weeds and upstarts showing up where they weren't wanted. Charlie's fingers tap-danced over his keyboard as he looked up the program. The man was Reverend Jebediah Whyte - Jeb to his friends, Reverend to his flock. On the screen, he flashed a set of pearly whites worthy of a toothpaste ad. They gleamed amidst a tanning booth shade of bronze. He exuded the typical blonde-haired, blue-eyed Jesus evangelical charm. Reverend Jebediah Whyte was broadcasting from the nation's largest megachurch, a whale of a structure renovated from an old football stadium in Eastern Texas. It could seat seventy thousand people . . . and televised to over two million viewers. The camera zoomed wide over a congregation that could have done a crowd scene for Hitler's biopic. The service had a production quality worthy of Vegas. Spotlights swept the stage. The choir could have performed on Broadway. Hollywood would have slit throats for their gospel soundtrack.

"Now, I myself," Reverend Whyte went on, "give praise to God for American democracy. My father fought for it. My uncle died for it. My brother brought it to Iraq."

Charlie snorted. The United States had delivered American corporate occupation to Iraq and seized their oil fields in an illegal war. Democracy didn't enter into the equation.

"But when I say *democracy,* I mean the brilliant system delivered to us by the Founding Fathers, not the anarchy making headlines these days." Jeb shook his blonde curls and rolled his blue eyes up to heaven in an appeal to the Lord. "If we're not careful, you know what those Dandelions will do? They'll be demanding that we replace God with a citizens' council!"

The megachurch congregation roared with laughter, but Jeb Whyte wasn't joking.

"Remember the last time someone tried to take God's place? Why, the Lord smote Lucifer down from heaven into the fiery depths of Hell! And that's the first and last place these notions of Zadie Byrd Gray's should go. Straight to Hell."

His congregation thundered with approval, clapping and stomping their feet.

"Did he just ... ? He actually named you," Charlie spluttered.

A look of pure wrath came over Zadie's features. Now, she remembered where she'd heard his voice before. She stalked across the room and clicked off the television.

"I hate that guy," she stated flatly. "He's poisonous."

At first, she refused to elaborate. She slammed around the hotel room like a whirlwind, shoving her clothes into her travel bag, knocking the plastic wrapped cups off the table with her elbow, bumping her hipbone into the edge of the doorjamb. When she tripped over the shoes she'd pulled out just moments before, Charlie grabbed her by the shoulders.

"What's wrong?" he asked, seeing the distraught and wild look in her eyes.

Zadie sank down onto the edge of the bed. Her hands clenched the comforter in a white-knuckled grip.

"You know why we can't have children? That guy. Jeb Whyte. He made abortions illegal, him and his millions of self-righteous evangelicals. Despite the facts, despite the decades-long evidence that banning abortions doesn't stop them, it just makes them more dangerous."

Zadie bit her lips, a storm of rage and sorrow shuddering within her. She'd had an illegal, back alley abortion at sixteen, nearly bleeding to death and destroying her womb in the process. She'd never have children now, not even with Charlie, who'd be ten times the father - no, a hundred times - that the abusive guy who'd knocked her up would have been.

"I see that smug face oozing with his self-righteous sanctimoniousness, claiming moral superiority on television, and I just want to punch walls and throw hard objects at the screen!"

His power kept growing, too, expanding year after year. Corporations owned the television networks, but evangelicals had bought up the radio stations, one by one, until you couldn't pass through the middle of the United States without being preached to on the car radio. Zadie had no gripe with Christians, on the whole. It was a faith like all others: marked by brilliant mystics who spoke of love, and marred by its history of institutional violence and oppression. Few faiths had escaped the living damnation of corruption and abuse. To her, the responsibility of living peacefully with others and correcting the wrongs of the church, temple, or faith leaders was a challenge in all religions.

This, however, was hardly even religion.

"Look them up," Zadie told Charlie. "Their end goal is global domination, a Christian empire that encircles the world. In the meantime, they're hard at work taking over the United States, installing christo-fascists in political offices and powerful positions."

Charlie shuddered. Capitalism, Christianity, and colonization made a sinister trinity. Each one had been used to justify and enrich the others, training foot soldiers and worker bees, oppressing millions around the world. Zadie was right: this wasn't religion. This was a corruption of faith so severe it resembled the very horrors it denounced: violence, hatred, murder, domination, intolerance. This was the underpinnings of genocides and hate crimes and lynch mobs and holy wars. It was syrupy self-righteousness poured over vitriolic hate. It was poisonous and seductive. It was as American as apple pie.

"So, that's why he's bent out of shape? Our democracy projects are getting in the way of his global domination?" Charlie wondered.

"That's part of it," Zadie answered, rubbing her eyes, "but it's also about hierarchy and control."

The Dandelion Insurrection's leaderful structure and radical equality dismantled chains of command. It challenged the idea of *the guy on top* . . . and that threatened everything from *father-knows-best* ideologies to God on High, white supremacy, the United States as a superpower, and visions of a christo-fascist empire. In Zadie's view, hierarchy was a dinosaur whose Ice Age was coming. Its mastodons and wooly mammoths may not have surrendered to elephants quite yet, but the handwriting was on the wall. The glaciers of those times were receding. A different way of life was arising. The social and political ecosystem was evolving, but the Jeb Whytes of the world were hell-bent on making sure the old worldview survived. If love had proven as enduring as the horseshoe crab, domination was the cockroach of humanity. It was violent, dangerous, and organized. Jeb Whyte's ideologies of Christian supremacy were a politics of extremism and hate, wielded by people convinced of their own goodness and right-to-rule.

People like Jeb Whyte held a mirror up to the world and saw distorted images of themselves. They assumed that all the violence and hatred they envisioned for other races, classes, nationalities, and faiths was felt back toward them. They could not imagine equality, only hierarchy, and so losing supremacy meant being ground down under heel. They had oppressed everyone, and suspected that everyone would oppress them if given the chance. They feared people would do unto them what they did unto others. They saw through the lenses of themselves and missed the truth entirely.

Charlie sat next to Zadie on the sagging hotel bed, shoulder touching hers, offering wordless support. He turned his hand palm up on his thigh, an offering. She slid her fingers into his.

"Want me to write a fiery denouncement of his megachurch?" he said.

She chuckled and wiped the shine of tears out of her eyes.

"No. Well, not today, anyway," she answered.

He shrugged. The offer stood.

Zadie squeezed his hand then rose. The evening awaited them. She wasn't going to let Jebediah Whyte ruin it.

She glanced at Charlie and saw the words writing themselves behind his eyes, a grim expression on his face. She let him be. Someday, they might need those words. Someday, they might be a line of defense against intolerance and hatred. That day was not today.

But someday . . .

CHAPTER EIGHT

· · · · ·

Rainbows of Democracy

Jeb Whyte and the evangelicals were not their only critics. The system of government designed in 1787 had been built to offer equality to dueling factions of rich, white men, not to all of the human beings it impacted. Over the years, waves of struggle had attempted to expand that framework. Suffragists knocked down the doors of the males-only club. Black, Chicanx, and Indigenous Peoples campaigned for equal suffrage. The poor and property-less classes waged constant struggles to stop the rich from exploiting them. It was a never-ending effort, tidal in nature, flowing forward as people advanced and ebbing backwards as elites rolled out gerrymandering, Jim Crow, unrestricted campaign financing laws, voter disenfranchisement, closures of polling places, and more. Racism ran rampant through this system's history, along with sexism, colonialism, and imperialism.

Like pulling out threads in the fabric of the empire, participatory democracy unraveled those injustices. It carved out space for equality to breathe, for people to decide their own fates, and to put the community in control of itself. Black people, in particular, had a long history of resisting racism through building independent institutions and insisting on community control. After their visit with Tucker and Alex, Charlie and Zadie went north to Freedom, Oklahoma, to see one of these contemporary projects firsthand.

They skirted the cities and followed the old country roads to an intentional community. Elisha had connected them, asking them to write a piece that could be shared with similar communities in Minnesota, North Carolina, Missouri, and California. People tended to think of white hippies when they heard the word "intentional community", but, due to segregation, Black Americans had long history of self-organized towns and cities. In the 1890s, Oklahoma had dozens, including universities, farm communes, worker co-ops, and Black-run governments. In the case of Freedom, Oklahoma, the farmlands were stewarded by the Cherokee Nation, but a self-sufficient, sustainable community of thirty Black families had been offered a low-cost, hundred-year lease for an off-grid community. They'd built not only a shared community center, but also crafted processes that drew from several cultural strands, integrating restorative justice, arts-based relationship building, and direct self-governance.

Freedom, OK, embodied a story that revealed the long history of self-governance as resistance to white supremacy. It showed how creative solutions could meet the needs of multiple groups. It was a story that showed the longevity and diversity of the very movement Charlie and Zadie had been tracking across the country. It was a story that encompassed the history and present, the resistance and resilience of the people who had demanded democracy because all other forms of government had utterly failed them. Community control of police departments, schools, and local government was a notion that never died. It was the simple, but radical idea that people should be in charge of the institutions that impacted their lives. Charlie and Zadie left inspired, humbled, and renewed in their commitment to participatory democracy as a vehicle of community justice.

This, however, was exactly why the old guard hated real democracy.

They were driving across Nebraska when Charlie's phone rang.

"Brad Anderson," Charlie groaned, answering. "I was wondering when I was going to hear from you."

"You're a hard man to get ahold of these days, Charlie," the flat tone informed him.

Charlie rolled his eyes and made a face. Zadie motioned for him to hang up. He shook his head; Brad would just keep hounding him.

"What do you want?" Charlie asked.

"I just want to know what everyone wants to know," Brad replied, his tone oozing ominous geniality. "What on earth are you two doing?"

Charlie frowned.

"Isn't that obvious from our essays?" he replied, jiggling his knee in agitation.

"Charlie, this isn't a good time to be confusing people," Brad answered. "People need leadership, not this joy-larking about, chasing rainbows and fairy tales of democracy."

"Is that what you think we're doing?"

"It's not just me, Charlie. It's everyone around here. We're all concerned about this little stunt."

I bet you are, Charlie thought savagely. The entire Capitol Hill gang must be having heart palpitations over the rising interest in direct - not representative - forms of democracy.

"If you and Zadie want to go on a road trip," Andersen was saying, "go visit the Grand Canyon - "

"- that's not - "

" - but don't go undermining the party in the primary season, Charlie. We need you on our side. We need the Man

75

From the North to help get this country up and running again. We need the Dandelion Politics crew out there stumping and campaigning, not organizing . . . what was that last thing you wrote about? Listening circles?"

The man's tone dripped with disdain. His scorn was withering.

"There's a time and a place for everything. You'll have a chance to do this work in two years . . . and imagine what we can do to support it. The House, the Senate, the Oval Office - help us make a clean sweep of it and you'll have everything on your side, Charlie. We can take these notions of yours out of idle dreaming and into reality."

"Why not do it now?" Charlie challenged, cutting Andersen off abruptly. "Why wait?"

"Too much, too fast, too soon," the DC man answered. "We've got to take it slow, secure the seats. Change doesn't happen overnight."

"What are you asking, Brad?"

"Let this go for now. Support the party. Set things up to do it right. You're not in the shadows fighting the corporate government anymore. You've won. This is the time to work with us, not against us."

Charlie grimaced. He didn't have much patience for Brad Andersen, and he resented being told to "get in line" and behave himself.

"Call me when the Democrats are ready for real democracy," he said, hanging up and silencing the ring tone.

Too much. Too soon. Too fast.

Brad Andersen's comment echoed in his ears. He'd heard it before, blaring out of the bullhorns of corporate media. Zadie's call for shaking up democracy provoked roars of objection from surprising quarters. Charlie had anticipated the conservative,

Constitution-loving faction's kickback. He had predicted the far-right Christians' reaction. But the opposition from the left-leaning power holders stunned him. It wasn't just Andersen. He'd been noticing growing counterarguments being made in speeches by academics and heads of universities. Talk shows hosted lopsided "debates", reinforcing falsehoods and myths about real democracy. If he had to hear one more pundit tell him that "democracy was two cats and a mouse deciding what was for dinner", he'd scream. The two-party duopoly railed against them, of course. In the midst of a multi-billion dollar rebranding effort, neither party was interested in dismantling the electoral system in favor of something as uncontrollable as real democracy.

In the comment threads, the online trolls' remarks made Charlie cringe:

That pair of infantile political superstars will wreak havoc on the greatest democracy in the world.

Once great leaders, they've devolved into demanding ingrates who want the impossible.

They got change. Now they want anarchy.

The pushback and criticism gnawed at Charlie's confidence. He fell silent for a long stretch, lost in his thoughts. They drove under a towering thunder cell that ached with lightning tension and bone rattling booms. It growled and crackled over the stretching prairie. Zadie rubbed the hairs down on her arms. She glanced at Charlie. She recognized that particular crease in his brow, deep as a gorge between his eyebrows, the way the skin above his jaw twitched like the hide of a nervous horse.

"What's wrong?" she asked, softly.

The storm dragged blue-black shadows over the half-veiled horizon's edge. Around them, the sunlight gathered in a huddle like a herd of antelope, ears pricked at a sense of danger, ready to bolt and run.

"Are we just kicking up a hornet's nest?" he worried, letting out his tension with a bursting exhale. "Is this democracy stuff *too much, too fast, too soon*, like Andersen said?"

"I know we're getting pushback, Charlie," Zadie answered, "but we can't live on accolades alone. We have to do what's right."

"Are you sure this is right?" Charlie asked. He breathed out the words in a hush of confession. A flash of lightning leapt the distance between cloud and earth. Their eyes jumped instinctively toward it, but in the infinitesimal gap between periphery and center, it vanished.

Was it too much, too fast, too soon? Or was it so long overdue that we've forgotten that it is a human right to be involved in the decisions that impact our lives? Power comes from the people. We bestow it upon leaders and systems through our obedience and cooperation. Perhaps our consent is gained under duress, despair, or distress, but at the end of the day, when we support the system, go along with it, or fail to oppose it, we give our tacit consent to the regime of the hour. We give them the power to rule over us. We let our inherent power lie dormant within us and accept the rules of their political games. For millennia, common people have been browbeaten and starved into giving rulers our consent. We've been strong-armed into accepting unjust rules and rulers. At sword-point and gunpoint, we've been forced to obey dictators and tyrants. Under the shadow of drones and nukes and bomber jets, we've been terrorized into accepting the politics of our times. With teargas and rubber bullets and sound cannons, we've been told over and over again to give up the power of the people and submit to the rules of the powerful. We've given our power away so many times that we've lost sight of the fact that rulers wield the borrowed might of millions. But it is ours. Ours to give. Ours to take back.

And when in the course of human events, it becomes necessary . . . we have the right and responsibility to alter and abolish the system of laws that oppress us.

"But what if these democracy practices *aren't* better than the old representative republic?" Charlie wondered aloud, plagued by the thought of leading lemmings off a cliff because the wolves were at their backs.

"It's about consent, Charlie," Zadie reminded him. "We inherited this system. We didn't design it. But in the past two hundred and seventy five years, we've won so much more equality, socially and culturally, than the Founding Fathers ever intended. It's time to revisit the political agreements, I think."

She wasn't talking about rewriting the Constitution. Not yet. She was talking about asking her people to explore what kind of politics they truly wanted. Until all three hundred and twenty million of them had sat in a wisdom circle or joined a participatory budgeting process or crafted policy with stakeholders or showed up at a citizens' assembly, they weren't consenting as fully-informed adults. They did not know their options. And without that knowledge, complicity could never be accepted as consent. This system wasn't created of, by, and for the people. From the Founding Fathers until today, it was created by the few to benefit the few at the expense of everyone else.

Zadie wanted to know what her fellow citizens would create if they had a chance, if they spent five to ten years building national awareness of their options, practicing the possibilities, and test-driving democracy systems to see how they worked.

"We need this, Charlie," she reminded him softly.

79

The Dandelion Insurrection had managed to reform the old system, to make it a little more fair and just, but it wasn't enough, not yet, and it was as vulnerable as ever to the creeping control of rich people and businesses. Like a poorly-built ship, the United States' political system would always tilt toward rule of the rich, not toward rule of the people. It had been designed to give extra weight to elites, to counteract the combined strength of the populace, to let the few have equal say to the many in the direction the ship was headed. A strong captain could try to avoid icebergs, but the problem lay in the design - uncapped hull sections, too few lifeboats, not enough capacity in the steering. The great mass of people was destined to drown in the inevitable collisions. They had to step off this ship. They had to remove the weight of their consent from this imbalanced structure and let it capsize.

But in order to get off, they needed to build another vessel.

"That's all we're doing, Charlie," Zadie said. "Working on another design."

Charlie let out a long breath. The furrow still divided his brow. The storm still rumbled ominously on the horizon. He realized that he and Zadie were just questioning and writing, introducing the notion of real democracy to the country. But they'd ousted the hidden corporate dictatorship. They'd thwarted the corporatists' attempts to steal everything that wasn't bolted down. They'd kept John C. Friend from sliding into power and unraveling everything they'd done. They had a track record of making big changes. Everyone knew it, for better or for worse. It gave some hope and courage. It gave others nightmares.

Those who feared their ideas also feared their power to make their dreams into reality, to unleash the people's capacity to change their world, to throw out the old and establish the new. Ideas were dangerous. You can't kill an idea. They burrow into hearts and minds, germinating at unexpected times and in surprising places. When they blossomed . . . they could turn the times on their head. The domestication of horses. The light bulb. The theory of evolution. Copernicus and Galileo. $E=mc^2$. Ideas could shape the world, unstoppably, irrevocably.

As for people-powered democracy, it was poised to upend the nation, a revolutionary idea taking root in evolutionary times. The people who feared its power also knew that Charlie Rider and Zadie Byrd Gray didn't deal in half-measures. They knew the revolutionary duo played for keeps.

And those people did not like to lose. Those people would not play nice.

CHAPTER NINE

. . . . .

Bloodsuckers

They landed in coastal Oregon amidst a downpour. It was a shock after weeks zigzagging through northern sagebrush and arid mountains. They had headed northwest from Kansas and Oklahoma, stopping in Nebraska to visit a grain co-op and a young ranchers' collective in Wyoming. They traveled through the sculpted landscape of South Dakota to attend a gathering of Sioux nations, posting an article on the long list of democracy practices Westerners could learn from the original peoples of Turtle Island. In Montana, they sat in on an intergenerational climate assembly that gathered Indigenous organizers and ranchers to resist an oil pipeline. In Eastern Washington, they picked apples with the farmworkers union.

As soon as they crossed over the Cascades, a veil of rain dropped down from the sky. They entered a land that seemed not quite awake, dreaming in grey mists and irrepressible greens. The downpour that marked their arrival at the coast was as natural as breathing. It was a rainforest, after all. The drizzle whispered hushing lullabies to the trees. The sun broke out through the clouds in a revelation of light.

They were here to meet a man named Oliver Lang and visit the renowned Democracy Lab. Charlie and Zadie received numerous requests each day asking: *how do we do this?* Even if they were experts - which they weren't - they couldn't handle the volume of requests . . . but Meera, Elisha, and Frankie knew who could.

"You've got to meet Oliver Lang," Frankie told them. "He's been advising our intergenerational climate council and our citizens' assembly."

"He's a bit obsessive," Meera warned them.

"And absentminded," Elisha added. "He once set his eggs on fire while telling me about the group decision-making practices of seventeen different Indigenous cultures."

He advised groups all over, troubleshooting, training, teaching, and facilitating. He was constantly on the road, a real roamer, but he lived in rainy Oregon and happened to be home. Charlie and Zadie met him at the entrance of the Tiny House Village where he lived. Oliver stood six foot six with impossibly long limbs and not an ounce of spare fat to his name. Jet-black hair flung out in every direction, just shy of punk-rock glory. When he paused in thought, he folded his hands one over the other. When he moved, he left the impression of an extremely large praying mantis. Though he was approaching forty, there was a touch of innocence to the man. Oliver - or Olli, as he insisted they call him - burst with delight in meeting them, pumping their hands with unrestrained glee.

"Can I just say . . . I am a huge fan. I mean, thank you, for - for everything. I read *all* of your essays, Charlie. Well, all that I could get my hands on. I think I missed a couple that got swept up in early raids - and - "

He paused, beet-red and sheepish.

"I'm rambling," he admitted.

"Gushing, actually," Zadie teased gently, tilting her head up at him. Her inky curls tumbled over the side of her face. Her hoop earrings caught the light and winked. "Maybe we can just pretend we've known each other for years?"

"Oh, yeah." He beamed. "I kind of have - I mean, everyone knows you two. I can still quote the first essay I ever read of the

84

Man From the North: *Democracy is not the circus act of elections. Democracy lives in the hills and valleys, the towns and kitchen tables throughout this nation. It's the way we decide things, together."*

Charlie hunched his shoulders self-consciously as Olli sang his praises.

"That essay made me realize that I wasn't alone in wanting something different," the tall man said.

Oliver was a wealth of knowledge. Despite his absentminded air, Olli focused like a telescope when working on a democracy problem. He was neither a professor nor a student. He was a mechanic of a political sort.

"I'm a democracy repair man," he offered cheerfully. "People call me when things go wrong. My job entails intense bursts of troubleshooting followed by long hours of mental tinkering."

He was a walking encyclopedia of participatory democracy projects across the United States - and around the world.

"You've got to look beyond our borders to see the full scope of this movement," he proclaimed, gesticulating with a broad sweep of his broomstick arm. Zadie ducked under his hand as it flung over her head. "Our country is backwards, regressive even, when it comes to democracy. It's like we're using switchboard telephones while others have high-speed Internet."

Olli's notion of democracy came with a hundred practices. He shared them with anyone who asked.

"I help anyone, anywhere," he said. "Even people I don't like or agree with. Democracy is a way for us to resolve our differences together instead of fighting. I'm all for that, even if I personally disagree with the beliefs and worldviews of some of the people I'm working with."

He offered to give them a tour of the Tiny House Village, passing out umbrellas from the stack near his front door. Oliver

Lang hailed from Seattle, originally, but for several years, he had dwelled in a Tiny House Village outside a mid-sized Oregonian town. For years after attending university, he had drifted, itinerant.

"Put all my meager earnings into paying back debt instead of rent," he admitted.

But as couch surfing lost its charm and cities cracked down on camping, Olli needed somewhere to crash between road trips. In the rainy climate, a roof beat a tent, hands down. Though the tiny house craze had started with aging upper middle class women, it swiftly popularized as a solution to the swelling tent cities of unhoused residents. Olli's village had once been a homeless camp plagued by police raids. Now, it had rows of shack-sized dwellings, a common kitchen, restrooms, and potable running water.

Olli had won his place by luck and skill. He happened to have pitched his tent in the encampment of unhoused persons just nights before one of the early raids. In the effort to defend his rights and get his tent returned, he rallied the local community to do something besides letting the authorities throw poor people's belongings into the trash.

"I was educated, articulate, and didn't fit into the usual biases," Olli sighed. "The critiques of the critics sloughed off my back like water from a duck. I had to step up and organize."

The Tiny House Village moved forward. Olli gained more than a roof . . . he found a home.

"We have internal governance, talking circles, democratic rules, restorative justice, and shared contributions for garbage, sewer, electric, and Wi-Fi. It's not perfect, but what town government is?"

Midway through Olli's grand tour, a man and a woman came racing around the corner. Their faces showed years of weathering, rough-skinned and wind-chapped.

"Hey, Olli! Just in time."

"For what? And where is everyone?" Olli asked, gesturing to the empty windows of the houses.

"Over on East Street," the woman reported. "The bloodsuckers are back."

"We've been trying to get them to leave," the man reported with a disgusted look, jerking his leathery thumb over his shoulder.

"Who is it this time?"

"Redemption Church volunteers," he groaned.

Olli cursed under his breath. He pulled the hood of his raincoat tighter and sighed. He gestured for Charlie and Zadie to follow. They navigated the large puddles in the gravel walkway, sneakers and cuffs soon sopping and squelching with each step. The bloodsuckers turned out to be a blood collection mobile that had pulled up alongside the village. Under the rollout overhang of a medical van, a pair of earnest-faced youths were trying to hand out pamphlets. No one took them. The village residents stood in a solid wall of stubborn resistance. Frowns carved each face. Arms crossed over chests. The volunteers laughed nervously. No one joined in.

Olli explained the strange scene to his guests. The blood collectors paid cold cash for pints of blood. In poorer neighborhoods, the monthly sales of blood kept the electricity turned on, bought food, paid bus fares for getting to work. It wasn't enough, but it was something.

"And the blood mobiles are run by Christians?" Charlie asked, blinking the rain out of his eyes.

Olli shrugged.

"Not always. This particular outfit is owned by an evangelical church out of Texas, the Redemption Church."

"We've heard of them," Zadie growled. This was that megachurch preacher they'd heard on television.

"These guys haunt the homeless camps, the soup kitchens, the shelters. Sometimes, they're run by the evangelicals. Other times, the bloodsuckers just pull up alongside another church's outreach work. They rope young students from evangelical colleges into handing out pamphlets - basically free labor disguised as missionary work."

The downpour thickened. A trickle of water slipped between the hood and zipper of Zadie's raincoat. She shivered. The grey deepened from gloomy to glowering. Olli kept talking as they took their places in the back row of residents. The horror story went on; truth was a bottomless pit once you started down this particular rabbit hole. Blood - plasma - was a trillion dollar global industry.

"In the affluent neighborhoods," Olli remarked, "they don't pay - it's all blood drives and donated pints. Think of the profits there."

But even those paled compared to the sheer volume of desperate people out of work and scrambling for survival. That's why the collection mobiles tracked the homeless and poor.

"The medical industry farms the poor," Olli commented darkly. "The blood is the funnel - it gives them a way to screen and scan the populace. Then they return for the organs."

Kidneys, ovaries, eggs, lungs, sperm, wherever the bloodsuckers found a relatively healthy body, they tried to collect the parts.

"Eyes are big money on the market," Olli murmured, gesturing discreetly to a man with a patch leaning against the wall of his tiny house. "Bone marrow fetches a high price, too. It's hard to get and painful to extract. I've heard of fathers who contracted their vital organs and committed suicide to support their families."

Zadie made a retching gasp. Olli nodded, somberly.

"Lots of young women sign up to be surrogate wombs, carrying rich people's designer babies."

It wasn't the blood collecting that worried Olli's community. It was the funnel of desperation that turned poor bodies into spare parts for the wealthy.

"That's . . . horrible," Zadie choked out.

"Yeah," Olli agreed, "that's why, about six months ago, we made a community decision to discourage them from pulling up here. Excuse me a second."

The village resident that had been serving as spokesperson had just thrown his hands up in frustration and stomped away. As the others exchanged nervous glances, Olli stepped up to the awning and pulled back his hood.

"Hey, I'm Olli," he said, talking to the woman with a stack of fliers and an umbrella.

"Have you come to join the Redemption Church's *Christ's Blood Saviors Program*?" the young woman replied, shaking his dripping, outstretched hand.

"No."

Olli's answer was toneless and uninterested.

"You need to leave. This community wants to be taken off your visitation rounds."

She stared at him blankly for a moment then remembered her spiel.

"But donating to save others is a holy act - "

"Yeah, I've heard. But this community has voted to do good in other ways. So, we're telling you to leave. Now. Please."

She wavered for a second and then went to get her boss. After a moment, he came out into the rain, pulling his hooded jacket up tight and standing under the awning, forcing Olli to duck under the runoff.

"We're on public property," he told Olli, loud enough for the others to hear. "We have all the permits."

"It's not a question of laws," Olli remarked quietly. "It's a question of respect. You aren't wanted here. We've asked you to go."

They stared at each other for a long, taut moment while the rain drummed loudly on the metal awning. Finally, Olli shrugged.

"You won't get any business here - "

"They're donations - "

"I don't care for the framing," Olli retorted harshly. "Working for survival money isn't a donation. You won't get any blood here, no matter how long you stay. If you choose to overstay your welcome, we might have some conversations with people in town. We can organize these types of protests in other locations. We can put pressure on your sponsors and hosts. You may find that your . . . donations . . . are plummeting and your access to church soup kitchens and street clinics is revoked."

"You can't do that - "

"Want to find out?" Olli remarked. "We have regional connections, too."

"And national," Charlie called out, speaking for the first time.

The doctor's eyes widened, recognizing Charlie Rider and Zadie Byrd Gray standing in the back of the crowd.

That did the trick. Silently and swiftly, they packed up and moved out.

Soaked, Charlie, Zadie, and Olli sloshed back towards the tall man's tiny house. The other residents also sought relief from the downpour. Faces peered out at them through windows, hands cupped to the glass panes in the gloom. A shudder rippled down Charlie's spine, chill and aching. This was the bottom of the downward mining of unbridled capitalism. Without laws, without limits, it was a system that devoured everything. As it scraped off the easy pickings, hunger pinched its gut. Its rapaciousness rose. It swallowed up fishing stocks until they collapsed. It gnawed down a continent of old growth forests. It dug deeper and deeper into the ground to lick up oil and minerals. It siphoned the lifeblood of the poor straight out through their skin. It shoved people into poverty, one generation after another, so it could break their backs and suck their labor out of them like bone marrow. It fastened them to a health care system that stole every scrap of wealth they managed to save and sent them into death or debt, or both. It took their houses and fined them for sleeping in the streets. It locked people up in cells and charged to keep them imprisoned. And then, it farmed their blood and bodies.

The only thing that stopped it was real people like Olli and his neighbors saying, enough was enough. They had organized space for people to speak up, to build tiny homes, to find survival together, and to draw lines in the sand to keep the bloodsuckers out.

"Democracy matters, you know," Olli said, holding open the door to his house. "It's how we speak up when things are wrong. It's how we discover that we're not alone. It's how this community - with all its many, serious problems and challenges - found out that no one likes the bloodsuckers and realized we could do something about it."

"But they had you," Zadie pointed out.

"Ah well," Olli admitted, ducking his head. "I'm an expert on tap, not on top. I'm a resource for my home community just as I am in other places."

"There should be more of you," Charlie insisted.

"Let's dry off a bit and then head up to the Democracy Lab," the tall man suggested. "There are a hundred people like me there."

Charlie hid a smile. He needed millions ... millions of people trained and training in the practices of participatory democracy. With a movement like that, they could change the whole world.

CHAPTER TEN

. . . . .

The Democracy Lab

The Democracy Lab's Forum took place in an old chapel which had been stripped of religious iconography. It had been converted into a theater-in-the-round by removing the pews and circling concentric rings of chairs around a central open space.

"Our mission, here at the Democracy Lab," Olli informed them, "is to empower citizens to engage in vast experiments in democracy, as if they were searching for remedies for what ails us."

The Democracy Lab was a wild, unruly beast. The people were boisterous, brimming with ideas and enthusiasm. They were all ages and backgrounds. They had come to explore one complex subject: democracy.

"There's no wrong way to make a democracy," Olli told Charlie and Zadie, "and no singular right way, either."

The more experiments, the merrier; that was the Democracy Lab's unofficial motto. Charlie and Zadie had been invited to speak at the Forum. Zadie planned to use the time to relay a request from Elisha Adams, Meera Sundaran, and Frankie Mirelli. The three teens had been following the cross-country journey avidly all summer. A couple of days ago, they had phoned Zadie.

"We've been thinking," Frankie began, their voice tinny on speakerphone. "Now that you've riled up the country for real democracy - "

" - you should ask everyone to *do* it," Elisha interrupted.

"Like the constructive programs that Gandhi did," Meera put in. "Every day, each citizen should do real democracy, practice it a little bit, put it to work in their lives."

Charlie and Zadie had explored this idea with the teens that day on the beach. They'd strolled to the far end, down by the breakwater jetty where the crowds thinned out. The wind had swept over their skin, siphoning off the seawater, leaving the salt, gritty and primordial, a reminder of the long journey of humankind's evolution. Meera remembered rubbing her forearm with her palm and thinking of her great-grandfather who had stood on the beach with Gandhi, lifting a fistful of sand and seawater, poised to shake the foundations of British rule. Salt and homespun cloth had set India free, giving millions a symbolic and tangible way to stop paying the British for imported cloth and the daily necessity of salt. By wearing the homespun *khadi* and making salt in defiance of the British monopoly, the two campaigns made a significant dent in the colonial government's tax revenues. They also galvanized people into opposing unjust laws, demonstrating their support for independence and defying British authority.

The question that kept Meera up at night was: what is our salt?

For the United States, a nation struggling to end the rule of rich people and giant corporations, what were our versions of Gandhi's salt and spinning wheel? Local food and small business, of course. At the heart of all constructive programs was the principle of self-sufficiency. Frankie, Elisha, and Meera had chatted about this as they beachcombed.

"A community reliant on imports, giant corporations, slavery, or other injustices is weak," Meera commented as they strolled northward along the curving shore. "It is dependent on those systems when it should be autonomous. Gandhi saw that. The early American Independence movement recognized that. If we're going to keep off the yoke of corporate and oligarchic control, we must build local self-sufficiency."

Charlie glanced westward toward the sedge-crested dunes, the dark forests, and the distant city. Ninety percent of their daily goods came from somewhere else. It made them dependent on the corporations that produced these goods. What would the nation be like if ninety percent of their food, clothing, entertainment, products and services were created within a hundred-mile radius of their homes? It would be a startlingly different world.

"Beyond local production," Meera went on, side-stepping the next brush of a salty wave, "Gandhi had programs for education because the colonizers shouldn't control the knowledge of the people."

Zadie nodded. Her Indigenous friend, Kinap Crow, had spoken to her at length about the efforts for food, water, energy, and education sovereignty among the Penobscot Nation and other Indigenous Nations. Local power built resiliency and responsiveness to the unique characteristics and strengths of an area. In many ways, local resilience *was* democracy in action.

"Gandhi also restored the local justice systems," Elisha put in, remembering her father speaking about this, "so the Indians could take the fate of their people out of the hands of the British court system. For us, the parallel is restorative justice. My dad was big on that. He helped keep kids out of the punitive justice system and used restorative justice to get at the underlying problems."

Now, Meera, Elisha, and Frankie thought it was time to add democracy to that list of constructive programs. A constructive program had to be symbolic *and* tangible. It had to be something everyone could do. With dialogues, public policy crafting, participatory polling, wisdom circles, and more, real democracy was as tactile as making salt from seawater or spinning cotton into thread. A constructive program should build the strength of the people and lessen their dependency on their oppressors. It should have revolutionary potential even if it wasn't directly confrontational. Participatory democracy was all of these things.

Democracy should be a daily practice. It was a family collectively deciding the week's dinner menu. It was teachers asking their students what they wanted to study. It was unhoused persons setting group rules for their encampments. It was joining an artist collective that created community-designed murals. It was the old guys on the block pooling their tools and turning one person's garage into a tool library. It was holding listening sessions with coworkers to find out how to improve life at the office. In the United States, these kinds of democracy projects held the keys to ending corporate rule, the rule of the rich.

These day-to-day democracy practices weren't just about democratizing the bread-and-butter staples of our daily lives . . . they were the training grounds for the skills we needed to self-govern as a nation on every level and scale. The ability to listen deeply could be used by the manager of a hair salon as much as by the president of the United States. The capacity to reflect on contrasting opinions was a skill both church members and congress members should have. Every schoolchild should learn how to be part of a student assembly, how to listen, how to use hand signals, how to speak succinctly and to the point, how to learn from others and how to share their truth. Then, when they grew up, they would know how to participate in a workers' assembly, a citizens' assembly, a neighborhood assembly, or a street assembly. The skills we learn in local democracy serve us in every other place real democracy erupts.

But Americans couldn't just read about real democracy online. They had to *do* it in their communities.

"Doing democracy is our version of Gandhi's salt," Meera told Zadie and Charlie. "It's our spinning wheel. It's something we can all do that helps us build our independence from the people who want to exploit and abuse us."

There were dozens of ways for communities to make decisions together. The problem was, people weren't using them. Like the Indians who nearly starved their traditional spinners and weavers to death because they wanted to buy imported British cloth, we had outsourced decision-making to politicians and bosses. The average citizen had little direct participation in the rules that affected their lives, and they were suffering because of it.

In order to have real democracy, the populace needed to learn how to listen to each other, talk with each other, and solve their problems, together. Like spinning yarn, democracy had to be a daily activity, part of a way of life. Like knowing how to work the fibers and turn the wheel, everyone should have practical skills for making decisions together. And, like wearing *khadi,* the plain-weave cloth in traditional style that became symbolic of Indian independence, every US citizen should find pride and powerful symbolism in the act of doing democracy.

Charlie and Zadie listened as the three youths explained. The teens wanted the pair to issue a call-to-action: don't just read about democracy. Go out and practice it. Try it on for size. Take democracy for a test drive.

"If we're going to scale up the movement," Zadie replied, "we're going to need more troubleshooters, teachers, and democracy repairmen than just Olli."

Fortunately, Oliver Lang had friends at the Democracy Lab. The organization had started as a street experiment and grown into a loose network of scholars, trainers, and practitioners. They crowd-sourced the funds to buy the old convent when it came up for sale, securing a roof, a common kitchen, and rooms for both office space and residential study programs. In the Forum, the community gathered to debate and discuss the best practices, emerging experiments, and challenging questions around this thing called democracy.

"It's not always this argumentative," Olli apologized as the lambasting harangues made them wince. "They're debating whether or not non-humans should have rights."

"Non-humans?" Charlie queried as they walked down the narrow aisle from the door toward the center.

"Oh, not corporations," Olli clarified, seeing the hard look on Charlie's face. "We've debated that many times in the past, but today they're talking about trees, animals, ecosystems, rivers, that sort of thing. Should the forests have rights and if so, then can the Loraxians really speak for the trees?"

"The Loraxians?" Zadie asked. The word evoked childhood memories of a fuzzy orange creature warning about the dangers of chopping down the Truffula trees.

"They use Seuss' Lorax as a name, but it's really the concept of humans offering representation to other species. That's controversial. I mean, can the Beef Industry be trusted to speak in the best interests of cows? What about PETA or other animal rights groups? Who knows what wooly sheep dream about, let alone electric sheep - and don't get me started on tech and robot rights!"

Olli rolled his eyes and slid into the second row from the front. Zadie squeezed in after him. Charlie eyed the stained glass windows and wondered if gods and angels, devils and mythological creatures would get representation some day - or maybe that was a good reason to maintain separation of church and state.

Olli glanced at the time and began rapping his knuckles on the back of the chair in front of him. The man to his right picked it up, then the next person.

"It's a point-of-order signal. You're on the schedule for the four o'clock slot," Olli explained as the whole assembly replicated the metallic rapping.

As a single person, the tapping was barely audible. Multiplied by the whole room, the din was deafening. The heated exchange of the debaters faltered. One glanced around as if emerging from a deep-sea dive of logic and argument. The other blinked, then stuck out his hand. The pair shook and sat down. The people in the front ring of chairs gathered notes and coffee mugs then shuffled back into the secondary rows.

"If someone wishes to enter the debate," Olli explained, "they step into the ring and sit in the first circle of chairs. The rest of us listen in the back rows until we have a point to make, then we step in. If we've had enough, we leave. It's a bit like boxing, I suppose, but without the violence."

He shrugged. It was one model. They used over a dozen more. On a whiteboard affixed to the stone columns of the cathedral ceiling, the names of the other formats were posted: *the Ring, the Shuffle, the Tides, the Soapbox, the Classic Debate*, and so on. Someone stood up on a chair and wrote a new model on the whiteboard. Their dry erase marker squeaked as the word *Matchstick* was scrawled across the surface. Charlie and Zadie had been invited to introduce their concept like a matchstick in a haystack and see what unfolded from there.

The knocking din died down. Zadie admired the elegance of it. If the assembly wished to disregard the point-of-order, they simply didn't knock. But, if they supported the shift, the noise quieted the debate and they could move on. Unlike a bell or loud whistle, it took general agreement to make the transition.

Olli nudged the pair onto chairs in the center ring and stood up to address the crowd. The floorboards beneath him had been worn black and shiny by countless feet. The hall quieted as Olli held up his hands. He introduced the visitors and thanked the assembly for allocating floor time to them. He did not mention their purpose, leaving the explanation up to them.

"As you undoubtedly heard," Zadie said, rising to her feet, "Charlie and I have been traveling the country, writing about the participatory democracy stories happening all over the place. Our young friends, Elisha, Meera, and Frankie, think it's time for participatory democracy to become a constructive program for this country, something everyone does, everyday, to build local and community control, self-reliance, and people power."

In the folding chairs, a keen-edged focus settled on the room. Faces stilled. Fidgeting stopped. Beyond the arches of stained glass windows, the rain slowed as if listening. The sky lightened. A kaleidoscope of diffuse colors painted the chapel.

"I've come to ask for your help," Zadie said, humbly, quietly. "Our nation has a steep learning curve ahead of us. The greater parts of our lives are deeply undemocratic. Will you . . . can you escalate the nation's learning curve? Can you scale up your experiments? Can the members of the Democracy Lab help us as we expand the good work already happening? If every single town or city in this nation called you tomorrow, how would you deal with such a glorious onslaught of interest?"

A hush of reverence hung, suspended over the gathered. Breaths poised in chests, hoping, longing for such a miracle.

"Because," she mentioned with a wry grin and a wink, "tomorrow, Charlie and I are thinking of asking millions of Dandelions to give you a ring."

Create, copy, improve, share: that was the viral operating principle of the Dandelion Insurrection. It's what had fueled their wild and unruly growth. All summer long, she and Charlie had told the stories of those who were creating new democracy practices. Now, by issuing a call-to-action, they could invite millions of Dandelions to take these ideas to the next level.

Zadie gestured for Charlie to speak up. He stood. The wind hissed through the trees outside, sending a shower of raindrops over the old slate roof, the drumming fingers of Earth, impatient and waiting.

"Democracy is the science of our times," Charlie said, "a social science, a field of inquiry and experimentation that involves all of us. The United States has fostered many waves of scientific curiosity from the natural sciences to atomic physics to space exploration and genome mapping. We can expand our laboratory to include the entire nation. We can catalyze a mass experiment - or rather, a mass movement of thousands of experiments."

"So, what do you say?" Zadie challenged them, flinging her arms as wide as she could stretch, a matching grin on her face.

The sunlight broke out from the clouds in luminous brilliance. A dazzle of gold and emerald, ruby and azure showered through the grey hall, illuminating smiles and grins. A murmur of excitement swept through the members of the Democracy Lab. A thrill of anticipation shifted through the group, an eagerness to begin. The conversation opened to the whole Forum. Ideas raced forward. Concerns over capacity were raised, met, and dealt with. When the vote came, they ayes had it . . . the Democracy Lab was in.

Charlie and Zadie released a new essay, a call-to-action to the nation to *use* one small act of democracy each day, and to *add* one more democracy practice to their lives each week. In one year, they pointed out, we, the People, will have infused fifty-two new practices into three hundred and twenty million lives. That math equated to more than nine billion moments of democracy added to our world.

It was a match laid to a web of fuse lines. The projects exploded in all directions at once. When the change agents in a system reach a tipping point of interconnectivity, it only takes one final spark to trigger an immense catalytic reaction. The democracy effort was in a primordial soup moment, a point in the evolution of this field, when the catalyzers and multipliers connected with the readiness of the nodes to transform. Everything was poised for change. The examples existed. The test models had been tried. One last touch and . . . *poof!* It was an evolutionary leap for both the Democracy Lab and the Dandelion Insurrection.

Elisha, Meera, and Frankie launched out of the gate with an enthusiasm that set the tone for the nation. They inventoried their city, giving out one-to-five star ratings in democracy to every business, institution, club, nonprofit, social network, and governmental department. They mobilized the youth and seniors in an intergenerational effort to infuse democracy into their city. The community centers launched public surveys to determine programming. The summer camps held world cafes with youth, parents, and camp councilors on next year's activities. One of the newspapers put together its first-ever community advisory board in a bid to beat their rival journal in moving from one star to two.

Small, daily acts of democracy catalyzed larger projects. Vermont burst into a wild frenzy of action; doing democracy was a local pastime, right up there with maple sugaring. Long known for its rebellious autonomy and local self-determination, towns across the state were the first to scale up participatory democracy practices in town councils, local schools, worker coops, and more. Milton, Vermont was the first municipality to declare a town-wide Democracy Revolution. Others swiftly followed.

In New Jersey, a state long regarded as a mere bedroom community of the New York behemoth, a Black and Brown-led housing justice movement shut down planning and zoning commission meetings with a Renters and Residents Assembly. They demanded immediate public referendums on anti-gentrification and rent control measures.

In Minnesota, the youth walked out of school to demand that the state hold intergenerational dialogues before approving any new pipelines or fossil fuel infrastructure. The youth of today objected to getting stuck with the long-term bills and cleanup costs of fossil fuels, and an unlivable planet, to boot.

Alabama's university students took the administration by surprise with an occupation for participatory budgeting. "We're paying for it," was their slogan as the students argued against budget cuts for the health center and the failure to pay graduate teaching assistants a fair wage. Their itemized list of suggested cuts included eliminating the million-dollar ice cream bar.

In Alaska, citizens demanded veto power on oil drilling. Since state law mandated that each person received a cut of the tax revenue on extraction, organizers launched statewide kitchen table conversations about economic justice, transitions to wind power generation, and what would happen when the ice melted and their unique way of life vanished along with the permafrost and polar bears.

State by state, city by city, the campaign for real democracy took off. In Detroit, Salt Lake City, and Phoenix, citizens demanded public governance of privatized water utilities. Towns and cities in New Mexico, Nevada, and Colorado launched stakeholder meetings on nuclear waste, giving down-winders equal say to nuclear scientists and public officials from the Departments of Defense and Energy. In the College Belt, students at Connecticut, Massachusetts, and New Hampshire colleges formed student assemblies to meet with administrators on governance of higher education. Arkansas, Tennessee and Missouri workers went on strike for the right to bid for worker co-operative ownership of corporations put up for sale. In New York, Houston, and Los Angeles, renters unions and land coops launched occupations at public offices, using world cafes to hash out policy for housing justice laws. In Denver, Atlanta, Seattle, and Baltimore, citizens demanded direct control of police departments.

After two hundred and seventy-five years of the representative republic, corporate dictatorship, and hierarchal domination at work and throughout their culture, people decided they didn't just want "voice". They wanted choice. They wanted agency. They wanted self-determination. They wanted more than input. They wanted to make the decisions. The screams of outrage from the Constitution-loving faction reached new heights of histrionics. They hollered bloody murder over the "treasonous insurrection" . . . and they weren't entirely wrong. It wasn't an insurrection. It wasn't treason, but it was a revolution. It was the only truly revolutionary change the Dandelion Insurrection had ever called for.

Their critics complained about the project's complexity. Why not just implement wisdom councils everywhere? Weren't the two dozen formats confusing to everyone?

"You don't put out beach chairs in a Montana snowstorm

and you don't hand out snow shovels to Floridians," Zadie answered. "Every place is different and these differences can and should inform what practices we try first."

The Dandelion Insurrection has never shied away from a certain unruly madness, Charlie wrote, championing the complexity. *We are a vast and complex country, with peoples as unique as the terrains we inhabit. We can embrace our diversity and use it as a saving grace. The trap of homogeneity is for authoritarian regimes, not us.*

But every action had an equal and opposite reaction. When Charlie and Zadie's article on *The Revolution of Democracy* hit the Alternet, it exploded like a sonic boom in all directions at once: the good, the bad, and the downright ugly. Democracy - real democracy - put decision-making capacity into the hands of those affected by the decisions. If implemented broadly, it would rattle the foundations of the entire structure of the United States.

It was simple, really, and yet, almost beyond imagination. If the shape of the world was made by an undemocratic ruling class, adding democracy would radically alter it.

"Business as we know it will collapse!" the critics shrieked as consumers called for greater say in what stocked the shelves. They demanded that businesses take responsibility for their products from "cradle to grave" and acknowledge that there are no externalities. They insisted that the full costs be taken out before profits, not shifted onto consumers and workers while owners raked in fortunes. Companies had to pay for cleaning up mine tailings and effluents. Corporations had to account for the particles churning from their smokestacks, the plastic packaging on the shelves, and the ultimate resting places of worn-out products.

Humanity had constructed ivory cities built on the bones of

the exploited and oppressed. Glittering fortunes amassed atop hidden toxic waste dumps. By ignoring the outcry against the innumerable abuses, humanity had built a shiny hell, a global economy whose maintenance required endless destruction, despair, and death, poison, pollution, lies, and war. Suffering was the hidden fuel shoveled into the furnaces of this economy. Why should humanity grant its continued loyalty to this?

"The economy keeps billions alive, day in, day out," the business moguls claimed, launching a massive counterattack as Charlie and Zadie's article crashed websites with its popularity.

The slave owners said the same thing, claiming they kept the enslaved alive as they fed them cornmeal mush in pigs troughs, Charlie wrote in his rebuttal. *That does not mean the enslaved should support their enslavement.*

"Millions have a high standard of living because of us," the pundits of money claimed.

But Zadie argued back:

"We have constructed a trap in which those who enjoy the highest standard of living require others to live in misery to maintain it. This is not normal. It's sociopathic. It behooves all of us to dismantle this so-called civilization and build a better world that works for all of us."

Democracy - real, functional, inclusive democracy - transcended arbitrary boundaries of state lines and even national borders. It offered the only governing system that could, by its very nature, end the current abuses and *prevent* new ones from arising. The process of identifying who was affected by a decision demanded a full accounting of the impacts of any action.

Humanity had circled the globe, met people who lived upside down and backwards to one another, gone to the moon and seen Earth rise on the horizon, stretched their imaginations to the ends of universe and inside atoms. There was no terra nullius anywhere. There was no place for adolescent fantasies of narcissistic freedom. There was only community and interconnectivity, a web of life and relationship that could not be ignored.

In a world where there was nowhere left to run, how would humanity live? What would people's lives look like when they took full account of their actions? When every place was somebody's backyard, how could there be any more sacrifice zones?

This, Charlie and Zadie discovered as the online commentators screamed in vitriolic protest, was the true revolution of their lifetimes. It wasn't about replacing one political party with another. It wasn't about inventing fancier technology. It wasn't even about ousting oligarchs or corporatists from power. It was about the rise of an ancient understanding, a truth so self-evident that the Founding Fathers in all their racist, colonialist, patriarchal, classist, Christian supremacist madness could not acknowledge or else their entire pseudo-nation would unravel at the seams. It was an idea that Dr. Martin Luther King, Jr. would articulate so clearly and poetically on scrap paper in a Birmingham jail in 1963: *Injustice anywhere is a threat to justice everywhere. We are caught in an inescapable network of mutuality, tied in a single garment of destiny. Whatever affects one directly, affects all indirectly.*

A living democracy was the only choice when presented with that reality. It was an inarguable, self-evident truth in a world where everything matters. In such a world, no one should abuse the next, or profit from another's misery, or ignore the destructiveness of their actions. In such a world, we can no longer justify war, exploitation, poverty, or ecosystem abuse. It sounded like a fairy tale as they sat in the midst of the current nightmare, but it was so, so, so very close, only a heartbeat away. The revolution would be a revolution of the heart, a remembering of ancient truths, a coming full circle for humanity, a healing from the millennia-long sickness of the soul, a return home to our one-and-only planet, a reunion of brotherhood and sisterhood with each other and the Earth.

This was the revolution of democracy.

CHAPTER ELEVEN

. . . . .

The Council of All Beings

They drove south from Oregon along the winding coastal highway, craning their necks at the explosions of surf and stopping every half hour to admire the wild coast. Craggy mounds of eroding sandstone skulked in the fog. Twisted trees clung to cliff sides. Grass-capped sand dunes sported wind-blasted comb overs. Charlie had seen the Atlantic Ocean's shores with sturdy pines and enduring granite coastlines. The West Coast was another world.

Zadie and Charlie had been working on a new essay at the Democracy Lab, brows furrowed in thought, heads bent close together, the rain pounding on the slate roof, when Zadie's phone rang. She glanced at the caller id and broke into a smile.

"Kinap!" she exclaimed. "Great to hear from you!"

"*Kwey, nitap,*" her friend greeted her in the traditional language of the Wabanaki People. "I have a democracy story for you."

"Sure. About what?"

"Why it's long past time for you newcomers to Turtle Island to learn how to include non-human *people* in your notion of democracy."

Zadie nodded. She'd been wondering how to remind her fellow Americans that although Benjamin Franklin and the Founding Fathers borrowed their ideas about democracy from the Haudenosaunee, members of those nations viewed the United States' system as warped beyond recognition. Where were the women? Where were the non-human creatures? How could a democracy that excluded most of the human population and all of the other relatives succeed? It wasn't democracy. It was simply a new set of rulers.

Kinap brought word that another kind of revolution was brewing, half-hidden, long overdue. The Earth, herself, was speaking, haunting the dreams of humanity. The rivers sang with the rocks. The forests whispered stories into the wind. The animals stared into the startled eyes of humans and would not look away. The land was alive, living, and refused to be objectified and exploited any longer. Nature in all forms - animal, plant, mineral, elemental - demanded that their rights be acknowledged and honored. It was the sacred contract, long ignored by certain strands of humanity, long defended by others.

As the climate crisis showed the dangers of destroying humanity's one-and-only planet, more and more humans were listening. Indigenous Peoples had never stopped. Humans ignored the beingness of non-humans at their own peril. When they die, we die. It was better to respect them and live.

"A global movement for the Rights of Nature is picking up steam," Kinap had told Zadie over the phone. "There is a resurgence of these beliefs among people who ignored the beingness of non-humans for centuries. It's happening at last - and it's beautiful. Lake Erie has laws that assert the lake's beinghood and limit the pollution of nearby cities. The Whanganui River in New Zealand has legal personhood status. Ecuador granted Rights of Nature to the entire nation's ecosystems. Even small towns are doing this. Crestone, Colorado passed a law recognizing the rights of the Crestone Creek. The wild rice beds of the Anishinaabe in Northern Wisconsin have rights as an ecosystem of species. The original inhabitants of Hawai'i are defending sovereignty for Indigenous People and for the islands, themselves. The bioregion of Cascadia is asserting its beingness in the Pacific Northwest, extending beyond state and national borders. A massive revolution is underway - no less profound than the abolition of slavery or overthrowing dictators - it's about a Democracy of All Beings. Come to the Council and see for yourself."

She thought Kinap was going to haul them back to Maine to talk, but instead, the Penobscot organizer said she'd be in Northern California for a gathering called the *Council of All Beings*. She invited Zadie and Charlie to attend. This was not an Indigenous tradition, but rather a way for the newcomers to the continent to begin the long process of learning how to relate respectfully to the community of beings that lived in these lands, too.

As they drove south, Zadie waxed poetic about the possibilities of a democracy that included both humans and non-humans. Charlie wrestled with his skepticism. He doubted the average American was ready for the revelation of equality between humans and bears, let alone with moss or gnats or a riparian woodland. Humans still had trouble seeing other humans as equal. Were they ready for Kinap's revolution?

"Ready or not, here it comes," Zadie pointed out.

"Here we come, anyway," he answered.

The gathering was held at a coastal wilderness area where redwood giants carpeted the mountains, drinking the moist ocean fog. Beneath their hushed canopy, the banter of human voices rose and fell. Thick mats of needles made the earth springy underfoot. The shade cut the dry heat of the September day with delicious coolness. Steep slopes stretched along a dry creek bed. Upon arriving, Charlie and Zadie wandered the forested area in search of Kinap. At a designated campsite, tents were set up. Small groups sat in clusters, talking in easy tones, faces serious, intense, and smiling in turns. At the edge of one such circle, a tall, straight-backed figure spotted them and waved.

"Kinap!" Zadie called out, bursting into a run. She crossed the glade and flung her arms around her friend. Kinap's laugh ran bell-like through the grove, clear as the hidden birds calling out in the overstory. The first lines of silver touched Kinap's dark hair. She carried herself with stillness and weighted presence.

Kinap Crow was a protector of water, an Indigenous rights lawyer, a member of the Penobscot Nation. She, too, came from Maine. She, too, traveled the continent helping people protect their communities. She and Zadie had met in Arizona, standing shoulder-to-shoulder as they blockaded a bridge to keep corporate extractors from plundering the water in the underground aquifer. Zadie and Kinap's friendship touched upon the sacred and transcended the short time they had known each other. Her deep brown eyes focused over Zadie's shoulder and caught sight of Charlie. She lifted her hand in greeting as he neared. Kinap recognized the strain of years of struggle in his face. She knew the weight of that. Kinap and her people had been fighting for survival for six hundred years. They were from the Dawnland, the place of first contact with European colonizers. The burdens of their souls ran deep. The sorrows they carried were genocides and generations wide.

He will need to learn when to put his burdens down and when to pick them up again, she thought. He did not yet realize how long this road would be. Charlie Rider was sprinting down the first leg of a marathon. If he didn't rest, he would collapse long before the finish line.

Kinap saw the gaping hole of understanding in the

newcomers, the immigrants and descendants of colonists. Millions of people in this nation held the delusion of a settings-and-object landscape. They saw ecosystems as ideas, rocks and water as objects, landscapes as backdrops to their lives, plants as scenery, and animals as dumb creatures of a lesser order than humans. At best, they saw themselves as stewards. More commonly, Americans saw themselves as masters and owners of this land, individually with private property, collectively as a nation, and by divine right according to Bible and arrogant superiority.

They would never survive this way. Any of them. Not the collapsing ecosystems, not the endangered species, not the descendants of colonists, and not the Indigenous Peoples. Unlearning these attitudes was no longer a luxury. Dispelling these beliefs was critical to survival. Kinap had joined both Indigenous-led gatherings and non-Indigenous workshops to help guide this culture back to sanity. The Council of All Beings was one of these.

"Come," she invited them, "let me show you around."

They started in the main grove. The gathering place was nestled in the natural amphitheater of the steep slopes of a redwood grove. The "floor" reverberated with impassioned poetry and prose, praise and promises. Charlie and Zadie sat on the soft carpet of needles next to Kinap and listened as one human after another conveyed the messages of mountains and the reflections of bogs. The Council of All Beings brought the world to life. It was a ritual, a ceremony, a creative summit in which the voiceless were given words in human speech. Rocks, rivers, estuaries, bays, kelp, humpback whales, plankton, moss, meadow grass, wild orange poppy, roe deer, spotted owl, blotched tiger salamander: hundreds were given voices through creative imagining and biological science. People translated the whistling bird songs of flocks. Those representing insects brought word from hives, nests, and swarms. One person brought the fog to life, chanting a tidal incantation of the poetry born of water, air, time, and tide.

Barefoot in the dusty carpet of cool earth speckled with redwood needles, a semicircle of speakers gave voice to the western forest trees: Sequoia, Live Oak, Madrone, Jeffrey Pine, Sitka Spruce, Coast Redwood, Douglas Fir, and more. Together, they came from a community of overlapping ecosystems that stretched from Alaska to Northern Mexico, crossing three nation's borders, encompassing a span that housed millions of humans and trillions of non-human beings. Red Cedar spoke, her voice lilting, words rising in prayer, prophecy, and promise.

"Once, the People sang to us," Red Cedar said. "Then the sounds of shouts and saws came, cut by the crash and boom of our sisters falling, followed by the silence, the long silence, of clear-cut ground. Humans are short-lived, but we live centuries. We were here before Columbus touched the eastern shores, before the conquistadors and colonists brought the diseases that silenced the original people's songs. We will be here after today falls into silence. We will hear tomorrow's music begin. But will you?"

On the slope, Charlie sat stunned, silent and intense, imagining the earth through different eyes . . . or antennae, or echolocation, or senses that defied human conception. Slowly, his human-centric perspective surrendered its stranglehold on his mind. He felt the clenched tightness in his chest that preceded tears. He would never think about his country in the same way again. As the messages went on, the Council of All Beings knocked him off his feet, captured his heartstrings, and swept him away into a world of perception so different from his usual worldview that there was simply no comparison.

"It's like I was . . . dead . . . or blind," Charlie stammered as he and Zadie lay curled together that night. "Like I've been sleepwalking through my life, a cardboard actor in front of a flat backdrop. I never realized how lonely it is to be human in a world full of mere objects or lesser animals. It's completely different to see oneself as part of a community of species."

The next day, they joined the small group sessions. Most of this Council came from the West Coast, but a few, like Kinap, came from further afield to share their expertise. Delegates from the Pacific Northwest came to learn from the riverkeepers of the Southwest. Coastal wetlands defenders exchanged stories with inland water protectors. Forests, deserts, mountains, mammals, fish and fowl, moss and shrubs, prairies and tidal zones: the list of beings was endless. They gathered in different circles, passing talking sticks, listening, sharing knowledge, expressing concerns, and brainstorming solutions.

Representing the Penobscot River - a being she considered her kin - Kinap joined not only the council of rivers, but also the circles of estuary dwellers, the headwaters summit, and the watersheds gathering. She sat in on the mammals discussion and the aquatic plants dialogue. She gave voice to her Indigenous perspective and reminded the descendants of colonizers to acknowledge the wisdom of the original knowledge-holders of the continent. She shared with - and learned from - biologists. She offered legal advice and traditional wisdom.

In all of the conversations, the Earth came alive and rose up with towering beinghood. The planet brimmed with personality and power. A river was not a flat ribbon of water, but an ancient creature that lived over eons, carving the landscape and forming an enduring community of fish and fern, reed and rock, serpent

115

and sand, deer and muskrat, otter and algae, and more.

All those voices had been denied by the conquerors and colonists as surely as Indigenous Peoples'. By relegating beings to objects, creatures to resources, and "nature" to a status separate from "human", Westerners had killed off the fertility of their imaginations and now strode across barren moonscapes of the mind.

The delegates were a mix of backgrounds. They were scientists and poets, activists and ecologists. One without the other was insufficient. The poets tended to anthropomorphize. The scientists habitually objectified. The two balanced each other, poets dreaming into the beingness of forests and moss; scientists lending detailed research into the ways ferns live, birds migrate, and frogs transform from tadpoles. Geologists spoke for the rocks, thinking in terms of eons. Entomologists spoke for dayflies that lived entire lives in a single day. Both poets and scientists were needed.

"Indigenous Peoples," Kinap pointed out, "have never separated the two, nor divided the spiritual from the scientific."

Indigenous Peoples were the original natural scientists, biologists, astronomers, and pharmacists of this continent. The lie of primitivism overshadowed the fact that Indigenous Peoples held both ancestral knowledge *and* detailed sciences of place. Their cultures and ways of life, forged by millenniums of living interconnectedness, had never separated science from spirit and story. Newcomers to Turtle Island would need to build ways to respect this knowledge . . . and create their own practices for living in right relationship with the rest of the living world.

"You cannot simply adopt our Indigenous customs," Kinap reminded them. "It doesn't work like that. That's why the Council of All Beings - created by Joanna Macy and others - is so helpful. It is an emerging ceremony that helps repair the splintered, or unforged, connection between newcomers and this land."

Six hundred years of colonizer culture had to be uprooted. Entire ecosystems needed to be protected and repaired. Regeneration and restoration had to be a priority even amidst the climate crisis - especially amidst the crisis. The invasion of the Europeans drastically altered the continent, triggering an environmental shift as dramatic as an Ice Age. Entire species were wiped out, from the passenger pigeon to the bulk of the bison population. Old growth forests were razed to the ground. The Great Plains were turned into corn and soy fields. Cattle grazing replaced antelope and deer. Cities grew like barnacles on whale skin.

"The Council of All Beings would not be complete without the cities," Kinap told Charlie and Zadie. "For better or for worse, they are some of the most impactful beings on the planet."

They devoured the resources of a globe. They churned out pollutants into the air and the water. They built mountains of their garbage and riddled the underground with holes in their consumption of minerals, oil, and coal. They sprawled for miles, creating concrete deserts where complex ecosystems once stood.

"We have to include the cities if we want to make change," Kinap explained as she steered Charlie and Zadie toward a cluster of people sitting on logs. One stared at a signal-less phone then put it in his pocket, shaking his head. Another gaped up at the cathedral of trees. A third nervously joked and wondered if there were bears around here.

"Not with all the noise," Kinap told him with a wry smile. "Charlie, Zadie, these are the people speaking for the urban cities."

"Los Angeles!" one said proudly.

"San Fran," another chimed in.

"Portlandia," said a third.

"Seattle."

"Vancouver, Canada."

"Vancouver, United States," said another person with a grin. "It's like having two girls named Sally in the same class."

At least a dozen cities had come to the council. Like mountain ranges or watersheds, their needs, choices, and behaviors weighed on every other system they touched. Their sewage, electricity, garbage, delivery and transport, heating and cooling, all connected to the surrounding ecosystems. The choices of those massive, human-centric beings rippled like shockwaves through trillions of other creatures, ultimately affecting the entire planet.

"These brave souls have come to learn and bring back the process to their regions," Kinap explained to Charlie and Zadie. "San Francisco does not stand alone, after all. She is part of an entire region of urban cities: Oakland, Berkeley, Marin, Richmond, and more. In these places, too many humans have forgotten the knowledge of the original peoples and beings: the Chumash, Ohlone, sturgeon, otters, pelicans, and so on. Once, these people and beings far outnumbered even the millions of humans who live there now, oblivious."

Charlie had never thought of cities as beings before, but if a river or an ocean or a forest was a being, then the behemoth of Los Angeles certainly was one, too. How would a city manage its beinghood in a manner that respected the existence of all others? Would they fight for survival like cornered bears, trapped by lack of food and water? Would they intentionally adapt, and perhaps shrink to a sustainable scale? The questions were endless.

And, Charlie mused, *if a city was a being, what about corporations?*

"Corporate personhood is not the same as beingness," Kinap clarified when Charlie brought it up. "Corporate personhood is how rich people push for their companies to enjoy all the privileges of the world's most entitled people, while avoiding all of the responsibilities borne by regular humans. When I talk about beingness, I'm speaking about honoring our rights and responsibilities in equal measure."

Kinap gestured to the group of urban representatives. If cities were beings, they had to take responsibility for their impacts even as they asserted their rights. At the Council of All Beings, people could start to think about what rights and responsibilities a human, a city, a bioregion, an ecosystem, a corporation, an element or a non-human being had.

Zadie plunked down beside them on the log and leaned forward, elbows on knees.

"So, how does one represent an entire city?" she queried. It seemed like a daunting task.

"We were just talking about that," the Latina representative from Los Angeles answered.

Every city's process was different. One used polling. Another used poetry and art. A third held public conversations. A fourth circulated statistics and studies. They asked similar questions: what does a city need to survive? What is enough? What is too much? How does a city harm others? How does a city help them? What emerges in a city's dreams? What wakes a city up at night?

They had no right or wrong way to answer those questions. There were no rules when it came to imagining the consciousness of a city. The residents were like gut bacteria dreaming of what a human thinks when she sees an apple.

Today, the twelve cities compared notes on how to listen to a being called a City. Yesterday, they had met with the rivers and continental plates. The Seattle Fault, a 50-60 million-year old being (you lose count after that many trips around the sun, the Fault admitted), warned the City of Seattle about the rising geological pressures under the ground. Are you ready for the Big One? the Fault asked. How will you shelter your people when the earthquake of the millennium hits?

In a few days, they would return to their cities with knowledge, warnings, and more questions. Los Angeles would invite the Colorado River to give talks about how she longed to reach the Pacific Ocean once again, how sad it was to dry up and vanish amidst the desert, siphoned off by the city's thirst. Portland and the Columbia River would gather the watersheds to offer *State of the Union* addresses. The Pelicans would go on a poetry reading tour, delivering poetic messages up and down the coast, following their migration route.

In other cities, regional convenings would take place every few months. Smaller gatherings and artistic expressions would pop up weekly. In Monterey, the sea otters and humpback whales wrote weekly blogs. In Olympia, the fog and tides planned to spin off that idea and launch a column in the newspaper.

"The goal of the Council of All Beings," Kinap told Charlie and Zadie as they thanked the cities and moved onward, "is to find ways to bring the voices of the rest of the Earth into human awareness."

For too long, humanity had objectified and ignored the beingness of all. It was killing humanity . . . and everything else.

"If our species is to survive, we will need to reawaken everyone's sense of community with the interconnected web of existence. Our process with the Council of All Beings has its shortcomings, but it is a start. Imagine these gatherings in twenty years . . . or a hundred."

The thought staggered Charlie and Zadie. It was hard to imagine their culture after a hundred years of practicing and using Councils of All Beings. They'd spent over six hundred years denying the beinghood of non-humans (and most of humanity). Envisioning their culture actively uprooting those delusions pushed their minds to the breaking point. They could see how the Council of All Beings served as a training ground, a school for stretching atrophied imaginations out of the narrow constraints of the human-centric worldview.

They crested the slope that served as amphitheater and returned to the full assembly. Sitting down on the soft carpet of pine needles, they listened to the speeches. The messages surprised Charlie. He had expected a litany of sorrow: collapsing ecosystems, species extinction, poisoned rivers, dead forests killed by beetles, extreme droughts and vanishing lakes. As he looked around, he couldn't see one single being that wasn't suffering because of humanity's behaviors. And yet, much of that had already been addressed in small groups and one-on-one conversations. In the full assembly, the messages centered on love and hope. The Beings had more to say than simply haranguing humanity. They had solidarity to offer one another. They had visions and dreams for a new way forward. They *remembered* the best of humanity from the times before extraction and conquest.

Delivered one after another, these messages moved Charlie more than the pleas of succor against destruction and exploitation. He heard the gray wolf speak of how close the packs came to vanishing, and how they felt when they finally heard the howls of mates in the distance after traveling thousands of lonely miles. He laced his fingers together with

121

Zadie's and thanked all that was holy that they had found each other. He heard the humpback whales express gratitude to humans for the web of protections that allowed their numbers to return to the levels of pre-whaling days. He wiped his eyes as the acknowledgement made him choke up with emotion. When the humpback whales sang in solidarity with the endangered blue whales, the tears fell down his cheeks. The rivers stood in interlocking connection, telling the epic story of how the dance of water extended around the entire planet. Shivers shot up and down his spine. Charlie dug out his notebook and pencil, scribbling down fragments of thoughts for later writings:

Who knew that plate tectonics had prophecies about collision?

Moss spoke about restoring mine tailings.

Fungi dismantles toxic waste as a love token for the world.

Eagles are taking down drones.

The marine sanctuary issued an open invitation to the ecosystem to come move in.

The grizzly and polar bear celebrated the birth of their baby pizzly, a new species emerging out of climate pressures.

As the afternoon stretched on, he and Zadie fell into a near trance state, the cumulative weight of the speakers shredding the veil of ordinary thought. They sensed a world hovering on the horizon of reality, a world where humans would pour their time into relearning the extraordinary beauty and mystery of the Earth. This world wasn't impossible. It hung on the edge of reality. The Council of All Beings helped dream it into existence.

CHAPTER TWELVE

. . . . .

The DNA of the USA

The next day, while Charlie sat hunched against the trunk of a redwood tree feverishly writing up his notes into a poetic essay on the Council, Kinap invited Zadie to take a hike with her through the deep shadows of the forest. They wound along a trail, snaking up the gulch and climbing toward the ridgeline. They walked in companionable silence until Kinap, at last, spoke.

"I want to speak with you about something hard," she began.

Kinap had followed their journey across the continent, reading the stories of participatory democracy in Cincinnati, Indianapolis, Chicago, Billings. In her mind's eye, she invoked another set of names: *Shawnee, Lenape, Iroquois, Kansa, Kiowa, Shoshone, Pauite, Sioux,* and so many more. Kinap's home nation was the Penobscot Nation, not the United States, and when Zadie and Charlie's writings spoke about *our* nation, *our* democracy, and *we, the People,* Kinap could only think: *who, exactly, is this "we"?* She had to remind Zadie that she wrote such words on stolen land, talking about a nation that, from Kinap's perspective and by its own violated treaties, had no right to be in existence in the first place.

"Would you dare to ask the real question?" she challenged Zadie. "It's not just what kind of nation should the United States be . . . but also, should the United States exist at all?"

Zadie blanched. Kinap saw the reaction. Between them, history rolled back six hundred years.

"You say you are a radical," Kinap told her softly. "You say you boldly go into ideas where few others dare to tread. This is one of them. You write about the evolution of your country, but stop short of asking another important question: should the United States even continue to exist?"

If it was wrong for Germany to invade Poland in 1939, wasn't it also wrong for the Netherlands, Great Britain, France, Belgium, Spain, and Portugal to invade and conquer the lands they dubbed the Americas? Six hundred years of colonial occupation did not make the presence of hundreds of millions of non-natives *right*. It just made the situation harder to resolve. Zadie could hear the violent howl of the nation, the clutching and loading of guns, the vitriolic intensity of the reaction to Kinap's question. She could see the *finder's keepers* attitudes of her fellow Americans kicking into hyper-drive. She could hear the accusations of *sore losers* hurled from the mouths of belligerent colonial-settlers. And yet, what ground of ethics or morality could they stand on in these beliefs? All they had was *might makes right* and a slew of toxic notions of supremacy.

"Honestly, it's hard to imagine my fellow Americans even taking that question seriously," Zadie replied slowly, uncomfortably, painfully aware that even being honest failed to rise to the justice required by the question. Too many people in this pseudo-nation had nowhere else to go; that's why they came in the first place. She could feel her bones tearing in two as she thought about returning to her European ancestors' homelands. She could feel her cells scattering on the winds with the roaming folk ancestors she'd never met. She could feel her very existence and identity shattering if she lost her country.

Then she looked into Kinap's dark, unwavering gaze and

saw that she was not unique in this. Did not Kinap and her people know that same sense of being torn apart? Didn't they know that feeling of having their nation and sovereignty denied? So many others had felt those things, often because of the actions of the United States. Zadie thought of Meera and Inez, children of immigrants propelled from homelands through the economic warfare of United States imperialism. She thought of Elisha, Will, and Tansy, whose ancestors had been stolen from their homes and brought in chains to this country to build the nation that enslaved them. She thought of Starling, Sparrow, and Elena, carrying both Indigenous and non-Indigenous bloodlines inside them.

"Is there any going back for any of us?" Zadie wondered.

Kinap did not falter.

"There is only going forward," Kinap said quietly, "but if we dare to imagine another future, it cannot be with a blind eye to the past. That is the same entitled attitude that led us here. It is a fantasy of terra nullius, a fiction of blank slates and empty land free for the taking."

To go forward meant understanding it all, not ignoring any of it to embrace some sanitized vision of a new nation. To Kinap, the United States was an occupying nation sitting atop a crisscross of occupied Indigenous territories. It existed in contention with the Indigenous nations that still endured. Colonization was an on-going process. It was largely hidden from United States citizens, but their nation continued to attempt to subjugate Indigenous nations each and every single day, violating treaties, stealing land, putting toxic waste sites in Indigenous territories, ignoring sovereign laws of Indigenous nations. In Kinap's home, the Dawn Land, the State of Maine was trying to claim - in violation of treaty law - the very waters of the river that was the heart and center of her culture, the river from which they drew their name. The Penobscot rejected this renewed attempt at colonial seizure. They defied the United States' attempts to erase their existence. They were still here. Still living. Still resisting.

Colonialist nations relied on a make-pretend illusion of permanence, a sense that their existence was now unquestionable, irrevocable, settled. But nothing was as permanent as it seemed. The British Empire collapsed. The Ottoman Empire dissolved, fractured by World War I. The Soviet Union's hegemony crumbled only a few decades ago as Latvia, Lithuania, Estonia, Poland, Hungary, Ukraine, Czechoslovakia, and more asserted independence through nonviolent struggle. The future is ever unpredictable. This land was no exception.

What would it be like if every immigrant to these shores, or descendent of immigrants from before, had to honor the treaties with Indigenous Peoples? What if the United States truly acknowledged Indigenous sovereignty? Could it endure the weight of its past without collapsing?

Zadie had her doubts that it could. If the United States went forward, it would be like a company in debt. It owed those it had stolen from, subjugated, and exploited. Dissolving the nation without dealing with these wrongs would be a cop out. It would be like the corporations declaring bankruptcy to avoid clearing up toxic spills and class action lawsuits over poisoned workers. The United States had debts to pay to women, migrants, the peoples it had bombed around the world, African-Americans, Indigenous Peoples, the Earth. It has stolen their lives, their labors, their freedoms, their children, their cultures, their lands, and their peace. These were the debts the nation had yet to pay. They spent six hundred years accruing them. Would they spend six hundred years repaying them?

These were difficult questions . . . but they were not buried ones. The continued existence of the original peoples of this continent demanded they be raised. These were the questions that removed the notion of terra nullius - empty land - from discussions of the future, the questions that dispelled myths of blank slates and level-playing fields. The present and the future were filled with landmines planted in the past. We had to clear them out, one by one, in a long and dangerous process.

Kinap and Zadie paused along the long trail up the steep gulch, catching their breaths. They spoke quietly back and forth, exploring the hard truths about this creature called the United States. In Kinap's eyes, the United States was an upstart nation, young amidst a continent of ancient cultures. If nations, like cities and forests, had identities and beinghood, what was the United States? A monster or an angel? An ecosystem or a parasite?

Zadie blinked and tried to answer that question - for herself, for Kinap, for her country, for all of them. This nation's history was carnivorous, voracious, all-consuming, destructive, violent, and yet . . . that was just one of the curling spirals of its DNA. In the double helix of the US' genetic code, one strand was dark and brutal, a toxic brew of racism, colonialism, sexism, and imperialism. The other was the enduring resistance to those injustices. The story of the United States was both. For every horrific act of violence, there were many who decried it, opposed it, and tried to stop it. From the first nascent glimmerings of nationhood, the shape of the United States had been forged between the oppressors and the oppressed. Rebellion against injustice was as American as the injustices themselves. The resistance was integral to the nature of this nation: suffrage, abolition, workers' rights, women's rights, civil rights, Indigenous Peoples' sovereignty, Chicanx rights,

LGBTQ pride, environmental protection.

All of these efforts aligned against the greed-takes-all mentality, the ideologies of conquest and colonization, the toxic belief in white supremacy and patriarchy. The arc of the moral universe is long, Dr. King said, but it bends toward justice. Slowly, painfully, with much sacrifice and tremendous courage, movement after movement separated the double helixes of the United States, opening the space to decouple from the patterning of the past and evolve into something else.

But, Zadie acknowledged, could this country change enough to deserve its place in a world striving for justice? Could the United States evolve into something worthy of continuing? These questions hung, potent, pregnant with the progeny of the future as they rocked in the cradle of the present. Zadie half-suspected that her nation was a dinosaur, unable to adjust, destined to go extinct. Much of the country stubbornly refused to change its colonial genetics. Constrained by hate, bound by arrogance, driven towards the cliff's edge by the hubris of exceptionalism, the United States might lack the resiliency to adapt to the imperatives of the times. If it didn't change, would there come a time when the United States would simply cease to exist? Was it possible that the country would balkanize, fragment, split into dozens of nations states and bioregions? Zadie could see the beauty and ugliness of that. She wanted to see her country grow into its long-stated ideals, but the massiveness of the empire bound its citizens and states in a certain holding pattern, for better and for worse. The question of what might come after the United States was terrifying and fascinating at once.

It was a question not just for her country, but for the entire species. Humanity's crossroads loomed. The climate crisis pushed them to choose, smacking them across the head with forest fires and superstorms and catastrophic droughts. *Homo sapiens sapiens* was about to change, by necessity, by force. A smart, greedy creature without reverence for the Earth would no longer be allowed to remain in the web of ecosystems. Faced with the imperative of making a choice, what would Americans choose for their country and for their species? Evolution or extinction? They could no longer be the extractive, consumptive society that they were. Would they release their former identity with all its trappings of empire, supremacy, and greed? Could they redefine who they were in ways that could last in an interconnected planet?

This was the referendum of the millennium - not the shape of politics or who would be the next president. The looming question was both individual and collective: will you abandon this abusive greed and learn to live respectfully on the Earth? At its heart, the question was cultural, not biological. It affected politics and economics, but it stemmed from a deeper place in the mysterious architecture of the human being. Were we willing to change to survive?

We had delayed answering for decades, stalling and dodging this question. But time was up. The deadline had come. Either we'd choose . . . or the choice would be made for us, and not in ways we liked. Zadie swallowed hard. These questions struck a raw and frightened chord in her; she could imagine how others would scream in resistance. But perhaps the answers to these questions were worth wading through our fear of asking them. Zadie was willing to confront her fears. Justice demanded that much, at least. She would talk to Charlie, too, and together, they'd find a way to bring these considerations to their entire country.

Looking to the horizon line of change, Zadie lifted her eyes to the far side of the dry meadow. She blinked and shaded her eyes with a frown.

"Hey Kinap . . . is that what I think it is?" she asked, squinting.

Beyond the crest of the hills, miles of forest opened in all directions, boughs dark and glossy, rippling in the wind. To the south, a bruised haze, discolored and sullen, covered the once-blue sky. In the distance, a tall chimney of smoke puffed up. At a higher altitude, the wind punched the haze like a sail, sending the mass of churning pink and grey eastward.

"Forest fire," Kinap agreed. Shifting uneasily, she added, "It's still a long way from here, but we'd better warn the others."

CHAPTER THIRTEEN

· · · · ·

The Phoenix Moment

By morning, the smoke had swallowed the sky. The day dawned in an eerie orange glow. The Council of All Beings disbanded and evacuated. Charlie and Zadie drove north, shoulders twitching and tensing as the fire tripped their evolutionary signal wires of animal unease. Charlie cast anxious glances in the rearview mirror. At the clearings, Zadie stared nervously at the thick plume towering like an eruption behind them. The wind spun around and licked their bumper, hurtling smoke and malice at their heels. Charlie fiddled with the radio and caught a brief report of the fast, roaring fire devastating hundreds, then tens of thousands of acres. Tiny mountain towns were evacuated then consumed. Asphalt roads heated into tire-melting rivers of molten tar. A gas line exploded in a boom louder than a bomb. The air turned toxic in the region. Hardware stores had long since run out of masks. The birds refused to sing, shrieking sharp warnings as they desperately winged north. Deer, skunk, raccoon, and all the larger mammals crashed through the underbrush and bolted across the road in front of their car, wild-eyed and half-crazed with primordial terror.

Around noon, the radio crackled and went dead. Charlie and Zadie threaded through one mountain ridge then the next. They passed caravans of firefighters headed south. At a gas station, the clerk watched the news, jittery. Prisoners, soldiers, and fire jumpers had formed a defensive line to the south, turning the fire away from the populated cities.

"But they won't stop it running from there to here, all the way up to Oregon," the clerk spat out bitterly. He turned to them and cocked his head. "My advice? Get as far from the smoke as you can."

They did, wondering what happened when forest fires and gas stations collided. By the next evening, they had traveled to the thinning edge of the smoke. The sky returned to hazy blue. The clerks and townspeople stopped staring warily at the southern horizon. They breathed deeper. The radio reports came through clear. The news channels showed heartbreaking footage of the fire. Giant fir trees transformed into blazing torches hundreds of feet tall. Helicopters with puny loads of water rushed back and forth from lakes. Yellow flame retardant dumped in showers of disturbing chemical plumes.

Thirty miles from the place of the Council's gathering, the town had been razed, reduced to blocks of ash and rubble. Strange, lone trees had survived. Seventeen people had not. The smoke choked people to death even when the flames were miles away. Two firefighters died when the wind trapped them behind an unexpected pivot of the fire. A family of campers had been caught in their car when the asphalt road scorched their tires to shreds. Thousands of people had crowded into the nearest towns and cities. Refugee camps had been set up in parking lots. Charlie sat on the edge of the creaking hotel bed with his elbows on his knees, staring at the television in wide-eyed horror.

"Zadie," he began.

"I know," she answered.

They checked out before dawn, heading south back toward the fire zone, to offer whatever aid they could.

They traveled to a town just outside of the fire zone where a relief center had been set up. The box store parking lot resembled an unruly flea market, laid out hodge-podge in a jumble of serpentine pathways. At the entrance, donations were arriving by the truckload: blankets, tents, clothes, camp stoves, canned goods, children's toys, stacks of diapers. Volunteer relief workers scurried in ant lines, sorting through the overwhelming array. In front of the store, the frazzled manager argued with the police, gripping his mousy hair with one aggrieved fist and slapping the other palm against his thigh, helpless. He'd called the cops on the open air relief network, only to be told that, since the mega-corporation had suckered the town into constructing a giant municipal lot as part of the deal to lure in the store, the citizens technically owned the lot. The mayor, up for re-election, could be spotted passing out baby formula and teddy bears to families.

Charlie and Zadie parked a quarter mile down the road and walked along the grassy ditch, fingers entwined, hands swinging. Smiles burst across their faces at the sight of a familiar gold, green, and white flag flapping in the smoky breeze, an iconic flower emblazoned on it. On the chain link fence, a hand-printed banner boldly declared: *The Dandelion Insurrection is here!*

They checked-in with a distracted coordinator caught amidst too many phone calls, text messages, and queries. She barely turned her head at their offer to help, simply pointing to where they could lend a hand unpacking a truck. She had a roll of toilet paper under one elbow and a clipboard in her other hand. She raced to the back section of the ever-growing mounds of donations, hollering that - no matter how much the kids loved them - that crate of week-old puppies had to go to the animal shelter in the next town.

Charlie and Zadie had been passing boxes and bundles for twenty minutes before the guy next to Zadie tossed her a flirtatious wink and asked her name.

"Zadie," she answered with a grin, catching the box of toothpaste tubes as he dropped it.

He stared agape at the slender woman in her faded rock band T-shirt and fire engine red skirt. Zadie bit back a laugh as she shoved the cuffs of her hooded sweatshirt past her elbows and passed the box to Charlie.

"And that's . . . that's," the volunteer stammered, craning around her mane of black curls to stare at Charlie as he waited with a bemused smile.

"Yep," Zadie replied cheerfully. "Now, keep passing the stuff before everyone starts hollering."

Too late. Pivoting at the hold-up, the other volunteers spotted the duo. Soon, an excited cluster huddled around them. The pair deflected questions, politely refused to sign autographs, and tried to get everyone back to work.

"What in Goddess' name is going on here?" a voice bellowed.

A short figure waded into the crowd, tapping shoulders and snaking between people to get to the center. A poof of frizzy and silvered honey-wheat hair encircled her face. Her skin hung about her knees as they stuck out of her shorts. She'd cut the sleeves off her T-shirt and a slather of sunscreen whitened her leathery skin. A tan line at her biceps hinted at long hours outdoors. The calluses on her hands and darker streaks in her fingerprint whorls suggested a lifetime of gardening. She peered up with the imperious, no nonsense attitude of all crones who claim their rightful place in human culture, and scrutinized the young pair with her squinted brown eyes.

"Well, that explains it," she remarked. "Back to work, all of you."

She snatched Charlie and Zadie by the elbows and pulled them along with her as the rest of the volunteers re-formed their bucket line.

"Bramble Ellison," she introduced herself.

"Are you in charge then?" Charlie asked.

"Not really. This community is like a bunch of ducklings I fuss over," Bramble answered with a twinkle in her eye. "Nice little flock, eh? Dandelions, the lot of them."

Her voice burst with pride as she gestured to the crew of volunteers.

"I can't tell you how glad I am to see you," Bramble declared, shoving her frizzy hair off her exertion-reddened face. "Needs to be written down and I haven't the time."

"What does?"

"The miracle unfolding in the wake of disaster. The phoenix moment!" Bramble exclaimed, gesturing around. "I tried to tell the reporters, but they just wanted to take photos of towering flames and burnt houses. That's not the real story."

The most eye-popping, heart-grabbing tale to be told wasn't the forest fire that flattened their town, but how years of preparation had readied the town to rise from the ashes, stronger - far stronger - than ever before.

"The corporate news chased the fire crew up the melting roads," Bramble griped, "I suppose *this* couldn't compete with the images of an apocalyptic inferno."

She gestured ahead of them to a grassy area running along the edge of the parking lot. Shade tents sheltered small groups gathered on picnic blankets and in circles of mismatched folding chairs. Conversation rose and fell in murmuring waves. The atmosphere's calm settled in Zadie's heart like beeswax

135

balm on chapped hands.

Peace.

It was the last thing she expected in the wake of a disaster, but it swept over her like a breeze. Not a bland, monotonous peace, but the peace that comes after the tears spill and the heart empties its anguish like the libations poured in a healing prayer.

"What is this?" she asked.

"A world cafe on how to rebuild," Bramble explained as she guided them through the clusters.

They had held empathy circles and listening sessions, too. When fire devours your home, you don't just need food, water, and shelter. You need community, understanding, and empathy. You need space to express fear and grief. You need a chance to comfort and be comforted.

"Typically, our society treats anything but happy productivity as a disease, an individual failing, and sends those who do not conform to therapy," Bramble said, shaking her grey hair, "but collective grief, mourning, anger, and shock is a different kind of tidal wave. We can't outsource it to specialists. We must cultivate ways for our communities to cradle each other as we grapple with our human emotions."

Our inner world was an ecosystem, entwined like mycelium and tree roots. Human beings were more than bundles of flesh. The emotions of one affected the whole, not just in families, but in entire communities.

"This is . . . incredible," Zadie said, looking around, awestruck.

Charlie nodded, his head bent over his pen and notepad, taking notes for their next essay. *This* was, without a doubt, a story everyone needed to hear. The world cafe facilitator rang a bell - a salvaged wind chime pipe still clinging to a string - and the small groups stretched and laughed, shook hands and exchanged hugs. They rose and looked around, then found a new group. Notetakers flipped to a blank page in their notebooks. The facilitators posed another discussion question on how they should redesign and rebuild. One person in each group began to speak.

"I'm a veteran of Occupy Sandy," Bramble shared proudly, "the Occupy protest-inspired disaster response to the hurricane that slammed New York City."

She pushed her glasses back up her nose and eased into a fluorescent green beach chair, gesturing to the two young people to sit as she continued her story. Bramble had been visiting her sister when the storm struck, battering the coastal city built precariously on backfilled marshland. Photos of flooded taxicabs in lower Manhattan shocked the nation, giving an image to the scientists' statistic-ridden warning about rising sea levels. But the disaster struck hardest in areas the news cameras never focused on. The shattered beachfront vacation houses evoked the concern of the nation, but it was the neighborhoods cut off from power, water, food, and medical care that bore the brunt of the storm. Shades of Hurricane Katrina in Louisiana haunted them, specters of people on roofs awaiting rescue, dead bodies floating in the street, poor hospitals abandoned while wealthy neighborhoods were evacuated. If Katrina brought out the worst of the nation, Occupy Sandy was determined to empower the best.

"We weren't a charity organization," Bramble told them. "The organizers detested the ways that the charitable-industrial complex's relief efforts demoralized and disempowered people. We were survivors. We had skills. We didn't need to sit around wrapped in Mylar blankets. We dug in our heels and got to work."

Collective organizing, mutual aid, self-designed relief systems, volunteer squads, barter networks, communal kitchens, and pop-up medical centers: there were dozens of ways people rose up to take care of their neighborhoods.

"Many of us wondered why we'd ever go back to 'normal'," Bramble mentioned with a sigh. "The life-as-usual downtown Manhattan was rebuilding was a disaster for poor people. In digging out from the storm, we found strength, resilience, and alternative systems that actually served our communities."

But the disaster of corporate capitalism was unrelenting. It never abated, even when the skies cleared, the floods retracted, and the mud was swept out. The drive to go back to business-as-usual swallowed up the neighborhoods again, leaving mere traces of the changes - a tool library, a renters collective, a mutual aid network - but nothing on the scale that erupted in the wake of disaster.

Bramble returned home haunted by two things: one, that the bigger disaster was the economic system, and two, that there must be ways a community could prepare the response that Occupy Sandy unleashed - not during a crisis, but before. Could they actually deal with the on-going economic disasters in ways that built their resiliency for other kinds of disasters?

Bramble looked around at the pop-up relief center that had reclaimed the box store parking lot for public use. It was astounding, really. The tents, the supplies, the mutual aid network, the world cafes, and empathy circles . . . with these, the people in her town were holding a revolution against the automatic defaults of the corporate empire, right in the shadow of the box store, right on top of the pavement the citizens had been duped into paying for. Well, they were taking it back! Not all revolutions happened with guns. Bramble Ellison's took place with volunteers and sharing, conversations and ideas.

Haunted and inspired by what she'd witnessed after Hurricane Sandy, Bramble began prepping - but not in a canned goods, basement-loaded-with-guns sort of way. She saw the handwriting on the wall. Fire was the disaster waiting to happen to her mountainous community. Drought plagued the region, worsening by the year. The conifer trees yellowed at the tips. The carpet of crackling orange needles thickened. Beetle-killed dead trunks dotted the mountainsides. The creeks dried up and took longer each season to return. Climate change turned up the heat and evapotranspiration sucked the moisture from the earth. She looked around her community and started asking: Disaster is a question of when, not if . . . so what will make us all stronger, together?

"I asked everyone: could we do what Occupy Sandy did? What would stop us?" Bramble explained.

The answers were surprising.

Fear. Isolation. Distrust.

"The default setting of US culture is individualism. We're socially organized around atomized families and isolation," Bramble declared with a disgusted snort. "It's terrible. We all stay home, scrolling the Internet or streaming videos in our dark little rooms."

To make a resilient community, she decided to start breaking the rules of social culture.

"Hostess with the most-est, that's me," she stated then laughed uproariously. She'd lived through the last vestiges of the wasp-waist, jello-laden nonsense. Her idea of hosting was more like convening potlucks and telling her neighbor to spread out picnic blankets in her front yard for everyone.

"It's amazing how much bossiness you can get away with when you're old," Bramble told Charlie and Zadie. "Meddling is part of the crone's ancient duty."

139

Bramble convened events every day of the week and circulated the schedule. She was the invoker, the outreach coordinator, the cheerleader, the catalyst for the social needs of the community.

"When people come together, they can do anything. We had to ditch our social dependency on corporate culture, replace movies with game nights, and Internet with interaction."

Before long, Bramble deepened the conversations from "get to know your neighbor" to "figure out how to take care of one another". From there, she challenged them to envision their collective future in ways that corporate culture never dared.

"We had visionary futures dinners and storytelling evenings and problem solving brunches," she reported with a gleeful chortle.

Connection was the key that unlocked everything, but, in the beginning, the people who showed up surprised Bramble.

"The people I thought would be at the top of the list to help weren't. They were too busy, caught up with the rat race, with careers and ambitions, hectic schedules and daily concerns."

The people who were interested in making immediate change were the ones already struggling to survive the economic disaster: the poor, students, the unhoused, migrants. That's who showed up to help. That's who wanted the communal kitchen, the tent medical centers, the bike repair shops, the clothing resale pop-up stores.

"But every system we tried, every idea we test-modeled, every seed we planted has borne fruit this week. Look around."

When the fires struck, the marginalized of the community weren't forgotten: they were at the heart and center of organizing the community's response.

"The quiet lines of connection we've been laying for years suddenly catalyzed into widespread action. The question some of us asked after Sandy is being asked by everyone now: should we go back to what was? Or should we go forward?"

Along the grass strips, under the trees, the world cafe brimmed with conversation. The wind chime bell rang out once again. The facilitators gathered everyone to "harvest" all of the ideas that had been shared. On large sheets of paper, scribes wrote down the comments as the notetakers reported back what they had heard from mothers and fathers, students and small business owners, artists and workers and activists, city planners and engineers, mechanics and teachers, nurses and doctors.

The ideas were visionary and practical, wide-ranging and sensible. Instead of rebuilding rows of big houses from flammable materials, some people suggested pooling land into a housing co-operative and reviving the commons. A team of architects wanted to design tiny houses made of less flammable, locally-available materials like rammed earth, adobe, cob . . . and at a fraction of the cost of the previous houses. The town officials were explaining how to put the schools and public libraries in the center of neighborhoods rather than on the outskirts. The department of public works was hoping to finally implement their plans for a citywide water catchment and management system.

"We are evolving. Here and now," Bramble declared to Charlie and Zadie, chuckling as she listened to her community's ideas.

They would take the fertile ash of disaster and compost tragedy into possibility. The old system had failed . . . and the next chapter was an unwritten book.

"It's time for courage," Bramble said, "for vision and for change."

A community would always rise to its potential in the wake of a disaster, for better or for worse. The seeds planted beforehand would grow. Disaster capitalists would exploit. Disaster collectivists would empower. People would rebuild in the shape of their imaginations, narrow or wide, cookie-cutters or visionary, inside the box of the old culture or outside the lines of the past.

"What we do today matters to our future," Bramble told them, "and your democracy challenge is helping us navigate this disaster together."

At their surprised smiles, Bramble nodded.

"Oh yes, we were one of the places that picked up on your essays after the Fourth of July. We started a Democracy School, a street assembly, and a participation challenge," she boasted proudly. "Come on, I'll tell you over lunch - or brunch or whatever meal we're at - I missed breakfast and am feeling peckish."

She rose in a creak of joints and a groan of muscles, and led them through the corridors of stacked boxes to the wide tent that served as a community kitchen. The core staff had run the Food Not Bombs group for years, making meals and sharing them with anyone who dared to throw off class distinctions and be human with one another. A sign-up sheet for chopping, cooking, and washing dishes was full of names of volunteers. The kitchen bustled with lunch preparations, but snacks of fresh fruit and trail mix sat next to the coffee dispenser. Bramble collected an assortment and settled down at the edge of the tent, where she could survey the terrain, keeping an eye on the kitchen, world cafe, and pop-up relief center all at once. She let Charlie bring her a cup of coffee and then told the young couple about how the Democracy Challenge had inspired her community.

Bramble had issued an adaptation of the Democracy Lab's constructive program called the *Participation Challenge*. She reached out to every group in town - everything from the Boys and Girls Club to writing groups to the Small Biz Association - and challenged them to try out one inclusive, participatory process. It might be a yearly agenda survey, a stakeholder discussion on the direction of the organization, an across-the-aisle dialogue on a divisive issue, a poll on what products to stock the shelves with, a mock participatory budget for the town - the list was endless. Hundreds of groups joined in, including the school sports teams whose listening circles revealed a surprising youth message: winning wasn't as important to them as having fun. They'd rather lose while having a great time than win under a drill sergeant of a coach.

"The Participation Challenge activated our community," Bramble reflected, eyes wide as her smile. "It was as if we suddenly woke up ... like a field of golden dandelions blooming in the spring."

Bramble had taken the flash of interest in those experiments, and issued a wide invitation to hold wisdom councils on the town's *500 Year Vision Plan*.

"We had just started the first of thirteen gatherings when the fire hit," Bramble said with a shake of her head.

In some ways, they just picked up where they left off . . . but with a sense of urgency. The visionary exploration suddenly became a very real question. They were in a phoenix moment, rising from the ashes. Redesigning had become designing anew. Redevelopment now had an unexpectedly clean slate. Previous attachments and fears had been burnt away.

"No one alive today was involved in making the blueprint of the town. It grew hodge-podge," Bramble explained, "but we're still a community. We know our strengths and weaknesses. We have a guess at our coming future needs. We can plan for them and fix problems that were literally built into our town."

Local democracy was about hardwiring resilience into the community. It was about being prepared to counter the inevitable predatory response of the worldviews that caused the disasters to begin with.

"Look at them," Bramble said, gesturing to the people in the world cafe. "This community is coming up with a vision and a plan. When the disaster capitalists try to sneak in and snatch up real estate at rock bottom prices or steal reconstruction funds and contracts, each person here knows that there are other options. They know who to talk to if they want to order bulk building supplies as a co-operative. They have already pooled remaining resources - and their larger resource web - to meet immediate needs. In this kitchen, there are plates for and from everyone."

The predatory vulture capitalists that would inevitably swoop in, trying to pick at the carcass of the burnt town, wouldn't find isolated, shell-shocked families huddled in despair. They would find an active community ready to shoo them away as superfluous annoyances.

"But the old representative system weren't the ones that made this happen," Bramble stated emphatically. "Our town councilors and county commissioners, the mayor - they would have made backroom deals with speculators. We stopped that with our real democracy project."

To politicians and officials, "getting back to normal" and returning to business-as-usual were often considered the only options. They felt the pressure of expectation. If Bramble Ellison's hadn't launched the local democracy initiative, their local officials would have had no idea that the populace was not only ready for a redesign, but already brimming with plans for it.

Fires devoured ailing woods - the Southern Rockies had

burnt like a row of matches, one beetle-killed tree igniting the next. Scraggly, overcrowded stands of clear-cut regrowth ignited from lightning strikes. The sparks of electrical wires in drought-weakened undergrowth set the Sierras ablaze. The forests kept burning year after year. But there were also species of mushrooms that flourished after forest fires, erupting from the ashes to begin the process of returning life to the woods.

"We are the mushroom spores," Bramble chuckled, "building the soil for what comes next."

Forest regrowth would take time. City rebuilding was a process.

"But we can grow differently, in ways far better suited to this place," Bramble insisted.

They could. They would. They must.

It was the only way forward for them all.

CHAPTER FOURTEEN

· · · · ·

Murmurations & Swarms

The bridge loomed in the fog. They came to it from the north, suddenly lurching out of a tunnel on a careening rollercoaster of a highway that clung desperately to the steep hills above the bay. Charlie and Zadie had stayed with Bramble Ellison for a week, interviewing people in the community, covering the story of collective re-envisioning and rebuilding. They had amplified the requests for support . . . and ultimately discovered that they weren't really needed at all.

"That's the ideal, really," Bramble told them with a chuckle. "Put yourselves out of a job. Wouldn't it be wonderful to get to go home and do this where you live?"

Charlie agreed. He also wondered where, exactly, was home for him and Zadie? They'd spent years on the road, living in other people's homes, caring for a whole country. Would they ever settle down in one spot? And where? He couldn't quite imagine Zadie living at her dad's farm, much as she loved to visit.

Bramble sent them south. *Go to San Francisco,* she told them. A large rally was being held to call for community-led relief and resilience funding.

"The city is a global wealth epicenter. We want the billionaires to put their money to work for the people and planet."

For decades, the wealthy had stockpiled money, property, and power. The Dandelion Insurrection had called the bluff on

147

the mythologies of trickle down effects and the fantasies of rising tides that lifted all boats. The money had to be dispersed, not hoarded. And it had to happen *now,* not ten, twenty, fifty, or a hundred years in the future.

"The resources for climate adaptation can't be in the hands of those who caused the crisis," Bramble pointed out. "We can't solve a problem with the same thinking that created it."

There was a group in the tech capital of the world pushing for radical redistributions of fortunes. They formed Community Funds governed by participatory budgeting, and pressured the wealth holders to give in big, bold, and boundless ways. Demonstrations were going to be held throughout the Bay Area in support of them, with a major rally in San Francisco's Financial District.

"You'll like this," Bramble promised them. "The whole event is one giant murmuration."

As they crossed over the Golden Gate Bridge, Zadie made Charlie park and walk back out along the pedestrian walkway, under the giant suspender cables, and through the metal gates. At the midway point, the reverberations of the vehicles pulsed eerily through the steel. They peered down on the inland side, watching the churning tide stride ferociously into the bay. Around them, wisps of grey fog whispered in their ears and then vanished.

"I love this city," Zadie sighed, a curl of a smile on her lips. "Of all the American cities, San Francisco tugs my heart strings."

New York was brassy and magnificent. Los Angeles was a beauty and a beast. Chicago was hard-edged and steely. But San Francisco was a portal, a brimming laboratory of possibilities, eyes forever on the west, the realm of night dreams and ocean secrets. She was a heartbreaker, this city, rife with casual cruelties. When the evening fog marched in, the streets stank with their musty secrets - but Zadie loved that, too. The day's end held reckonings, an invisible tally sheet for squandered hopes and deferred dreams. There was a madness to this place. San Francisco held forth a shining promise for the pains that ailed the nation's soul - but there was a price. Every city had its price. New York was crazy. Chicago mad. Los Angeles insane. San Fran? Delirious. A city of dreams and delusions, unrequited passions and fog visions that faded when the sparkle of sunlight burnt through.

"Come on," Zadie said abruptly, pulling Charlie away from the edge.

They went the full length of the bridge and crossed under the highway at the far end. The pedestrian walkway was emptier on the ocean side, lonelier. The sharp scent of salt and fog whipped them. The sea opened like a gaping maw. Its grey cloak failed to conceal its naked immensity. This side of the bridge was wild, unconquered by the tourists' cameras and fussy kids.

"You have to see both sides," Zadie whispered in Charlie's ear, threading her arms around him as goose bumps prickled their skin and beads of fog bedecked their hair, "to truly see this place."

On one side, the modern city. On the other, an ancient being born from the crosshairs of tide and time. Charlie shivered. How long had this churning channel watched the city? Did anyone else sense that an unseen creature crouched here? Did the commuters perceive this being as they thundered over the bridge? Did they tap the dashboard or lift a hand in greeting as they passed?

"I feel it," Zadie confessed. "I don't like to come to the city without paying my respects."

When they left, Charlie had the prickling sense of eyes trailing him, watching without a word. What beings of place resided across his country, rendered invisible by ignorance and prejudice? What else would he see, now that his human-centric superiority had been stripped away like a pair of blinders pulled off a horse?

The questions haunted him until they reached the financial district where the distracting bustle drove them from his mind. There, murmuration trainings swarmed through the streets like a wild dance class released from studio walls. The murmuration was a flocking movement, modeled after the ever-shifting groups of starlings that swooped and flew in formations at dusk. Zadie had introduced the concept to the Dandelion Insurrection and it had grown into a popular, versatile street action. Conducting the training from the sidelines, a small pair of figures passed a megaphone back and forth as a sea of bodies moved in synchronized gestures, mimicking the motions of the temporary leader at the front of the group.

"Remember," one of the trainers said into the megaphone, "this is a leaderful structure. As the 'flock' turns, the leader changes. Whoever is in front leads until they turn. Look for the new leader now. Who is that person?"

The trainers reoriented the demonstrators as they lost sight of the changing leadership. Laughter rose up like bird wings. The murmuration pivoted and worked through its awkward moments, bumbling hiccups, and confused stumbling. As they practiced, they gained skill, speed, and grace.

"Can't see the front?" the co-facilitator asked, taking the megaphone. "Follow your wingmate's cues. Stay equidistant. Keep moving forward. That's it! You've got it!"

The pair cheered from their perch on a concrete garden planter. Charlie and Zadie made their way closer, skirting around the edges of the moving flock of humans, arriving near the trainers just as they called a break.

"Great work, everyone. Remember, those guiding principles will determine how we'll fly through the city, swooping in groups, splitting into smaller clusters, and rejoining with others once again. Go get some water and get ready. We'll start at the top of the hour."

The megaphone squeaked as it shut off. The pair of petite organizers hopped down to greet the new arrivals.

"Well, if it isn't the Mother of All Murmurations," the first said, grinning at Zadie and sticking out a hand. "We were part of the DC Swarm, but we're from Chicago, originally. Lately, we've been migrating westward training people in cities all over."

They were a pair of siblings, almost mirrors of each other, twins with identical features. They were in their thirties, compact and muscular. Caramel skin creased around the deep dimples in their cheeks. Laughter lines formed around their eyes. They flirted at the edges of gender, refusing to be male or female. They wore jeans, blazing yellow T-shirts, and a set of hoodies, black and blue. Zadie noticed a tattoo of a dandelion seed on the back of one twin's hand and tucked the distinguishing mark away for later reference.

"I'm Sparrow," the one with the tattoo said.

"Starling," the other offered, extending a hand to shake.

As the mass of protesters readied for action, unfurling banners and fetching signs, Starling and Sparrow filled the pair in on the objectives of the day's protests.

"We're trying to remove the moral legitimacy of stockpiling wealth at this pivotal time in human history," Starling said, pointing out signs and banners that decried the concentration of wealth. "We'll swarm around the financial district with dozens

151

of messages, all pushing, compelling, and demanding that the ultra-rich give big and give back."

"They've gained unprecedented wealth in the last decade. Now let's see them *give* at an unprecedented rate," Sparrow chuckled.

"People know how to solve the problems we face," Starling chimed in. "Like Bramble Ellison's community, they have good ideas for moving forward. But in order to move them forward, they need the resources that the ultra-wealthy have."

"We need to democratize wealth along with democratizing everything else," Sparrow stated emphatically.

At the stroke of eleven, the sun burst through the fog, the twins gave the signal, and five hundred people moved into action. Soapboxes were scattered throughout the district on the street corners. People swarmed in ever-shifting groups from one to the next, leaving when they felt ready, staying when the speaker held their attention. They carried signs and banners calling for democratizing wealth. They stopped traffic and blocked roads, bogging down the pulse of the city's traffic patterns. They swept into lobbies of finance centers for two-minute speeches then swept out before the managers could call the cops. They picketed the luxury skyrises and deluxe hotels. They flooded the sidewalks near expensive boutiques and hair salons, asking wealthy women to give to the Community Fund. Zadie and Charlie split up, each shadowing one of the twins, trying to witness as many of the flash actions as possible.

"If that woman gave away a million dollars a day for a whole year," Sparrow whispered to Charlie, pointing to a wealthy patron of a high-end salon, "she'd still be a multi-millionaire."

A billion was a thousand millions - a fortune impossible to spend in one lifetime. It was the wealth a whole species needed to transform a broken world into a whole one, to rebuild after

152

the ravages of not just fires and floods, but centuries of greed and exploitation.

Sparrow and Charlie tracked as many actions as they could, taking photos of small pods of protesters holding up banners in front of high-end art galleries, filming a flash mob and die-in at the Palace of Fine Arts during its fundraising soiree. Charlie posted photos online as groups painted a giant message across six city blocks in under twenty minutes: *Invest In Resilience Not Destruction.* Each letter was the size of a bus. Artist-activists used roller brushes to paint the enormous letters onto the street. With Sparrow, he slipped through the revolving doors of a financial district skyscraper while the guards gawked. They rode the elevator as high as they could and snapped a photo from the twentieth floor. From there, they could see Zadie and Starling down the block, recognizable by the twin's blazing yellow shirt. They were in the middle of an immense murmuration dancing in the street.

On the ground, Starling and Zadie turned slowly, following the motions of the nearest people as they stood in the heart of the giant murmuration. Zadie had never seen anything so beautiful. Elegant. Masterful. Peaceful. Strong. Here, a sense of calm settled like sunlight. The bustle of the city fell away. They lifted their arms and rotated like a field of sunflowers. They stepped forward in the rhythm of antelope herds. They stilled like watchful birds then darted into motion, swooping and diving. The shape of the mass of people rippled and contracted, shifting direction from moment to moment. They flooded the streets. They drifted onto sidewalks. They charged along crosswalks. On the outermost rims, murmuration monitors in orange vests halted traffic. They also handed out fliers that explained that the murmuration was a reminder, a dance of respect for all living beings, a way of invoking the ecosystems of

153

the world in the heart of a financial district whose decisions affected the entire planet.

They moved like rivers, curving and churning. They rippled like shoals of fish and mimicked the swooping wings of manta rays. They banked and turned in avian spirals. All of life swept through them: the patterning of clouds, amassing, swelling, breaking open into rain; the upward curls of unfurling ferns, the loping gamble of the wolf pack, the thundering gait of bison herds, the leaping flight of deer and dolphins, the slow sunning of turtles on logs.

The Earth thinks in circles. She dreams in spirals and nautilus shell revolutions. She paints in sprays of wildflowers, clusters of lichens, stands of trees. She moves in tidal dances, forward and back, in stretches of time too long for human conception. She tells her stories across eons. Her epics are epochs.

Humanity is not excused from this dance. Every breath of air entering our lungs weaves the ever-shifting formations of clouds into our blood. The circumambular journey of the sky feeds into our cells. The phytoplankton riding the ocean swells winds up in our veins, transformed. Invisible, they hitch a ride on water molecules, climb the elevator of evaporation, gather into cloudbursts, and split into rivers, only to reunite in our bodies after a journey across entire continents and ocean currents.

Awe - sheer wonder - was the only acceptable response to the majesty of the Earth.

This murmuration, pulsing in the heart of a glittering city, swarming through the streets like salmon runs of old, swooping and diving in a flock hundreds strong, was more than a protest ... it was a prayer, a ritual, an invocation of the Earth in the places that had forgotten how to think in circles and cycles, curves and spirals. With it, the rules of natural systems crashed the opium dream fantasies of the line-and-grid urban world. Their feet, lifting and falling - not in march-step unison, but in patterned waves of rippling, subtle drumrolls - reverberated through the tar into the ground, down, down to the shivering fault line that trembled beneath the city, a reckoning built by plate tectonics and continental shifts.

It was more than a protest statement; it was a return of reverence. With it, they laid their human lives upon the altar of the planet, and swayed and swarmed back into the ancient dance their species had forgotten. They did not speak, they listened, and their rusty animal alertness crept back into their limbs. They let their presence proclaim their message. They allowed the unexpected sight of hundreds of humans embodying the primal patterns that had birthed and nurtured their species for millennia shock and baffle the passersby. Spectators gaped, still caught up in the doings built by humans. Drivers blew their horns when the murmuration blocked the street, resenting the interruption of their headlong rush toward extinction.

And still . . . there was the woman in tears on the street corner, filming with her camera, unable to explain why this movement evoked despair and hope in the very marrow of her bones. There was the old man at the outdoor cafe, cream overflowing his coffee cup as he stared in wonder, a smile crinkling his face. There were the children who tugged their harried mother's arm, pointing to the magic breaking through the bustle of commercial mundanity.

There were those who saw and understood the beauty dancing before them, those who paused amidst the day and let the murmuration call them back to their human nature . . . the human nature birthed in ocean wombs and built in primordial times, the one entwined to moon cycles and seasonal minuets and a world more wild than tame. When the murmuration turned the corner, these humans stepped forward, transformed, and they, in turn, transformed their world in small and large ways, choosing the smaller footprint, stepping lightly and gently on this beloved Earth, cradled by their abiding interconnection with a living world.

Zadie danced with the murmuration until she tired. Then she stilled in the shade of a building, watching the movement sweep through the intersection. She rested for a spell then followed, catching up to Starling as they stood back to record a video.

"It's ... beautiful," Zadie sighed. She had been part of dozens of murmurations, but this one transformed the protest tactic into art. She felt transformed, exalted, grounded, and broken open into awed vulnerability.

"It's modern-day magic," Starling agreed. "It's a ritual dance in the ancient sense. It deepens with time. Duration matters. If you watch the old dances - think Sufis spiraling or stamping dance rituals of African traditions - the movement is not performative so much as experiential. The length and repetition is what works the magic."

They tracked the murmuration down the next street. There was an abandon to the participants' motions, a surrendering. They settled into the space between leader and follower, alert and receptive.

"I could watch it all day," Zadie sighed.

"Or move with it all day," Starling added.

They shared a grin. Starling and Zadie had just turned the corner when Zadie froze.

"What?" Starling asked, spotting her stricken expression.

The world fell away. The blare of car horns faded. The

bustle of passing crowds sped by, invisible. There, on the street corner soapbox in front of them, surrounded by a white-clad, fawning crowd, was Reverend Jebediah Whyte, pulling one of his favorite publicity stunts: street preaching. It was second only to feeding the homeless for fifteen minutes or visiting orphanages on photo-op charity missions. He planned these stunts to coincide with his speaking gigs, exhorting others to donate to the poor while he raked in huge fees at Christian universities and conferences. He made a show of standing with the downtrodden, like Jesus, while flying across the country in a private jet and dining at five-star restaurants. Today, Jeb Whyte rode his high horse in opposition to the murmuration swarming through the streets.

"This is paganism, heathenism!" he was saying, slamming a fist onto his palm for emphasis as his followers nodded and clapped. "There is a natural order of the species. The handprint of God can be recognized in this order. We, who are made in His image, were given dominion over the Earth - not the other way around. The sensibility of this can be seen by any true believer."

The startling sight of Reverend Jeb Whyte in his tailored suit filled Zadie with loathing. His cluster of worshippers - one holding a sign that declared the end times were near - swayed and rocked to the rhythm of the preacher's incantatory tones. Behind him, his wife Evelyn stood with her head bowed, Bible clutched to bosom, one manicured hand lifted heavenward in supplication.

"The social order is breaking down. There are those who promote anarchy! There are even those who want us to embrace bestiality!" Reverend Whyte's Texas twang drawled out sentences into proclamations and prophetic revelations. "They wish to bring back the sinful days of paganism and animal worship. In this time of lawlessness, not only are the young disobedient to their parents, but the entirety of society is losing its sense of place. Workers want to be bosses; students think they should be instructors. Soon, humanity will have the arrogance to proclaim themselves God."

Zadie gagged. The rhetoric reminded her strangely of John Adam's rebuttal to Abigail's demands for equality. The Founding Father had bemoaned the fact that his fellow rich white men's quest to make themselves kings of a new country had spurred Black people, women, Indigenous Peoples, and lower classes to actually believe the rhetoric of revolution and imagine that equality meant their equality, too.

"This alarming trend must be stopped," Reverend Jeb Whyte proclaimed, "wherever it lifts its unruly head. God meant us to rule. Wisely, as He does. For the greater good, as He does. With a natural order, as He does."

A flurry of amens rose up.

"With the white man on top, no doubt," Starling muttered in a disgusted undertone to Zadie, tugging at her arm. "Let's go."

Zadie stayed frozen in place, eyes narrowed dangerously, hands balled in fists on her hips.

"There are those - false prophets - who claim a time of change is upon us, who say the natural order should be turned upside down, who want us to think that ants and flies should be greater than humans! We shall not fear these lies. We shall not forsake our Lord and His divine design. We shall remain loyal and obedient."

Zadie winced. Their essay on the imperative of including all beings in this burgeoning democracy movement had been met with more than the usual derision. Apparently, there was a limit to how far they could push the envelope before the people's sense of revolutionary potential met with kickback. She and Charlie had argued for hours before releasing the writings about the Council of All Beings.

"It doesn't matter if they're not ready for it, Charlie," she had told him. "It's what they need to hear."

Against his better judgment, she posted the essay. Within minutes, the vitriolic scorn roared out of the dark corners of the Alternet.

They've lost it.

Gone batty.

Crazy treehuggers.

Are plants the new race card?

The nation split into three camps of reactions: the eco-minded who had been saying this for years, the scathing mockers, and those who thought the environment should be protected, but not because mountains and rivers were beings.

Charlie and Zadie have gone too far, they said, shaking their heads from the comfort of a superiority built on centuries of human-centric worldviews.

From the cheers and amens coming from Reverend Whyte's crowd, his true believers belonged to the clique of vitriolic critics who couldn't stomach the notion that God hadn't granted them dominion over the Earth, nor the right to dominate the world. Zadie had to concede that it was a long way down to fall, particularly for the white male. In under a century, they had plummeted from the apex of global dominance into the bewildering terrain of equality. The oldest among them would have been raised in the remnants of the father-knows-best culture of the fifties.

But the fact that they were livestreaming Reverend Whyte's sermon with their cellphones proved those old dogs could learn new tricks. Surely, respecting women, the Earth, and people of color wasn't as difficult as keeping up with the breakneck pace of ever-changing technology? Surely the concept of the Rights of Nature wasn't as mind-bending as the ability to video chat with someone halfway around the planet with a computer translating one's remarks into another language?

A shudder whipped through Zadie's thin frame. She shifted, ready to go. At that moment, Jeb Whyte's eyes dropped down from the fog-cloaked, skyscraper-lined heavens. For a brief, excruciating instant, his gaze caught hers. A twist hardened in his fixed smile. A jolt of adrenaline shot through her - primal fear. Beneath the blue-eyed charm, she saw it.

Hate.

Sharp as a knife, hard as stone, it flashed for a second and then vanished. Zadie didn't wait for him to speak to her. She grabbed Starling's arm and ran.

CHAPTER FIFTEEN

. . . . .

Crashing the Atrium

"You didn't see it, Charlie," she exclaimed. "It was like staring at the face of evil. He *hates* me. It was like he saw the Devil or something."

"You are *something*," Charlie answered with an appreciative grin, throwing an arm around her.

Zadie shrugged away, irritated that he didn't take her worry seriously. They strode briskly down the concrete sidewalk on the heels of the twins. The evening fog had rolled in, dense and chilling. Zadie's skin prickled, a trillion tiny warning signals lifting along her bare shoulders. She grimaced and tugged her T-shirt up where it slipped off her shoulder. She hadn't known they'd be out this late or she'd have brought a jacket. San Francisco autumn nights chilled in the fog, which swept in eerie wisps around the top of the skyscrapers. She shivered. Her cut-off shorts halted mid-thigh, leaving her wishing she'd worn blue jeans like Charlie.

"Tell me about this gala again?" she urged Sparrow.

"It's *the* party of the year for the Bay Area rich and powerful. Starling and I have been trying to crash it for years."

After the street murmuration, Charlie and Zadie had offered to treat the twins to dinner, but the pair declined with mischievous looks.

"We've got a gala to crash. Wanna come?"

The twins had wrangled entry out of one of their friends on the kitchen staff. At precisely seven o'clock, Carlos would open the backdoor and let them sneak in through the maintenance entrance of the Atrium. Taking their campaign to the next level, they planned to storm the mic and hoist a banner that said: *Champagne on the Titanic?* They planned to read an itemized list of how many months of a poor person's rent went into a single bottle of wine, how many meals for children one truffle hors d'oeuvre could buy, how many electric bills could be paid with the price of the gala tickets, and how many fire-destroyed homes could be rebuilt for the cost of throwing this party.

Of course, Charlie and Zadie wanted to come!

The Atrium sat a few blocks west of the financial district. They circled around the block, avoiding the growing media circus camped out alongside the red carpet. Together, the four crept into the alley behind the Atrium and waited for Carlos to let them in.

"With you two involved," Starling enthused, "we'll make national news, not just regional."

The Atrium's signature party space was an open mezzanine under a glass ceiling. Two curving waterfalls of staircases connected the upper level to the lower. A third story was accessible only by guarded elevators. From the balconies, the uber-wealthy looked down their noses at starlets and tech start-up millionaires. To one side, a string band on a stage played orchestral adaptations of pop songs. A swirling set of figures danced, diamond rings glittering, gold watches glinting, and bracelets shining. Zadie felt underdressed, but spending anything less than fifty thousand dollars on clothes and jewelry would still have left her feeling naked.

"Who'd you take to prom, Charlie?" she asked. This was the

162

closest she'd come to a prom. She had run away from home as a teen and spent her prom night waiting tables.

"Marie-Claire Thibodeau," he answered. "Remember her?"

"I thought she was gay."

"She was. Is. She came out in the fall and no one would go with her."

"So, you did," Zadie said with a smile.

"Well, it's more accurate to say she took me . . . I didn't even want to go."

"Why not?"

He gave her a pained look.

"The girl I wanted to go with wasn't available," he reminded her. She had broken his heart by running off and leaving him behind.

Zadie threaded her arm through his.

"I'll claim my waltz now, okay?"

They were supposed to make a distraction so Starling and Sparrow could get up on the stage. They'd discussed tipping over the crystal punchbowl or the stacked tower of champagne flutes, but settled on the optics of Charlie Rider and Zadie Byrd Gray waltzing in blue jeans and cut-off shorts at a black tie affair.

They managed to step on each other's toes only once before they spotted security guards mouthing commands into their collars. Flashes of cameras burst dizzyingly all around them. They blinked, unable to see beyond the winking pseudo-starlight. Just when the band faltered and they thought the guards would rush them, a woman in a gold dress with a tiara in her blonde coif stepped forward.

"Well, well, if it isn't the famous love birds. Surprise!"

She smiled to the crowd and waved to the security guards to stand down. Then, she pivoted on her heel and snapped her manicured fingers at the band to resume playing.

"I'm cutting in, dahling," she informed Zadie, nudging her aside. "It's the least you can do after crashing mah party."

The woman gestured imperiously. A movie star stepped forward to offer his buff arm to Zadie. She cursed under her breath, but she was already being swept off. She scanned the sidelines and spotted Starling facepalming.

"Chah-lie, dahling," the wealthy woman drawled, "I cannot tell you how glad I am to meet you."

She smiled like an alligator.

"Um, who are you?" he replied, twisting to find Zadie.

"Mona Gold," she answered, yanking him back with a shockingly firm grip. "A fan of yours."

Charlie blinked in surprise, looking her up and down.

Mona Gold reeked of money. She was a petite woman - the kind destined to shrink with age until they distilled their power into a sour-and-salty, pickled plum kind of a punch. Charlie didn't like to speculate on how many hours each day it took to preserve her flawless skin and perfectly coiffed blonde hair. Mona wore her wealth like a vanguard announcing her arrival. Trumpeting fortune in silks and diamonds, she held out her manicured hand as if Charlie should kiss the backside. At the last minute, perhaps spotting his baffled disdain, she rotated her gold-bedecked wrist and extended her handshake.

"Chah-lie, I must tell you: you are my hero - no, don't blush. It's true."

"I would have thought our anti-wealth stance would, uh, insult your sensibilities," he confessed.

She laughed.

"You're cute. Dahling, I am richer than Gawd. You could slice my fortune in half and I'd still have more money than I'd know what to do with. A little pruning at the top strengthens the roots, right?"

Little wasn't the adjective he'd apply to his comments on trimming back excessive wealth.

"What do you want with me?" he retorted.

"Dance with me, dahling," Mona drawled. "People are staring."

She held out her arms expectantly. Charlie hesitated.

"I don't bite," Mona promised. "I want to offer you a job. Now, be a gentleman and dance."

She shook her hands imperiously. Warily, reluctantly, Charlie took her hand and let the woman slide her nails over the shoulder of his T-shirt. In his periphery, Zadie whirled past, a skeptical laugh bursting out of her at something the actor had just said. Charlie shuffled his feet into the rhythm of a waltz.

"I want to syndicate your writings and put the Man From the North column in every major news journal in the country."

"I already have a bigger circulation on the Alternet," he answered.

"But you don't make a dime on it, do you?" Mona pointed out. "My media network could make you *millions*. You could be rich."

"Those news journals all require subscriptions," he argued back. "Right now, everyone can read my posts for free."

"Annoying, isn't it?" Mona drawled, clenching his shoulder as he moved to get away.

"I have to go - "

"Chah-lie, the party's just getting started. Everyone wants to meet you."

"I'm not here for the caviar," he pointed out. "I'm here to demand that wealthy people like you return the money you've stolen from ordinary citizens. The country is like an engine

165

spluttering, trying to run on too little fuel. We need the wealthy to open the coffers and pour the resources back into circulation again."

"Pfft," Mona scoffed. "Regular people don't have a clue how to use money wisely."

"Do you?" Charlie shot back, skeptical. The designs of the wealthy had led them to the brink of extinction, plummeted millions into poverty, and collapsed the economy beyond fixing. It was *structural* change that mattered. It was ending the pay-for-everything economy and investing in shared resources accessible to everyone. If Mona Gold funded nothing but tool libraries, she would infuse more resources into communities than if she walked around handing out million dollar checks to mega-corporations.

"You could be the Carnegie of the new millennium," he tried, smiling persuasively.

"I'd rather buy an election, frankly," she retorted, wheeling him around the dance floor while the media crashed into each other, snapping photos.

"That's exactly what we need you *not* to do," Charlie exploded. "We need you to get your money out of our politics. They don't belong to you . . . or any of the wealthy people."

"Dahlin', this country's politics have been in our pocket since 1776," Mona laughed, batting her eyelashes. "By hook or by crook, we, the Wealthy, own this country. The government jumps to our tune, not yours."

Charlie jerked away, angry, but she clenched him in a grip toned by a lifetime of personal trainers. She smirked.

"Newsflash, Charlie Rider: rich people rule. Always have, always will. Your precious Dandelions have won one round of a never-ending class war. That's all."

Her icy eyes raked him up and down. He felt flayed into a

bloody carcass hanging in a meat factory's abattoir, pinioned on a hook, mouth gasping breathlessly. She licked her lips, suggestively, seductively, and leaned close to his ear.

"The question is: do you have staying power?" She bumped her hips against his. He squirmed away. "I've got money, guns, laws, billionaires on my side. What do you have, Charlie Rider?"

He shoved her off. They froze, still amidst the swirling crowd.

"I have the people," he told her flatly. "And we have an endurance you can't even imagine. We've turned the gears of your economy for centuries. We've fought your wars of profit. We've outlasted all your genocides and ecocides and daily grinds and starvation. Not alone, but together. We always will. And in the end, you will lose this war."

The mocking smile on her lips faltered under the intensity of his certainty. His dry laugh barked soundlessly.

"You don't even know why, do you?" he asked her, shaking his head, half disgusted, half astonished.

She gaped at him. Her eyes narrowed in thought, the beady abacus of her brain clicking away, trying to calculate what ordinary people had that she didn't.

"Love," Charlie said. "We have love. Millions of parents who love their children more than life itself. Millions of people who never surrendered their love for the Earth. Millions of people who care more deeply about one another than you've ever cared about anything. You have money. We have love. We have community. We have courage. We have justice. We have truth. We have the Earth, herself. You will never win this war."

He burned with something hotter than fury, stronger than steel. He took a half step closer. She flinched away.

"You should surrender now," Charlie warned her. "You all

should. We've been waiting for you for years."

He turned away then. The people and the earth wouldn't wait any longer. They couldn't. The clock was ticking. In the eleventh hour, the wealthy would either surrender the class war, or all of humanity would hurtle into oblivion. The people had solutions. The people had the dispersed, wild creativity needed to save them all. The people needed the stolen wealth returned so they could build a chance of survival for them all.

Charlie could feel the eyes in the room pivoting toward him as he stalked off the dance floor. He was fairly certain half of them had tried to kill, arrest, or stop him in the past few years. He jumped as a dancing couple nearly crashed into him. Muttering an apology, he slid sideways between a pair of tuxedoed men on the sidelines, scanning the crowd for Zadie. Squinting into the distance, he could see Starling and Sparrow crouched behind one of the amplifiers. As he ducked beyond a marble column, the pair walked boldly up to the mic, unfurled their banner, and started their recitation as the band stumbled to an abrupt halt. The dancers paused. The whole room turned to see what was going on. Their faces contorted as their anticipation of the host's speech gave way to consternation over the twins' proclamation of the shamefulness of extravagance. Charlie dodged around the partiers, searching for Zadie with increasing worry.

"Long live the Dandelion Insurrection!" Sparrow shouted as the security guards seized the twins and hauled them off the stage.

Just as the band frantically struck up a tune, Charlie spotted Zadie in an alcove off of the main room, a look of utter fury on her face, eyes narrowed at a trio of sniggering men.

"What the hell do you think you're doing?" he heard her snap.

"Come on, do a little dance for us. We know you can," one of them said, leering.

They gyrated in a poor mimicry of a strip dance while her cheeks flamed. As Zadie edged away, one of them grabbed her arm just above the elbow, fingers hard enough to bruise.

"Let go," she told him, twisting away and grabbing her faded T-shirt as the motion pulled it sideways.

"C'mon," he teased, reaching for her other shoulder.

"No!"

Zadie yanked back. She heard a ripping sound as the shoulder fabric caught and the flimsy seam gave way. She wrenched free and spun out of the area, whirling toward the main room. A flash of cameras blasted her. She winced and flung one hand up to shade her eyes.

"Charlie?" she called, shoving between reporters as a slew of questions slapped her from all sides.

"What's going on?"

"Where were you?"

"What happened to your shirt?"

"Wardrobe mishap or secret tête-à-tête?" a reporter shouted.

Here we go again, Charlie thought.

CHAPTER SIXTEEN

· · · · ·

Strippers Strike

In less time than it took them to get out of the gala, the online fashion sites had posted the photos of a disheveled, wild-eyed Zadie clutching a falling-down shirt and the guy's one-line quote:

"Once a stripper, always a stripper, I guess."

Zadie wanted to punch his smug face.

"We crashed the gala to make a point about hoarding wealth during a crisis," Zadie snapped back to the reporters. "*That's* the story. The assault on my body is nothing compared to what those people do, day in and day out. They evict families. They condemn millions to poverty with low wages. They hoard money while children go hungry. They destroy our only planet."

She's hiding something, the reporters concluded. *Is Zadie Byrd Gray having an affair?*

Zadie gritted her teeth and bit back her scream of frustration. She was so tired of her "bad girl" reputation avalanching into these rumors. The vicious cycle had only grown with every attempt to discredit her. Public opinion swung toward Charlie. He started receiving love letters and marriage proposals from hopefuls who couldn't wait for them to break up. The four major media channels spun the story out like stretched taffy. The corporate "news" networks pretend to investigate the incident while simply rehashing the rumors of

171

her infidelity. The comedy shows whipped out satirical soap operas about her and Charlie. *Limelight* did a documentary on her teen runaway past. *Dateline* held a date-off competition for Charlie Rider's new girlfriend. *Deep Dive* explored her rumored affair with Will Sharp, neglecting to inform the viewers that those had all been debunked. Worst of all, Mona Gold's network, Golden Media Corporation, released a special series on infamous strippers in American history, featuring the notorious Zadie Byrd Gray in the opening credits. The United Strippers Union took umbrage with the show and rose up in protest. A Bay Area strippers strike was declared, calling for the cancellation of the show's scheduled six-week run.

"The show misrepresents both the industry and the individuals portrayed," the President of the United Strippers Union declared as she and her colleagues occupied the steps of the Mona Gold's network offices in downtown San Francisco. "It sensationalizes sexuality while framing our bodies and profession as immoral and sinful. It fails to bring up the real concerns of sex workers or to amplify our repeated demands for basic worker protections. Featuring Zadie Byrd Gray is an attempt to slander her by association with our profession ... but we say this: stripping is not immoral. What is immoral is the shaming and shunning of our profession to the point where we are excluded from the legal protections offered to other workers: fair wages, healthcare, legal recourse for harassment and discrimination, and the respect and dignity due to all human beings."

The Strippers Strike hit hard and fast, shutting down the industry from San Francisco to Los Angeles, expanding to cities nationwide with the demand for the show's cancellation and the immediate inclusion of their profession in basic worker rights.

"Sex work should not be secretive or shameful. It should be

consensual, non-coercive, and safe," the United Strippers Union proclaimed.

Zadie had stirred up a hornet's nest. A very loud, very public uprising erupted. Sex workers marched in broad daylight for mandatory healthcare coverage. They carried photos of her on signs that read: *No shame!* Meanwhile, evangelical counter protesters demonstrated with banners reading: *Have you no shame?*

As Zadie awkwardly became the center point of a broader struggle, the president of the union gave a speech in her defense.

"Why should Zadie Byrd Gray be shamed for this? It is the thousand-year history of suppressing sacred sexuality and denying both the validity and complexity of human sexuality that is shameful. We are not ashamed of - or for - Zadie Byrd Gray."

Their bodies were glorious, sacred, and beautiful. *All bodies were.* In their curves and folds, bellies and breasts, hips and limbs, in the swing and sway of their steps, in the softness and strength of their flesh, in the hidden heartbeats and secret pleasures, in all skin tones and hair textures, in all eye colors and heights and widths, in freckles, birthmarks, scars, and tattoos. For too long, the human body's simple, extraordinary beingness had been the source of shame. Entire industries existed to profit off our dissatisfaction in our bodies. Everything from cultural bias to religions to workout programs eroded our love of our bodies. They made us miserable in our most immediate homes. Sexuality was deemed sinful and stifled, along with sensuality, pleasure, and embodiment. The bodies of humans had a long overdue liberation to declare: we are whole, we are human, we are beautiful. Each and every one of us. We deserve to live in our skins, to love our bodies . . . and to love *with* these bodies.

The Strippers Strike stood up for sexuality and sensuality, for an industry stigmatized by the broader repression of bodies. With every step they took and every action they held, they declared the beauty of their bodies' limbs and hips, curvature and crevasses. They proclaimed their right to sexuality, safe and sacred, secular and commercial. They danced burlesque in broad daylight on the steps of City Hall. They delivered declarations of liberation in six-inch heels and tassel-swaying miniskirts. They announced a sex workers Bill of Rights that gave conservatives apoplexy. The media gluttonously feasted on the strike. They couldn't look away.

"The Strippers Union is right, you know," Zadie told Charlie as they watched the latest reports streaming on the Alternet. "Why should I feel ashamed about what I did?"

Charlie's eyebrows drew into a scowl.

"You were stripping for money, Zadie."

"So?" she answered, hands on her hips. "In pursuit of money, the military-industrial complex foments endless, illegal wars. In pursuit of money, coal companies blow up mountain ranges. In pursuit of money, Wall Street forecloses on millions of families and evicts them from their homes."

"Two wrongs don't make a right," Charlie pointed out.

"Yeah, but is it wrong to have the powers of Aphrodite and be remunerated for it?"

Sparks crackled from the tips of her curls. Charlie chewed his bottom lip and tried to think of a response that wouldn't get a lightning bolt flung at him by this goddess of a woman. He remembered the tight mask of pain and shame she had worn after secretly stripping to earn cash when the corporate regime froze their bank accounts. He remembered her courage crumbling in court as that snake of a lawyer hurled her past in her face to try to discredit her.

"These places you worked at," he said slowly. "They weren't exactly . . . sacred or respectful."

"I'm not denying that I've worked in hellholes," Zadie told him. "But that's what the Strippers Union is saying. It doesn't have to be that way. It shouldn't be that way. It's only because of this legacy of Christian supremacy that it is that way."

Charlie lifted both eyebrows over that claim. Zadie sighed. It was complicated. Sex always was. But the dirtiness of sex in their culture came from patriarchy. It came from shoving humans into cultural attitudes toward sex that had no correlation to biological reality. It came from tacitly giving men the wink for disobeying these strictures while condemning women to poverty and shame for doing the same thing. It came from making women financially dependent on men for survival so that working in the one industry still open to them required stepping into a lifetime of shame.

"When do we break that cycle?" Zadie demanded. "When do we restore the sacredness of sex to our society? When do we stop pornography not because sex itself is shameful, but because of the way so much pornography debases and demeans people?"

"Are you saying every seedy strip joint should be replaced by a Temple of Love?" Charlie joked.

"That's one idea," Zadie answered. "But for starters, sex work should be decriminalized, de-stigmatized, and sex workers should have the same rights and protections as any other workers."

Fair wages. Healthcare. Protection against violence and discrimination. If the Strippers Strike was willing to rise up in defense of her honor, Zadie was willing to return the favor.

"I'm going to speak out for their demands," she declared. "How can I not?"

Charlie shifted, unsure of what to say. It twisted something in his gut, this piece of her past. It hurt to think of Zadie stripping for money. He'd always thought it was *wrong* . . . but now she was saying it was right? He'd gotten uncountable messages telling him not to let her cuckold him, telling him he was being played. They said he was being unmanned by the ways Zadie's sexuality was eternally a subject of national discussion.

"If you speak up on this," he replied, lifting his head, "you'll be stirring up a shit storm on a side issue."

She spun, eyes full of ancient wrath.

"This. Is. Not. A. Side. Issue."

She snarled out the words. Her conversation with Elisha, Meera, and Frankie stung in her mind. The issue of sexuality and gender had dogged her heels every step of the way, every moment of her life. It had slapped her in the face over and over again as their political opponents tried to discredit the Dandelion Insurrection and sabotage her relationship with Charlie. The disparity was stark and clear. Only a few days ago, they had crashed the same gala; both had been manhandled by rich people, but he came away with a million-dollar job offer. She came away with yet another tabloid sex scandal slapped in her face. Gender and sexuality were not side issues. They were at the core of their lives, at the heart of their revolution, in the middle of so many of the attacks on their efforts for change. Zadie explained this, trembling, pushing the tears off the rims of her eyes as fast as they gathered.

Beneath the familiar rhetoric of workers rights, health and safety, fairness and respect was a resurgence of a divine and sacred worldview, a demand to end the attitudes toward sex that left women raped and strangled, tossed in gutters and murdered in back alleys. It was part of a global movement to restore the holiness of bodies, male, female, transgender, non-binary, straight, queer, lesbian, gay.

"I have to speak up, Charlie," Zadie repeated, certainty growing stronger with each breath. "How can I not?"

When Zadie Byrd Gray took her public stand with strippers and sex workers in support of their basic rights, she might as well have painted a target on her forehead for every patriarchal, misogynistic hater in the country. She'd seen some nasty smear campaigns in her life; this one put them all to shame. The far right printed out her image and put it up at the gun ranges for target practice. The evangelicals preached that the Whore of Babylon had incarnated as Zadie Byrd Gray. Total strangers spat on her in the street, men and women alike. She was dubbed the nation's biggest threat to family values.

Charlie hated every minute of the debacle. He stalked around San Francisco in a foul mood, taking the rattling old car out of the city to avoid people, leaving Zadie to hangout with Starling and Sparrow. He detested the headlines, the slander, the whole damn mess. He wrote a thousand words and threw them all away. For once in his life, he didn't know what to say or do.

"You don't need to do anything," Zadie kept saying with increasing exasperation. "I don't need you to be my knight in shining armor. I'm not a damsel in distress."

And it was true. Zadie was fine. Bold as always, stronger than ever, laughing in the face of vitriol. From the moment she stopped running from her past and claimed it - *owned* it - an unstoppable surge of power had blasted through her. They could sling their worst at her. She'd already heard it a thousand times. The only voice that sent a tremor through her was Jeb Whyte. The man gave her the willies. He'd been televising a series of saccharine sweet prayer circles for the salvation of her soul. His wife, Evelyn, offered to counsel Zadie like the Virgin Mary might have counseled Mary Magdalene.

"Yeah, I bet they'd have a lot to talk about," Zadie grumbled.

She, Starling, and Sparrow were standing on the steps of the Golden Media Corporation with signs demanding the removal of the Strippers Exposé show. Zadie craned her neck up at the glass plates of the skyscraper's windows, imagining Mona Gold staring down her nose at the strippers from the penthouse office. Zadie didn't care. Starling and Swallow had joined the picket line in solidarity. They waved their cardboard signs at passing cars and chatted amiably in the breaks between the traffic surges.

"The day Peter kicked Mary Magdalene - whom Jesus called the 'greatest of his disciples' - out of the early Christian faith was a sad day for humanity," Starling sighed. "He set in motion two thousand years of patriarchy and buried Christ's radical feminism, egalitarianism, and non-hierarchical beliefs in the dust of 'lost' scriptures."

"Hey," Sparrow put in, turning to Zadie in excitement, "*there's* a democracy story for you and Charlie! Did you know that the Gnostics - the group Mary Magdalene was part of after Jesus' resurrection - selected their priests, bishops, and prophets by sortition, drawing lots at each meeting?"

Zadie blinked in surprise. She hadn't known that. She scowled, thinking about how - if Mary Magdalene had won the struggle for the Christian faith - their world might have been democratic, egalitarian, and on track to dismantle the patriarchy and restore women's rights two thousand years ago.

"The results of that showdown are one of our greatest tragedies," Sparrow agreed, grimacing. "It turned Peter into one of the world's most influential misogynists."

"Oh, he's got some tough competition, though," Starling countered. "That guy who wrote *the Malleus Maleficarum, the Hammer of Witches*, was pretty bad. Eighty thousand women burned at the stake because of him - and the actual number of murders is probably over a million."

A chill swept over the bright day. Ghosts of the past ran cold fingers down their spines. From medieval times to today, strippers and streetwalkers had long resisted - and flat-out rebelled against - the patriarchy. Zadie lifted her sign aloft as the next wave of cars roared out from the intersection. Horns honked, setting off a cascade of sound down the block. Some rolled down the window and whistled at them. Catcalls interspersed with cheers of support. A pick-up truck thundered past, coal-rolling plumes of black smoke, the engine's rumble drowning out the expletives hollered at them from the driver. The light changed. The block quieted again.

"You know what else should go on the scorecard of Mr. Hammer of Witches' crimes?" Sparrow said thoughtfully, lowering their sign and rolling their shoulders. "This continent. The genocide of Indigenous Peoples here is directly related to the persecution of women, pagans, and earth-based practices during the witch hunts. It's during the same timeline. The two stories run in parallel lines of hatred."

The traumatized sons and husbands who watched their mothers and wives get burned, drowned, and hung wound up on this continent. They came here stewing in trauma and toxic beliefs, which they then unleashed on the Indigenous nations.

"I'd put the genocide of twenty million Indigenous Peoples onto Mr. Hammer of Witches," Sparrow said bluntly.

"What about the Pope who issued the 1490s papal bulls?" Zadie mentioned, remembering something Kinap had told her. "Those religious edicts told kings, priests, and men to go out and conquer the savages and the pagans. You can't understand the United States without knowing about that."

"Pope Alexander VI," Starling sighed, naming the man. "A couple short declarations, tens of millions of lives lost, hundreds of nations destroyed, continents conquered, and millions enslaved. He's definitely up there for the *Worse Than Hitler* award."

"The 1500s and 1600s were a nightmare," Sparrow reminded them, "the Enclosures of the Commons and the Black Plague, Columbus, Cortez, the Papal Bulls, the witch hunts: it was a perfect storm of earth-hating and women-hating violence. All of this wouldn't be happening without that."

Sparrow gestured to the strippers chanting slogans as they marched up and down the sidewalk in front of the media headquarters. Across the street, a cluster of counter protesters shouted, "Shame on you! Shame on you!" Two of them lifted up crosses as if to ward off the Devil. Zadie eyed them warily as she listened to the twins chat about the criminalization of sex, the seizure of women's bodies for monogamous and forced childbearing by Christian beliefs, the enclosures of both common land and women's labor. The twins ranted about how the wombs of European women were turned into factories to reproduce the feudal work force after the Black Plague wiped out a quarter of the population. The Christian doctrine of *go forth and multiply* kicked into hyperdrive as the church forbade herbal reproductive care and banned women from being doctors and midwives. Women often gave birth to fifteen, twenty children; many were kept bearing children until they wore out and died.

"The current abortion debate in the United States stems directly from this period," Starling said. "It's a direct outgrowth of the subjugation of women, the enclosures of the land, the persecution of pagan and Indigenous beliefs, the rise of capitalism, and the drive to expand the worker population."

"Then there's chattel slavery," Sparrow said with a scowl, "and the legal doctrines of one of the nastiest bits of patriarchy crossed with racism: *partus sequitur ventrem*."

Partus sequitur ventrem was Latin for *that which is brought forth follows the belly*. It was a law invented by slave owners that decreed that if your mother was free, you were born free. If she was enslaved, you would be a slave. It gave rise to mass rape of African and African-American women to perpetuate chattel slavery in the Americas. Sparrow shuddered, a disgusted look twisting their features. The horrors of this continent knew no end. Everything was connected, far more directly, deeply, and disturbingly than most people imagined.

"How do you know so much about this?" Zadie asked, turning to the twins.

"Oh, our big sister, Elena, is obsessed with this stuff," Sparrow groaned. "She's doing her PhD in capitalist exploitation of women's bodies and the women-led resistance to the enclosures of the commons across three continents."

It was a mouthful, but Elena's fascination was also personal, the twins explained.

"We're from Mexico, originally," they explained. "Part Indigenous, part Spanish colonizers. Our great-great-great-something grandfather fled his Spanish village after his wife was burned as a witch in the Inquisition. He came to the New World with his daughter to save her from her mother's fate."

"Maybe Zadie should go to Chicago and talk to Elena," Starling suggested to Sparrow with a nudge. The twins beamed. It was a logical next step for the democracy effort. After asserting the rights of people *and* nature, those two groups had to sort out how to work together. And one of the many answers

181

to that was the Commons . . . and Elena was an expert on the past, present, and future of those.

CHAPTER SEVENTEEN

. . . . .

Solutionary Rail

Deep night. An eternal darkness surrounded the train. Zadie leaned her forehead against the cool press of the window and sighed. The glass caught her sorrow in a foggy circle. She traced a heart with her finger, shattered it with a crack, and then swiped it clean with her palm. Charlie curled on the fold-down sleeper bed opposite her, back to her, flat planes of his shoulders solid as a closed door between them, the knobs of his spine pressed against the twisted fabric of his shirt.

Charlie's irritability and sour mood had only deepened over the past week. She couldn't blame him. The tabloids deemed him *Cuckold Of the Year*. He was mocked for having an unfaithful slut of a girlfriend. The evangelicals referred to him as *the Beast that Layeth with the Whore*. By the time they had packed for their trip to Chicago, the tension between them had reached a painful pitch. Even the success of the Strippers Strike was soured when Charlie's only response was a bitter:

"Great. Hurrah for strippers' rights."

Then their car died. It was the last straw on his frayed temper. Patience vanished.

"Let's take the train to Chicago and search for a new car there," Zadie suggested when the weight of car shopping and dwindling bank accounts smacked the hard slap of reality across their road trip. Bay Area car prices ripped the breaths out of their chests.

183

"Maybe I should have taken Mona Gold's job offer," Charlie grumbled.

"Yeah, and maybe I should go back to stripping," Zadie snapped back, sarcastic. "That way we can both sell ourselves for money."

"No shame, right?" he mocked her.

Zadie wanted to throttle him. His foul mood worsened as they tried to pick up their coach tickets and got upgraded to a sleeper car by an overly enthusiastic station agent.

"Just write about rail riding, please," the man begged as he slid their tickets under the old-fashioned bars and the bulletproof glass at the counter. "Rail is the wave of the future, especially for a country the size of ours. An article from the Man From the North and Zadie Byrd Gray would really help popularize rail travel."

"But a sleeper car?" Charlie argued. "It's kind of elitist. They're expensive."

"You'll cause a commotion in coach. Neither you nor anyone else will get any sleep."

"I told you we should have flown," Charlie muttered to Zadie as she accepted the sleeper tickets and elbowed her ungrateful boyfriend out of the line.

"Two words: climate crisis," she hissed, hauling him along by the arm as the all-aboard whistle blew. He knew as well as she that the carbon emissions of rail travel were a small percentage of air travel, even on a diesel-powered train.

This route, however, ran on renewable electric. The Solutionary Rail line had been an early victory for the Dandelion Insurrection, part of the WPA-style climate jobs bill they'd managed to push through Congress in the glowing days of insurrectionary hope. Zadie frowned. Those times seemed long past. Their second bill had stalled in committee as the oil companies rallied to block the transition plans. Just because the Dandelion Insurrection had annoyingly barred them from buying elections didn't mean they weren't bribing and blackmailing behind the scenes and off the books. Business-as-usual for them. The stalled rail energy conversion bill was yet another example of why people-powered democracy mattered. Eighty percent of the populace wanted renewable rail. The jobs, the ease of travel, the economic stimulus to forgotten rail towns, and the carbon emissions reductions made nothing but sense to the people. Yet, in the representative system, a handful of rich people could block all of them from moving forward.

Solutionary Rail was the future for the continent-wide country. In fact, there was nothing new about electric rail; up until the 1960s, many rail lines had run electrically. Then, the greed of oil companies had flipped the switch on the system.

The rail right of way has space for solar and wind technology, explained a pamphlet tucked into the pocket of the sleeper car door. Out the window, a line of solar panels lined the tracks, feeding the railroad a continuous supply of power

On cloudy days, the FAQ section stated, *the rail line transmits energy like the rest of the power grid, sending energy from sunny Nevada to snowy Rocky Mountain sections.*

A quarter of the world's rail lines were already electrified. Winter-bound Russia moved seventy percent of its freight on electric rail. India had converted its train system years ago. Even when electrification didn't draw from renewable power sources, the pamphlet reminded them, it opened the door for that possibility in the near future - unlike reliance on fossil fuel powered engines. Even before the San Francisco to Denver route had been converted, the first rewired electric Solutionary Rail line had been built through the northern-most parts of the United States. If they could build it there, they could build it anywhere. Thirty percent of climate emissions came from transportation. Shifting passengers and freight onto renewable-powered rail had to happen if they were to meet the demands of the climate crisis.

Solutionary Rail should have been the perfect story to pull Charlie out of his funk. Ordinarily, he would have been pacing the corridors, talking to the conductors, interviewing the cafe car workers, hanging out with the passengers in the lounge car and scribbling down their stories. Instead, he spent the day sitting silent and moody in the sleeper car, staring at the receding landscape in his backwards-facing seat.

"Want to switch?" Zadie offered.

He shook his head without meeting her eyes.

"What's the matter with you?"

"Nothing."

"Want to talk about it?"

"No."

She gave up. They rode in silence through the Central Valley's flat fields and perfect orchards. The train climbed into the foothills of the Sierras, winding through twisted oaks and golden hills contoured by the rings of cattle trails. The mountains loomed and vanished as night fell. They woke in the Eastern Range, diving into the wide, hot desert. Charlie remained untalkative, though the black stain of his mood had lightened somewhat. Zadie let him brood. She could only guess what unspoken thoughts he chewed on, mile after mile.

He was mad at the world, at the scorn of others. He was a young man forced to reckon with the constraints of a patriarchal world. He'd seen many injustices with painful clarity - race, class, militarism, ecocide - but the Strippers Strike's demand for justice had rattled him. He'd been raised by his mother's French Catholic family. *The Guy in the Sky* lurked somewhere in his subconscious. He'd grown up plagued by the whispers about his "wild" mother, askance glances at her son born out of wedlock, fistfights when the kids mocked him as a bastard, a seething resentment at his father for exposing him to the scorn of others.

He'd made up his mind early to be a better man than his father, to not expose his loved ones to those kinds of criticism. But Zadie was playing by a different rule book altogether. She shook her fist at thousands of years of patriarchy. She turned shame on its head and said the scales of sin and shame were weighed wrongfully. She upended his thoughts. He didn't know what to think and it made him confused, short-tempered, and scared. He could feel Zadie glaring at him, annoyed. He didn't want to lose her. He felt weird, hopelessly old-fashioned. She had refused to marry him once. *Someday,* she said, but he had a bad feeling that *someday* would never come.

Charlie had no words for now. He had to weigh everything he'd assumed or been taught. So he sat silent as the train rocked rhythmically through the open desert. Out one window, the landscape of withered tans and sun-bleached earth spread to the shimmering horizon line. Huddled creosote shrubs brimmed with dusty autumn pollen, revived by the late summer rains that had rolled like clockwork through the August afternoons. On the south side of the rumbling passenger train, the route followed century-old history, tracing the path of a river that submerged underground and then re-emerged in sparse patches of green. In the old days, steam engines had relied on that water source to keep chugging as they traversed the vast valley between the continental ridgelines. The vanished Sierras receded in the west. The Wasatch Range grew slowly in the east. They passed through places where the train seemed to tread water, advancing nowhere as it raced through endless stretches.

When darkness fell, he pulled down the sleeper bed and curled up on it. Zadie shook her head when he glanced at her. He could see the weight of her thoughts pressing on her shoulders. He rolled over, leaving her to stare at the blackened windows.

The darkness was meant for dreaming. In the places where no light shone, the imagination had room to blossom. At night, absolute darkness pressed against the train. In a land haunted by its past, bound in the chains of its present, who would dare to dream of a future?

Zadie would.

She let her mind drift into times to come - not the horrors of apocalypse, but the breakthroughs gleaming in the cracks of every breakdown. On the train, she imagined a future where a woman's body was not simply bearable, it was sacred. She imagined a future where the entire spectrum of skin colors was as beloved as the Earth, herself. She imagined a future where reverence extended beyond church walls across the sky and into the curves of land and river, plant and animal and mineral.

The deep, taut band of tension she carried like a corset in her gut suddenly unwound. Tears unleashed like floodgates in a dam. It was not until she dared to imagine the world-to-come, or *a* world-to-come, one of the infinite possibilities, that the absence of fear revealed the ways her soul had shriveled to fit into the constraints of the current world. She was like an ancient juniper twisted by wind and clinging to a rocky cliff. She did not begrudge the beauty of tenacity, the wisdom of rugged endurance, or the strength of resilience in her being . . . but she glimpsed the towering height and glossy boughs of trees growing in a sheltered lee, nourished by sunlight, clean water, and fertile soil. Unencumbered by the pressures of the current reality, she would be an entirely different being. They all would.

Zadie could almost imagine what her body would feel like in a world where people spoke of last night's dreams and tomorrow's hopes and today's joys. Where one paused as the sun rose and set, following the change of light and returning to reverence and gratitude again. Where she knew the names of every species that was her neighbor in this world. Where stories came from elders and artists instead of televisions and screens.

She let her eyes fall shut, soft as feathers, light as snowflakes. Her thoughts slipped across the threshold of the present into the imaginings of a wild future. Every bone in her body yearned to live in those times, when all people - women and men and those defining gender differently - felt welcome to the core of the beings; felt beloved in their skin and celebrated in their bones, cherished in their hearts and minds, bodies and souls and spirits. It was a world where no one went hungry so long as everyone had enough, where no more bombs fell from the sky and no more toxins bled into rivers. It was a world teeming with life, where humans thought less about unpaid bills and more about the dreams and visions longing to be shared. It was a world where time was no longer a brutal taskmaster doling out one's days, but flexible and fluid, graciously stretching when small children wanted to play.

This was the world she wanted to midwife into existence. *This* was a vision worth the blood, sweat, and tears of a lifetime's labor. Zadie sensed the ferocity of mother bears and the tenacity of cataract-leaping salmon singing in her chest. *This* was a world worth braving the inherent dangers of challenging the current paradigm. This was the dream shared by peoples throughout time, against all odds. They had cherished it with the endurance of mountains and the determination of baby birds cracking the shell to be born. Zadie would fight for this. She'd heal for this. She'd die for this. She'd live for this.

189

She'd love for this. She'd dismantle barricades of beliefs and build bridges across cultures for this.

She could sense the millions of others striving alongside her. Human and non-human, every living thing that yearned for a life of balance, ease, and hope. The movement for this overdue change encompassed trillions of life forms on a scale that defied human conception.

But something blocked the movement. Something stoppered the resurgence of life like a cork in a bottle.

Show me, she requested, shivering as echoes of that question rippled through her memory.

Silently, like a pair of curtains drawn aside, the edges of her vision peeled back, revealing what stood between all of life and the future of the world. The hackles of ancient animal instincts kicked in. Her hairs rose on her arms, one by one.

Before her, the flaming cross howled its misery and rage against a blackened sky.

A pair of ice-blue eyes stabbed her heart like daggers.

CHAPTER EIGHTEEN

. . . . .

Stinky Onion

Charlie and Zadie staggered out of the glass doors of Chicago Union Station into the chilly blast of the Windy City's welcome. Like sailors who had just stepped onto shore, they reeled as the ground heaved beneath them. In a daze, they had wandered through the station's labyrinth of underground corridors, the press of people overwhelming after days on the rocking train. Commuters raced in madcap dashes to catch departing light rails. Mennonite families departed from the Midwest terminal in old-fashioned dresses and suits, white bonnets and straw caps atop their heads, incongruous sneakers on their feet, fathers carrying cellphones, mothers holding sandwiches on homemade bread. Above the long, wooden benches in the vaulted ceiling of the iconic lobby, statues of *Night* and *Day* watched over the travellers.

"You alright?" Charlie asked as Zadie gasped in the slap of wind. "You look tired."

"Just a little travel-worn," she answered, shaking her hair back from her face and blinking into the cold blasts of city, traffic, and steel.

Somewhere between Denver and Chicago, the fight had gone out of them like a dying wind in a listless sail. They bobbed, be-stilled in their hearts as their bodies hurtled down the track. Charlie offered an apology for his moodiness and confessed his inner turmoil. His hours of soul-searching had revealed only one thing: he loved her . . . and everything else was irrelevant.

Zadie nodded. She bit her lower lip, considering if she should pry into the terrain he wasn't willing to talk about yet. She let it go - for now. Everyone had their hidden pockets of their soul, the places that even their loved ones weren't allowed to barge in. Instead, she mentioned a Solutionary Rail factoid like a balm to their raw scars. He followed up with a question and by the time the conductor stopped by, they were sitting side-by-side reading the pamphlet together. They bantered with the rail staff about solar panels and energy corridors as they passed under massive windmills that dotted the farmlands on Chicago's outskirts. Arriving in the city, they stepped forth with matched strides and hearts beating in tandem once more.

Sparrow and Starling's sister met them two blocks down from Chicago Union Station where the traffic abated slightly and a curbside drop-off zone gave her room to hop out of her electric vehicle to greet them. Elena was a curvaceous woman, all smiles and effusive greetings. She wore her dark hair pulled back in a messy pile on her head. The sleeves of her shirt were rolled up. Her jeans had colorful patches at the knees. She drove a shocking pink tiny van, an electric vehicle that was not much more than a glorified golf cart.

Seeing their wan faces, she gestured to her canvas bag.

"Sandwiches, coffee, sliced veggies, whatever you need. I thought we'd swing by the shore on the way to the house. If you don't mind, I have a friend you've got to meet."

Her friend was Lake Michigan, whose name came from the Ojibwe's *michi-gami*, large lake. It was giant and immense, sparkling in autumn's pale sunlight. They walked down to the gravel shore with the wind scraping the skin from their cheeks and the roar of traffic at their backs. After rumbling through so much desert on the train, it was startling to see such an enormity of water. The pounding behemoth tossed up ocean-worthy waves. The wind picked up speed like an ice skater on a long, flat stretch and hurtled, full-bodied, at the skyscrapers aligned brashly at the shore. The lake and wind battered the city, toughening its inhabitants. Charlie and Zadie flinched in its gusts.

"You have to meet the lake on its own terms," Elena told them. "No matter the weather. Go to the water's edge and pay your respects."

As they had in San Francisco on the Golden Gate Bridge, they stood on the buffeted shore and greeted the beingness of one of the world's largest bodies of fresh water. They chanced getting soaked by the choppy waves, crouched down by water's pebbly edge, and outstretched their fingers for a watery handshake. They quieted their hearts and stilled the motion sickness of travel. The cold air, the whipping wind, the crash and hiss of the lake's shore song called them home to the here-and-now.

Beside them, Elena murmured greetings from the commoners of the Great Lakes Commons, an international group of people from the United States, Canada, and the many Indigenous nations surrounding the lakes. They managed their collective relationship to these vast beings in ways that had no parallel in the legal structures of nation states. The commoners gathered to spend time with the Lakes, to forge living relationships with them, and to protect the water from the insanity of their fellow human beings.

Elena watched her guests rise from a crouch, shoes water-splashed, the blessings of the lake shining in their eyes. She hid a smile. It changed everything to forge a connection, soulful and meaningful, to the beingness of place. It opened the human heart and awakened our aliveness. She pivoted to greet Chicago, noticing her differing relationship to this immense beast of a city: wary, loving, exasperated, worried. Elena felt a million things for her home city, not all of them pleasant or comfortable to acknowledge.

"Come," she said to the pair. "Let's take a walk. I want to show you something."

From the shore, they traversed the jammed intersections and headed northwest along one of Chicago's diagonal streets. It crisscrossed the city planners' relentless grid with a sense of whimsy, leading to confusing five-way intersections. The uninformed eye might bemoan the idiocy of design that stuck a set of miles-long roads at odds with the rest of the city, but this street was one of the time-honored footpaths of Indigenous trails from forests to shore. The diagonal streets were not at odds with the city; the city was at odds with the contours of the curvaceous earth and the sinuous curls of lakeshore wetlands. As Elena explained this, Zadie's mind spun, disoriented and grounded by the knowledge at the same time. Suddenly, she saw the grid for what it was: a poorly-designed overlay planted atop another, older civilization. The city's name, Chicago, also hinted at its past. It came from a French rendering of an Algonquin word, *Checagou*, meaning *stinky onion*. The place was named for a wild onion that grew along the shore, the delicious taste of its pungent kick flavoring meals of fish and deer. The namesake of the city grew at the destination of those diagonal roads; *checagou* once flourished along the shores of the windy lake.

Names and origin stories matter. Their living presence in human imagination influences our relationship to place. Their absence leaves a void that changes our impressions of the world.

"Did you know," Elena offered, "that Mt. Everest has at

least three original names? The Tibetan one, the Nepalese, and the Chinese."

They shook their heads.

"The Royal Geographic Society, in all their colonialist attitudes, decided to name it Everest after the first European ascender. But Sir George Everest didn't want it named after him. He thought it was ridiculous to rename a mountain to something none of the locals could pronounce."

"But they named it after him, anyway?" Charlie remarked, lifting his eyebrows.

"Yeah, they claimed that they didn't want to insult any of the peoples by using the name of the others. But here's the thing: the Tibetan name, *Qomolangma;* the Chinese name, *Zhūmùlǎngmǎ Fēng;* and the Nepalese's more recent name, *Sagarmāthā;* translate to Holy Mother, Earth Mother, and Goddess of the Sky, respectively. An appropriate English translation might have been, Great Mother Mountain or Goddess Mountain."

"Wait," Zadie blurted out, "you mean Mt. Everest is *female?*"

Elena nodded. Zadie halted on the sidewalk, an astonished expression on her face.

"Wow," she murmured, blinking up at the crack of sky between the buildings. "That . . . that really changes . . . well, everything."

She didn't have words for it. She couldn't explain why it staggered her to know that the tallest mountain in the world, with its famous peak and snow-cloaked slopes, was regarded as female by the three cultures that surrounded it. Cultures, she realized, that totaled more than a quarter of the world's population.

"Makes sense when you think of her as the mother of

hundreds of watersheds," Elena explained. "The Great Mother Mountain feeds the Ganges, the Yangtze, the Yellow, the Mekong and many other rivers, ultimately supplying water to half the people in Southeast Asia."

Names and knowledge matter. They mattered to the conquerors that stripped the beinghood from the world's tallest mountain and renamed her after a mortal man. They mattered when the twelve-month calendar unhinged the year from the moon cycles and women's periods and the ancient magic of thirteen. They mattered when Daylight Savings Time disconnected an entire nation from the annual rhythm of falling darkness and rising light. They mattered when we forgot that Chicago means *stinky onion* and that the old roads crisscrossing the grid lead straight to the namesake of the city.

"Does that wild onion even grow within the city limits anymore?" Zadie asked Elena.

"Oh yes," she assured them. "Back when they lived here, Starling and Swallow loved to plant them guerrilla-style in the sidewalk edges and drain spout runoffs. We didn't dare eat them because of the toxins, chemicals, grime, and asphalt leachings that contaminate the water. But then we won a chance to plant them in the city parks."

"Don't they spray pesticides?" Charlie asked.

"Not in those areas - actually, in fewer and fewer areas each year."

"How'd you manage that?"

"By connecting urban gardeners to Parks & Recreation," Elena answered.

They had test-piloted a volunteer corps of people longing to stick their hands in the dirt. The city claimed it didn't have the funds to pull weeds, so Elena and her twin siblings had demonstrated that they had the people power to pull it off.

Capitalism, Elena asserted, made a wasteland of the populace's riches. Time became a commons to strip mine rather than a wild field of possibility. They had a situation in which the City couldn't stop using dangerous chemicals and grass monocultures because it didn't have people to pull weeds. Meanwhile, the Chicago Urban Gardeners Club languished because they were trying to collect fees to access land.

"Put the problems together and we found a solution," Elena enthused.

The world brimmed with creative solutions and untapped potential. Opportunities astounded. Possibilities seethed beneath the surface of things.

"Come on," Elena urged them, guiding them back toward her tiny van, "there's more. Let me show you our wild neighborhood."

She drove them home to her nestled checkerboard of streets just outside the denser urban districts. Here, the lots widened slightly and the old houses had been remodeled into four-family dwellings, quartering the architecture. Behind the buildings, small gardens opened up. Elena led them down a narrow alley, past the garbage cans, and the neighbors' locked up bicycles, to her backyard. The season was wrong to see it, but beneath the frost-etched branches and cold-withered shrubs lay a wild miracle.

"You are looking at a restoring ecosystem that stretches across three nations and this entire continent," she told her guests.

At first glance, Elena's backyard looked scraggly and feral. Brown and silvered stalks, withered clinging leaves, dropping dried husks of seed heads. Here and there, a bright spark of red berries.

"Everything in that yard is native to this place," Elena offered.

A decade ago, a group of neighborhood naturalists had launched a wild and native backyards effort, teaching about the plants that the local ecosystem relied on for food, shelter, egg laying, and more.

"For some reason, the idea caught on. Nearly the whole neighborhood got involved," Elena explained, smiling as she remembered.

Kids came back from school with science projects to track backyard species. When school let out in June, the summer camps picked up the project. The Girl Scouts joined in. Rotary Club sponsored a youth project to redesign backyards from unnatural and pesticide-guzzling grass lawns into native plant gardens. Elena, like many in the neighborhood, had a pushpin board nailed to the wall near her back window. A wildlife guide hung on a string next to a pair of binoculars and a camera phone. A massive chart tracked dates and species. Red felt pen checkmarks scattered across a chart, indicating birds, insects, squirrels, and more.

"Then some university graduate students got a grant to track bird species in the neighborhood and we discovered something extraordinary," Elena reported.

This residential suburb had reconnected a vast and ancient migratory corridor of species that traveled from Canada to Mexico. The residents had restored a missing link to the migratory highway, creating a place for the animals to stop over in this wooded urban neighborhood. Scientists proved that even this seemingly small project had a noteworthy impact on species count.

"Then there was no stopping us," Elena laughed. "We started reaching out to other neighborhoods and expanding the project. We leveraged our network to block destructive city plans and industrial developments near us."

They were proof that change was not impossible and that the suburbs did not have to be devastating to the original ecosystems of an area.

"We had to ditch the colonizers' mindset that wanted to shave, pave, carpet, and tame this land," Elena confessed. "We had to let the wilds into our homes and make peace with what Western cultures had been warring with for so long."

It was simple, really. It was a relief to stop fighting the land, to lay down the weapons of the lawnmower and chemicals, to scatter seeds and plant odd-looking shrubs, to love the scraggly weeds . . . and then to watch the tiny beings - beetles, ladybugs, earthworms, butterflies, spiders, ants - return, followed by birds with flashes of wing and warbles.

"Any regrets?" Zadie asked.

"Only that we didn't start sooner," Elena answered with a rueful expression, "and that we haven't gotten the entire city to organize like this. Yet."

Elena explained that their backyard efforts were small compared to what needed to be done nationwide. She mourned the fact that the Colorado River no longer reached the ocean, that the salmon runs of the Pacific Northwest still faced barriers of dams, that the resurging bison population still struggled for open prairies amidst the barbed wire fences of cattle ranges.

"Plus, right here we still haven't figured out the streets and fences problem," she admitted. "The mammals and ground-dwellers are impeded by those, though there are raccoons nesting under porches and skunks behind a shed a few doors down."

"Some places have figured it out," Zadie mentioned, eyes slightly distant as she remembered a story. "There's a town in

199

Japan where the deer wander freely. They're revered and given right of way even over cars and human pedestrians."

"And don't forget animal corridors over or under highways," Charlie mentioned, thinking of the wide bridges planted with meadow grasses and trees to let the animals pass over human traffic unharmed.

"Or the way Vermont closes down highways during salamander crossing season," Zadie added.

"Would it really be so bad to live like this everywhere?" Elena mused. "To be in and of nature, part of it once again?"

It was the healing humanity so desperately yearned for, the medicine they craved without knowing its name. Up the street, a man who taught astronomy at the university was trying to get a "Dark Skies Night" passed by the local municipalities - one night each year when the lights would go out and everyone could see the stars. For some kids, it would be their first time seeing even the Big Dipper. He hoped the annual night would be one of storytelling, peacebuilding, and cross-cultural community exchange. He had reached out to local tribes to see if there was interest in sharing their legends of the constellations - after all, the stories of Orion and Cassiopeia came from a distant continent.

What would this country be like, Charlie thought, *if we all knew the stories of the stars from the original peoples of this land?*

Zadie found herself growing teary-eyed at Elena's next tale: the astronomer had started gathering people from the many cultures that lived in this urban area: Somali immigrants, African-Americans, Syrian refugees, Mexican and El Salvadorian migrants, asylum seekers from Honduras, the descendants of Swedish, German, and Russian immigrants, the Potawatomi, Ojibwe, Chippewa, Ho-chunk, Sac, Fox, Miami, and Odawa. Each month, they gathered at the dark moon to tell star stories of the hidden sky overhead.

From this, a new myth emerged, a new prophecy whispered in the elders' ears: the stars had vanished because of humans' misunderstandings and hatred of one another. They were hidden by the fears that kept electric lights burning through the city, hidden by the injustices that caused poverty and crimes of desperation, hidden by the myth of Western civilization's conquest of the natural world.

But if they gathered and shared their stories, this new legend promised, if they built peace and justice instead of fear and inequality, then one day the stars would return. When humans made peace, this new legend said, the stars would shine again in the sky overhead.

"The astronomer has been reaching out to local gangs, the police, and residents," Elena finished, "to see if we could have one night of truce, a night of peace, a night where we trusted each other enough to sit in the darkness together and tell the many stories of the stars."

It was a haunting vision, a dream so possible it could almost be touched, a dream so impossible that it felt as distant as the invisible stars.

How will we know when this continent begins to heal? Elena asked them.

When we can finally see the stars.

CHAPTER NINETEEN

. . . . .

Reclaim the Commons

The next day, Elena corralled them into volunteer work for the Great Lakes Commons. She told them to bundle up and handed a stack of fliers to Zadie. She asked Charlie to grab the bag of pins and pledges. They set out into the dazzle of day and pinch of overnight frost. October burned bright and chill as the dry leaves tumbled off the city trees. Mounds of leaves collected in the iron grates that protected the feet of buckthorn and ash trees. Flurries swirled in the wind and whipped up on the cross currents of car traffic.

"It'll warm up midday and turn glorious," Elena promised as they stepped off the downtown bus straight into an icy blast of cold lake wind. The buffet nearly knocked them flat, but the howl of air was no match for the steel skyscrapers of the financial district. They soldiered on, colder than cold, their inscrutable glass window eyes glaring out at the city.

She led them between the buildings, down an alley, into a concrete courtyard. Amidst skyscraper towers, a lively rebellion of color and laughter bubbled up.

"Welcome to Reclaim the Commons Day," Elena announced with a flourish of a gesture and a broad grin at their surprise. "Once a month - on the full moon, actually - we take over a different space in the city to teach people about the Commons and the Enclosures."

This patch of a concrete park was managed by the office building next to it. Though they termed it a "city park", private security patrolled it and the corporation reserved the right to throw the commoners out at any time.

"We have a list of six places in this area we'll go if they kick us out of here," Elena explained, "but this park is a particular target of ours, since it was donated to the city as a public park for a tax deduction, and their security throws out anyone who isn't wearing a business suit and staring at a phone full of stock exchange reports."

Like the Levellers and the Diggers of the 1500s who knocked down the fences that blocked off the grazing pastures, Reclaim the Commons Day reoccupied spaces enclosed by privatization or by elitist control. Some months, they set up permit-less flea markets in lower income neighborhoods, defying the enclosure of market space in ways that made commerce accessible to those shut out of the storefronts. Other months, they set up pop-up tool libraries in community centers or temporary toy libraries on street corners.

"Good day for it, eh, Elena?" a man called out, pulling his knitted hat down on his shock of white hair.

Next to him, a man with massive thigh muscles set down his bicycle bag. Zadie hid a smile as she spotted the college students on the next picnic blanket eyeing him. The park was full of people of a range of backgrounds. Folding tables and picnic blankets held fliers and signs. Rocks weighted down the edges. Beneath someone's lunch pail, Zadie read a flier about the Childcare Commons, a collective that swapped playdates and babysitting, and maintained play spaces in multiple neighborhoods.

The fliers on the next blanket announced the formation of a collective mechanic shop. Nearby, a group of open source tech designers spread out a checkerboard cloth and set laptops down on the corners to hold it flat. Beyond them, a group of mothers had part of their Toy Library available and were signing up new members.

"Reclaim the Commons Day brings all the scattered projects out of our hidden nooks and crannies, and puts them on full display," Elena told Charlie and Zadie.

A commons was a shared resource stewarded by shared decision-making by the users. Commons existed everywhere: the acequia irrigation ditches of New Mexico, the lobster shoals of Maine, the digital public domain archives, the Anishinaabe's wild rice beds, the Hawaiian surf spots.

"What about the national parks or forests?" Charlie asked, thinking hard for examples.

Elena shook her head.

"Direct participation in stewardship by those who use it is a requirement of the Commons. That's why it's important that you and Zadie meet the commoners - it's the most essential, vital, widespread, and ancient democracy movement alive."

Ask the average citizen about the origins of democracy and they'd parrot back the standard line about Ancient Greece. A particularly informed citizen might mention Benjamin Franklin's observation of the Haudenosaunee and Iroquois Confederacy; democratic governance was common among Indigenous Peoples.

"But the Indigenous Peoples of Turtle Island weren't the only ones with those traditions," Elena reminded them.

All around the globe, the democratic stewardship of the global commons was under-researched and long-ignored. Significantly older than the Greek Forum, commons systems were some of the most enduring, resilient, and effective democracies in human history. One of the goals of Reclaim the Commons Day was to revive the forgotten past and return the practice of commoning to living memory. In a society ailing from privatization, individualization, and atomization, it was medicine for their culture.

"The reason so many aspects of our liberation are tied together is because the sources of our oppressions are tangled together. To understand the present, you have to understand the past," Elena explained. "The history of the United States is intimately connected to the Enclosure of the Commons. The land lust of settlers is tied to the theft of their lands in Europe. We are here because of the Tragedy of the Enclosures. And we can't heal until we deal with it."

"I thought it was the Tragedy of the Commons, not the Enclosures," Charlie said in confusion, referring to the 1960s article so famous everyone remembered the title even if no one knew its contents.

"That essay was a terrible piece of propaganda," Elena sighed. "The tragedy isn't the failure of the commons - it's the intentional destruction of the commons via the Enclosures."

The 1960s article claimed that the commons could never work because everyone would take too much, but that wasn't true. The commons described in the article were, ironically, not a commons at all, but rather a description of unregulated extraction. The article did not deal with collective governance, only collective use. Steeped in Social Darwinism, the article claimed that greedy humans would take and take and take until the resource was depleted and destroyed.

"And that's not a commons, not by a long shot," Elena snorted.

A commons was a resource plus democratic stewardship wherein the well-being of the resource mattered to the well-being of everyone involved. Before European feudalism in the 1300-1500s, and the rise of global colonialism, the commons flourished throughout the world. And they did not collapse from over-use. They were stolen by the colonizers, destroyed by enclosures, plundered by extraction, and exploited under the rule of the rich.

"What is an enclosure, exactly?" Charlie asked, frowning over his notebook as he tried to articulate the concept for his readers.

Elena launched into an explanation. Enclosures were the fencing-in of a commons by law or literal barriers. It was putting a private gate on a shared resource and then charging access fees. It was erecting a fence around a once-open pasture. It was a law forbidding entrance to a forest unless you paid the fee determined by the lord or landowner. It was getting kicked off the land your ancestors had lived on for centuries and being replaced by sheep or cattle. It was unaffordable - and unequal - prices to access the Internet that we all built together. Enclosures took a thousand forms, but in each, the common people lost access, paid steep prices for resources, and no longer had direct say in the decisions.

Privatization came across the oceans with the colonizers, as destructive and deadly as small pox. The Indigenous Peoples of Turtle Island, with their widespread view of nature as beings and their traditional teachings, often used a commons-like approach. But, that all changed with the genocidal invasions of colonizers. Privatization was imposed upon subjugated tribes, often with devastating consequences. The imposition of private property had been a disaster for most of humanity. And, in half a millennium, it had brought the species to the brink of annihilation.

At a time when the Earth demanded her due, not as a resource, but as a being, the practices of commoning offered a path toward living in relationship, together.

"Look at these business people," Elena pointed out,

gesturing to the people in suits streaming in and out of the revolving doors of the skyscraper. "All educated, all misinformed about the history of the Commons. And that is the missing puzzle piece to understanding the past six hundred years."

That, she said, was why the commoners not only shared about tool coops and childcare collectives at their monthly gatherings. They also enjoyed a street theater production that debunked the myths of that infamous essay on the *Tragedy of the Commons*. The performers were a community theater group with a social justice twist who built giant puppets with school children, choreographed participatory dances with workers, created circus acts with seniors, and made shows with anyone who yearned to strut their stuff across a concrete and asphalt stage.

The performance, entitled *The Tragedy of the Enclosures*, began at ten o'clock with the boom and crash of a cymbal-wielding kid. A band of actors clad in green carried wooden staves and bended bows. They doffed their pointed hats as Robin Hood bounded into the middle of the concrete park.

"Who better to narrate this tale than I," he proclaimed, his voice bouncing off the steel and glass buildings, "the most famous resister to the enclosures of the commons and enslavers of the poor?"

A cheer lifted at his words and the pageantry of the production began. It was an impressive undertaking with a thirty-person cast, giant puppets, and a horn band for music. Sherwood Forest - sculpted out of painted cardboard boxes - narrated its own story of being a people's wood since time immemorial. It offered timber and firewood, food and herbal medicines, accessible to all who treated the woods with respect. Then Prince John banned the commoners from the forest and outlawed deer hunting for anyone but himself.

"Thus came Robin Hood," the man in green narrated, "a legend of resistance, a popular tale that never died, but arose whenever the rich stole from the poor - through taxes, laws, and land enclosures. And they did . . . over and over and over."

A dance came next. People swayed as open fields as a herd of cattle puppets grazed freely. A group with fence poles marched in, thundering and drumming a rhythmic, relentless drive to enclose the space and drive the cattle out. Once the field was caged with fences, the commoners had to pay fees to access the pastures. But the peasants who couldn't pay refused to starve. They became the Levellers and Diggers, and tore down the fences and filled in the ditches, cheering as their herds grazed freely once again. Then the soldiers of the rich marched in and massacred the protesting commoners, leaving a die-in of men, women, and children lying in the square. To one side of the open plaza, a pair of sign holders kept track of the acts and scenes, holding aloft the historical footnotes:

Act 1, Scene 1: Robin Hood & Sherwood, 1300s.

Scene 2: The Early Enclosures, 1500s.

Scene 3: The Midlands Revolt of 1607.

In Act II, the timeline backtracked to introduce a second theme to the drama: the persecution of women. The sign holders held aloft the setting: Italy in the 1500s, and the show began with a group of women gathering herbs in a field. When the nobles enclosed it, the women led the resistance. Instead of soldiers marching upon the commoners, this time it was a priest who came, pointing his finger and shouting: *witch, witch, witch!* Pyres were built. The resistance leaders were burned with rippling flames of brightly-colored silk. Their white-clad ghosts rose from the ashes in a chorus lamenting the persecution of women's bodies and women's knowledge and women's connection to the land.

"This will come back to haunt you," they prophesized, foretelling how alienation from the Earth would lead their species into extinction.

Robin Hood closed out the act with the dead women in the background and the rich people counting their gold on the sidelines.

"The real Tragedy of the Commons," Robin proclaimed, "is a tragedy of the enclosures. The Commons were destroyed by the greed of the few, stolen from the people by violence and murder. Once upon a time, the Commons were pharmacy and fuel source, pantry and hardware store. They offered substance and succor. They were taken by force, enriching the few while the many were driven into poverty."

The sign holders flipped their cardboard signs:

Act III: The New World, 1492-today.

In an elaborate dance across a blue, rippling ocean, the patterns of the Old World were replicated in the new. The land was seized and made into private property; the original people were driven off their ancestral homes. The earth-based practices were banned. The women were subjugated. The rich counted up their gold. The ships sailed to Africa and back, enslaving Black men, women, and children in a massive enclosure of not just their lifetimes of labor, but their children's lifetimes, too. Plantation capitalism replicated like a cancerous growth, ensnaring cheap labor from group after group in order to build the riches of another. The pattern repeated over and over and over. Act III, Scene 2: The Industrial Revolution stole the time of the people, amassing the profits of machinery for the already-wealthy, not for the ranks of the working poor. Act III, Scene 3: Globalization & Neoliberalism turned world disparities into a shell-game dance of cheap labor, cheap goods, and differing values of the dollar.

Only in the final scene did a glimmer of hope appear. The sign holders displayed a clock face poised at the eleventh hour. The chorus brought out an immense cardboard mural collage of the ravaged Earth. The actors brought forward illustrations of the enduring and reviving commons around the globe: online, encyclopedias, community gardens, healing arts, volunteer fire departments, graphic design materials, community forests, irrigation systems, housing commons, shared parks, and so much more.

"The final act is in your hands," Robin Hood told the viewers as the ensemble gathered in the stage area. "Will you rise out of the ashes of this tragedy? Will you tell the true history of the Commons?"

He began to walk forward with the entire cast alongside him, trees and ghosts, Merry Men and Italian herb women, peasants and immigrants. They all passed through the crowd, weaving through the picnic blankets and tables to connect the past to the present, and put today's commons on the center stage of the long show. Silence turned into clapping; applause grew into cheers. The Theater of the Commons bounded back to shake hands with the viewers, to bow and share lunch with them all.

Charlie and Zadie shifted on the cold stone benches of the financial district's sterile park. Charlie murmured a phrase from their friend Idah Robbins, a schoolteacher in a nearby district:

"Those who don't know their history are doomed to repeat it . . . and it looks like some of us have a lot of homework to do."

Elena overheard and nodded at the words.

"Without knowing this piece of history," Elena said quietly, "it's hard to understand the tragedy of *this*."

She swept her hand up to the skyscrapers and along the grid of crammed streets that ran counter to the older, diagonal roads.

"The theater show needs an Act III, Scene 4," Elena sighed, "about the rise of on-demand culture and the ideologies of unrestricted access in these times."

"Access?" Zadie asked.

"Yes, open and unrestricted access, anytime to anything," Elena explained.

Access to land. Access to wealth. Access to power. Access to the wilds. Men's access to women's bodies for pleasure and reproduction. Unregulated access to markets and resources. Twenty-four hour supermarkets. Instant streaming. Overnight shipping.

"It's the notion that a few people should have the ability to do whatever they -often 'he' - please, whenever they want, wherever they want. Basically, the world on-demand. That's the vision. But to do that means subjugating everything and everyone to meeting the whims of the few."

Twenty-four hour stores meant night shifts for millions. Overnight shipping required warehouse workers whose every footstep was monitored. Two-day delivery across a country the size of a continent meant air freight that worsened the climate crisis. It was patriarchy and colonization taken to the extreme, gendered and often racialized. The ideologies of access were the enclosures repackaged into modern expectations of on-demand culture.

"That's why those guys can't stand the commoners," Elena said, pointing to the sidelines.

A row of suited men stood with scowls and crossed arms. One loudly demanded that the security guard clear the courtyard park. In the windows above, Zadie spotted a cluster of young men staring down, faces pale above the stranglehold of white button-up shirts and nooses of ties.

"The young economists hate us because we disrupt their fantasies - just as the commoners always have. We're an inconvenient truth. We get in the way of their entitlement wet dreams." Elena's bark of laughter shot out. "Entitlement is their automatic default. Their convenience justifies - in their minds - the subservience of millions. They want the world on-demand. And we refuse to oblige."

Elena broke off. Behind them, a commotion erupted at the edge of the gathering. Just as they turned to look, the first cry of alarm broke out. A pair of police officers grabbed the arms of an unpermitted seller in the mini-maker's market. Another flank moved forward to arrest others, only to be blocked by a group of commoners that stepped forward holding out their wrists. Behind them, a flurry of others dispersed into the street. The commoners had organized the more privileged among them to step forward to stall and delay the security forces to allow others to avoid arrest. On the opposite corner of the park, a shouting match broke out. The police looked up from handcuffing the commoners with zipties. A group of young men shoved their way into the square.

"Alt-right," Elena said in a strained, worried voice. "They've been stalking us lately, following us to be nasty and intimidating."

Zadie looked around grimly. The world of patriarchy was lined up against them: the private security of the moneyed worldview, the police state enforcing the laws made by the wealthy elites, and the far right's vitriolic hatred of everything but themselves. She moved to step into the fray, to stand up to the faces of hate and greed.

Charlie snatched her back.

"We've got to go."

Charlie's voice cracked at the end, taut and tight. He gripped Zadie's elbow in a vice of fingers. She resisted.

"We have to help - "

"No," he cut her off. "We have to go. Now."

Elena followed his worried glance. She paled.

"He's right. Let's go."

She grabbed Zadie by her other arm. The two dragged her hastily away from the tumult.

"What in the world?" Zadie started to say, craning over her shoulder. Her gaze fell down the slight steps into the park, down into the melee of flying picnic blankets and hurled pamphlets. She choked, whitened, and gasped.

The words of the shouting chants shifted from a meaningless roar of hate into phrases that stabbed her like knives between the ribs.

Screw the Whore. Burn the Witch. Kill the Bitch.

Suspended on a pole with unmistakable black curls, iconic jean jacket, and short red skirt, was an effigy of Zadie Byrd Gray.

They had hung her with a noose.

CHAPTER TWENTY

. . . . .

The Unholy Alliance

They returned to the house, shaken. Elena had hauled them down the block, shoved them in a taxi, ordered them to leave, and then returned to check on the commoners.

"The best thing you can do is stay safe," she insisted when Zadie protested. "They're targeting you. Deny them the satisfaction of your presence."

"I'm not afraid of them!"

But she was. Back at the house, Zadie's hands shook so hard, she dropped the spare key three times before managing to unlock the front door. A silence heavy as a tombstone hung over them. She and Charlie had chattered nervously on the ride back, shocked by the violence of the attack, patching together what had transpired out of the shards of chaos and fear.

A pack of men, white-skinned with shaved heads, had charged into the plaza, seizing blanket corners and ripping them out from under the commoners. Picnic baskets went flying. Lovingly-prepared sandwiches were crushed under heavy boots. Parents grabbed their small children and ran. A bike messenger was punched in the face as he attempted to stop the assaulters from hurling the contents of the Toy Library at screaming children. Fliers were tossed in the air like the scattered feathers of terrified birds, littering the wreckage in the park. Robin Hood and his Merry Men got into a brawl with the attackers. The witches were seized by their hair and dragged across the cement. Police stood by and watched until shouting commoners compelled them to intervene. By the time they did anything, the thugs had dispersed, leaping into vehicles that pulled up curbside. They peeled off with skidding tires and the stench of burnt rubber. It was a haunting clash, a scene straight out of the theater show, eerily familiar despite its modern costuming. History had stormed out of the past and tried to smash the fragile hopes of the future.

Zadie shuddered. The shouted insults - *kill the bitch, burn the witch* - had lodged in her body like bullets. One by one, she extracted them, breathing deeply and steadying her trembling hands. Charlie held Zadie's cold fingers in one hand as he turned the knob to the guest room with the other. Just as Charlie groped for the light switch by the door, the table lamp on the bed stand clicked on.

Someone sat in the armchair.

Zadie yelped. Charlie instinctively threw his body in front of hers. The door banged into them both and knocked them off-balance against the wall.

"Oh, for the love of . . . it's me."

The intruder held up his hands, palms out, to show he was unarmed.

"That's not reassuring," Charlie snapped, recognizing the voice instantly. "What the hell are you doing here?"

"Will?" Zadie gasped a second later, clued in by Charlie's cold tone more than anything else.

Will Sharp sat in the armchair, dark skin backlit by the window's glare, legs stretched out in front of him. He was a lean-muscled youth, catlike. An air of secretiveness clung to him. He was the last person they expected to see.

"I'm not here to cause trouble. Shut the door so we can talk."

"We can't trust him," Charlie stated through gritted teeth.

216

"Charlie, I've been hiding under tighter cover than the Man From the North ever did. There's a price tag on my head among private security mercenaries. It's a risk to come within half a continent of you two."

"Swear on your mother," Zadie said suddenly. "Swear by Angelica that you will do us no harm."

Will grumbled, but complied, vowing on the one thing he held sacred that he wasn't there to hurt them, but to warn them.

"About what?" Charlie demanded, suspicious as an old dog, hackles up.

Will Sharp had helped them, betrayed them, lied to them, and tried to sabotage the Dandelion Insurrection. In the end, he flipped loyalties and blew the whistle on the Interim President's plans to discredit them ... but that didn't make him trustworthy.

"I'm here to warn you about the unholy alliance of your old enemies with religious fanatics," Will said.

That got Charlie's attention. His eyes met Zadie's. She nodded. They untangled from their startled position. Zadie sat cautiously on the edge of the bed. Charlie remained standing, arms folded stubbornly across his chest. Will looked worn. Purplish circles hung under his eyes. A greyish tinge clung to his dark skin. He'd lost weight, sleep, and muscle. The stress of hiding from his former associates had taken a toll. He'd changed as he hunkered down in a series of safe houses, waiting for the fury over his whistleblowing to subside. Charlie tried to muster sympathy for the young man and surprised himself with a faint spark of understanding. He, too, had lived hidden, hunted by the corporate government for his words. He, too, had worn the same shadow that touched Will's brown eyes. He, too, had a slight hunch in his shoulders from anticipating the bullet in his back.

217

Will Sharp had made enemies of his friends, the team of infiltrators and saboteurs called the Roots. Since coming clean publicly, he hadn't had a solid night's sleep. He doubted he ever would. His only consolation was that, while John C. Friend had been indicted on criminal charges and incarcerated in a rich man's prison, the Roots had scattered and vanished. He'd done them the small favor of a tiny head start, a code warning to disperse and lay low. Not that they had appreciated it. He'd exposed them and their identities with the information he'd sent to Tucker Jones. All twelve of them would give their right pinky to see him dead. Without Tucker's quiet help tracking them online, he'd be feeding worms.

And it was his discrete surveillance of his friends and enemies that brought Will Sharp here today. Will sighed. He could be in the tropics right now, secluded on an idyllic and anonymous island, doing nothing, swimming with sea turtles in aquamarine waves. But he owed these two. So, he took a risk and came to help them.

"For the record," Charlie said grudgingly, "thank you for saving the Dandelion Insurrection from your own sabotage."

"Charlie!" Zadie exclaimed at his bitter words.

"No, he's right," Will acknowledged, meeting Charlie's eyes. "The Roots and I put you in that mess. It was only fair that I try to fix it. That's why I came. You've got problems."

"And you couldn't just call?" Charlie grumbled. "Scared us half to death. How'd you even get in here?"

Will shot him a pained look. This was his *profession*. He had a hundred ways of getting into places he wasn't allowed.

"Your security stinks since I left," he told Charlie.

The pair rolled their eyes. Since he'd left, fewer people had been trying to assassinate them.

"Water and bridges," Will said swiftly, tapping his fingers

nervously on the armrest. "I caught word of something disturbing."

He flipped a stack of printouts over on the side table.

"Know this guy?" he asked.

"Jeb Whyte." Zadie said flatly. "Unfortunately, yes. Did he have something to do with the attacks today?"

"Attacks?" Will asked, eyes leaping from one to the next in alarm. "What happened?"

They filled him in. His scowl deepened, carving furrows in his face.

"Why did you think he was behind the attack?"

"Just something I heard on the radio," Zadie muttered.

That morning, as they ate breakfast, Elena had flipped on the radio to catch the weather forecast. A familiar twang slid over the airwaves.

"If we look around this country, we see many people unraveling our great traditions."

Elena started to change channels, but Charlie asked her to wait. After Jeb Whyte's diatribes on Zadie during the Strippers Strike, he'd been trying to keep tabs on the man's sermons. Today, Reverend Whyte was in a full froth about the Whore of Babylon.

"She parades around - shameless, blatant - a modern Whore of Babylon. Is she not the harlot of prostitutes? Does she not call for the worship of nature, sheer paganism? Applauded for sin, idolized for her wickedness, she has upended our nation and destroyed the order of our world."

"Is he . . . is he talking about me?" Zadie had exclaimed with a gasp, wrenching the volume up.

"She would have us revert to bestiality, lay down with the red bull and fornicate with those beings."

"Yup," Charlie confirmed. The references to the Strippers

Strike and the Council of All Beings and the Rights of Nature were undeniable.

Jeb Whyte ranted on. He accused them of trying to steal the hard-earned money of the fortunate with their demand that the wealthy give their fortunes to Community Funds.

"God rewards the Just, the Faithful. The whore and her consorts would upend God's will, take the money from those who work for it, and give it to the lazy and the sinners."

Charlie and Zadie exchanged looks.

"Wait until we write about reviving the commons and destroying capitalism," Charlie commented as he glanced at the Great Lakes Commons fliers on the table. "He's going to hate the idea of *democracy transcending arbitrary borders, flowing with water and wind.*"

"No doubt," Zadie agreed with a short laugh.

But they stopped laughing as the radio church service went on. Reverend Whyte cued the choir. His wife took the stage to lead a prayer for the unborn souls aborted by wicked mothers seduced by sin. At the end, she made an appeal for their Birth Centers, asking for donations and calling out to those 'lost and lonely lambs, the young girls who find themselves blessed with child, but lost in the world.'

"Come home to us," Evelyn Whyte pleaded. "We will grant you comfort and shelter. We will protect you and your blessed child."

Zadie switched it off. She couldn't bear to listen. She'd heard those very words on the radio years ago after a back alley abortion had left her broken and bleeding her insides out. Because of the evangelicals' campaign to shut down women's clinics, she had been stuck hundreds of miles from a doctor that wouldn't jail her for manslaughter under anti-abortion laws.

"It's too fine a day to be caught up in Jeb Whyte's hatred," she said, shaking off the feeling of unease.

But the violent attack on the commoners put the radio sermon in a different, darker light.

"He could have sent those thugs," Zadie suggested.

Will frowned thoughtfully, looking at his computer phone.

"Hmm, it is possible that your hecklers listened to Jeb Whyte's sermon. Interesting."

Will stilled, scowling, his eyes flicking from side to side as he considered the notion.

"Who do you think they were?" Charlie demanded. *Hecklers* seemed too mild a term for them.

"No idea, but the last thing you need is a nationwide *Kill Zadie* mission involving vigilante extremists."

Will had been watching these kinds of groups for years. The worse climate instability got, the more their prophecies - Revelations and such - seemed to come true, the more people joined the far-right churches, the more power and sway those fanatics amassed, and the more dangerous they became. They'd been targeting Black and Brown communities for years - centuries really - but left-leaning organizers and feminists were also among their favorite targets. The foot soldiers of this army were stockpiling guns and canned goods in anticipation of the Rapture and Apocalypse, but their leaders were preparing for more earthly rewards: namely power and money.

As the country's brief unity against corporate dictators splintered into political factions, the rich people started casting around for someone they could scapegoat as the source of the escalating tensions and crises. Zadie Byrd Gray made a perfect target. The centrist politicians already threw her under the bus with their *too much, too fast, too soon* rhetoric. Outspoken, female, and untamable, she made a perfect bullseye for the conservatives. They could rail against her style of dress, her history as a stripper, and her abortion backstory. They could scream about her boundary-pushing views. She personified immorality to the christo-fascists. For them, there was nothing worse than a liberated woman dismantling hierarchy and domination.

"You're skating on thin ice," he warned Zadie.

Will's tone sharpened like shattered glass, cutting and slicing the words. The sound ignited the fire in Charlie, the old irritation at Will's smug know-it-all secrecy, his air of superiority and arrogance. Will Sharp hoarded knowledge, gripping his cards tight to his chest, waiting to win, and smirking as he collected all the poker chips. Worse, Will had sabotaged Zadie in the media with a highly-publicized kiss and rumors of an affair. Charlie wasn't ready to forgive him for that one, not with the echo of that scandal rearing its ugly head in the recent slander campaigns.

Hearing the silence, sensing the taut reaction, Will sighed.

"Sorry," he apologized unexpectedly. "I . . . I'm worried. Jeb Whyte is charming and crazy - a historically dangerous combination - and his followers are violent fanatics. He's been under surveillance for years. A former colleague of mine tipped me off that he's getting renewed interest in the backroom deals made by certain politicians. He's been having sit downs with the old power players who miss the good old days of stealing with impunity. He's been meeting with the corporations you kicked out of power. We all know they aren't looking forward to picking up the price of all the externalized costs they've foisted off on people and environment for decades."

The growing ranks of behind-the-scenes christo-fascists worried Will. They had worked for years to infiltrate and take over every major institution in the country from the police departments to federal bureaus all the way up through the halls of government. They were hell-bent on re-establishing a global Christian empire, but many couldn't outwardly campaign - they needed a white-toothed front man who looked like the blonde haired, blue-eyed Jesus. A megachurch televangelist aligned with the corporate elite, the christo-fascists, and street vigilantes was a nasty sort of beast. A guy like Jeb Whyte could ooze charm and Christian goodness while the shadow-guys took power behind him and the white supremacist rank-and-file terrorized the populace.

"*That's* the problem," Will said flatly. "The Unholy Alliance of corporate fascists and christo-fascists. There's a lot of money changing hands and no one turning over the tables. Your real democracy efforts must have the rich and powerful running scared."

Charlie snorted.

"Who's afraid of democracy?" he asked.

Will blinked owlishly at him. A twist of an ironic smile flitted across his face.

"That is the trillion dollar question, isn't it?" he murmured. "Who's afraid of democracy? Count the answers to that question and you'll have a list of the people who would send in those thugs today."

Find the answer to that and the tangled web of money and power unraveled at the seams. The history of the United States shattered its myths and platitudes, propaganda and lies. Standing stark naked in the rubble and ruins of patriotic hubris, caught red-handed in a conspiracy theorists' wet dream, were the string pullers of political puppets. No one would be surprised to see them. Any one of them would send in vigilantes, several of them already had.

"Jeb Whyte probably did it," Zadie answered immediately, the smarmy insincerity of the man flashing through her mind.

But the list went on, Charlie acknowledged. They had scores of enemies, two former presidents, the military-industrial complex, the mega-corporations, the tech billionaires, the oil moguls, the fascists, the supremacists. Everyone loved the idea of democracy - right down to schoolteachers and parents - until the *practice* of it weakened their power. And the more power they held, the more Charlie and Zadie's real democracy efforts threatened them.

Charlie scrubbed his face with his palms, pulling down on the flesh of his cheeks before letting it spring back into place.

"We knew ousting the *président illégitime* would be risky," he confessed, "but it was nothing compared to working for real democracy."

"That's fascism for you, corporate, christo, and classic," Will said dryly.

"So, what are we supposed to do?" Zadie asked.

Will rubbed his brow.

"Keep a low profile and let me do some digging. We've got to buy time to find out if today's culprits were isolated individuals or the start of something bigger."

"Stay out of sight, out of mind?" Charlie groaned.

"Where are we going to do that?" Zadie burst out, furious. "We can't put Elena at risk, or anyone else."

Will's Cheshire cat smile curled. He knew a thing or two about hiding.

CHAPTER TWENTY-ONE

. . . . .

The Twain

No cameras. No press. Not even consistent cell service. Will Sharp knew the perfect place for them to hide out.

"You can stay on the Twain with my friend Affina's father," Will suggested. "I'll ring her and ask her to introduce you."

After he blew the whistle on John C. Friend, Will had hunkered down in his safe house in the apartment next to Affina Barrie's. They weren't friends at the time - more like acquaintances - but her fourteen-year-old son liked to hang around and Will couldn't help trying to keep the kid out of trouble. No one had done that for him, and he had a soft spot for kids that defied his tough reputation. Affina's father was a riverboat man, born and bred. When the worst of Will's danger passed, he finagled a chance to meet the old man . . . and wound up drifting downstream on the Twain for a few weeks. Huck L. Barrie had lived on the Mississippi all his days - and by "lived on", he didn't mean in a riverbank or floodplain house. He meant on a houseboat, a raft really, with a short shed of a sleeping quarters with a tin metal roof that clattered madly in the rain.

"Huck L. Barrie?" Zadie repeated, incredulous when she first heard the name.

"His mother gave him that name," Will explained with a grin. "He told me she wanted to name him Huckleberry Bunny, but his father told her emphatically that if she wanted her son to survive to be a man, she couldn't name him that. Don't tease

225

him about it. He's sensitive still. Just call him Barrie or he'll kick you off the boat - likely right into the water."

Will had Affina pick them up and drive them down to the border of Iowa and Illinois, where the Mississippi wound modestly through a series of river towns - all of which had flooded in the recent spat of rain and early snows.

"Climate weirding has been a disaster here," Affina Barrie told them on the drive, shaking her head. "The early snows almost wrecked the entire crop. Then the rains came and melted it all, then the ice clogged the tributaries, which backed up and flooded, then it dumped into the Miss all at once during the worst week of downpours on record. Now the whole region is flooded."

Her father was headed south to warmer climates for the winter months, but he had refused to get on the Mississippi until the worst of the floodwaters ran past. He'd weathered the floods out, hunkered down on a tributary, tethered off to a stand of half-submerged trees on the edge of an eddying field that was now a pond. The trio planned to meet him in the nearest town. Affina parked on High Street. Main Street was blocked off by sandbags. First Street was submerged. The old river wharf on Front Street had been devoured by the river. Affina shaded her eyes as she stepped out of the car, scanning the water's edge for the boat.

"He should be here, somewhere. He said he'd be around."

"He didn't say where?"

Affina flashed them a long-suffering grin and shrugged. Her old man had a cellphone - he charged it on a solar panel and called her at one in the morning to wax poetic about the moonlight on the water - but he refused to let the device control his life. He nicknamed it Mammon, the False God, and kept it hidden in a coffee can.

Affina's mother called him a mad genius, impossible to live with, infuriating to the extreme, but admirable in his convictions. He was a one-man resistance to the entire churning juggernaut of modernity. Her father refused to bind himself to dates and places, specifics or hard-and-fast promises. The river obeys no man's beck-and-call, Barrie often said, she keeps her own time. A man who foolishly promises to run on the clock will find himself mocked by her. The Mississippi delivered all things in her own time and fashion.

"He may be upstream, downstream, stopped to visit a landbound friend, inspecting the eddies for salvage, who knows? We're on river time now."

In their waders and rain slickers, backpacks slung over shoulders, they sloshed through the frigid water to the concrete steps of a flooded-out grocery store. They waited under the overhang as the sky greyed and cleared, promising sunlight in one moment and snatching that hope away in the next.

At last, Affina spotted her father rounding the corner of Front Street, poling his raft down the sections too shallow for the outboard motor. He moved with the languid ease of one who has repeated the motion every day for a long life. He was a thin man, skin the color of wood darkened with age. Close-cropped grey hair curled against his skull. His cheekbones perched over hollow cheeks that matched his angular limbs. Muscles clung unexpectedly to his arms and shoulders. He had a look of indefatigable endurance. He would weather time and age as surely as the stones along the riverbank. Deep set amidst the crinkle-lines of a lifetime of good humor, his brown eyes shone.

He drew up close, gripped Affina's hand and let her pull his raft tight to the edge of the storefront steps, tethering off to the handrail. Barrie kissed his daughter on both cheeks, holding her by the shoulders to get a good long look at her.

"Can you believe this high water?" he exclaimed. "Come hell or high water, the old saying goes, and now that I've seen the one, I'm not so scared of the other. Just hope I get to take the Ole Twain with me."

He patted the metal roof fondly. In his view, there were two great landmarks that defined the United States: the Grand Canyon and the Mighty Mississippi. Similarly, there were two great folklorists: Mark Twain and the inimitable Zora Neale Hurston. Barrie had named his boat after Twain and the outboard motor after Zora - because she was a real powerhouse.

Barrie studied Charlie and Zadie in detail, brown eyes sweeping up and down. He'd heard an earful about them, first on the news, then from Will Sharp. If ever there'd been a young man that needed an older man's counsel, it was Will Sharp. As they'd drifted downstream, Barrie had teased out the whole long story of the fugitive whistleblower's complicated life. Barrie'd been around the block, done his share of stupid things, sold his soul to the Devil and won it back in the game of cards that was earthly life. He passed no judgment - hardly spoke at all - but gave the young man time to think and talk and work out the things that weighed on him. Somewhere around Missouri, he'd gotten the impression that Will Sharp hoped he could call this pair of young revolutionaries his friends one day. And Barrie was old enough to hope that wish would come true. He looked the pair over carefully. They waited while he huffed and hummed to himself. Finally, he leveled a knowing glance at Zadie.

"You have the look of the roaming folk."

"Well, the spirit of one, certainly," she confessed, "and perhaps some blood relatives somewhere back."

Next, he turned to Charlie.

"She may be roaming folk, but not so for you. You are a man of place, of land and farmers, and yet, a restlessness pulls you. I do not envy you, pulled in two directions, longing to move and yearning to stay put."

Charlie felt unexpectedly exposed, as if the weathered old man had seen straight into his soul.

"Dad, please, you have plenty of time to play river oracle for them," Affina interrupted. She caught his eyes and held them, reminding him of the real world. She wanted him to drop by a health clinic for a check-up in the next three months. If he called her from St. Louis or New Orleans, she'd find out where the nearest clinic was and set up an appointment.

"I'll take care of the bill, so have them - "

Barrie flipped a hand at her, cutting off her fussing. Affina rolled her eyes and turned to Charlie and Zadie.

"If he annoys you, or goes truly mad, just jump off and swim to shore. I did that once, when I was fifteen."

"Scared the living daylights out of me," Barrie remarked with a loving look. "Used to take the kids each summer to get them out of their momma's hair."

"Those were the days, Pop," Affina chuckled. "You can relive them all with your grandson this summer. He can't wait to get away from me and spend time on the river with you."

Affina had a plan for her old man; Barrie wasn't immortal. She was already worrying about the coming years, sorting out friends who would ask to ride with him or let him moor at their riverfront properties. She'd put her fourteen-year-old through CPR and First Aid training. The river life held romance, but it had harsh realities, too. Aging alone was not easy, on land or water.

Discretely, she handed Zadie a roll of cash and asked her to hide it when Barrie wasn't looking. His unexpected "windfalls" kept him going and fed his guests - he'd never accept money from them directly. Affina kissed her father on the cheek, waved to Charlie and Zadie and sloshed back up Main Street. Barrie poled to the intersection and made a show of stopping at the stop signs before turning right down Springer Street and heading for the river.

In the days before the automobile and the interstate highway system, he told them, the rivers rivaled the railroads. The rivers *were* the early highways of the country, shipping goods upriver, timber and furs downriver. Mail was sent by boat, travelers moved by ship. Zadie thought of Kinap's home, a series of islands in the Penobscot River, the water connecting them all as surely as the paved roads now interlocked the towns and cities of the world.

"The river is slow," Barrie conceded, "but do we really need to go so fast? Do we need robot drones whirring overhead just so we can have on-demand everything?"

The river hissed and hummed around them, mumbling in gurgles and currents the way a child murmurs deep in daydreams, or a writer's lips move along the next lines of the story. The wind licked small shivers of ripples across the surface. Along the banks, the trees shrugged and showers of leaves lifted like birds. Autumn plucked their nerves like harp strings, stroking chords of urgency and nostalgia at once. The afternoon passed in quiet, interspersed with low, slow comments that hung on the air like autumn leaves before falling into contemplation.

"Affina was right," Charlie remarked. "Time really does flow differently out here."

"Wait until tomorrow or the day after," Barrie replied with a secretive smile, "or until you've spent your whole life out here, never yielding to the tyranny of the clock. Mother Earth never surrendered. She runs on tides and seasons, moon cycles and rhythms as old as plate tectonics. We are made of times such as those. This tick-tock, follow the clock, instant coffee, world-on-demand, assembly-line insanity will kill us all. Fast or slow, it steals our soul and sanity."

As the afternoon rolled into evening, Barrie tethered off and they made simple sandwiches for dinner. The night cleared, sharp and cold, and he suggested they spread sleeping bags on the deck.

"The stars are worth the nip of frost," he promised, "and the river tells stories at night."

In the darkness, the language of the river grew more distinct. It was an ancient tongue, older than humans of all ancestry. But it knew the stories of the Quapaw and the Chickasaw. It had seen the first European fur trappers, the French traders. It had listened to the cries and prayers of the Cherokee and the Choctaw being driven west by colonialism. It had heard the first chop of settlers' axes and caught the blood and tears of Black people striving to escape to freedom. The land, the water, and the wind were old; they had watched humanity for eons. They had gossiped and chatted daily. What sorrow had they not shared? What stories hadn't the wind relayed to the trees and clouds, rain and river? Every time a factory dumped toxins under the cover of darkness, the river shuddered up and down her thousand-mile length. Her currents had choked and gagged on nitrates, runoff from hog farms, releases from nuclear power plants.

The river could tell horror stories about humanity - but she could also tell of a coming time when the polluting stopped and the waters ran clear. She could prophesize about a time when the muskrat, trout, snapping turtle, and herons came back, a time when humanity understood how to sit quietly and listen, a time when healing took precedence over hoarding.

In the morning Charlie and Zadie woke, rested and feeling like they had journeyed a hundred thousand miles and a million years through the past, present, and future. They felt as if the river of the world had flowed through them as they slept, rocked by the current's surges and eddies.

"I feel like I've learned to dream in another language," Zadie confessed to Barrie, curling her hands around a cup of coffee.

"The river speaks its own language, for sure. It takes a world class education to understand it," Barrie chuckled, a twinkle in his eye. He gestured broadly to the trees and churning waters. "This is the world. It is my teacher, classroom, textbook, and fellow students all rolled together."

He was not an uneducated man. He had read a library's worth of books and pondered deep philosophy. He'd never wasted a day of his life earning money in an office doing *matters of consequence* as Antoine de Saint-Exupéry put it. His life was simple and free. He worked a little, lived a lot. He had time for friends and adventures, travel and visits, and long hours learning from his ever-present stack of books.

Still, this nation wasn't easy on the itinerant. It was a cultural judgment against the unsettled, a holdover of colonizer mentality. *Good* people owned and cleared land, planted monocrops and lawns, established dominance and control over nature. *Bad* people drifted, lived wild, and remained untamed. The laws favored those who owned or rented property. They outlawed those who didn't.

Barrie grew solemn and quiet, thinking about his fellow boat people and their counterparts on land: the unhoused, the nomadic, the senior citizens living in trailers in state parks, the migrant workers on endless rounds south and north and back again. The mentality that privatized the shoreline so boat people couldn't dock, anchor, or land was the same mentality that criminalized camping in urban areas and put up barbed wire across the plains and herded Indigenous Peoples onto reservations. It was all the same. The fact that he couldn't vote - even for the president - because he didn't rent or own a house with a foundation in a certain district was the same line of thinking that denied him a driver's license.

"You know it's an Empire of Money when you are a non-person simply because you don't buy their houses or use their banks."

He laughed, but there was a bitter edge to it. He and his wife Charlene had nearly lost their kids to foster care . . . and in the end, he lost them and her to the pressures of settler culture. Charlene moved to town with the kids for the school year, and he only saw them in the summers or on short visits.

Barrie felt this pain as keenly as a cut-off limb. The ache of his loss was part of the vast tapestry of pain woven into this land, starting with the Indigenous Peoples who had been robbed of cultural continuity, had their lands stolen, their people massacred, and their children abused in residential schools. The suffering of Black people formed another thread from slavery times through Jim Crow and mass incarceration. A third strand belonged to the migrant workers laboring twelve-hour days far from their homelands because of global economics. The poor of all backgrounds entwined through this sinister pattern, downtrodden and exploited. And what must the animals of this continent feel, to see their families so reduced? To fly, not in massive flocks that blackened out the sky, but in tiny handfuls. One's own pain could be a window into compassion and empathy with others. Barrie's dole of human suffering give him the grace to comprehend the hardships others faced, and to stand with them in solidarity as they sought to stop the injustices.

As they drifted downriver, the trio spoke of these patterns. The history of the Commons weighed on Zadie's mind. Elena had told them that, to enforce feudalism and enclosures, harsh laws against vagrants and vagabonds had been passed throughout Europe. The homeless could have their feet cut off or be shipped to the colonies in the so-called New World. Sixty percent of the Europeans who came before the Revolutionary War came as indentured servants or prisoners. In a world where private property reigned supreme, those who did not surrender their right to roam paid harsh penalties for merely existing. Those who refused to own or be owned - to be tenant or landlord, peon or feudal lord, slave or enslaver - inevitably led lives of risk and uncertainty.

"People think this is progress, a natural and good evolution from the Dark Ages to modernity," Elena had said, "but there's nothing natural about how we got here. And, if you know the true story of the commons, you understand that the Tragedy of the Commons is not a description of the shortcomings of democratic stewardship, but rather a description of the very worldviews that systematically enclosed them with every brutal, horrific, torturous form of repression known to humanity."

Poverty. Eviction. Execution. Rape. Subjugation. Greed. Enslavement. Genocide. Political oppression. Violence. War. *That's* what destroyed the Commons, not mismanagement by people who cared deeply for one another, the land, and the myriad creatures that once belonged within the Commons. The brutality of Europe's privatization was exported around the globe through colonialism, beginning new chapters in an ongoing story of destruction. That tale continues to this day. Our world was constructed on the back of tragedy. It is a world that serves the few at the expense of the whole, including the pillage of the Earth.

A culture built on wealth and property, borders and boundaries, would always be at odds with the natural world. Here on the Mississippi River, state lines were irrelevant; the river ran through them all. Overhead, a flock of Canada geese called out their haunting cries as they headed south for the winter. The rain clouds sprinkling them came from halfway around the globe. The river waters would journey ever onward when they reached the sea. But humanity walked around in cages of invisible lines. They bound each other up with greed and fear in ways no other species - plant or animal - did.

"See that?" Barrie said, pointing a weathered hand toward the shore.

A pod of milkweed, wind-brushed, released its silken fibers.

"The dandelion of North America," he told them. "Your symbolic, golden flower is actually an immigrant from Europe. Milkweed, on the other hand, stands at the heart of this continent's ecosystem."

Zadie smiled softly, watching the silken seeds drift on the cool October air, journeying to new homes. Immigrants brought the dandelion to this continent as food and medicine, but now gardeners and farmers detested it as much as the milkweed. The extermination campaign against those plants had ravaged the Midwest lands, causing dead zones and leaving behind broken ecosystems. The small cluster on the riverbank was a hopeful sign. It was part of a continent-long constellation of milkweed patches that mirrored the Milky Way overhead. The Great Milkweed Corridor was an international effort to reseed the endangered plant and protect the migratory route of the monarch butterfly. The orange and black beauty flew a thousand miles in multigenerational waves to Mexico and back again on fragile wings. It was miraculous.

"I helped plant those," Barrie confided proudly, "all the way up and down the river. I planted the seeds for all those who wander, the migrants and the migratory, and in honor of the opening of the Mariposa Gate last spring."

Tears sprang to Zadie's eyes, touched by the gesture of solidarity. Last year, she and Charlie had campaigned long and hard with Inez Hernandez to push through immigration reform. As the river tugged the Twain gently downstream, Zadie and Charlie spoke about the effort. Barrie had followed the news on the radio, but the sound bites and headlines left out the most interesting parts of the story. It had been a tough and painful fight, underscored by the knowledge that people had migrated from north to south and east to west for thousands of years. In Chaco Canyon in the desert of New Mexico, the feathers of Mexico's ancient macaws from the jungle and conch shells from the ocean proved the long history of trade, kinship, and cultural exchange between Indigenous civilizations. Migration and travel was as ordinary for humanity as for the geese and monarch butterflies, the wide-ranging wolves and the humpback whales. The walls and laws of recent years had interrupted ancient pathways, and were constructed on greed and fear and hate. Last spring, Inez's efforts bore fruit and, at long last, the Mariposa Gate opened on the US-Mexico Border. Zadie smiled as she told Barrie about that day, how the hot sun turned white in a sharp blue sky, how the voices of the crowd rose in Spanish and English, how she would never forget Inez' words honoring the historic moment.

"*Hoy es un día de milagros, un día en que las paredes se derrumban y los niños se reunidos con sus familias,*" Inez had proclaimed. Today is a day of miracles, a day when the walls crumble, and children are reunited with their families.

Inez Hernandez was barely five feet tall in heels, yet she towered like a giant with a microphone. Zadie and Charlie had stood behind her, looking out at the swelling crowd that packed both sides of the international border. On the Mexican side, hundreds of black and orange butterfly flags waved in the wind. A massive cloth-and-wooden jaguar puppet the size of a school bus crouched. Kites of condors and eagles spiraled overhead. Nearby, Inez' gristle-tough mother fought back tears. The wall that had stretched hundreds of miles along the border had grown as odious to Pilar Maria Ignacia Hernandez as the Berlin Wall was to Germans. Far more Mexicans, Guatemalans, El Salvadorans, and Hondurans had died trying to cross to safety than had ever perished along the notorious wall in Germany. Thousands had perished in the Desert of Death as they fled US-manipulated terror, violence, and poverty. Tens of thousands made it to *los Estados Unidos* only to be deported back into the crosshairs of the dangers they had fled. Hundreds of thousands had their children ripped from their arms and locked in detention camps. The ones that "made it" worked harder than imaginable and fought decades-long struggles for immigration status.

No more.

Inez had rallied the Dandelions to wrestle and wrangle an immigration bill through the new Congress that worked miracles. Pilar already heard heretical rumors about her daughter's sainthood in the streets of their New York City neighborhood. Now, at their local Catholic Church, she spotted colored candles with Inez' photo pasted on them. Saint Inez, they called her, adding a drop of teasing to assuage their passionate seriousness, calling her the matron saint *de Viajeros, Migrantes, y Milagros* . . . travelers, migrants, and miracles. The burden of that cross would make even Jesus stumble. Inez had already worked miracles for millions of people; her stigmata came from the crosshairs of snipers. She could have rested on her laurels, but instead, she stepped up and took on a struggle nobody thought could be won. She turned it into a stunning victory.

The fight over immigration and migrants was rooted in two things: xenophobia and greed. With one hand, Inez' bill streamlined naturalization, borrowing from Canada's sane and effective policy. With the other hand, she closed loopholes in corporate exploitation of undocumented workers and raised the minimum wage to a living wage for everyone. The corporatists screamed. The regular people cheered. It was a once-in-a-lifetime bill, one that could only be passed in the aftermath of insurrection, in the open space of upheaval, at a time when the clearinghouse of departing politicians allowed a wave of new ideas and fresh faces to champion justice in the halls of power.

When the Battle of the Mariposa Bill turned into trench warfare in the House, Mexico broke the gridlock by offering to come to the structure with steel cutters and metal saws and take down the border wall. Pride stung the legislators. They refused the offer and found the funds to remove the hated metal structure. When the Senate struggle came, Pink Floyd Tribute bands held a two hundred city multi-nodal rock concert rally to perform *The Wall* calling for the removal of the border barrier. Germans called from across the Atlantic, flooding the phones of key legislators, offering pro-tips on how to dismantle walls.

"*Ich bin ein Berliner,*" the calls began, echoing the words John F. Kennedy had once said to them.

When the legislation headed to the Oval Office, some of the immigration officers went on strike, vowing not to return to work until - and unless - the law was signed. They picketed their own offices with signs declaring: *We are not Nazis. Ellis*

Island is closed. Give us the tired, the hungry, the poor. Close the camps. Cut the paperwork. Let us welcome people instead of terrorizing them. The other half of the officers were quietly put under review. In the following weeks, over two thousand employees of INS and ICE, and the Border Patrol, were fired for gross violations of human rights, bribery and corruption, blatant racism, discrimination, brutality, and cruelty.

"The Mariposa Bill pays for itself in the legal fees we save from getting rid of those human and civil rights violating agents," Tansy remarked caustically, disgusted by the scope of criminal behavior that ran rampant in the old immigration system.

When it came to the bill's fine print, Pilar Maria had a request for her daughter: that when the border wall came down, a second Statue of Liberty would go up.

"Take that metal wall and pound it into *una nueva estatua de la Libertad*," Pilar urged her. "Put a concertina wire crown on her head and let the rust run down like the *sangre de los mártires.*"

Pilar Maria wanted to see the Virgen de Guadalupe towering along the border like a southern Statue of Liberty, but in the end, the legislation simply called for a mutually agreed upon, culturally appropriate, public sculpture akin to the symbolic nature of the famous lady that lifted her torch in New York Harbor. Inez and Zadie were pacing through Central Park when the answer to the statue question came.

"Remember that orange sculpture?" Inez reminisced.

Zadie nodded. *The Gates* had stunned the city with its bold evocative intensity in a time shocked by death.

"What if it was orange and black like the monarch butterfly? *Una bandera de mariposa* . . . a Monarch Butterfly Flag."

Zadie's eyes lit up. It was perfect.

239

"Forget statues," Inez continued. "Take the steel away, melt it down to build bridges. Along the border, let's fly the symbol of migrations: the monarch butterfly, black and orange with white spots, fragile and resilient at once."

Where the wall once stood, the Mariposa Flag rose in fluttering silken beauty, flying in the wind. The gate was a giant sculptural banner that arched over the international border, swaying in the breeze. Orange, black, and white, it welcomed those coming and going. It was a reminder of the courage of ancestors, and a tribute to the determination of a fragile species that was returning from the brink of extinction. It was an emblem of resilience for all cross-continental wanderers. The flags flew over five new bridges - each built from reclaimed steel - at remodeled border crossings. When Inez was asked to speak at the unfurling of the first Mariposa Gate, she brought Pilar Maria with her.

"Ready?" Inez had asked her mother, handing her the scissors to cut the strings for the ceremony.

To Inez Hernandez, the honor of this moment belonged to the woman who had raised her, the woman who had made the perilous journey across borders, a woman who had survived a lifetime of being called illegal, a woman who had navigated the cruelties of modern times and raised her daughters to be humans with courage and heart.

Pilar Maria pulled the lever. Above them, a furl of orange released its wings into the brilliant blue of the sky. The Mariposa Gate opened. The people, the coyote, the cougar, the deer, and all the land-walking creatures could now travel like the geese and butterflies, traversing back and forth along the ancient pathways.

All these months later, the story still moved Zadie to tears. As she and Charlie drifted down the Mississippi River with

Barrie - a man who had spent his life following the currents across invisible state lines - she thought of how humans were just one more species on this immense Earth. Like countless others, they traversed the planet's ecosystems in migrations and evolutions, following eternal tides and the constant of change. Whether they were monarch butterflies, milkweed seeds, migrants, or the Mighty Mississippi, all beings longed to follow the rhythms of Earth. Someday, humans would remember that those cycles and seasons, the heartbeat and pulse of the planet, beat in their veins and sang in their bodies, too.

CHAPTER TWENTY-TWO

. . . . .

Hurricane Eve

A high wind smacked the water, kicking up waves that glinted grey as the overcast sky. Barrie eyed the river warily as he slurped his coffee. He set the mug down and tied a second bowline to the copse of trees in the eddying inlet. The first smatter of raindrops hit the half-bare branches and withered leaves of the trees. Barrie flipped on the radio. He fiddled with the knob, adjusting the signal. A crackled report came through. Amidst the garble, Barrie picked out the words: gulf, hurricane, superstorm.

"Won't be moving today," he murmured. The Gulf storms had ratcheted up in intensity year after year as climate denialism flourished under the corporate-controlled government. Every year of delay and inaction destabilized the climate further. The high tides crashed further into coastal cities, surging up through storm drains, flooding whole neighborhoods. The centers of continents crisped with 110° degree heat bombs. The droughts were trouble enough, but it was the weirding of the weather in extreme oscillations that spelled doom for humanity. Over the Great Lakes, polar vortex blizzards crashed miles of power lines down. Snow in the Midwest in late June killed thousands of acres of crops. Tornadoes tripled in size and ferocity, hurling towns across the prairie like gods in a temper tantrum.

But it was the hurricane season superstorms that terrified Barrie. This far inland, they'd be plastered with monsoon-worthy rain, but the brunt of the one hundred and twenty miles per hour winds would be slowed. The winds would trip over New Orleans, drag their feet into Louisiana's swamps, and stagger through Mississippi. By the time they got here, they'd be strong enough to strip the branches bare, but not to flip the Twain over. As the rivers flooded, the currents would surge, unpredictable and treacherous.

"We'll be hunkering down here for a few days," he informed Charlie and Zadie.

They nodded, eyes wide and worried over the weather report. From its coffee can prison, his cellphone jangled. He opened it and scowled as he stabbed at the touchscreen trying to turn it on. Managing it at last, he answered.

"Hello? Yeah, was just about to call you. Hmm. No, sorry to say she's running high and wide. Newbury's looking like Venice. The wetlands are full up? Ah. I see. Well, I'll come down right after the storm passes and lend a hand. Sounds like you'll need boats."

He hung up and closed his eyes for a long moment.

"What's happening?" Zadie asked, a clench of worry seizing her.

"The Sisters of St. Joseph in New Orleans called to check on the Miss. These floodwaters are hurtling downstream and will collide with the storm surge. The Maribeau Wetlands are already brimming. The city'll flood."

"What are the Mirabeau Wetlands?" Charlie asked.

They were a miracle borne from the wreckage of Hurricane Katrina. The twenty-five acre grounds had once housed a Catholic convent. The buildings had been completely flattened by the storm. The Sisters, praying for guidance, spent years contemplating how best to rebuild and serve their ministry . . . and the planet. For theirs was a double mission: shepherding the people and stewarding the Earth. Twenty-five acres in the heart of New Orleans had reckless developers salivating over the potential, but God interceded and sent the nuns a vision: make the area into the nation's largest urban wetlands. Using a natural design, the area mitigated the heavy rains and frequent floods that hit the region. The wetlands could offer recreation space in dry times and water catchment in wet weather. With the rebuilt levee system of the Army Corps of Engineers already sinking beneath tidal surges, the Mirabeau Wetlands offered to serve an entire city of four hundred thousand people *and* nature.

But even that beautiful garden couldn't stop the mighty collision of river water and hurricane. Hurricane Eve would hit land with all the vengeance of a woman scorned. She was coming. There was no stopping her.

Charlie, Zadie, and Barrie waited out the storm north of Jackson, Mississippi. Even this far inland, the trees whipped and the rain lashed and the Twain rocked and sloshed on its moorings. Barrie offered to take them to a hotel, but they declined. Hundreds of thousands of families had evacuated the mouth of the Mississippi. Charlie and Zadie stayed on the Twain and organized disaster relief among the Dandelions. They crowd-funded to make entire regional hotel chains available for poor families. They connected local insurrectionists with evacuees to provide shelter. They pressured inland town officials to open their gymnasiums and community centers to those fleeing the brunt of the hurricane.

It is time, Charlie wrote, *to once again live up to our motto: be kind, be connected, be unafraid.*

Be kind ... let your compassion lead you into action.
Be connected ... be the indivisible nation that we aspire to be.
Be unafraid ... and show up to take care of each other.

From the makeshift office of his Twain shack, Barrie helped them mobilize shelter for Hurricane Eve asylum seekers. He lined the tin roof with blankets to muffle the din of the downpour. He charged the battery packs for their phones, first off the solar charger, then with the diesel converter rigged up to the outboard motor. He brewed coffee at midnight and brought an extra blanket for Zadie when her teeth started chattering. *Perhaps*, he grudgingly conceded as they worked, *there was a time and place for technology*. He had planned to sail into New Orleans as the storm receded and rescue those who couldn't or wouldn't leave, but even as he sat here waiting, Charlie and Zadie and the Dandelions had assisted millions.

Charlie's grandfather called, both of them hollering over the deluge of rain. Valier rattled on in French for several minutes before Charlie understood the gist of the old man's message.

"Wait - you raised how much?" he blurted, shocked.

"*Deux millions!*" Valier answered proudly. "Two million, Charlie!"

He had called every single French Acadian family in the St. John Valley, invoking their cultural connection to the Cajuns to gather relief funds for the city. During *Le Grand Dérangement* in 1755-1764, the British had expelled most of the Acadians from Northern Maine and New Brunswick, sending many of them south to Louisiana. Thousands died along the way. Years later, some returned to the northern lands, reclaiming homes and farms, but the Acadians who remained in the south became the Cajuns.

"They are our brothers and sisters, my grandson Charlie's distant relatives!" Valier had declared, pestering his neighbors nonstop until they turned out their pockets to contribute to the relief effort.

"That's amazing, *grand-père*," Charlie shouted, plugging his other ear so he could hear above the howl of the storm. "I didn't think our valley had two dimes to rub together."

"*Bah, voyons,*" Valier exclaimed. "They don't. We only raised a thousand, but I got the churches involved and *les Canadiens.* They started calling the French on the continent, and *voila! Deux millions.*"

The old man was fit to burst with pride. Charlie hung up, deeply moved, and relayed the news to Barrie and Zadie.

"Disasters like this will be the making or breaking of America," Barrie remarked. "Hearing this gives me hope that the best of us will show up to redefine patriotism from *love of one's country* to *love of one another.* We can build our identity not on corporate brands or short-sighted nationalism, but on how well we rally to take care of each other."

Charlie glanced up from the screen. The bluish light reflected in his eyes.

"May I quote you on that?" he paused as he choked up. "That was . . . beautiful."

"Just get my name right: H. L. Barrie, i and e, no reason y."

As the hurricane slammed the coast and dropped continent-sized armloads of water inland, the Mississippi spilled her banks. She hit historic high-water marks, hundred year flood lines, all-time records . . . and then she kept on flooding. She swallowed farm towns and cut off cities. She turned roads into canals and fields into lakes. Still, the clouds kept raining, the river continued rising, and there was nowhere for the water to go except into the thousand mile-long river valley basin.

Whole cargo containers were dragged off train side rails. The waters tore out dikes and shoved up into industrial areas. Box stores and warehouses turned into island archipelagos. The water table rose beneath the ground, bubbling up in old basements far above the river. Foul water seethed out from

247

drains carrying the stench of sewage. Old diseases from medieval times resurfaced as sanitation systems broke down. Bloated corpses from hog farms washed downstream in nightmarish scenes. Green algae-filled sewage and sludge ponds overflowed and poured their toxic soup into the brown and angry floodwaters. The factories along Cancer Alley oozed with leaking containment ponds. The military was recalled from overseas bases to help with the rescue operations. Dramatic footage of helicopters and ocean vessels collecting people from rooftops of homes, hospitals, even clinging to a church steeple, deluged the media.

As soon as the brunt of the storm passed, Barrie's boat sped southward. New Orleans drew closer on the horizon. On either bank, the damage and destruction increased by the mile. They closed in on the city. The devastation around New Orleans shocked them. There was no river edge, only a sea of flooded streets. As they approached, a second boat motored into sight. The captain lifted her hand to Barrie. A third boat came up behind them, then another and another, until a veritable fleet sailed down the Mississippi to help with disaster relief. Some bore supplies; others brought volunteers. One carried a deck full of white-robed doctors and nurses in green scrubs.

The flooded neighborhoods teemed with activity, much of it odd and startling, tinged with a sense of surrealism. In the streets-turned-canals, a group of men, waist deep and shirtless, hauled a floating house against the pooling currents. A bantam rooster perched on a roof next to a supremely aloof tabby cat. On a church ridgepole, a row of people sat in resignation, waiting for deliverance in the form of a boat. The debris of a bouncy ball hut bobbed colorfully against the grey walls of the cemetery crypts. On the next street, a pack of kids poled an inflatable mattress down the streets, salvaging and scavenging.

The strangeness grew as they got closer to the coast. One hundred and twenty miles per hour winds had ripped roofs off houses and left walls splayed like half-opened boxes. The entire contents of a superstore had washed out the broken sliding doors into the submerged parking lot; plastic toys knocked against the windshields of abandoned cars. There was a line of people pushing seniors in wheelchairs up a turnpike bridge, rescuing the residents of a nearby retirement village. Houses had been blown off foundations, crushing cars underneath them like metallic wicked witches of Oz.

Much of the devastation was marked by loss, the absence of the ordinary. It was an invisible wreckage that only the locals could see: the lake with a neighborhood hidden beneath, the place where a store should have stood, the absence of landmarks, the water-surged relocation of an anguished Virgin Mary statue who opened her arms on the front step of a demolished school.

They motored in near silence until they reached a Spanish-style convent. The pink plastered walls darkened at the waterline. A bustle of activity teemed near the covered porch that encircled the building. Boats congregated around as black-robed nuns coordinated supply, delivery, and rescue operations. They cheered at Barrie's hollered greetings and without a moment's fanfare, he and his guests were drafted into helping. The Sisters were repackaging donated food goods into smaller boxes to deliver all over the city. Charlie teamed up with Barrie, grabbing crates and lending his young back to loading and unloading. Zadie joined the nuns - specifically, a tiny bird of a sister who worked indefatigably and spoke with boisterous French and Spanish-accented enthusiasm. Her habit was scandalously tucked up into her belt, revealing no-nonsense jeans underneath. She refused to wear a wimple, and the rising heat made her dark brown hair curl in a furious wrestling match with the humid air. They spoke in snatches between hauling boxes.

"Sister Theodesia is my name, just call me Theo," she insisted.

The nun's compact strength belied the weathering of five decades. She bent at the knees and hefted a cardboard box that clinked with jars of peanut butter. Zadie stacked packages of crackers into her arms and followed her into the other room. The day passed in a blur. Zadie remembered only a whirl of faces. At dusk, her back ached with the recollection of innumerable box loads moved from hall to kitchen to porch to boat. She saw Charlie only twice amidst the fleet of small dories and larger skiffs that moored against the old convent to load and then departed to deliver sustenance to water-trapped families. The next day was the same. And the next. They slept on the Twain. Barrie docked each night alongside the convent's porch rails. In between hauling boxes and handing out relief packages, Zadie and Charlie made sure the nation poured their hearts into helping out their fellow citizens.

They called millions of Dandelions into the relief effort in an historic appeal:

"We are a continent of a country, larger than our fears, bigger than our petty greed. We must rise to care for one another, to help our fellow citizens in the wake of disaster. Let us open our schools and churches, auditoriums and gymnasiums to take in those displaced from their homes. Let us give from our pantries and gardens. Let us volunteer to deliver supplies. Let us staff emergency shelters. Let us help clean up the debris and offer our help when the time to rebuild arrives."

In the crisis, the best and the worst of the nation were revealed.

"If we cannot find common cause in caring for ourselves as one country, indivisible, regardless of background or political beliefs, then we have no right to think of ourselves as a nation. If we will not care for each other in times of need, if we will not bend our collective strength to this task, calling upon our citizens, businesses, institutions, government, and whole society to take care of each and every one of us . . . then who are we truly? Are we the people we aspire to be? Or are we merely three hundred and twenty million miserable crooks and criminals robbing each other for our own comforts and pleasures?"

To say it was a watershed moment was an understatement. As the floodwaters began to recede and the worst of the damage was revealed, Charlie and Zadie called upon Congress to pass a Relief Bill and a New Deal-style work program to provide jobs for the people as they helped their nation in its hour of need. Charlie rang up Brad Andersen and corralled him into helping.

"You'll owe me for this," the DC fixer told him.

"Maybe you owe me for putting your heart in the right place," Charlie countered, "and for saving your soul from its usual state of perdition."

He hung up with a disgusted sigh and turned his attention to other things.

Zadie, always outspoken about greed and inequality, called upon Dandelion Insurrectionists to disrupt all the luxury affairs of the rich, demanding that they put the suffering of their fellow citizens ahead of their social pleasures. Starling and Sparrow mobilized murmurations in ten major cities. Fifteen thousand people participated. Tens of millions of private dollars poured into citizen-led relief funds and mutual aid networks.

We cannot accept the highway robbery of business-as-usual in times like this, Charlie wrote. *We cannot be a country that continues to selfishly profit from the wreckage and upheaval that greed has wrought.*

"And why stop there?" Zadie asked as she worked with Charlie on their latest appeal. They were huddled in the head nun's office, using the spotty wifi running off the generator. "Shouldn't the richest country in the world also be the most generous? Not just in philanthropy and in donations, but in mutual aid networks and fair wages, affordable housing, healthcare, and free college education?"

"But Zadie," Charlie argued, fingers poised over the keypad, "if we did all those things, those fair and ethical things, we wouldn't be the richest country in the world anymore."

She tossed him a contemptuous lip curl.

"Of course we would," she countered, "but we wouldn't measure wealth by adding up rich people's hoards and private stockpiles. We'd measure it in collective wellbeing, health, quality of existence, access to opportunity, and happiness indexes."

She had a point. Charlie wrote it down.

We can forge a new spirit for our country based on how deeply we care for one another. In our hour of need, we can judge patriotism not by our willingness to wage endless war, but by endlessly expanding our capacity to care.

A sense of national pride could be found, not in narrow lines of race or class, but in the deep upswell of care shown by ordinary people to their fellow citizens. The generosity pouring into relief funds and mutual aid networks, volunteering and sheltering evacuees, revealed that the citizens had cast their vote for compassion. Patriotism had to include taking care of one's fellow citizens, indeed, all of humanity. Charlie made sure the memo reached the desks of politicians, demanding that they open the public coffers as generously to the people as they had for the corporations. He insisted that the government raise the taxes on the wealthy and put those funds to work for the wellbeing of country. A poor person who donated their last dollar was as generous as a millionaire who gave away their entire fortune, he reminded them. The rich should aspire to be as radically generous as the working class and the poor.

The message was loud and clear: *we, the People, love our people.*

And if you do not . . . then what exactly do you mean when you claim to love this country?

CHAPTER TWENTY-THREE

· · · · ·

Twilight of the Empire

One evening, just after Charlie called Zadie to report that he and Barrie were doing one last round of welfare checks before nightfall, Theo nudged Zadie to put down the box of supplies they were repacking.

"Come," the older woman told her, "you look grey. Take a break with me."

Sister Theo snatched a loaf of bread, a jar of peanut butter, and a butter knife, and hauled Zadie up the stairs to the rooftop. Her herb garden was already shaking off the storm's battering. The rosemary bared its greenness, utterly undaunted. A bedraggled oregano plant woefully strove to emulate it. A calendula bed already lifted a few ragged stalks up to the fading sun.

"Twilight is beautiful, don't you think?" Theo remarked, swiping the raindrops off the metal bench with the hem of her habit. "I've always loved it best. It's the time when the dust settles and the soul naturally pulls inward in communion. It's the perfect time to reflect on the activities of the day."

Most people thought the twilight mournful, eerie, haunting. But to Theo, the darkness brimmed with resplendent gifts. The close of day offered unique solaces and rare understandings.

"There is a time for everything . . . including ends, collapses, decays, and closures," Theo said as she broke bread with her young companion.

Zadie twisted the peanut butter jar open and gratefully slathered the slice with it.

"In my younger days, I wandered a lot," Sister Theo confessed. "At twilight, I'd stop wherever I was and reflect on all I'd seen and heard. It was an odd little ritual for a young woman. All of my friends were getting married or breaking glass ceilings. Not me. I liked to watch the pattern of things."

Theodesia had drifted and dreamed, observing the cycles of commuter traffic and the way the grass grew. She watched the rhythms and repetitions of tides and turning seasons, the iterations and incarnations of the world, day after day. She studied the moon and stars, the seasons, the ebb and flow of rising rivers and dwindling droughts, the migration patterns of animals and the lifecycles of ecosystems.

"In ancient times," Theo admitted with a laugh, "I might have been a druid. These days, in the United States, pattern-watchers like me tend to be systems analysts or computer programmers. I missed my era, one way or another. Instead, I toyed with poetry and biology, but never quite settled anywhere."

She just liked to walk the patterns of this land. She read the flight of birds and the color of the setting sun. She listened to the insects' songs and the silences where they had been poisoned into extinction.

"And what do you do with all this knowledge?" Zadie asked, curious.

Theo gave her an odd look.

"Must something be done with it? Isn't it enough to listen and see, to pay respect through observing?"

"Yes, of course," Zadie answered, flushing a little.

Sister Theo smiled in absolution. This was one of the more insidious patterns of the modern world: everything was ascribed a value, a price tag or lack thereof. Nothing existed simply for its own beauty, its own joy. Each plant, animal, and mineral had to *do* something, serve consumption's hunger, feed humanity's voracious appetite for products, experiences, knowledge, and entertainment. Such thinking colored the gaze of many people. Theo was still trying to unravel these strands within herself. It was a terrible thing to look at the world and see objects to exploit rather than beings to admire.

Theodesia chuckled and swung her feet.

"I had quite an ache for the days when women could be hermit oracles. Closest I could find was joining a convent . . . and I've been a bit of an odd duck in the order ever since."

"You don't strike me as, um, nunlike," Zadie confessed.

Theo's smile bloomed. The Catholic Church was a billion people, saints and sinners, angels disguised as ordinary people, and devils masquerading as holy figures. The history of the church - like any nation of similar size - was blessed and sacred, wicked and sinful.

"Many of my superiors have shared your impression," Theo admitted with a laugh. "I am the bane of control freaks and the blessed sister of chaos. I thrive in adversity and go batty in routine. But I was raised Catholic, right here, with a Creole mother and Cajun father. The Church always had my soul. Back when I joined the convent, I wanted to be part of the quiet revolution of the liberation theologians. I felt the Church should stand in solidarity with the oppressed and all those striving for justice."

Theo bit into her bread with a sigh. Persecuted protector, oppressed liberator, wounded healer: to be a woman in the Church was to wrestle with faith and corruption on a daily basis.

Not unlike being a US citizen, Theodesia thought wryly.

257

They were called to have faith in the ideals of the nation while wrestling with the corruption and injustice of the empire.

Zadie shaded the gold of sunset out of her eyes. The light burst across the flooded city. The stains, discolorations, and high water marks softened. The water shimmered. For a moment, the disaster site came alive with beauty.

"So, as a pattern watcher, what do you see?" Zadie asked her straightforwardly. "What is brewing in the pattern of this country?"

"Mmm," Sister Theodesia murmured, "excellent question."

They were at a crossroads, undeniably. Disasters like this, or the forest fires out west, put the handwriting on the wall. The old way of life was collapsing, the new way just barely emerging. Everything was in flux. She saw wild oscillations in the old systems, crazy swings from one extreme to the next. She noticed people doggedly clinging to tradition as if keeping a white-knuckled grip on a sinking ship. She spotted blind leaps of desperation, visionary impulses, and unruly adaptations. Feedback loops were amplifying, echoing, bashing in chaotic collisions.

"If I were an oracle," she stated at last, "I'd advise you to prepare for what comes next. To imagine the possibilities, for better or for worse. Because these times are coming to a close."

Theodesia stared at the lengthening shadows that darkened the waters and drowned the gold.

"We face a perennial choice," she told the young woman, "to be or not to be an empire. Whether 'tis better to overextend and collapse in the gory tradition of empires past. Or whether 'tis upon us to embark on a new destiny."

Empires followed a natural cycle: they began, grew, over-extended, and disintegrated. They were systems that transgressed against limits, employing violence to amass wealth and power. They could not be sustained; it was not in the patterning of their nature. The question was: what would follow the collapse of an empire? Would they descend into violence and fighting? Or would they evolve toward smaller assemblies with greater equality?

The sun dipped. The gloaming hour descended over the flooded streets, a time of greys and hushes.

Had anyone gracefully deconstructed an empire? After the fall of the Roman Empire, a rash of walled city-states cropped up, rife with internecine wars. The British Empire had deflated through one independence struggle after another, bitter years of wars and occupations, inglorious retreats, and vain delusions of resurging power. The struggling Ottoman Empire was dismantled by European powers after World War I. The Aztecs crumbled when Cortez fomented factional wars and spread deadly disease through the region.

"If we voluntarily abandoned the ways of empire, what possibilities might arise that we couldn't have foreseen?" Theo murmured as the first bright star - a planet, actually - appeared on the horizon.

"If the empire didn't require a global military force," Zadie muttered, "Americans would get a double boost of social services. Can you imagine what we could do with all of that?"

Empire strangled life. By its nature, it gave wealth and opportunity to a few by taking those things from others. It was costly, time-consuming, and ineffective.

"Hurricane Eve," Sister Theo murmured with a chuckle, staring at the water-soaked city.

"What?"

"Oh, well, it's just that I find myself contemplating the Fall - or rather the many Falls in the Bible, Eve's especially. Typically, we're taught these stories as cautionary tales: obey the wise father and stay in the patriarchy, or bad things will happen like getting cast out of Eden or condemned to hell." Theo paused, reflecting. "But from a feminist perspective, one must wonder if a heaven or Eden constructed on ignorance and domination is really all it's cracked up to be."

Zadie shot her an askance look for such a heretical thought. Theo grinned, unperturbed. A faith that couldn't bear the rigor of critical thinking and blasphemous questions wasn't very strong to begin with, was it?

"What if we told these stories differently? Eve chose to learn, to know more than blissful ignorance - and yes, it is painful to have your eyes open to Truth, to see the suffering in the world. It means you can no longer wander like an innocent, unaware. You feel the cold and hunger, the heartbreak, the fear and danger. But are these not the trials of being human? The tests for our souls? The measure of our hearts?"

This aptly-named hurricane came to wake them up, to reveal the nation's hubris and arrogance along with its strength and kindness. She came bearing the hard fruit of truth, which, once tasted, changed everything. She showed the reality of a changing climate and an empire unwilling to care for its people. She unveiled the necessity of utter transformation. When she contemplated the coming times, Sister Theo saw a flickering stream of intuitive snapshots, like an old film rolling into motion, sequences full of looming possibilities, disparate and even contradictory: the metal of military smelted into bridges, petty warlords in feudal states, corporate colonies on Mars-like surfaces, backyard gardens and simple living. Cities that cared for citizens, cities that gnashed cruel teeth. Watershed alliances replacing states. Civil wars over water.

Theo looked ahead to a future few dared to imagine: the United States dissolving, fragmenting, vanishing like empires before it. In its place, a primordial soup of possibilities, some terrifying - feuding states and regional warlords - and some extraordinary, like bioregions with permeable boundaries, tribal nations resurging, local communities self-governing with autonomy and respect.

"We really could go any direction," Theo said. "Our next waking breath could change everything."

"It's a good time to be alive, then," Zadie replied, eyes gleaming with the potential.

Amidst every breakdown was the chance of a breakthrough. Times of great change were times of great possibility. Zadie thrived in such times, when the whirling coin toss on the fate of humanity hung in midair, when the slightest breath of kindness could sway the results. Anyone could be the person to tip the scales of the world. The outcomes of this pivotal moment could be determined by any of us. Everything rested on the choices of more than seven billion people. Each person's life mattered to the way the coin fell. One single act could alter the course of human history . . . indeed, could ensure that humans had a future at all.

Zadie and Charlie had instigated hundreds of local democracy projects, but there was another kind of participatory democracy: the trillions of choices made by people every second of every minute of every hour of every day. This everyday democracy didn't wait for polling or voting or televised debates. It tallied and enacted in real time. The training ground for participatory democracy was here, hidden in glib phrases like "vote with your wallet". Yet, even the rich and powerful behaved as if they didn't matter, as if it made no difference if they hoarded their stockpiles of wealth, as if there would be another and another and another day to support important change, as if they would always have more time to do what was right, as if it didn't matter if they didn't.

But everything mattered. Tomorrow was only a possibility. Now was the only time to act. If you knew that everything counted, how would you live your life? If you saw that your choices could be the ones to tip the world - one way or another - what would you do right now?

The night fell, deep and gentle. A motored boat flicked on a light. Below them in the convent, the sisters sang a hymn.

"Darkness," Sister Theo said softly, "is not the horror it's cracked up to be. It is the other half of life. We must imagine the twilight of our times not as a tragic fading, but as a graceful crossfade into the fertile darkness, the landscape of wombs and tombs, rest and incubation, inward reflection and gestation."

Zadie agreed. Their culture had always been afraid of the dark. Certain strands of humanity had spent two thousand years fearing and shunning the night, the womb, the darkness. But it was time to let the lights dim, to turn them out, to look up, and remember that stars shine most brightly in the dark. In fear, they had grown accustomed to snapping on the lights and blaring the TV screens. They had forgotten the gift of the stars. But, as Elena had told Zadie in Chicago, the stars held stories, wisdom, and prophecies. If humanity overcame its fears, they would find, hidden in the depth of night, that the stars held the secret to navigating the dark. The constellations still blazed overhead, waiting to guide us to the dawn.

CHAPTER TWENTY-FOUR

. . . . .

#ShelterUs

Zadie woke to shouting. The morning broke, overcast and drizzling. The boat knocked gently against the convent's porch rails. The water sloshed in the wake of a vessel motoring by. The convent doors were thrown open to allow the cooler air to circulate indoors. In the foyer, a cluster of nuns argued in loud voices.

"We can't force him - "

"Shelter them that come unto you - "

"- it's his church, not ours - "

" - that is not a church. It's a football stadium, a rock concert venue for that prancing prat - "

"*Charity*, Sister Theodesia," the head nun warned in a sharp snap.

"Vengeance is mine, sayeth the Lord."

"If you quote scripture at me one more time - "

"Oh, throw me out, Mother. I'll go to Texas and call the wrath of God down on his head."

Zadie shook Charlie awake. They rose, bleary-eyed, and hurried to find out what the commotion was about.

Jeb and Evelyn Whyte had just issued a televised call-to-action so outrageous that they had to see it to believe it. Sister Theo pulled the video up on her phone to show them.

"They - they didn't just . . . ?" Charlie spluttered.

The Greatest Race, as the Whytes called it, pitted their evangelical followers against the Dandelions in a match of generosity. Who will give the most? Who will give the biggest? All proceeds would go to build temporary shelters for those displaced by the hurricane.

Jeb Whyte stared straight into the camera with his ice-blue eyes.

"I challenge Zadie Byrd Gray . . . and Charlie Rider," he added almost as an afterthought, "to a friendly competition between our followers. Will she - they - accept?"

Let us pray, he concluded, for the strength to meet this challenge. The camera panned over a sea of white faces dutifully bowing their heads in the stadium tiers of the megachurch.

"Don't rise to his bait. It's a trap," Sister Theo grumbled. She'd been grinding her teeth over Jeb Whyte's antics for years. His megachurch was just over the state line in Texas. Sister Theo heard all the sordid gossip on him from the Sisters in Redemption.

"Maybe he's trying to work with us?" Charlie wondered aloud.

"He will stab you in the back and feed your kidneys to his dogs," Theo predicted contemptuously.

"Yeah, I got the sense he doesn't like me," Zadie replied with a sigh.

Theo rolled her eyes. That was an understatement. Jeb Whyte made Sister Theo hope there was a special place in hell for the believers in the blonde-haired, blue-eyed Jesus. Or a special place in heaven. She didn't really care which so long as she didn't get stuck in all eternity with that xenophobic set of Bible-thumpers.

"He *literally* told southern racists to be good Christians so God would segregate heaven after the Rapture," Theo reported. "He organizes border patrol vigilantes to turn back migrant caravans. He preaches that God made women - wombs included - to do His will and not the Devil's, namely to produce a Christian army for the purposes of a global Christian empire."

She was trying not to scream or vomit, since neither would help.

"I could throttle him," she spat. "He's raising money to build more temporary relief shelters, but he doesn't *need* temporary shelters - he's got a whole big megachurch. His church is the size of a stadium; it used to *be* the sports stadium. The entire town of Redemption, Texas, could fit inside it."

"Why can't people stay there, then?" Zadie asked, confused.

Theo shot her a pained look.

"Jeb Whyte won't let them. He'd rather charge fees at his temporary shelters."

"What can we do?" Charlie asked.

"Pray God opens his heart," the head nun sighed.

"I'd rather wring his neck than pray - "

"Theo!"

The nun crossed herself and muttered a Hail Mary for the uncharitable impulse to shake Jeb Whyte by his glossy curls. The sordid story of Redemption, Texas, convinced her that Satan had bought a vacation house there. Lord knows, it was hotter'n hell in the spring and fall, and hell on earth in the summer.

"Do you know why the low income neighborhood is nicknamed the Purg?" Theo asked. "It's named after Purgatory, the interminable waiting room of the dead. Those cardboard houses and overrated doublewides are nothing more than a flimsy shantytown built by the Outreach Ministry of Jeb's father, Joe Whyte."

The below sea level neighborhood was a development scam from the get-go. The levee wasn't designed to stop storm surges; it was an old seawall, a breaker over the marshland connected to the sewage treatment plant. When the football stadium was built, they scraped ten feet of topsoil off the area and heaped it up into a hill. Back then, Joe Whyte ran a storefront church in the suburbs of Redemption. He eyed that open space like a God-given miracle and snapped it up cheap.

"He made his fortune fleecing low income tenants displaced by waves of gentrification," Theo explained. "He was known as The Slumlord of Purgatory until he died."

Jeb Whyte was a chip off the old block. He leveraged good looks into televangelism, and solicited charitable donations for "doing the Lord's work in Redemption". Like his father, he raked in the profits, never paid a dime in taxes, and the Whytes now resided in a seventeen-thousand-square-foot mansion on the high and dry end of town.

"That levee broke because no one cared if the Purg was flooded," Sister Theo muttered. "Jeb Whyte's Greatest Race is just an attempt to solicit hundreds of millions in rebuilding donations and relief funds . . . all the while charging the residents an arm and a leg for temporary shelter. That's why he won't open the church - that and his wife Evelyn's ungodly fear of dirt, trash, and anything darker than a lily."

"Racist?" Zadie asked, not in the least surprised. Evangelical megachurches had been hotbeds of racist indoctrination for decades.

"Purity Consciousness is her term for it," Theo snarled. She pinched her nose and mimicked the woman. "Think pure, act pure, enter God's Kingdom pure of heart, mind, body, and soul."

"Have you even seen that woman in anything darker than lavender?" Sister Constance groaned to Theo.

"Cream, butter yellow, mint, pale pink . . . nope."

"Racism and megachurches are a scary combination,"

Charlie commented, a chill running down his spine.

"Given the track record of the Catholic Church, we don't like to cast aspersions. Glass houses and stones and all that," Theo replied piously, folding her hands into her sleeves, "but if it takes one to know one, we recognize the rhetoric, the leanings, the *code* of religious oppression, if you will."

"That husband and wife team is a nightmare," the head nun agreed with a sigh.

Charlie and Zadie exchanged long looks. Something had to be done. Someone had to do something. And in the leaderful movement, that someone meant them.

Together, they released a video statement in response to the Greatest Race challenge.

"A crisis is not a sports game," Zadie said. "This is not the time for competitions - friendly or otherwise. It is time for unprecedented generosity and cooperation. We need to work together, to pool our resources, not pit them against one another in petty games of ego."

"We cannot measure generosity in numbers alone," Charlie added. "A single dollar from a struggling family is worth more than a billionaire's entire fortune. Generosity is relative to the sacrifices we personally make to offer the gift. Keep giving. Keep helping. Keep showing up. We know we will."

They didn't have time to follow the reaction to their refusal to play games with Jeb Whyte. They didn't track the mutterings and rumbles, the outrage and insult that swept through those among his two million followers who took the rejection as a slap in the face.

Sister Theo had come up with a wild idea for resisting Jeb Whyte's disaster profiteering . . . and there's nothing a dandelion likes better than a wild idea.

CHAPTER TWENTY-FIVE

. . . . .

Crashing the Megachurch

In the uppermost balcony of Jeb Whyte's megachurch, Zadie, Charlie, and Theo crouched in the shadows just over the main stage. They'd traveled through the night, an odyssey that began with Barrie ferrying them out of the flooded-out neighborhoods, walking several miles to an ad-hoc car rental place, then driving through the darkness across Northern Louisiana to avoid the worst of the road closures. At dawn, they'd arrived in Redemption, Texas, and managed to find a much-needed cup of coffee at the only diner that was open on Sundays.

They had slipped into the megachurch with the rest of the worshippers and made their way up the multi-tiered corridors. Zadie peeked over the balcony, glaring at the spectacle below. Charlie kneeled beside her, loosening the ties on a roll of fabric. Sister Theodesia, dressed in plainclothes with the beads of her rosary tucked discretely under her white polo shirt, muttering disparaging remarks - interspersed with *Hail Marys* for penance - under her breath. The nun would not describe the charade of a service below as holy, but most of the seventy thousand worshippers crammed into the tiered seats would. An enormous television screen expanded the image of Jeb Whyte and the immaculately-attired Evelyn into looming giants as they sanctimoniously prayed for God to help the storm victims.

In the folding chair section near the front, the residents of the Purg shifted angrily. They didn't need God to help them -

269

except to intervene in Jeb Whyte's greed. In the best seats in the house, the plush armchairs embossed with donors' names, the uniformly white faces scowled at the restless poor. If there seemed to be more Purg residents than usual, it stood to reason: the insubstantial doublewide house of worship they usually went to was submerged. If they seemed nervous, the regular worshippers from the high and dry suburbs of Redemption chalked it up to awe at the enormity of the megachurch. The backpacks they shoved under their seats had passed through the metal detectors at the front entrance. Flooded out of home, they now carried their belongings on their backs and slept in a burgeoning tent city not far away, unable to afford the steep prices that Jeb Whyte charged at his temporary shelters.

The Reverend was in a holy-rolling high fervor. Just as the choir launched into song, Zadie caught Charlie's eye. He winked at Theo. On the count of three, they dropped the banner:

SHELTER THOSE WHO COME UNTO YOU.

One hundred feet long and twenty feet wide, it was bigger than a semi-truck. As it unfurled, startled gasps and surprised cries lifted throughout the congregation. Seventy thousand heads turned to gape. At that moment, the residents of the Purg surged onto the stage. Two youths pulled a second banner from under their shirts and stretched it out.

#ShelterUs

A group of mothers with children grabbed the microphone.

"Please. We're asking that this church shelter us in our time of need. Make the shelters free . . . or let us stay here in the church. Thousands of people can sleep in these tiers, in the aisles, across the cushions of the seats. Let us stay. Like Mary and Joseph, we have nowhere else to go."

Their appeal was televised to two million worshippers. The eyes of the children fixed on Jeb and Evelyn. The shape of their plea hung on their lips. The mothers fell to their knees to pray for divine intervention.

"If you believe in doing your Christian duty, join us in asking this church to give us shelter from the storm," they asked the shocked worshippers.

Dead silence greeted their words.

Then, one of the children grabbed the mic. She'd been in a children's theater production last year, playing one of the Lost Boys in Peter Pan. With that show in mind, she implored the crowd to show their support.

"If you think Reverend Whyte should help us, clap your hands!" the kid piped with youthful surety, fully expecting the adults to do the right thing. They had clapped to revive Tinkerbell last year; why wouldn't they clap to help her family find shelter?

Jeb Whyte made a slicing motion at his throat, urging the sound technicians to cut the mic. Evelyn gestured for the security team to clear the stage.

Then someone began to clap.

No one knew that the lone woman in a white shirt and pleated trousers was Sister Theodosia clapping as a way of calling down the power of God to open their hearts, but one after another, people joined in. At a ragged cheer from the kids, a wave of sound erupted, leaping up from the seats, crashing like a thunderous waterfall onto Jeb and Evelyn Whyte.

The Holy Spirit was at work in the unexpected interruption of the Sunday service. Many thought the Whytes had orchestrated the whole affair. They often pulled stunts like this in their services: an "unexpected" altar call, or a miracle boy rising from his wheelchair through the power of prayer. Every move of their show was carefully rehearsed, but the congregation assumed this was just yet another one of the surprise miracles they had come to expect at the Redemption Megachurch's Sunday Service. In minutes, caught in the public eye, the phone line flooded with messages from congregation members. With their biggest donor leading the standing ovation, the Whytes forced matching pairs of tight smiles over their lips and agreed to shelter the displaced residents of the Purg, and to make their temporary shelters free of charge. Reverend Jeb turned the unexpected action into a fundraising appeal and doubled his weekly haul by invoking Noah and the Ark. By the time Evelyn Whyte spotted the tiny sharpie-inked message in the bottom of the giant banner, the instigators of the clever action were long gone.

She hacked the words off with her wardrobe assistant's scissors. Her eyes narrowed into slits in her make-up laden face. Her lips pinched in fury as she read the words.

God works in mysterious ways. Love, the Dandelion Insurrection.

CHAPTER TWENTY-SIX

. . . . .

Texas Billboards

Texas. A state so wide that, on a windy day, the clouds stampeded like cattle. Charlie and Zadie sped west across the immense landscape in an electric rental vehicle powered on the huge Texas windmills that dotted the horizon line. Theo had agreed to stay with the Purg residents and make sure the megachurch didn't renege on their promises. Charlie and Zadie dodged the wrath of the Whytes - for the moment.

As soon as they left the coastal regions, evidence of the dry season abounded. The land rose and fell, surprising Charlie, who had imagined Texas to be as flat as a checkerboard with alternating squares of oil fields and cattle ranges. Instead, sprawling cottonwood trees lined the stream gullies. The repetition of fields and patched-together wooden houses was interrupted by the occasional august ranch mansion set back from the highway behind a cattle brand bearing gate and a row of trees. The summer had scorched the life out of the earth. The fall withered to a crisp in the drought. The hurricane had rolled northeast from the mouth of the Mississippi, sending no relief to Western Texas. The cattle hung their hot, tired heads as they stood in the crumbling edges of gullies.

In between country twangs and Christian scripture, the radio bemoaned the hell-on-earth that had arrived that summer in Texas. Temperatures had rivaled Bombay. Heat stroke became the leading cause of death. Energy bills spiked as air conditioners stopped being a convenience and turned into a life-saving necessity. Radio hosts joked that if NASA wanted to terraform Mars, they could do practice maneuvers in Texas. The air still tasted smoky around the edges from a series of summer brushfires that had been nicknamed the Texas Barbeque.

God is testing us, folks, the radio announcer commented, *pray for rain and praise His name. Amen.*

Zadie switched the radio off.

"Evangelicals bought up all the stations in the Bible Belt," she informed Charlie. "It's impossible to cross Texas without being told you're going to Hell."

"One more scorched earth summer," Charlie replied grimly, "and they'll be right."

They drove through a recent burn area, the blackened ground still smoking. Charred cattle carcasses heaped up on the roadside; they'd run trying to escape the flames only to asphyxiate from the smoke. In the distance, fracking well towers rose, the release vent pipe waving its flaming flag in a plume of heat and invisible carcinogens. They breathed a sigh of relief when they reached the far side of the burn.

Then the billboards started.

Guns 'n ammo.

Sex 'n titties.

Abortion stops a beating heart.

Jesus saves.

Family and Birth Centers.

The Rapture is nigh.

Adoption is a woman's right.

Lock, Stock, and Smoking Barrel.

Girls! Girls! Girls!

The themes repeated without a trace of irony or chagrin, the images standing twenty feet tall and executed in the classic

Texan larger-than-life style. The crowning glory was a pair of giant cutout figures towering outside the commercial district of an upcoming town: an eighty-foot Jesus in agony on the cross and a gun-toting cowboy tipping his hat across the highway. On one side was a church. On the other was a topless bar and whorehouse named the Rapture. The slogan, scrawled in neon flashing lights, proclaimed: *It's a man's world.*

Just after the church was one of the advertised Birth Centers, a bland set of buildings with a pastel pink logo faded by the sun.

"Quite a racket they've got going," Charlie remarked as he craned his head to catch a glimpse of the fertility and adoption clinic on the next block. "What's a baby going for these days? Fifty grand?"

On the other side of town, increasing in size and frequency as they neared, were a repeating chain of anti-abortion billboards, fertility clinics, adoption centers, and the birth homes for women denied access to any other form of reproductive healthcare in a three hundred mile radius.

"Do you think the mothers get a check if they hand over their babies?" Charlie wondered aloud.

Zadie didn't answer. She spoke only after they'd circled the next city's bypass and the last Birth Center had faded from the rearview.

"It's illegal."

"What is?"

"Baby farming," she answered in white-lipped fury. "But this racket weaves in and out of a dozen loopholes. I wouldn't be surprised if one person owned all of this, raking in the dough because abortion is banned, charging expectant mothers steep prices for staying in the Birth Centers, and then collecting fifty-thousand-dollar adoption fees, too."

"Let's go back," Charlie said abruptly, a flash of anger hitting him. "Let's go pretend to adopt and write an exposé about it."

"No."

Zadie's answer was flat and hard. Her eyes fixed on the western horizon like the end of Texas couldn't come soon enough for her. They had to pick and choose their battles. They couldn't fight them all, not all at once, not everywhere. They were in enough trouble with the evangelicals as it was. Zadie's shoulders prickled and her gut clenched. She wouldn't sleep easy until she and Jeb Whyte no longer shared a state.

"Keep going, Charlie."

Texas went on forever.

CHAPTER TWENTY-SEVEN

. . . . .

God's Will or the Devil's Work

"Turn around," Charlie growled.

"What? Why?" she exclaimed, startling, twisting at the wheel to look at him.

They had switched turns in the driver's seat in the middle of Texas near a series of endless feedlots. Charlie had his head bowed and his fingers swishing over his phone, reading a message. Zadie swerved around a tumbleweed as she waited for him to explain.

"Because I'm going to wring his little neck," he threatened.

"Who?"

"Jeb Whyte. He just issued a public challenge to debate. Strongly worded, almost a dare."

He held up the phone, showing her the video of Reverend Jeb Whyte at a press conference. The preacher called for an open debate on whether or not Hurricane Eve was caused by climate change.

"He's claiming the hurricane was either God's Will or the Devil's Work, or both, but it isn't climate change . . . and he'll debate anyone who says differently."

"Oh, for heaven's sake," Zadie groaned. "There is no debate. It's science. It's happening. It's caused by humans."

They couldn't debate fact. Not against an evangelical convinced that data was a hoax and the Doomsday was nigh. Zadie listened as Charlie played the video clip. Reverend Jeb Whyte wanted to turn this challenge into the Scopes Monkey

Trial of the new millennium. Evolution vs. creation. God vs. science. The Lord's servant vs. the Devil's minions. He'd use climate to put everything else in the line of fire: the Rights of Nature, democracy, women's rights, the beingness of elements and species, whether or not the Earth was alive or a dead object, whether mankind should have dominion over it, whether the United States was intended to be a Christian Nation. In three short minutes of an announcement, Jeb Whyte managed to link them all together into one debate on climate change.

Zadie blew out a hot breath of frustration.

"Tell him to go jump in a lake. Why should you - "

"No, not me," Charlie interrupted.

She frowned, confused.

"You, Zadie," he said. "Reverend Whyte wants to debate you."

Shocked, she pulled over on the shoulder of the road. The sagebrush quivered in the harsh winds outside. A semi-truck thundered past. A tumbleweed bounced across the pavement, coming to rest against a wire fence. They talked for an hour, started driving again, weighing the pros and cons, considering their options. At last, Charlie suggested that she just meet with Reverend Jeb Whyte.

"Ask him to meet us in Albuquerque," he suggested. "Neutral territory."

They could at least hear him out. If Zadie managed to cream him in a debate, it could tip the scales on climate action.

It sounded reasonable, but two days later, when the meeting had been arranged and she waited for Jeb Whyte to arrive, Zadie felt like bait left out for a shark. Her nerves fluttered in anxiety. Gnawing cannibal butterflies chewed her up inside. Purplish bruised bags hung under her sleepless eyes.

It's just a meeting, she kept telling herself as panic attacks stole the breath from her chest. Zadie hunched her shoulders under the florescent lights of the meeting room. The collar of her blouse tapped her throat with a tickling, choking sensation. She jiggled her knees, wondering again why she had agreed to this.

She suspected Jeb Whyte's entire church had been praying for a lightning bolt to smack her dead. Short of God's clean intervention, they had laid their hands of divine power on Reverend Jeb Whyte in daily televised pray-ins, imbuing him with God's might to conquer demons and drive out the Devil. She'd been referred to by every woman's-name-turned-epithet that the Bible could sling at her. Jezebel was the least of it. Last Sunday's sermon had warned that the Anti-Christ had appeared in heels and a short skirt, and that Zadie - who they called Satan's spawn - tempted the flesh as well as imperiled their immortal souls.

"I think that was a compliment," Charlie tried to joke, squeezing her hand and attempting to make her smile.

Charlie had offered to stand in for her in the debate, even leaping in last minute so Jeb Whyte couldn't back out.

"I'm not afraid of him," Charlie declared gallantly, striking a pose of bravado.

But Zadie shook her head. There was no victory in sending Charlie in like a knight in shining armor while she stayed locked in an ivory tower wringing her hands. If they did the debate, people had to see the truth that gender mattered, that her curves and breasts and female form *was* at stake here, along with every other woman's. She'd rather stand up there with Inez, Kinap, Elisha, Meera, Tansy, Bramble, Alex, and every person targeted by Whyte's hate. But one person had to stand and that person was she.

If she agreed to the debate, that is. This meeting was a

prerequisite. They had to lay down ground rules, agree to the terms and format. Zadie had insisted on doing it in person. She didn't want to officially meet Jeb Whyte for the first time on national television. Their encounter in San Francisco hardly counted. Zadie unclenched her fingers from their whitened and reddened fists. She stilled her agitated fidgeting. She took a deep breath. She rolled her shoulders.

The door cracked open.

Jeb Whyte stuck his head in.

Charlie was just down the hall, on the phone with Tansy. Their conversation was running overtime and Zadie silently urged him to hurry up.

"Hello, hello," Jeb greeted her, entering and flashing his set of pearly whites as he sat down in the chair opposite her. "This was a good idea, this meeting. Takes the tension out of the debate. Nothing like a face-to-face before we show our faces to the whole world."

He gave a taut chuckle, a dead thing divorced from humor and warmth. Zadie stared coldly back.

"I haven't agreed to debate yet."

"Zadie . . . " Jeb shifted and hitched his chair closer.

Too close.

Zadie's panic flared. Her chair was backed against the wall. She was cornered, trapped. She bit back her bile. He eyed her with the gentle compassion of a Hollywood Jesus rescuing one of his wandering lambs.

"I thought we might start by praying," he suggested with a crocodile smile.

He reached out and patted her knee.

"Take. Your. Hand. Off. Me."

Zadie gnashed out the words. Rage boiled in her eyes. Every fiber of her body wanted to backhand him across the jaw.

How dare he! The arrogance. The presumption. They were not friends. Not acquaintances. They were not even neutral strangers. He was the closest thing she had to an enemy. He would be, if she hadn't set her heart against the notion of enemies long ago.

His palm hesitated, hot and heavy on her knee. She stabbed him with her eyes, waiting until he pulled away. She could have moved, jerked her knee away, but in this moment, the shame of retreat belonged solely to him, not her. She had not invaded; he had. She would not back away from her space; she would force him to move back. Something ancient bubbled in her veins, a seething fury from the depths of millennia. There, in this moment, was the pattern of the patriarchy: Presume. Grab. Smirk. Repeat.

"This stops here. Now."

He attempted to look confused, but she saw it: the startled flash of understanding, the many layers of story that lay between them, past, present, and future. Perverted faiths and persecuted beliefs, burnt bodies of women, rapes of the feminine and the Earth, the assumption of access, primacy, privilege, and importance.

Memories of men assaulted her. Suddenly she was ten, pinched and squeezed by an uncle-in-law at a Christmas party. She was twelve, spinning bottles in a defiant attempt to climb the school pecking order. She was thirteen, unable to say stop. She was sixteen, alone, afraid, and pregnant. She was seventeen, stripping in clubs for money. She was twenty-five, still stripping because it was the only avenue of work left open after the government labeled Charlie a terrorist. She was twenty-six, lies about her sex life smeared across the tabloids to ruin her relationship with the man she loved.

She was caged behind bars. She was hiding and silenced.

She was hit hard across the cheek. She was herself and a thousand others. She was the midwife of the world. She had been outlawed long ago, called a witch, whipped, dunked, hung, and burned. She was the living Earth, objectified; she was women turned into property. She was the feminine enclosed, the commons raped and plundered. She had been through every trial - fire, water, earth, and air. She was eternal and still rising. And nothing would stop her now.

Zadie sensed the words of wrath boiling and toiling in her chest, demanding to be unleashed, the promise and the prophecy too long ignored. She knew, right then, with the histories - no, the *her* stories - of a trillion lifetimes churning through her that she would not play his game. She would not let him set the terms, would not let the weight of her notoriety draw attention to his words.

Hundreds of millions of people would tune in to see her take him on. Half were hoping she'd annihilate him. The other half lusted after a modern-day witch burning. If she debated him, they might see her take him down, word by word, point by point, view by view. But he'd get to proclaim his beliefs from the largest pulpit ever offered to him.

And she would have handed him the audience.

"I'm not playing that game," she said.

The debate was a trap. She refused to walk into it. For thousands of years, this trap had been laid, snaring them all into a toxic horror story. People like Jeb Whyte had farmed outrage for fame and fortune. He'd make millions no matter the outcome of the debate. His megachurch viewership had only grown since he began attacking her.

Enough was enough.

"I'm not debating you," she said.

Women, the Earth, the lives of other humans . . . they did

not exist for his pleasure and profit. She told him this in stark, uncompromising tones. He spluttered objections. She stopped him. His turn to speak was done. She had eight thousand years of history's time to reclaim. And not just her, but all those who had been silenced.

"We don't have time for you anymore. You are done. You had centuries to build your vision of the world. We've seen how that turned out. You're done."

She rose, a rare clarity coming over her. She was reclaiming her time. She would not debate his pettiness and narcissism. There was too much else to do. The world was moving too fast to get stuck in the mud with him. The changes - for better or for worse - were coming too soon to let him set the terms of this debate.

"You're chickening out?!" he squawked, shocked.

Zadie paused at the door.

"You know what happens when someone chickens out of a car-to-car bullheaded charge?" she asked him softly.

His face contorted in confusion.

"Nothing," she told him. "That's the beauty of it."

"You can't walk away from this," he warned her, smirking. "It's like letting me win."

Zadie chuckled softly. War and debates all worked the same. You lined up on opposite sides, charged in, and someone came out declaring themselves the winner. That didn't mean the winners were right. Only that they were the last ones left standing.

"You can't win if I don't play along," she said.

She was turning the game on its head.

CHAPTER TWENTY-EIGHT

. . . . .

Blackout and Boycott

Jeb Whyte claimed Zadie Byrd Gray wasn't well.

"The poor thing's out of her mind. We must pray for her. She's sick," he and Evelyn said in their next televised prayer circle.

"Yes, I *am* sick," Zadie answered. "Utterly sick of this disgusting charade. I refuse to let that man use me to boost his twisted messaging to millions of viewers. If people want to hear my views, they should tune into what the Dandelions are doing."

Zadie called for a blackout and boycott of Jeb Whyte. He thrived on their attention; even negative press served his egotism. They had to starve him with silence. Instead of screaming about the offensiveness of his last sermon, she asked the Dandelion Insurrection to talk about the solutions, alternatives, and efforts of people working for positive change. She asked them to lift up the people who were building real democracy, working for justice and inclusivity, promoting respect and dignity and equity in the world. She asked them to flood the Alternet with the world they longed to live in.

When the press wanted their reactions to Jeb Whyte's Doomsday and Apocalypse rhetoric that claimed the climate crisis was God's will to bring on the Rapture, the Dandelions talked about getting the stalled green jobs bill back on track. When the press tried to interview the Dandelions about Reverend Jeb Whyte's racism, the Dandelions spoke exclusively about the racial justice programs working for real solutions. When the press wanted comments on Jeb Whyte's obnoxious prosperity gospel sermons, they bought up economic justice campaigns. Each time someone tried to line them up on the battlefield of Good and Evil, the Dandelions refused to be conscripted. War wasn't just fought overseas; it was being fomented here at home. The two-party duopoly and the media both profited from the divisions, fears, and animosity of a nation divided by lies, half-truths, slants, and spins. Zadie asked the Dandelions to resist all attempts to be recruited and conscripted into hatred. Instead, she asked them to use love, vision, courage, and solutions to take up time and space in the media. Sound bite by sound bite, line by line, column by column, they stole the focus away from Jeb Whyte. They reclaimed the airtime his vitriolic followers had tried to take from their efforts for real democracy. They turned him into a ghost passing through this world without a voice.

And they didn't just take his time, they also popped up at his events and stole his show with demonstrations and banner drops. It got to the point where Jeb Whyte couldn't make a public appearance without one of the Dandelions' ideas becoming the talk of the nation. Everyone had to dance to their tune ... it was the loudest, boldest, catchiest, most popular music around.

"We're dandelions," Zadie reminded the country. "This is how we roll. We dance. We swarm. When they try to box us in with one option, we burst free with dozens of others."

All across the world, a tidal shift was underway. The changes had been flowing in, wave after wave, inexorably: civil rights, human rights, women's rights, LBGTQIA rights, Indigenous Peoples' rights, poor people's rights, the Rights of Nature ... nothing could stop this tide, not the seawalls or dams or genocides or corsets, not prisons or bombs, or chains of poverty or racism. They could slow the people for a moment, make them batter like droplets against hard stones, but the next wave would go crashing over the top. Zadie unleashed this tidal wave into the political sphere, chasing Jeb Whyte's heels with the incessant rhythm of change. Wherever he went, there they were: hordes of people, protesters, hounding him, haunting him . . . and yet, they never said his name, never mentioned his opinions, never spoke of him at all.

They simply stole his airtime, one camera after another, with their giant banners and songs and chanted slogans.

Another world is possible.

Imagine the future.

Be like the Dandelions!

They lifted up banners with paintings of community gardens, circles of people talking, marches for peace, laughing children, cities turning green with urban agriculture, the earth gleaming in her beauty. Image by image, day after day, they reclaimed the time stolen by the dominators of the past. They set the stage and told the story of the world in a whole new way.

Jeb Whyte didn't like it . . . but he didn't matter. He could scream to high heaven until smoke poured out of his ears. The Dandelions cut off his megaphones, one by one, leaving him wailing like a tantrum-throwing toddler at an ever-shrinking volume.

"If you don't want to see a world promoted by hate," Zadie said, "starve it. Boycott it. Abandon it. Organize every other person to do the same. Invite the supporters of hate to join the party of love. Reach out the hand of reconciliation. Build bridges off that lonely island of contempt."

Bit by bit, the silencing and shunning muffled the hate, shrank it down, narrowed its power, and undercut its fear mongering. They turned the volume up on the world to come, the vision of the future where every person was valued and cared for, a world where the Earth had rights and the children had a chance, a world where all races were welcome, a world where all people sat at the table of decision-making.

An hour went by without a mention of Jeb Whyte in the corporate media. Then a day. Then a week.

Then, he retaliated with an announcement no one could ignore.

CHAPTER TWENTY-NINE

. . . . .

Whyte Makes Right

Reverend Jebediah Whyte had heard *the Call*. Like George W. Bush before him, he was running for president. The Lord had spoken to him and said that America had a crisis of morality that could only be addressed by God's appointed spokesperson bringing sanctity and godliness back to the highest office in the land.

Whyte Makes Right was his running slogan. His followers helpfully rolled out other taglines:

The Whyte Guy For the Job

That's Why They Call It The Whyte House

Whyte On!

#WhytePower

In forty-eight hours, Reverend Jeb Whyte's announcement shattered the news cycle. The Democratic Party had a slew of less-than-inspiring candidates. The Republicans had a Christian revivalist prophet with a glittering smile and a rock concert stadium. Charlie had four hundred emails and his phone wasn't taking any more messages. They'd heard Jeb Whyte's announcement on the radio during the four hour drive north from Bangor to Northern Maine, headed home for the holidays. When they arrived in the St. John Valley, they saw that, despite the snow squalls and frigid December weather, a herd of reporters had taken up residence at the bottom of Zadie's father's driveway. They burst into action as Charlie and

Zadie pulled up, shouting out questions and demanding their reaction to Jeb Whyte's announcement.

Charlie and Zadie waded through the barrage of questions without a word, but as night fell, the blizzard thickened, and the news reports rolled in, it was clear that some kind of response was required. Jeb Whyte's candidacy shook the nation. The specter of a megachurch doomsday preacher in the Oval Office cracked the country into two camps - the terrified and the elated.

Over the next week, political shock rattled the country. *Whyte Power* groups marched in the streets with *Whyte Pride* banners. Evangelicals held pray-ins as rallies. The stock market roller-coasted between panic and pragmatic expectations that a climate-change denying president like Whyte would preserve fossil fuel extraction projects. Stock in tear gas and rubber bullets leapt to new heights of investment, a chilling warning of clashes between citizens and cops. Redemption Megachurch members went around singing *Joy To The World.*

But for millions, the idea of a Jeb Whyte presidency unleashed a cry of horror. Nightmares, old and buried, living and looming, rose up and reared their ugly heads. Reverend Jeb Whyte embodied the fears of half the nation and the hopes of a small, but vocal subset. He was a Christian family man with staggering personal wealth and a prosperity gospel that goose-stepped in perfect alignment with myths of meritocracy and the "work ethic" of wage slavery.

To feminists, he was the hammer of witches resuscitated, misogynistic hatred wrapped up in the pseudo-sanctity of higher authority.

To Black Americans, he was a modern version of the wealthy slave owner, toasted in circles where racism and white supremacy went unquestioned.

To Jews, he was the popular demagogue, the shadow of Hitler with a built-in Third Reich, millions of fanatical followers hanging on his towering speeches and thinly-veiled metaphors of hate.

To Indigenous Peoples, he was a renewed assault of Manifest Destiny and might-makes-right. His winner-takes-all conquest ideology renewed the threat to their existence.

To the poor, the ones who knew from direct experience that hard work is rarely rewarded fairly, he was the new face of feudalism, the self-proclaimed lord and king, the boss and billionaire, the next plutocrat who would throw their lifeblood into the machinery of profit.

The list went on: migrants, transients, activists, LGBTQIA, Muslims, Asians, Latinx, Indigenous Peoples . . . in short anyone who wasn't a cookie cutter of Jeb Whyte and his wife was appalled by the announcement of the presidential run.

The only ones not horrified were his opposing political party.

"We'll knock him out of the park," the Democratic Party chair boasted, almost gleeful at the immense outrage Whyte's announcement triggered. Where else could the appalled voters run but straight into the arms of his party?

"He's a maniac. He won't make it past the primaries," predicted their leading contender for presidential candidacy.

"We're already raking in millions," the head of fundraising reported. Nothing worked as well as fear for generating donations.

For a solid week, terror built, fueled by fundraising appeals and news reports filled with a litany of comparisons to Nazis, apocalyptic predictions, warnings of pogroms and lynchings. It was a well-oiled approach to greasing the wheels of fundraising:

donate now or the end of the world will come! The Democratic Party didn't need to promote a visionary platform. They just had to be less scary than the nightmare that was Jeb Whyte. People came running to them in droves. Millions poured into the party coffers. Milquetoast candidates, long denounced as corporate shills, shone like knights in shining armor by comparison. Faced with a christo-fascist, people were willing to back the Democratic Party's agents of empire and corporatist puppets. They were forced to ignore the unspoken agenda of rebuilding power for the wealthy. Already, the progressive candidates were being squeezed off the field as too "out there", "fringe", and "unable to unite the party to defeat Jeb Whyte".

Brad Andersen watched it all like a chessboard, projecting thirteen moves ahead, tracking the swings of voters left, right, down the middle, and those who threw their hands up in disgust and planned to stay home on Election Day. He calculated the odds and told his bosses they would lose.

"You're making a mistake - or a hundred mistakes - you're underestimating Whyte's appeal on the right ... and overestimating the attraction of your candidates on the left."

Jeb Whyte would win because he had a vision - God-sent, he claimed - and a plan for America. He could explain it in thirty seconds without mentioning the hated word: corporations. He promised to restore the good old days and stop the discomfiting upheaval of change.

"When you don't stand for anything," Andersen warned his party, "you'll fall before everything."

No one listened. They were too busy counting dollars instead of people. Andersen slammed up against brick walls and deaf ears. He was close to conceding defeat, but he still had one trick left, a magic card up his sleeve. Brad Andersen dialed the number he held in reserve for the most dire circumstances. The name of his old flame still made his atrophied heart flinch. To pull off this maneuver, he would need money, and lots of it. A Texas billionaire jilted at the altar for a political campaign was nothing to trifle with ... but he knew Mona Gold like few others. It would take a miracle to get her backing for a presidential candidate. Fortunately, Andersen had a once-in-a-lifetime chance - the kind of long shot Mona Gold couldn't resist.

"Andersen, dahling, what can I do for you?"

The very tone of her voice made his heart go cold ... and his veins burn hotter than fire.

CHAPTER THIRTY

. . . . .

Run, Charlie, Run

Two weeks before Christmas, Brad Andersen knocked on the front door of Bill Gray's farmhouse. Snow plastered the earth. Early dusk gathered its long shadows. A row of rainbow twinkle lights gleamed inside the frost-glazed window. At the sharp rap on the door, Charlie and Zadie looked up from making popcorn chains while videoconferencing with Inez, Tansy, and Kinap.

Dealing with Jeb Whyte's toxic brew of christo-fascism was like shoveling the porch steps in the middle of a blizzard. They cleared off the most pressing dangers, de-escalated tensions, countered hate, calmed fear . . . but the icy storm of animosity kept charging forward until they felt blinded by the constant assaults. Passions ran high. Polarizations deepened. Antagonism reached a heated pitch. Screaming matches erupted on talk shows. Fistfights broke out in the streets. Jeb Whyte literally frothed at the mouth one Sunday. Doomsday predictions - both scientific and spiritual - increased.

Brad Andersen's knock on the door was the least of the unpleasant surprises thrown at them that week. Zadie's father got to the door first, mistaking the man for yet another pesky reporter.

"They're on vacation," Bill Gray barked at the man. "That's what Charlie's mom put out in a statement and that's what you should have respected."

The DC fixer murmured something back that triggered an explosive snort of disbelief from the short, temperamental farmer. Zadie and Charlie rose from the table to help forestall a fight.

"What are you doing here?" Zadie asked.

Brad flashed a slick smile that strained at the edges. Bill Gray scowled back with all the suspicion and dislike of a radical confronted with the stench of Capitol Hill politics.

"I'm here to ask Charlie - "

" - if he'll run for president," Bill interrupted, spitting out the news, annoyed with the man.

"I'm too young," Charlie answered, surprised to the core, "and I'm not even a party member."

"There are some in the party - myself included - who are willing to make exceptions . . . and get the age requirement lowered," Brad Andersen explained glibly. "Your rankings are higher than all the other political frontrunners combined. Why, in the next election, we could make a clean sweep of it: House, Senate, Oval Office. Think of the power!"

Charlie privately thought that Brad Andersen and his party thought about power far too much already.

"I don't support dinosaurs like the two-party system," he pointed out bluntly.

"Zadie," Brad appealed, turning his charm on, "talk some sense into your young man. It's the opportunity of a lifetime!"

Zadie wore a matching expression to her father, dark brows furrowed into a single line, lips nearly white with tensed irritation.

Watch out, Brad, Charlie thought silently.

"Which leading party member did you have in mind for vice president?" Zadie demanded to know, mentally going through the list of powerful potentials that hoped to ride into the White

House on Charlie Rider's famous coattails. The bidding would be fierce; this term's vice president would be next in line for the presidential nomination in the following election.

Brad Andersen flashed a triumphant smile.

"That's a matter of debate, but I'm rooting for you, Zadie Byrd Gray! I think *you* should run as Charlie's VP."

The young couple's expressions contorted. Zadie made a strangled sound. Brad Andersen's smug smile broadened, assuming they were stunned with the honor.

"Have a great trip back to DC," she choked out. "Watch out for moose on the drive south."

"But, but," Andersen stammered, confused by the reaction.

She clapped him on the shoulder.

"You blew it, Brad," she confided with a shrug. "You got us all wrong."

The man's mouth fell open.

"Wait - it's - I don't understand," he cried.

"We're revolutionaries, not politicians," Charlie answered.

"And of the two of us," Zadie added, "I would have been your candidate. Charlie's really just a glorified speechwriter."

She closed the door firmly between them.

"Charlie, wait!" the man called, voice muffled, gloved fist pounding on the door.

"Oooh, the arrogance!" Zadie groaned as she stormed back into the kitchen.

"At least he didn't expect you to be a mere first lady," Bill pointed out.

"You weren't even a little bit tempted?" Charlie asked, frowning. The words *glorified speechwriter* echoed harshly in his ears.

"Maybe last fall we would have talked it over," Zadie confessed with a shrug, "but participatory democracy is the way forward, not putting brilliant, but hamstrung-by-the-system, candidates into office."

"But what about Jeb Whyte?" Charlie reminded her. "Doesn't that change the game a little?"

Zadie shrugged.

"Not for me."

Charlie scrubbed his face with his palms. For him, the political landscape had suddenly, irrevocably changed. Instead of questing toward a vision of people-powered democracy, the citizens had pulled an about-face to deal with the sudden danger at their backs. Just by announcing his campaign, Jeb Whyte had sent tremors through the nation. The real democracy projects had been reeling. Hundreds of nascent projects withered. Entire systems of beneficial programs collapsed. The democracy experiments were abandoned for the fistfight of a high-stakes electoral race. They were all gearing up to fight a desperate battle for the presidency . . . and even if they won, the next eight years would be caught up in Capitol Hill politics, trying to survive a political system designed to disempower them.

"It's just not fair," Zadie muttered. "Jeb Whyte should never have been allowed to run."

Charlie grimaced. Technically, it was fair. It was Constitutional. Anyone could run for president. But he knew what she meant. On a cosmic level where the gods and demons duked it out, and the Fates tied and snipped the threads of human life, it didn't seem fair that their country could be on the verge of the most exciting political shift since the 1770s and be derailed by a supposedly-Christian worldview so regressive that even Jesus would be ashamed to be associated with it.

The next week was hell.

Someone - Andersen, they suspected - had leaked that

Charlie Rider was considering a presidential run. It put him in a tough spot. Charlie felt pressured to respond. Demonstrations erupted across the country. People chanted: *Run, Charlie, run!* Counter protesters morphed the slogan into a sinister warning: *Run, Charlie, run.* He shut off his phone ringer and let the message box fill up. Unable to reach him, their friends called Zadie.

"Why didn't they ask you?" Inez blurted out, straight up, for which Zadie loved her. The feisty Latina told her not to commit any felonies in the next few years. "Someday, you and me, *chica.* We've got a date for the White House."

"Is he insane?" Kinap asked. "It's a rotten job. He can do more by staying out of it and pushing whoever is president to do what's right."

Zadie agreed.

Tansy uncharacteristically had no opinion.

"I'm proud as brass tacks of y'all no matter what. Can't say I fancy the job of White House counsel for you, though, not with y'all's penchant for breaking laws."

Tucker and Alex got into a shouting match over it. Alex, a public servant in her heart, thought Charlie should run. Tucker argued that the job would break his friend's heart and steal his soul.

Olli opposed a presidential run on the grounds that it would undermine the participatory democracy movement even further as the campaign heated up.

"Everyone will just give up and phone bank for Charlie as president," he warned Zadie in a panicked phone call. "The *Vote For Charlie and the Democrats* machine will distract everyone from our efforts."

Elisha, Meera, and Frankie felt similarly.

"Don't get us wrong," Elisha exclaimed, her voice tinny

through the speakerphone, her two friends agreeing in the background, "we'd vote for him . . . if we could vote."

"But we can't," Frankie put in. "So, don't give up on the kinds of democracy that we can be involved in, please."

"By the next election, it'll be too late to act on climate," Meera pointed out, "and instead of having a role as decision-makers through participatory democracy, we'll just be teens begging politicians to do something sane for once."

"I mean, to be totally honest, we'd be okay with both things," Elisha added, "Charlie as president and participatory democracy. But, he can't be in two places at once."

"And neither can you," Meera told Zadie. "You'd have to campaign with him."

"Then be first lady," Frankie put in,"which is just another way of saying you're nothing more than Charlie Rider's sidekick."

Girlfriend, wife, lover, whore . . . first lady or vice president was a step up from the usual litany, but it was still a step down in the equality of their relationship. That grated on Zadie's nerves. She tried to gloss it over, transform it into a pearl, put a shine on the situation and make something beautiful out of it . . . but she couldn't. She wouldn't.

The tension between them seethed and tightened over the next ten days. Charlie disappeared for hours at a time, claiming that he had to help his mother put up Christmas lights or that his grand-père needed a ride to the doctor's. But one afternoon, Charlie's grandfather put lies to his grandson's claims by driving over and pounding on Zadie's door.

"Brad Andersen is in our driveway," he huffed, "waiting like *un loup garou*, a bloodthirsty werewolf, to snatch up my grandson. You have to come talk to him."

Zadie groaned, grabbed her coat, and drove over to

Charlie's mom's house with Valier. The place was mobbed by reporters. Even Brad Andersen couldn't get close, hollering at her from the back of the pack, his voice barely audible over the shouted questions of the media. Natalie Beaulier-Rider shot Zadie a frosty look as she stepped inside. She was bursting with pride at the thought of her son as president. The glare threw Zadie back in time to middle school, when Natalie didn't hide her dislike of Zadie's short skirts and wild looks, and the way *the little hellion* got her son into so much trouble. Valier ran interception with his daughter so Zadie could dart past and leap up the familiar, carpeted staircase. She shouldered in the door of Charlie's room without knocking.

"We need to talk," she announced. She shut the door behind her, pulled off her winter coat, and tossed it on the back of his desk chair. Hands on her hips, the toe of one wool sock tapping in frustration, she raked her angry gaze over him. Charlie lay on his bed, arms crossed over his chest, face turned towards the window, watching the gaggle of reporters stamp their feet on the freezing sidewalk.

"Everyone wants me to run," he muttered. "Everyone but *you.*"

He threw the word at her like a knife. Zadie staggered back, surprised by the intensity. On the desk, his phone pinged. They lunged for it at the same time. She got to it first and danced away, holding it out of reach with her extra inch of height. The text was from Brad Andersen, begging him - again - to consider a run for president.

Only you can stop Whyte, the DC hack argued in a series of texts.

Please. We need you.

Your country needs you.

Just meet with me and hear me out.

301

"Andersen's right," Charlie blurted out, surrendering the fight for the phone. "We do have to get involved. We owe it to everyone to keep this guy out of power."

"That's not a reason to run for president and you know it," she snapped, jerking away from him. "You can't be serious."

One look at his worried eyes warned her that he was. Zadie snorted in disbelief. He squirmed uncomfortably.

"Andersen wants to meet with me. I think we should hear him out. I mean, Jeb Whyte is crazy," he said. "He'd *use* the nuclear codes to bring on the Rapture."

She gritted her teeth.

"Is it so wrong to secure the apparatus of the government from people like him?" Charlie argued, swiveling to face her. "Don't we have a responsibility to keep him out of office?"

"Yeah," she answered, "but not like this! Use people power to prevent him from gaining traction or force him to resign if elected, or back some other opposing candidate . . . but don't run yourself, Charlie! That's just ego. Fear and ego."

She glared at him, leveling the same knowing look at him that she'd used since eighth grade.

"We could do a lot of good," he shot back.

His bright blue eyes reminded her - for one horrible moment - of Jeb Whyte's.

"He's only asking you because you're white and male," she muttered.

"Only? Thanks a lot," Charlie snapped, furious.

"You know what I mean. Inez, Tansy, Alex, Idah . . . they all gave as much or more to this movement, but somehow they're unelectable."

"And you, you mean?" He glared at her. "Why not come out and say it, Zadie? You're pissed because he asked me, not you."

Zadie stilled. Her narrow shoulders stiffened. Her lips tensed. Slowly, she pivoted, catching her breath then pausing, fighting the swift boiling fury that seethed within her.

"No," she corrected him through gritted teeth, "I'm pissed at how this country's history makes guys like Brad Andersen assume you're the guy to talk to. I'm mad as hell that Christian domination and misogyny is still gaining traction two thousand years into this fight. I'm furious that ten thousand years of time hasn't turned over the lie that might makes right and therefore men should rule. I'm furious that Black and Brown women like Inez aren't considered obvious first choices for presidential candidates."

Her tone climbed a notch in intensity with each line until she shouted at him.

"I'm pissed that all this history boils down into the fact that even though we won a revolution, Brad Andersen is still headhunting a white male for the next president of the United States and telling me that I'm going *too fast, too much, and too soon.*"

Zadie screamed the last in Charlie's shocked face. Her features contorted, transforming her into a creature of pure wrath. Like a smoke detector and sprinkler system triggered by heat, tears stung his eyes. He slapped up a shield of resentful anger, a last ditch defense against the onslaught of her emotions. His jaw clenched. His throat worked.

"Tell me," Zadie demanded in a low, quiet voice, sharp with fury, "just how slow should I go? How many more thousands of years should women wait? How many more centuries should Inez or Tansy or Elisha let white people churn out deadly policies? How long should Kinap's words and warnings go unheeded?"

She let the question hang in the air. They both knew there

was only one answer: they had no more time to spare. The earth was on fire, drowning, tearing herself apart. Time was up. Change had to come now.

"Come on, Charlie," she said, her voice softening as she looked at him. "You aren't cut out for that sort of politics. You don't compromise; you tell the truth, you demand justice, you do what's right. You despise the middle ground that throws people under the bus. If you run for president, it'll be the death of you. Either you'll stay who you are and they'll assassinate you, or you'll change beyond all recognition."

Just before his face closed, expressionless, she saw the flash of hurt in his eyes.

"Guess I won't ask for your endorsement," he muttered, trying to pass it off as a joke.

"Charlie," she started to say.

He jerked away, rising.

"No, you're right. It was a stupid idea."

He banged through the house, grabbing his coat and hat, shoving his feet into boots, muttering about needing air. She gaped after him. Sure, he could beat Jeb Whyte. Hands down. In a heartbeat. He was even one of the few people she thought was worthy of being president. He had no experience, but he had tremendous love for his people.

But she knew him. From getting a presentable haircut to knowing the nuclear codes, he'd hate every minute of it. Then there was the ex-presidents' code. She grimaced. There were unspoken rules, a long list of things that former presidents did or did not do. They retired from politics, more or less, and limited their activities to motivational speaking, writing their memoirs, and fundraising for the party that put them in power. How could he possibly make commencement speeches and cut ribbons for the rest of his life, refusing to speak out against the injustices of the world? Zadie was sure Charlie didn't want to spend his days founding a library and sitting politely silent at state dinners.

His silence for decades would cost his fellow citizens more than his refusal to run now. From today until the election, he could organize relentlessly for real change, not deliver empty promises in stump speeches. For four years, he could support worker strikes and environmental blockades of pipelines and community democracy and a million things that would never make it to the president's desk - not until the entire culture of the country changed. For eight years of the next two-term presidency, he and Zadie could hold the administration's feet to the fire in the way they did best - by mobilizing people power, by awakening the innate strength of the people, by making sure the spirit of resistance they'd stirred up never settled down.

He doesn't understand, Zadie realized. *He thinks I just don't believe in him.*

She did, though. Too much. She'd barely managed to survive the Dandelion Insurrection with them both alive and their relationship intact. They wouldn't make it through a presidential race . . . or two. It would cost them everything - the things they couldn't say, the truths they couldn't speak, the ability to stand alongside the people and hold the powerful accountable, their sanity, their passion, their love for one another.

Zadie burst out of the house with her hair flying wildly in all directions, wind-howling at her back, and flakes of snow chasing her heels. She leapt the steps onto the driveway just as Brad Andersen's car peeled out. She cursed. Charlie rode shotgun in the front seat.

CHAPTER THIRTY-ONE

. . . . .

Money Talks

"Chah-lie, dahling, we need you."

Mona Gold owned the house next door to the presidential summer home and lost no time in telling him how nice it would be to be his neighbor. Her private jet had picked them up at the tiny municipal airport in Frenchville and whisked them south to Coastal Maine. The ocean tossed up sheets of ice onto the granite shore, then melted them away with its salt. Hidden in the grey trees, the mansions of politicians and movie stars dotted this bit of winding coast. They drove through a cluster of estates, down an unmarked drive, and up to a gold-gilded gate where the driver keyed in the passcode to Mona's sprawling house. A butler escorted them to a stately living room with a vaulted ceiling and enough silk to open an emporium. Brad Andersen smirked as Charlie and Mona shook hands. The political hit man exchanged air pecks on both cheeks with the billionaire. Charlie sat gingerly on a couch with gold tassels that would not have looked out of place at Versailles. Andersen plopped down on a chintz armchair. Mona arranged herself on the chaise lounge.

"I'm gonna cut straight to the chase," Mona drawled. "You do not strike me as a man motivated by money."

"Er, no," he answered, confused.

"Therefore, you wouldn't be interested in my vast fortune, and the ungawdly sums I could pour into the coffers of your Dandelions if you ran for president - "

"- they're not my Dandelions - "

" - so, I'm gonna make you an offer you can't refuse."

She deadpanned the line. Charlie's heart rate increased as he eyed the marble columns for concealed mafia strong-arms.

"I am prepared to use my not inconsiderable leverage and influence among the rich and powerful to clear the way for your Dandelions."

"They're not my - " he tried to interject again, but there was no derailing the barreling freight train of Mona Gold.

" - if you will do one eetsy, weetsy little thing. A thing, I might add, that any twenty-eight year old in his right mind would leap at the chance to do, a thing that is a once-in-a-lifetime opportunity, a thing that this country desperately needs you to do."

He could see where this was headed.

"Run for president, Chah-lie," she insisted. "For the good of your fellow citizens. We cannot have Jeb as our commander-in-chief. For gawdsake, we have got to keep that megalomaniac out of the White House. As a Texan, I would kill myself in disgrace - except there's no need, since he'll bring on the Apocalypse the minute he gets the codes to the nukes."

The speed at which Mona shifted from seduction to flattery to threatening terrified him.

"Zadie isn't keen on the idea - "

"Zadie."

Mona's drawl flattened the name like the meteor that extinguished the dinosaurs.

"You are a young man, so take my advice: have a heart-to-heart with Zadie and explain how she'll make a fine first lady."

Charlie bristled on Zadie's behalf.

"Why won't anyone consider *her* for president?"

Mona threw him an appalled look.

"The girl is unelectable. Plain and simple. She's got a mouth the size of Texas, her opinions are about as palatable as dog shit, and she's the face of everything our opponents, the centrists, *and* the corporatists hate. She's a target and a half."

Mona paused.

"But, as first lady, her political views don't matter, and her sense of style is an asset. Zadie Byrd Gray is a powerhouse, so long as she's attached to the right engine."

He steeled himself for the next word.

"You."

Unexpectedly, his heart swung full circle, slamming into alignment with Zadie's furious outburst. She was right. There was no difference between his political views and Zadie's. They just came wrapped in different packages. Radical views in a wild, female body was intolerable. The same views in a young, white male who never could shed the last hints of his small town roots . . . now, that was electable.

"I'm sorry," he said, rising and wiping his sweaty palms on his jeans. "This was a waste of our time."

Mona's mascaraed eyes narrowed in her porcelain face.

"Oh, take your time. Think it through."

Her voice dropped into dangerous tones.

"There are a lot of doors opening up to Dandelions these days. I'd hate to see them slam shut over some fool's decision."

Her smile gleamed like a shark's. There was more than one race at stake. Young Charlie Rider needed to learn to be a team player. A leader, not a maverick. Mona Gold already envisioned him walking out to the podium for the Inaugural Address. She fanned the blush that rushed her cheeks. Lawd Almighty, that would be a sight for sore eyes.

Her teeth glinted. Even if he lost, he'd be worth the millions she would pour into the campaign. She'd make billions in advertising on her news network. A presidential race between Charlie Rider and Jeb Whyte would rake in a fortune. She couldn't make a dime off the nonsense of this *real democracy* stuff. Boring meetings, circle discussions, online polling? Ugh. Ratings hell, that's what that was. But a showdown between the forces of Rider and Whyte? That was the ticket of the century. Those pesky public financing laws had wreaked havoc on the revenue projections for her media network in the electoral season. Fortunately, there were work-arounds. With a feisty election and her monopoly on debate hosting, she could jack up the prices of prime ad space. Not to mention the possibility of booking Zadie Byrd Gray for tell-all interviews dressed in a line of designer fashion she owned stock in. Mona Gold needed a flashy presidential race. The Democratic establishment was banking on a boring corporatist. She needed something young and handsome . . . Charlie Rider. The tension between Jeb Whyte and Zadie was an added bonus. Like a hot Sotheby's auction, they'd driven up the prices for the best advertising slots. Millions of dollars could change hands if Charlie ran against Whyte. For once in her apolitical life, Mona Gold couldn't wait for the primaries.

Charlie pivoted to Brad Andersen.

"I'm surprised the party establishment wants me to run," he said bluntly.

"They don't," Brad answered with equal bluntness. "They'd rather run a corporatist. That's why they got Jeb Whyte to run."

"Wait - the Democrats got Whyte to run?" Charlie asked, shocked and confused.

"Yes," Brad confessed with a look of disgust. "They figured he'd make a centrist candidate look good by comparison. Jeb Whyte's just a straw man, a monster tossed up to scare people into voting for a weak Democrat."

Mona laughed at Charlie's appalled expression.

"If you can't stomach the sausage-making, Chah-lie, you'd best stay out of the kitchen," she drawled.

"But the Democrats miscalculated Whyte's appeal," Brad went on. "He's going to win."

He set down his whisky snifter and leaned his elbows on his knees, eyes intent on Charlie.

"Unless you stop him, that is."

Charlie looked from one to the other. A boiling fury simmered in his veins. He couldn't believe that the two parties would collude to pull such a dangerous stunt. The two parties didn't care who wound up in the Oval Office so long as *one* of them did. The old enemies were now united against a common enemy: the Dandelions. They couldn't let the participatory democracy movement put them out of a job, cut off their access to power, and stop them from manipulating government to make trillions. Charlie had never been so angry in his life. He refused to be a pawn on their chessboard. He suppressed the urge to throw punches and smash glass. Instead, he kicked his journalistic skills into high gear.

"Tell me more," he urged them, leveraging their desire to see him run for a chance to pry more information out of them.

He would stop Jeb Whyte, alright . . . just not the way they expected.

CHAPTER THIRTY-TWO

. . . . .

Dancing on the Chessboard

The farmhouse went silent when Charlie entered. The click of the front door's latch snapped loudly in the sudden vacancy of chatter. The kitchen was packed with people. He cursed under his breath. He'd forgotten about Bill Gray's notorious Winter Solstice Party. Half the people in the valley came, including his neighbors and relatives. Charlie spotted his mother, grand-père, and cousins among other familiar faces. It was more crowded than usual. Everyone was hoping to hear if he was going to run for president. Charlie backpedaled, banging his elbow on the doorknob, not ready to face their questions. Bill Gray hastily swigged a gulp of whisky-spiked eggnog and nudged his daughter to get her attention. Zadie whirled. From the kitchen, straight down the narrow hall, her eyes pierced Charlie, pinning him to the wooden door for a brief and excruciating instant. He took a deep breath and braved the perils of his nosy neighbors to cross the room.

"We've got to talk," he murmured to Zadie.

"Yeah, I've got news for you, too," she answered.

Their eyes met, electric. She squeezed his upper arm in a cryptic code that he couldn't decipher. Her hand felt jittery with excitement, though. Something was up.

"Let me get my coat. We'll go up the hill," she told him.

An audible groan of disappointment ran through the room. A sudden eruption of babble broke out. Speculative whispers ran in an undercurrent through the resumed chatter.

313

Charlie fumbled out the door onto the enclosed porch, feeling the frigid air press its palms against his flaming cheeks. Just as the heat of his nervousness cooled down into a shiver, Zadie came out, bundled up in a winter jacket and woolen hat. She handed him a pair of snowshoes and dumped an armload of warmer clothes on the floor at his feet. When he started to speak, she shook her head. Whatever her news was, it was too big to risk the skillful eavesdropping of his Acadian relatives. Wrestling with his impatience, Charlie laced up his boots, shoved on his hat, and carried the snowshoes out into the driveway to strap them on.

Their footsteps crunched loudly in the silence of the night, guiding each other by sound as the darkness swallowed them. Starlight fell on the blank canvas of the snow, illuminating the barest hints of wind-sculpted ridges in the drifts and swells. They still didn't speak. Zadie fizzled and burned and sparked at the edges, a hornet's nest of information buzzing inside her, desperate to get out. Will Sharp had called, interrupting her frantic pacing after Charlie had left with Andersen.

"How come Chuck isn't answering your calls?" Will had demanded, not bothering with hellos and niceties.

"How do you know that?" Zadie asked.

"I tried ringing him with your number."

"That's spooky. And probably illegal."

"Oh, definitely," Will answered, unperturbed. "Why is Charlie being such an idiot?"

Zadie sighed.

"He's not. He's just - "

"Don't defend him, Zadie. Not to me."

She rolled her eyes. The relationship between the three of them was beyond complicated. She wished she didn't hold a grudging respect for Will Sharp. After all the trouble he'd caused, it would be easier if she could simply detest him.

"Did you just call to gloat over our fight?" she snapped at Will.

"No," he replied. "Remember how I told you I'd dig into Jeb Whyte after that attack in Chicago?"

"Did you find anything?" she asked, hardly daring to breathe as a fragile bloom of hope opened in her chest.

"Man, did I ever."

Will Sharp had unearthed enough dirt on Jeb Whyte to bury the man six feet under and drive a stake through the heart of his vampiristic empire. He had the evidence to not just stop Whyte's odious presidential run, but to topple his entire spider's web of industries.

"We could use Chuck's help breaking the story . . . but not if he's going to run for president. They'd cry foul so fast the information dump would be worthless."

So, Zadie held the knowledge like a caged bear roaring to break loose as they climbed the snowy hill. The incline pounded exertion-heat into their thighs, firing up the body's natural furnace against the icy night. When their next footstep unexpectedly fell level with the previous, they knew they'd crested the top of the hill. They crunched onward, across the buried farm road, onto the open field where an old tractor had once stood as a shrine. Frigid air scraped their throats and pinched the hairs in their nostrils. The night gleamed, magnificent, a small consolation for the cold. Stars blossomed like wildflowers above. Faint outlines of spruce trees shivered on the edge of their vision, dark against a darker world. On the top of the rise, they paused.

Charlie sensed Zadie's presence more than he saw her. He drew a short, quick gasp, recognizing how long that sixth sense had brimmed in his veins. He could remember turning in middle school, alert to the instant she tossed a grin across the hallway. When she ran away, he'd sometimes get a tingle down his spine and think of a distant city. Two weeks later, a postcard would arrive, confirming his sense of where she was. Like birds that see the magnetic fields of the earth, his life had been guided by an unwavering line of love that shot from his heart to hers across time and space and impossible odds.

"I love you."

The words leapt out of them both, merging and blending until neither could tell whose regret and hope and passion and apologies spilled over the banks of unspoken thoughts and flooded those three short words.

"Are you - " she started to ask.

"I'm not running," Charlie answered.

He launched into an explanation of the political collusion he'd heard about from Brad and Mona, but Zadie barely listened. The hard knot of fear wound in a tight coil around her ribs loosened in a gasp of relief. Tears sprang to Zadie's eyes and froze on her lashes. She drew a shuddering breath. Her sigh frosted on the cold air. Beside her, Charlie's voice rumbled on, outlining the ways the two parties were working together to sabotage the Dandelions' democracy efforts.

"And that's beyond wrong. It's despicable," he said.

Zadie whirled and threw her arms around him, knocking him backwards into the soft snowdrift with a fierce and wild kiss.

"Thank you," she murmured against his lips.

"For what?" he asked, breathless.

"Not running."

"It wasn't worth it," Charlie answered. "Even before I knew what they were doing, I'd already decided not to run. It wasn't worth the cost."

"What cost?" Zadie asked, suddenly alert, wondering what horrible bargains Mona and Brad had thrown at him.

Beside her, Charlie chuckled, reading her reaction even through the dark. He reached out and hugged her, arms bulky in the winter coat, hands thick in their mittens.

"You."

His answer hung on the air like the white breath of their lives, tender and fragile and unstoppable as their next heartbeat. The awed hush of winter wrapped them in its reverence. The cold crept through their gloves, jackets, and hats, stealing the warmth of their lives one degree at a time. He wouldn't trade Zadie's love for any amount of power or position. He'd rather pick potatoes on her dad's farm with her than live in the White House without her. Zadie would never surrender to the political niceties of politicians. She'd never swallow truth to speak polite lies. And why should she? The world was changing. Swiftly. Rapidly. Unpredictably. Their place was with the people, standing shoulder-to-shoulder to stop the raging forest fires and surging floodwaters. Their place was in the trenches of changing democracy. Their place was standing in solidarity with the innumerable struggles rising up for justice. The kind of politics that put them in this mess would not get them out of it. Their place was with the emerging solutions and the movements mobilizing to support them.

"For what it's worth, I think you'd make a great president," she confessed. "I probably should have said that earlier."

It was not quite an apology, more of a peace offering. Charlie smiled. His cheeks twitched as he did, unused to the expression.

"You were right, though," he admitted. "We can't win that way. Not by their rules. Not at their game. Even playing it is losing for us. I was just ... trapped. They had me - us -

317

cornered on their chessboard."

"Horrible game, chess," Zadie grumbled. "I always hated it."

"I know," Charlie answered. "You used to flip the board over."

A sliver of a smile curled on her lips. She pushed to standing and held out a mittened hand, hauling him to his feet. The dazzle of stars shone over them, eternal and breathless.

"Do you remember," Charlie asked, his voice husky with the past, "what we played instead of chess?"

He could sense her smile curling in the cloak of night.

"Some crazy game of hide-and-seek crossed with treasure hunting and collecting matching pairs of chess pieces without getting caught," she reminisced. "There may have been some pirating involved . . . and a dance-off. A lot of dance-offs."

"Hah. You always won those."

"Hey, if you don't like the game . . . change the rules and play to your strengths, right?"

"Maybe we should challenge Jeb Whyte to a dance-off," Charlie joked.

She smiled.

"We dance better, for sure." She nudged his shoulder with hers. "Even you."

"Thanks, I think."

They fell silent, memories curling in their hearts like a purring cat, warm and tingling through their bones. The wind lofted, suspending like a held breath before sighing back toward the frozen ground. As it landed, it wisped in Zadie's ears. It tickled the edges of Charlie's thoughts. It hissed across the snow, sweeping up tiny flakes and scuffing their frozen crystals against the ice in a symphony of shushes and silences. In the spruces, falling flakes played the xylophone of the needles. Clumps of accumulation fell in soft *floomps*. The ice on the beaver pond groaned and moaned, cracking and popping. Across the sky, time spoke through the dark expanse. The language of starlight winked its million-year-old secrets in twinkling Morse code. The constellations tickled ancient memories of myth and prophecy. The wind shook the darkness like a blanket. A ripple of cold shimmered.

All around them, the winds of change were blowing. They didn't speak of presidents and kings, dictators and destruction. They spoke of ecosystems and communities, healing and reconciliation, change and transformation. They hummed with unexpected hope in the dark night of humanity's soul. The winds told these stories to anyone who would listen. Not all could hear their messages. Not all who heard them had the courage to follow their instructions. Some people were deaf dinosaurs who refused the imperative of change, destined and doomed to slide into extinction.

But Charlie and Zadie? They were dandelions. They were born to fling their wishes to the winds, seek out fertile ground, and bloom. Their movement danced in murmurations, ready to fly and soar on the changes that swept the world. Winter solstice stretched long and deep around them, but tomorrow, the light would come a minute sooner. Every day, the world would shine a little brighter.

"What were you going to tell me?" Charlie asked, his voice half lost in the whispering wind. "Down at the farmhouse, you said you had news."

"Oh!"

Zadie bolted as if lightning struck. She'd nearly forgotten!

"Will Sharp called to tell me that you're an idiot - "

" - that's hardly news - "

" - and that he knows how to get rid of Jeb Whyte."

Charlie's head whipped around. Their eyes met. Smiles grew. He gasped. She nodded.

Behind them, unseen, the wind swept up to dance across the stars.

CHAPTER THIRTY-THREE

. . . . .

Blow the Whistle Day

Tweeet! Tweeet! Tweeet!

Jeb Whyte rolled over in bed, reaching for the alarm clock only to realize that the infernal racket was coming from outside his sprawling home. He cursed under his breath and thrust his bare feet into his slippers. The blaring chorus of whistles grated his nerves like nails on a chalkboard. Hundreds blew the shiny metal instruments at the same time in a synchronized, heart-pounding pulse of sound. Jeb Whyte stumbled to the window and threw back the curtains.

#BlowTheWhistleDay

The banner was painted in the same gold, black, and green lettering as the one that had been dropped from the balcony of the megachurch a few months ago. On one end, a nun in a habit puffed her cheeks out and blew ferociously into the whistle. Around her, a crowd held signs with statistics printed on them. He squinted. Gasped. Nearly choked. How did they know those figures? It was as if his accounting books had been blown up and pasted onto cardboard signs. He reeled as the residents of the Purg shrilled their whistles in tandem.

Tweeet! Tweeet! Tweeet!

Brad Andersen bolted awake at dawn in an unmemorable motel. For a dizzying moment, he couldn't remember what state he was in or which politician he'd come to hustle. The cacophony outside set off a clamor of furious voices. Even as Brad peered out the window, he heard the slam and bang of doors being thrown open. From the motel rooms, shouts lobbed down at the protesters in the parking lot. There were dozens, all with sports whistles, shiny and ear-shattering. They held a giant banner that read: #BlowTheWhistleDay. A painted graphic showed the head of the party in bed with his avowed nemesis, the two of them rocking Jeb Whyte in a baby cradle. Brad Andersen lunged for his phone and clicked on the television at the same time. His eyes bulged. His veins pounded in rhythm with the whistles' sharp noise.

Tweeet! Tweeet! Tweeet!

Mona Gold had just lifted the first sip of her slow-drip, French-roasted coffee to her lips when her maid dropped the breakfast tray with a shriek. Mona followed the woman's alarm, looking out the window, beyond the balcony doors, over the snow-dusted pines, and out into the coastal waters where an armada of lobster boats slammed their horns and clanged their bells. Four boats had lined-up bow to stern and had words painted on the inland side.

#Blow . . . The . . . Whistle . . . Day

Mona's phones all rang at once, adding their chaos to the boats' blaring and honking. She ordered her staff to shut off the ringers and unplug several lines, and turned on her television. The channel was set to her networks - which still churned through their regular morning programs - so she switched to her main rival's newscast.

"Charlie Rider, the infamous Man From the North, declined to run for president and posted a bombshell exposé in the early hours of the night. He alleges that the two major political parties colluded on presidential candidate selections, and even offers testimony that - hard as it is to believe - the Democrats pushed the Republican contender, Jeb Whyte, to enter the presidential race. Rider also released shocking information on Whyte's internal finances and business operations."

Mona clicked furiously to the other news networks. Same story. She clenched her fists, drawing blood with her nails. Everyone had this story but her!

"This," one newscaster warned, pausing with a dramatic flair that made Mona want to hurl her coffee mug at the screen, "is only the first of several articles Charlie Rider says he will post throughout the day . . . a day that activists across the country are calling #BlowTheWhistleDay."

Mona Gold's furious shriek shattered a crystal champagne flute and cracked a mirror in her marbled hall.

Tweeet! Tweeet! Tweeet!

Outside a bloodmobile in a rainy city in the Pacific Northwest, the poor and unhoused picketed the street, blowing screeching whistles. Their black umbrellas bore a golden dandelion flower on the crown. Around the edges, a slogan was written: *Be kind, be connected, be unafraid . . . and blow the whistle!*

Oliver Lang knocked on the door of the mobile blood collection clinic, armed with a written citizens' eviction notice. The confused interns opened the door.

"Time's up," he told them. "You're all being evicted by popular consent of this community. Your secret's out. We want your organ and blood farms out of our town . . . and out of every city in this country."

The Man From the North's second article had laid out the horror of the bloodmobiles and revealed that the nationwide operation was run by none other than Jeb Whyte and the Redemption Megachurch. Even more shocking, the article shared the financial reports on the obscene profitability of organ harvesting and plasma sales. Charlie Rider and Will Sharp had spent the past week holed up in his grand-père's cabin by the lake, taking turns stoking the woodstove and splitting wood, writing the series of whistleblowing articles that laid bare the inhumanity - and illegality - of Jeb Whyte's enterprises. The evidence was beyond damning. Olli's local action was one of hundreds taking place at soup kitchens and church parking lots, near thrift stores and shelters, alongside encampments and low-income neighborhoods. The article called for nonviolent, but determined, citizen-led evictions to oust Jeb Whyte's Christ's Blood Redemption Centers from their body-harvesting across the nation.

Tweeet! Tweeet! Tweeet!

Throughout Jeb and Evelyn Whyte's empire, the whistles screeched in protest. They showed up outside the couple's hospital chains, where organ donation clauses were part of the price of admission. They showed up by the Birth Centers across Texas, where unwed girls and surrogate mothers gave up babies that the Whytes then sold for six digit figures to desperate couples hoping to be parents. They blew whistles by the private prisons run by the Whytes where parole dates could be moved up if you donated a kidney, eye, or other body part. Every town in the country was shocked to learn that body harvesting was happening in their backyard . . . and by a presidential candidate, no less.

Tweeet! Tweeet! Tweeet!

Starling and Swallow and the San Francisco Murmuration joined the United Strippers Union on the steps of Mona Gold's media corporation. The racket they raised could be heard from the penthouse - and in the shareholders meeting taking place. Starling managed to deliver a print-out of Charlie Rider's third article that detailed how Mona Gold had fanned the flames of hate and fear simply to profit off a high stakes election. The hardcopy was followed up by thousands of emails to the board, sharing the article and demanding that Mona Gold be ousted from the company.

Tweeet! Tweeet! Tweeet!

Elisha, Meera, and Frankie mobilized thousands of teens to blow the whistle on the two-party duopoly's failure to address the climate crisis. Neither flat-out denialism nor profit-driven inaction was acceptable. Their lives and future were at stake. The adults were playing with fire. The youth were tired of getting burnt. The latest election manipulations showed that the system was broken, and corrupt beyond redeeming. They demanded immediate climate action and a climate transition plan led by citizens' assemblies.

Tweeet! Tweeet! Tweeet!

The whistles screamed from coast to coast, from mountaintop to rolling hill to valley floor, everywhere! They blew from the Statue of Liberty. They echoed over the Grand Canyon. They blared from the Golden Gate Bridge. They sounded from Mississippi steamboats. The Rocky Mountains reverberated with their calls. They erupted from the trains on Solutionary Rail lines. They shot out along the shores of the Great Lakes. Everywhere and anywhere the corporatists and christo-fascists tried to conceal their injustice, the Dandelions blew the whistle with the truth.

"They tried to control us through our fear of Jeb Whyte's hatred," Zadie Byrd Gray said in a public address. She had come to New York City to kick off the metropolis' whistleblowing parade with Inez Hernandez. "We refuse to be scared into compliance with their destructive greed. We are dandelions! When fear is used to control us . . . "

She paused and held out the mic to the teeming crowd. The end of the phrase came roaring back:

325

" . . . love is how we rebel!"

Instead of waiting for Charlie Rider to save them, the people would save themselves.

It would be comforting if I ran against Jeb Whyte, Charlie wrote in his public statement refusing to run for president. *Like champions of old, Jeb and I could have faced off on the battle field of the election. With our political armies amassed behind us, we could have duked it out as you all banged your shields with your sword hilts. But this is not what our world needs right now.*

Their world didn't need more wars and warriors, battles and duels. It didn't need saviors and superheroes. The time had passed for knights in shining armor. Those models were dinosaurs, antiquated species in the evolution from monarchies to democracies. It was time for humanity to spread its wings and fly.

We are meant to work in flocks and swarms, he and Zadie wrote, *to figure our problems out together rather than abdicating our authority to powerful leaders.*

The time had come for leaderful solutions, for ecosystem thinking and living democracies. The era of cooperation and collaboration was dawning. Stopping the Jeb Whytes of the world meant they had to stop handing over their power to leaders of armies - both literal and metaphorical. It required them to think like an ecosystem instead of warring militaries or pairs of charging football teams. It required not one perfect answer, but a swarm of responses, all brilliant, all flawed, all overlapping. It required dispersing power away from a handful of authority figures, out into the edges and margins.

Shift the rules. Flip the board. Change the game.

If you can't win, don't play. That was their motto. Don't let the bullies bait you into a fistfight. Don't let the bigger kids trick you into an arm wrestling match. Don't use the tools and tactics your opponents are better at using. Charlie and Zadie refused to play a game they'd always lose.

Instead, from every street corner, in every hall of power, in homes and schools and workplaces, Dandelions erupted into action. They burst forth in a ferocious swarm, the natural response of thousands of tiny birds alerted to danger in their midst, united by shared principles, and determined to protect all that they held dear. Love is what called them into action, and love what was moved them forward now.

"Our strength has always been in our numbers," Zadie reminded them. "Our superpower has always been our wild creativity. You don't need a president to save you. You've stopped tyrants and ended dictatorships. You've thwarted countercoups and halted corporate plundering. The Dandelion Insurrection's strategies have worked because we found the courage to reject silver bullet solutions and swarm into action from all sides."

Meera, Elisha, and Frankie mobilized protests in a movement-of-movements style, countering Jeb Whyte's anti-everything hatred. Starling and Sparrow rallied multicity murmurations. The representatives who had joined the Council of All Beings held Processions of the Species in the streets, with trees marching like myths of old, giant blue whale puppets swimming through intersections, and monarch butterfly kites soaring overhead. Neither corporatists nor christo-fascists held any hope for people or planet. Better candidates were required . . . and real democracy had to be at the core of the evolution of all politics.

Instead of abandoning real democracy in a heated election year, it was time to *apply* real democracy for an election cycle unlike any other. Olli and Zadie called upon citizens to organize local community conversations, across-the-aisle talks, and discussions on the political issues. Instead of surrendering democracy to the talking heads, media spins, and scripted debates; the Dandelion Insurrection and Democracy Lab asked people to be wildly creative in "doing democracy", including using street murals, community theater, street corner soapboxes, and potlucks on politics. The laboratory of democracy set out to dissect all the candidates and all the issues, inch by inch, policy by policy, view by view. In small Midwest towns and large coastal cities, at kitchen tables and in workplaces, in online forums and in-person gatherings, Zadie called upon citizens to throw Jeb Whyte into the crucible of real democracy. She told them to subject his catch phrases to the blinding light of scrutiny, unravel the net of false logic in his speeches, and pick apart his policies until they collapsed into the hollow promises that they truly were.

The planet couldn't survive politics-as-usual. The nation couldn't endure a duopoly of christo-fascists and corporatists. They lived in times of tremendous change. Survival required revolution, transformation, evolution. Somewhere, somehow, a different kind of politics had to come onto the scene, dancing to a different drum: the heartbeat of people and planet.

Inez Hernandez declared she would run for president like a Dandelion - independent, bold, and wildly unpredictable. Inez launched a People's Choice platform using participatory polling to determine what issues she should campaign on. Her opponents screamed that it was unconstitutional, but it wasn't. The Constitution set up who votes on bills. It doesn't say anything about how or why a representative or senator or even the president voted a certain way. Inez simply asked the people how they wanted her to represent them. It was simple. It was revolutionary. It rattled the foundations of the United States oligarchy. It was unstoppable. #Inez4Prez swept the popular polls. She stole the show. She was bold and outrageous, indomitable and kind. Where others battled, she danced. Where they fought, she laughed. Inez inspired dozens more candidates for local and state offices to integrate participatory democracy practices into their campaigns. Together, the Dandelion Politics cohort challenged incumbents and office holders to truly represent their constituents.

"We're supposed to represent the people," Inez reminded them, "but do you even know what your people truly want? Have you asked them lately?"

In contrast, Jeb Whyte's platform was decidedly undemocratic. Still, he had millions marching in lockstep behind his campaign. More to the point, he had millions of dollars backing his presidential bid. The rich people still needed a friendly face in the Oval Office ... and Jeb Whyte's prosperity gospel was enough to make believers out of them.

The Dandelion Insurrection had weakened his position, cut off the overt support from the left, kicked the Democratic corporatists out of the running with Inez' brilliant campaign, and pushed the media to do more than profit from Whyte's insanity and hatred. They'd countered threats from many sides and isolated Whyte from much of his support. But the wealthy wheeled and formed ranks behind Jeb Whyte, blatantly revealing that their pursuit of riches outweighed their concerns over a candidate who cared nothing for the people's demands for respect and dignity ... or for the very existence of millions of people.

Tucker Jones and Alex Kelly had a plan, however, a simple and brilliant plan for how to de-couple the wealthy from the megachurch preacher. Together, they launched an online calculator that tallied *The True Cost of Jeb Whyte*.

CHAPTER THIRTY-FOUR

. . . . .

The True Cost of Jeb Whyte

Down to the last dollar, Alex and Tucker calculated the costs of electing Jeb Whyte. They factored in the economic impacts of his policies. They added up the price tags of climate disasters and humanitarian relief. They totaled up the corporate bailouts and benefits he promised at each campaign stop. They worked out the price of his plan to expand the military and launch a global Christian empire. Then, they estimated the cost of the massive resistance movements that would rise up against him if he took office. Boycotts, shut downs, strikes, walkouts, noncooperation, the overtime wages of police, the court fees over arrests: Tucker and Alex put a number to it all and added it to Jeb Whyte's bill. With Charlie's help, they told the citizens what parts would come out of the taxpayers' pockets. More crucially, Zadie worked with Starling and Swallow to warn the wealthy how much it would cost them to put Jeb Whyte in the Oval Office. Work stoppages and strikes, consumer boycotts, and the disruptive impacts of mass resistance would put a dent in their profits. And now it could all be calculated down to the last nickel and dime.

The cost of oppressing and exploiting people should never be ignored, Charlie wrote. *It should be calculated and made visible.*

The price tag was not caused by protesters, he told the wealthy, but by the policies of hate and destruction. It could be avoided by pulling their support away from Jeb Whyte's campaign *now,* and not letting him get any closer to the White House.

We are raising the stakes of this choice, Charlie and Zadie wrote. *We are showing you the consequences of trying to enact his worldview. There will be resistance. This is what it will look like.*

Tucker and Alex connected the calculator to a Pledge of Resistance that put price tags on each nonviolent action. Unions, clergy, mayors, school teachers, soldiers, and others could sign up to resist. The total impact on the economy added up to hundreds of billions, even trillions of dollars. One million, two million, three, ten, twenty million people pledged to boycott, strike, divest, and blockade. The system calculated how nonviolent action translated into economic power. It showed them exactly how much leverage they had over businesses and politics. It put wattage to the idea of people power and illuminated how brightly the movement would shine when they decided to throw the switch. It built courage. It offered hope. It gave people the strength to demand real change.

The calculation on *The True Cost of Jeb Whyte* sent shockwaves through the electoral establishment. The rich and the powerful broke into cold sweats. It showed them that the cost of electing Jeb Whyte vastly outweighed the gains of supporting his campaign.

Incrementally, the veneer of charm that covered Jeb Whyte oozed, thinned, and cracked. The Dandelion Insurrection's swarms of popular resistance chipped away at his power. The murmurations and democracy projects shifted former supporters away from him. Tansy's legal team struck gold and discovered that he had used the church's tax-exempt status as a laundromat and funneled millions of dollars through it for his inner circle. Four women came forward with claims of sexual assault from him and his key staff. The Redemption Church's former backstage manager did a tell-all interview about the horrible narcissism of both Jeb and Evelyn Whyte.

More witnesses and whistleblowers came forward. Other stories surfaced. The dominoes of Jeb Whyte's empire toppled. The Whytes had fingers in the entire cannibalistic industry of human farming. There was no end to their blood sucking. Wherever a dime could be squeezed from the people's bodies, they set up shop. Armed with fliers chronicling the vampiristic empire of the Whytes, thousands of Dandelions took to the streets. Every news channel in the nation covered the dramatic showdowns, protests, blockades, and citizen evictions.

Soon, Reverend Whyte stumbled into defense, justifying his stances to increasingly sharp critics, defending his positions with growing desperation.

Then, the final straw arrived . . . just in time to break the camel's back.

One of the women in Evelyn Whyte's inner circle put her adopted baby back up for adoption. She claimed that the child was *impure* and *tainted*. Evelyn Whyte had promised her a white baby from a white surrogate mother . . . but this child had been carried by a Black mother in one of the Birth Centers. The news ripped open the sheer fury of Black women across the nation. After centuries of enslavement and rape, bearing and raising slave owners' children, being treated like livestock for the perpetuation of slavery; after centuries of forced sterilization and covert eugenics programs, laboring in shackles while imprisoned, grieving high miscarriage and infant mortality rates due to unequal access to healthcare and blatant medical racism, the disgusting racism of the Whytes and their circle could not be tolerated.

With the support of Tansy Beaulisle and Zadie Byrd Gray, they organized Operation Stork, staging a walkout of mothers from the Birth Centers across Texas. Nothing could withstand the footage of scores of pregnant mothers exiting from the pink double doors and climbing into a waiting fleet of rescue vehicles. They held plastic bags of belongings in one hand and cradled their round bellies with the other. The fate of the babies was a legal nightmare. Some mothers chose to keep them. Others still wanted the parents of the surrogate baby to take their child and pay for it. Evelyn Whyte didn't help her cause when she accused Zadie Byrd Gray of stealing thirty-six million dollars worth of babies. The outrage of the nation reached a new pitch. The whistles would not stop blowing.

The news hit the Whytes like the knockout blow of the Great White Hope. The FBI and the IRS raided the Whytes' offices and seized the rest of their records mid-shred. Jeb and Evelyn were taken into custody for questioning, but not before Evelyn Whyte was booed off the stage of her scheduled speech to the Women's League. Reverend Whyte's megachurch opened on Sunday, as scheduled, with his son giving the sermon and the stadium echoing emptily. The camera crew tried to recycle old footage of a packed house, but someone posted a video of the empty seats. Only a few die-hards remained.

By the end of the week, facing a FBI investigation, the revocation of the church's tax-exempt status, patrons bailing ship like rats off the Titanic, and his party's shocked denouncement, Reverend Jeb Whyte withdrew from the presidential race to "spend more time with his family during this challenging time". Citing the trials of Job and Jesus on the Cross, he called upon God to bear witness to his persecution. Perhaps the Almighty sympathized. Certainly no one else did.

One hour after he conceded the race, another video hit the news cycle.

Someone - an undisclosed person or group - had set fire to

every Birth Center billboard across the vast expanse of Texas. They lit up the night sky, signal fires blazing in a row, foretelling the arrival of change.

CHAPTER THIRTY-FIVE

. . . . .

The Clock

The earth pulsed soft and warm. Gentle winds ruffled the green grasses and unfurling leaves. The air tasted of hope and flowering fruit trees. Somewhere, a pollen-drunk bee hummed contentedly to itself.

Zadie sprawled on her back in a sea of spring, savoring the rare sense of ease and rest. Nothing pressing, no meetings or deadlines, no revolutions, no political fires that needed to be quenched. A tiny flicker of hope dared to blossom in her heart, not the hope of matchsticks on dark nights, but the hope of a springtime bird singing on a bare branch. Life burst forth with all its delicate, indomitable determination.

A dandelion seed floated across the blue canopy of the sky. Another danced on its heels. Zadie rolled her head to the side. Beside her, Charlie lay on his stomach, elbows digging into the soft earth. The grass flattened around him. His sandy hair blew into his eyes. He stared pensively at the white orb of a dandelion tuft. He was worlds away. Shadows darkened his gaze: climate change and economic challenges, a nation still reeling from revolutionary turmoil, a world with more hard questions than easy answers. Zadie could almost read the words of his next article in his somber expression.

"The clock is ticking," she murmured, mimicking the tones of a public radio announcer, pretending to read his next essay on air. "The clock is ticking for people and planet. It's not enough to restore democracy, says the Man From the North, we must *use* democracy to address the pressing concerns of our times."

"Oh, stop," he groaned, ducking his head and laughing at her.

He tossed a handful of grass stems at her. Zadie snatched up the white orb of dandelion seeds and brandished it like a sword. He caught her wrist, pulling her close enough to kiss. The heat of the sun and the dark solidity of earth pressed them together. Youth seared in their veins. The flush of spring's sensuality blossomed across their faces. Zadie released the dandelion to caress him. The last seeds scattered. The wind lifted them up in a silent invocation: life wants to live, but more than that, it wants to love. Simple survival is not enough.

Beyond the idyll of this wild field, the world seethed and burned with centuries of history yearning to be healed. It brimmed with injustices longing to be made right. It teemed with new ideas just waiting to be born. It stretched to bursting point with the future hovering at the edges of today. All across the nation, Zadie saw the Dandelions dispersing in a million directions, spreading out to plant the seeds of change in the fertile ground of the present. And it wasn't just Dandelions. Other movements were also rising. Other leaderful efforts were emerging. She and Charlie would always be dandelions - so would the millions who unleashed their golden souls in dark times - but people could also be roses or ivy, oak or sunflower, grasses or marsh reeds or mosses. A landscape made only of dandelions was as imbalanced as a lawn devoid of them. The world had room for them all.

"Do you think the Dandelion Insurrection will ever truly end?" Charlie asked her, tracing his fingers down her back.

Zadie shook her head. They would never stop tracking down stories of hope. They would never stop telling the tales of bright, golden souls. They would always call bold hearts into action, and always stand up for what was right. The Dandelion Insurrection could never end. In truth, it never really began. It had always been there, in one form or another, an endlessly reincarnating movement of resistance, rooted in kindness and hope. It was eternal, immortal, as old as time and as new as life, itself. Could the air end? The water? The earth? The Dandelion Insurrection might go dormant for a season, subside for a time, but it would always rise up when it was needed. It could pop up in a different place. It could deepen and mature over time. It might grow older and wiser . . . but it would never truly come to an end.

Not so long as one heart yearned for justice. Not if one person still cried out for change. Not when kindness still blossomed and courage still bloomed and wishes still flew on the wind.

Months ago, when Charlie refused to run for president, people had asked him how he could walk away from all that power. The answer, when he thought about it, was simple: they were rooted in a different kind of power. It was the power that ran in the veins of ordinary people, the power that put food on the doorstep of the hungry and spoke gently to the lonely and afraid. It was the power that illuminated solutions. It was the power that pushed forward for change. It was the power of growing vegetables and sharing tools and helping out neighbors. It was the power of blockading destruction and boycotting greed. It was the power of schoolchildren on strike for their futures and grandmothers stopping bulldozers in their tracks. It showed up when tenants resisted evictions and workers walked out on strike.

It erupts in our friends, our communities, and our neighbors when the changes of tomorrow insist on happening today. This is the power of movements throughout time, of people all over the world. It is a power that rises, unstoppable; a power that puts presidents and dictators, kings and tyrants, billionaires and bullies to shame. It emerges when outrage spills the banks of our hearts, when our love demands that we act. It surges in us when vision outshines despair, when hope burns more brightly than fear.

This was the enduring power of the Dandelion Insurrection, as infallible as life, itself. The movement had arisen as a rumor. It had whispered into existence in secret. Its seeds had flown across the country in Charlie's writings. They found fertile ground in the hearts of ordinary people. Its stories grew into action. Its courage gave rise to great change. Those changes turned into new chapters, and those stories started the cycle again.

The Dandelion Insurrection was still as small as baking bread in the oven. It was still as large as bringing down dictators. It was still practical and metaphorical, symbolic and literal. It was real. It was legend. It spread hope. It grew kindness. It sowed the seed of resistance in the ground of adversity. In the soil of oppression, in the shadow of fear, in the stranglehold of tyranny, in the death grip of greed . . . anywhere - and everywhere - the concrete of control tried to pave over the goodness of the heart, the Dandelion Insurrection still sprang up in the cracks.

Nothing could ever stop that.

"Did you know," Charlie asked Zadie softly, tracing her cheekbone and pulling her black curls back over her shoulder, "that a head of dandelion seeds is called a clock?"

She didn't . . . but all around them, the fuzzy orbs shivered in the winds of change. Seeds rose onto the air and marched across the sky. A cloud passed in front of the sun and the shadow ran its cold finger down her spine. They were two young lovers in the middle of a flowering spring meadow. They had won a revolution, ousted a corporate dictatorship, thwarted a countercoup, and evolved their nation's democracy. But even that was not enough. For everyone, everything, for the whole Earth and all her species, even for them, the clock was ticking.

The greatest adventures were yet to come.

Charlie held up the fuzzy clock of sunlit seeds, all its potential woven into gossamer-fine down, fragile and resilient, designed to carry wishes across the air to fertile ground. The seeds clung to the clock, ticking, trembling, poised on the edge of a great, vast journey.

The wind lifted. They breathed. And on the next exhale, the dandelions went soaring onto the winds of change.

- The End -

ACKNOWLEDGEMENTS

. . . . .

From Rivera Sun

I would like to thank a wide ecosystem of people. All books come into existence with the love of a thousand hearts. *Winds of Change* emerged with the help of so many kind people.

First, deep thanks to the Community Publishers of *The Dandelion Insurrection.* Way back then, that yellow book was a strange and new project, untried and untested. You took a leap of faith and here we are. Three amazing books in circulation at a time when the world needs them more than ever. *The Dandelion Insurrection* has come so far. It has been read by thousands of people. It has inspired people around the world. When *The Roots of Resistance* was published, the circle of Community Publishers expanded, and their generosity got me through a very challenging part of my life. Now, this people-powered publishing effort is gearing up to launch *Winds of Change* into the world. Thank you. Everyone who has been a Community Publisher over the years has made these books possible. I couldn't do it without you. We're rounding out eight years and over half a million words (if you include all the revisions!) together. It's been an honor making this journey with your support.

Winds of Change has been blessed by input from many strands of wisdom and many wonderful people. I'd like to specially thank Tom Atlee and Rosa Zubizarreta for their guidance and inspiration. I know my portrayals of democracy in these pages are mere baby steps compared to the giant strides you are doing with Dynamic Facilitation and Wise Democracy. I aspire to follow in your footsteps. It is an honor simply trying to keep up. Thank you for all of your support and for including me in the Co-Intelligence Institute Fellows Program despite being a novice among masters. I learned so much about wise democracy through all of your questions, reflections, and sharings! All missteps in this story's portrayals of democracy are my own. All brilliant leaps of thought are inspired by you. I hope everyone will check out Tom Atlee's work these websites: www.co-intelligence.org and www.wd-pl.com; and Rosa's work at: www.diapraxis.com.

I extend my gratitude to another ecosystem of brilliant people doing wonderful things. So many of my scenes are inspired by real life stories. Specifically, I would like to thank and acknowledge:

Joanna Macy and the Work That Reconnects have long inspired my writings. Starting with scenes in *Steam Drills,* and leading all the way up to the Council of All Beings in the California redwoods in *Winds of Change,* these practices and rituals have woven their magic into my novels. I encourage all of my readers to check out: www.workthatreconnects.org

Shareable and The Response contributed to many of the scenes in this novel with their excellent reporting on "disaster collectivism" during Occupy Sandy, Puerto Rico's Hurricane Maria relief work, and more. These reports directly inspired Bramble Ellison's phoenix moment in her community. I hope my readers will enjoy your podcast and pdf, and perhaps bring these stories to life in their communities, too: www.shareable.net/the-response/

With permission (more like enthusiastic cheers), I lifted Backbone Campaign's brilliant Solutionary Rail program off the pages of their campaign manual into a fictionalized existence in this book. We don't have Solutionary Rail lines yet . . . but we could and we should. I'm rooting for it. With a country the size of ours, it makes nothing but sense. Visit: www.solutionaryrail.org

Years ago, David Geitgey Sierralupe and I interviewed David Bollier on Occupy Radio about his book, *Think Like A Commoner*. His research introduced me to the scope and scale of the commons. It reminded me that, with my puppetista friend Teresa Camou, I saw a Bread & Puppet theater production about the Levellers and the Diggers in a field near some painted school buses in upstate Vermont. This inspired the *Tragedy of the Enclosures* theater show in *Winds of Change*. On the theme of the commons, thank you to Paul with the Great Lakes Commons for a fascinating Zoom conversation last spring. Also, my gratitude goes out to Peter for the unforgettable experience of growing squash on a New Mexico acequia.

Sherri Mitchell - Weh'na Ha'mu' Kwasset gave me the great kindness of naming Kinap Crow and making sure my character reflected the beauty, strength, and honor of her lineage. I want to also thank Lyla June Johnston for her article about both her Diné and Scottish ancestors. It gave words to the growing sense in me that the witch hunts of Europe and the genocide of Indigenous Peoples on this continent shared an important connection.

Historians hold a special place in my heart - and in my books. Thank you to Walter Conser, Jr. whose groundbreaking research on American Independence struggles changed how I view "revolution" forever. CELDF's Democracy School taught me about the blackout curtains, secrecy, and sealed records that handed us the 1787 Constitution. Also, to all the feminists who wrote those excellent articles on *The Tyranny of the Petticoat* exchange between John and Abigail Adams: you rocked my

345

world. Thank you for that priceless gem. I want to thank Ellen Freidman for hosting me in Austin, TX, years ago, and introducing me to Silvia Federici and *Caliban and the Witch*. Riane Eisler is a legend, and I, like countless others, owe her a debt of gratitude for many things, including reminding us that Mary Magdalene and the Gnostics tried to give us sortition and egalitarian democracy rather than patriarchy and church hierarchies.

There is a very long list of activist friends that have contributed to these stories. Some are movements like Extinction Rebellion, Partido X in Spain, the Pirate Party in Iceland, the 2011 Occupy Protests, Standing Rock, Black Lives Matter, #ShellNo, and so many more. Others are individual activists like Kevin Zeese (Rest In Power, my friend) and Margaret Flowers at Popular Resistance, and Tom Hastings with Peace Voice. Mary Pendergast, hats off to you . . . you know why. Ken Butigan gets credit for telling me about the diagonal roads and namesake of Chicago. It was an unforgettable lesson. I want to thank Judy from the Wild Backyards program in the suburbs of Chicago for inspiring the scene with Elena. Artist-activist David Solnit gave me (and so many others) hope all year long by creating giant street murals and posting photos online. Barbara Ford also deserves thanks for similar creative activism. She inspired me to create a dandelion umbrella as a spin-off from her sunflower umbrellas for climate justice. Thank you. My gratitude also goes out to all the organizers who hosted trainings and book readings for the Dandelion Trilogy. It has been an honor and a pleasure working with you.

The Dandelion Trilogy would not be so fun or intelligent without the wisdom and knowledge shared by my colleagues at Pace e Bene (especially Veronica Pelicaric), James Lawson

Institute, Peace Voice, Backbone Campaign, World Beyond War, Code Pink, Liisbeth and the Feminist Enterprise Commons, CELDF, Nonviolence International, International Center On Nonviolent Conflict, the Albert Einstein Institute, and more. A deep thanks goes out to Kit Miller at the M.K. Gandhi Institute for helping me clarify Gandhi's struggle with racism. Thank you to Michael Nagler, Stephanie Van Hook, and the Metta Center for teaching me about constructive program and asking the evocative question: *What is our salt?*

In early 2020, a circle of friends and I held once-a-month online conversations that informed some of the revisions in this book. My gratitude goes out to everyone who participated in those Dandelion Discussions. I always like to thank my dance teacher at Bennington College, Susan Sgorbati, for introducing me to murmurations as a "movement" structure. My sister, Leah Cook, deserves special thanks for all the amazing stories of Acadian resistance, including *tintamarres,* and potato-dumping blockades of border bridges, and railroad closures during paper mill strikes. My dedicated beta-readers, including Cindy Reinhardt and Jenny Bird, have been with me through the entire trilogy (and more books, too). Your feedback has been invaluable and helped the stories grow more powerful each time. Dariel Garner, you are my first, last, and best reader, my companion through life and creating these stories. Thank you for the laughter, tears, finding the typos, and cooking the best food in the world.

I could continue expressing my gratitude for the length of an entire novel, but I will conclude with this: thank you to the brave, beautiful, and beloved Earth. You have carried me all of my life. I owe you.

With love,
Rivera Sun

About the Author

Rivera Sun is the author of *The Dandelion Trilogy, The Ari Ara Series,* and many other books and novels. She is a nationwide trainer in strategy for nonviolent change and the editor of Nonviolence News. Her essays are syndicated by *Peace Voice* and have appeared in over one hundred journals. Rivera has red hair, a twin sister, and a surprisingly useful degree in dance. Rivera has been an aerial dancer, a bike messenger, and a gung-fu style tea server. Everything else about her - except her writing - is perfectly ordinary.

Rivera Sun also loves hearing from her readers.
Email: info@riverasun.com
Facebook: Rivera Sun
Twitter: @RiveraSunAuthor
Website: www.riverasun.com

Tell a friend. Spread the word.
The Dandelion Insurrection is here!!!

Love the Dandelion Trilogy? Share it.
You can buy the whole set for a friend at:
www.riverasun.com

New! The Dandelion Collection

The Dandelion Collection includes all three novels in the
trilogy and also the *Dandelion Insurrection Study Guide to
Making Change* and *Rise and Resist*, a set of fictional essays that
Charlie Rider wrote as the Man From the North.

You can find all these books and more at:
www.riverasun.com

The Ari Ara Series
by Rivera Sun

The Way Between

Between fight and flight lies a mysterious third path called *The Way Between* and young orphan Ari Ara must master it before war destroys everything she loves. A true high fantasy adventure with a shero full of spunk and spark!

The Lost Heir

Going beyond dragon-slayers and sword-slingers, the second book in the Ari Ara Series blends fantasy with social justice in an unstoppable story that will make you cheer! Mariana Capital is in an uproar as Ari Ara resists the forced labor of the desert people.

Desert Song

Exiled to the desert, Ari Ara must help the women restore their place in society. But, every step she takes propels her deeper into trouble. Her trickster horse bolts, her friend disappears, and time is running out.

The Adventures of Alaren

In a series of clever escapades, the fictional folkhero of Ari Ara's world rallies thousands of people to take bold and courageous action for peace. Each short story is accompanied by a "real life inspiration" in waging peace.

351

Other Books & Novels
by Rivera Sun
www.riverasun.com

Billionaire Buddha
- Inspired by a true story -

Money, fortune, wealth, billionaire Dave Grant has it all . . . until the shell of his heart cracks open to the misery created by his success. From the heights of luxury to the depths of poverty, he topples through the truth of inequality, colliding with his beliefs about capitalism, privilege, charity, property and love. Turned out on the street, locked up in prison, starved on the sidewalk, and brought to his knees, Dave Grant **crosses the distance between the 1% and the rest of humanity.**

Steam Drills, Treadmills, and Shooting Stars

With her infant in her arms, Black single mother Henrietta Owens shakes the nation awake with some tough-loving truth about coal, climate change, and the future of humanity. The coal company wants her stopped at any cost. Coal company lawyer Jack Dalton's morality and career collide as Henrietta rallies people to her cause. The stakes are high: life, death, the extinction of humanity. One question hammers in Jack's ears: what are you going to do?

Printed in Great Britain
by Amazon

67420052R00220